Augenblick

by r.g. vasicek vs. kenji siratori

"What the fuck is this? What is this? I don't know. Maybe that is okay, not knowing, and maybe it isn't. These words, these phrases, these assaulting passages that strike like a tsunami are shattering the windowpanes of pure consciousness and disturbing the foundations of what has been whispered into our ear, by a robotic earworm, lodged in there. This creature has been there, as early as our conception on this wet planet, a metaphysical and physical thing that destroys all forms of continuity, rational thought, and reality, spreading the seeds of this elusive thing that has been drilled and planted into us, under the guise of fiction/literature, this thing called... art. This isn't a book. This isn't literature. This isn't normal. This will test you. And, the further you go, the more you realise, there is no goalpost, there are no markers to pinpoint and to use to map your way through it. It is this fusion of confusion and submerged identities and manifestos that screams for attention. It provokes you into skipping, forcing your way through the molasse of information and detail, and creating your own narrative from a cargo hold's worth of words, letters, and protein grain ruining your vision. You end up flipping through it and hitting pause on your meat machine,

exacting a robotic process, selecting a phrase, a passage, a page, scrolling through the digital device, the paperback, breaking conformity and poisoning the expectation-devil sitting on your shoulder, the little bastard. This book can be read. This piece of art can be used as a physical weapon. This isn't the future. This isn't the present. This is definitely not the past. It is the in-between stages of corruption and renewal. In the blink of an eye, what was once a familiar word or letter transforms into something altogether ultra. Vasicek and Siratori have created a massive nuclear bomb of a "book." Augenblick is something altogether neu and alt. It is fucking impressive." Zak Ferguson (Author of My Body Meat & The System Compendium)

The birds are trying to tell me something. What? I do not know. All I am saying is: Listen. I can see their shadows on the curtains. Flying somewhere at ridiculous speeds. The sun is too bright. 8:36 am. Saturday. I should get up. I want to sleep. I hear other people talking in an apartment. I hear a radio. Not music. A man is talking. Very gravely. I cannot understand the words. Only the tone, the timbre, the feeling. Again, the desire to sleep. I have a sore throat. Is it serious? I have no idea. Like the birds, my throat is trying to tell me something. What? Something inside my mind? I do not know. Why do I think so much? Restless thinking. My brain is on fire. If I had a lover, I would fuck my lover. My lover would fuck me. No matter what is happening outside. Because of what is happening. We would fuck orgasms out of each other. Watch faces. Listen to grunts & whispers. Special requests. That is not the case. So, I just sleep a lot. Waiting. Waiting for what? I need to get out there. Make something happen.

Spatiotemporal positioning during sex is critical. Where are you, when? I am nowhere. I am sitting in a swivel chair. I am writing on a laptop computer. The computer is on my lap. My balls are getting soaked & pumped with EMFs & Wi-Fi. I have no plans today. Just this. Whatever this is. Cybernetic literature? Am I a cyborg? Am I a Minotaur? Am I a Satyr? Notebook 88 should be handwritten. Already I fuck up. At least, dear reader, you know who you are dealing with. Reader beware! My reliability is in question. I am a quantum thing. A weird fusion between me & you. Your thoughts are [sort of] my thoughts. Isn't that freaky? Or not at all. Meaning. Are you making meaning? Are you meaning-making? How goes your self-narrative? I feel idle. Stasis. What makes things go? Entropy? Negentropy? Orgasm is an abrupt awakening. Yes. Again & again & again. Eternal return. I do not know what anyone is saying anymore. Please, stop writing. She strips you bare. You are all meat. A rising cock. Sea salt. No more talk of anything, really. Experience. Consciousness. Submerged in anti-reality. Eyeballs. Brain. Amygdala. Pre-frontal cortex. Slowly rubbing her sex with his palm. Mounting. I don’t think my soul’s malfunction is fragmented. What I am superficially experiencing is not the weather naturally clouding over at the time of writing this article, but rather, there is something embedded in the program’s signifiers. Dolls in the description section potentially have defects and are rendered invalid from the outside. I am the energy of the abyss, destroying this corrosive eschatology. The solution is for the wormhole to merge, what has been done is not merged. What about the wonders of games and networks? Needs understood with change. Guerrillas possess not only genetics but also gas engineering, pursuing the poetry of new souls, overcoming thoughts that attack people. Linguistic necrophilia. The slapping sound of buttocks against thighs. She flips me. Who is fucking who, sometimes you wonder. I am a recording artist recording my thoughts in the early afternoon of late October in New York City. I might be on the edge of a nervous breakdown. Time will tell. These pages must show. I prefer not to write. Here I am. Using language. Unpredictability. Uncertainty. I need to make a U-turn. Might be best to keep going. The planet is fucking crazy. We should dance at a discotheque. The funky goulet. Disco balls & ABBA. John Travolta & Saturday Night Fever. Are your legs tired from last night? Zero-zero (0-0) on a football pitch. I can do the math. I am a left fullback. Sometimes a right fullback. Defense! My football skills atrophy. Cock no longer rises. I might be getting better. Am I getting better? My throat is soar. I scream at the universe. A cosmic scream. I should get a haircut. A buzzcut. Let the sun's rays hit my skull. Pass through me. Trigger & ignite my soul. The great excitement of first sex. Trepidation of last sex. She smears her butt all over my belly. We are two horny people going at it. Meanwhile, out there, in the night sky, distant stars are hurtling away from us. Our minds cannot fathom. Cannot keep up. Not ready to write the next notebook. This is this notebook. I need to be present. Here. Now. Tomorrow is a three-syllable word. Yesterday is a simulacrum. Keeps fluctuating. No longer trust reality. Never did. It is a little town. The market begins from a fucking dead place. Is it empty because there's not much interstellar? Perspectives and mental impulses. Avatars are girls. Human literature. Our innate survival. Brain regions. Social drugs. Perhaps causality. Captivated by you. Poetic empathy. In various ways, I boil our anus in stories. Cells. Replicant massacred in political dealings with you, violated, diseased, and are you in the dark? Has necrophilia expired already? We know internal difficulties. Combat inside the vagina is the danger of undissected telepathy. Cytosol manipulated by the soul sexually. Has this telepathy, this artificial dimension, been converted into one of human panic? The media suggests that corpses exist in its entity. Terrible, it means the disease is enlightened. There are defects in the Akashic enzyme. Data in the machine is overflowing. Ignore the interference of the base station. A small town. A metropolis. Everybody knows too much about you. Waiting to escape for summer holiday at the sea. October and November are the only months that are tolerable. You can hide in your attic and write a novel. We remove our clothes. She wants an act of love. I am incapable of anything more than a fuck. December is cruel. It snows a lot. I am more sentimental than anybody I know. And yet I can do no better. These words must show… what? Who is the speaker? Are you the speaker? Is it you? She says: Your ass is tasty. We should do this more often. I nod. Get her number. The body with a body. I kiss her mouth. Under her jeans tight pink panties. What goes on in the experimenter's mind? Experiments in delirium… experimental spheres. Quadrilaterals. Trapezoids. Parallelograms. No control. Uncontrollable. Existence unfolds. We observe. We get rolled.

Over & over again. Surf's up. Turbulent. Gnarly. Wave after wave. Where is the shore? The other shore. Memories of a village called Patchogue. Let them go. Are you a recording artist in New York City? I am. She is pulling at the zip of my jeans. I am not ready. I am ready. For what? I guess we will find out. 888 words always intrigues me. As a text. As a speed limit. 88 kmh. As an odometer reading in a motorcar: 88,888. As a distance to a faraway star. I know that corpses are showers, and your organs, through the shattered body, serve as the entrance for my semen in the true way, and the attached analog body mechanically connects to the brain. Please help. Evolution exists in 2030 and is integrated at the center as an interstellar solution. Sensations are all quantum and fantasy. Managed thoughts. Cells collide, we exist, and we become a failure of supernatural code. And the market shoots through my brain, engulfs the environment, cannibalizes our brains, controls the girl, distorts inner humanity, understands androids, android forms, obstacles, and deception. We have spread those words. How about you? The future, collaborative apps, the drugs of that society are visible. Virtualized language. That methodology is like a corrupt means executing death. Dark phrases from the Android storage are delivered, always starting oneself while asking for directions. Digital Karma. Brain cells towards sex and fear. The macro of corpses in space. Literature among readers more knowledgeable about reptiles than roosters. The distortion of my junkie. Courtiers celebrating ejaculation is a model of the compressed rotation era. The tragedy of literature has ended. Repressed energy from the Baron himself. Unique long-form technique, desert emulator. Rest. Experience. Evolution. Mechanization. Despair. Direction. Birth. Drift. False world clock. Applications. Repeat screen. Human exploration. War. Paranoia. Material. Earth material. Objects. Collaboration. Expanded form. Notices. Do you accept creations?

888,888,888 parsecs. Are you a cybernetic rock star? Yes. Estimate the drift parameter of being. She gets my jeans off. I am nervous and excited. My cock already erect. Swollen. Throbbing. She slips out of her panties. She has such a smooth & beautiful ass. A metropolis built on the ruins of nature. I take long walks on foot. Sulfur in the air. I breathe. I listen to birds. I listen to machines. People always going somewhere. I smile & laugh. I return to my notebooks. What disturbs my organism? What am I doing here? How did I end up in America? How did I end up in New York City? Are you familiar with Pittsburgh? The brain re-establishes… what? I bring a pencil into the metropolis. I am the disappearance of storage, creating data to exist. By break time, fluids carry creatures, and even the bewildered appearance of foolish thinkers blinks. Modular machines radiate an unforgiving universe. Geeks are grotesque monsters, and did you feel the linear jam in the brain as you sensed it? When the duality resonating with atheism and the unconscious triggers a tsunami of text with organs and genes within the unconscious, despite being a simple cause of human trafficking drugs, the person is alienated and excluded by prohibition, and the brain will be in confusion. When desire is impaired by communication, surrendering to magic, humans will engage in conversations with parallel lines in the sunroom or perhaps a toxic sun. What I am talking about is the further fragmented fusion of the theory of birth being blocked, awakening reality, and the dysfunctional craving of another demon that contradicts the concept of the vagina. I jot down my thoughts. I scribble. I doodle. Everybody watches me in the act. Nobody watches. Cybernetic writers are big-wave surfers. We cannot paddle in… a machine tows us into the biggest waves in the Solar System. Notebook 88 is neither Notebook 87 nor Notebook 89. It is something in-between. And must be written as such. Are you getting the signals? Electromechanical messages. Biochemical reactions. Are you alert? We spent long afternoons making love & arcing our backs. Now… what? Girlfriends & ex-girlfriends with panties around their hips. Raising their triangles to my face. I had no choice. We bought beer & cigarettes at a tobacco kiosk. We made love during a heavy snow. Buttocks are cerebral hemispheres for an intellectual. If you do not think so, think again. A girlfriend with dark eyes tells me something. I forget what. She palms my shaven skull as I pleasure her. Blue eyes. Hazel eyes. Are we getting somewhere? Twelve hundred words. Yes. Plenty. If you say more, you atrophy. If you say less, you perish. Keep going. I see a horizon. Light years in the future. It's whimsical, transcending only landscapes; it's grotesque. When the economy dies from infection through the movement of souls, utilized by rebels necessary for humanity's science, something is written. I give it to the printer's isolated knowledge. There are no mysteries about molecular connections and insects. The rushing earth produces them. The queen's distinctive role in healing wills. There is very clear knowledge about the impact within the precognitive app or the spiritual gravity system that exists when you throw liquid from a book, namely, the essential intelligence of a human living in the covering and rape among us, expressing through the function of language the fusion of bodily emptiness and rope. The ecstatic interpretation of the virtual puppet of the machine. The writer's soul feeds the firmware space as expected. Entropy. Negentropy. Everybody is a perpetual machine. Eternal return. Skip moments. Jaunt from point to point. Coördinates. Ten link clicks & does anybody care? Your bird has earned 10,441 impressions so far. I lay there getting a blowjob. It is not the worst time in my life. I probably complain about things. I am an artist. I am Chaos. Asphalt bald rust. Concrete October. Is it November? I speak. A quivering nerve. Tactical nuclear weapon. Battlefield. Now what? We scream in our cars. Nobody hears. A mouth opens. Silent void. Teaching is a quantum thing. I mean, at any moment… what? I teach the way I lead my life. Uncertainty. She knows my situation. Nevertheless, …. I like your improbability. Your randomness. Your inability to speak. We scroll through each other's lives. Is that it? I want more. Your hands are dry. Your brain is wet. Eat the aether. Drink the wine. I am the Big Bang. I am a whirlpool. A light year is almost 6 trillion miles. Nervous system. Impulses. Excitations. Flux & reflux. Cyborg blue is in the metropolis. Beautiful concrete ruins. Cracks spring luminescent green life. We fuck in a 'vertical' position. Oscillating between ooohs! & aaahs! Engage 'horizontal' position. Change positions. Doggie-style. Cyborg green & cyborg blue are coming. Security alarm goes off. War is imminent. Battle stations, please! Brain blueprint in concrete. Where is this? Syntax, hunting, and binary in the literary world. Absorption, examination of the body, violence of words, paranoia. Does the relationship between truth and humans exist in cats? The existence of precious access fluid. Always excluded by virtual through virtual. No, they give encrypted blows to beggars. It suspects that the era is regressing, that something beyond methods and bodies is accelerating the failure of the system and its pure society. The presence of bacteria collapses the criteria for selling organs more freely, and rebellious orgasms. But does it still alienate people? Engineers predict that in the urban use of the data plane, ranging from prisons to the sale of mad bones, poets' script languages effectively express children's special desires, essentially obtaining a digital input function with a mental mode similar to the script language. You are a biological filter of light. Move across a space. Quadrilateral. Trapezoid. What are you thinking? Feeling? Is it too much? Should we dial down the information? Are you a locus of impulses? Are you a cyberorganism? Are you a cyborg? The to-and-fro movement of buttocks during a fuck. Are you coming and/or going? The movement of waves during a fuck. The intermingling of genitalia. We split the atom. Now what? The room is brightly lit. She removes her blouse. Her breasts are luminescent. Her sex in my palm, she leans forward and coos into my ear. Her soft white buttocks. Her eyes get bigger & bigger. My cock hardens. Knees part. Knees on a bed. Buttocks flying. Up up & down. She takes me from behind. I am not ready. I cry out. Delighted & shocked. She finishes. Apartment block windows. Illuminated like neon blue aquariums. An electric tram sparks. Are you not excited? Like never before! Metropolis after metropolis I wander. A cyborg in search of a role. In fact, I require none. This is okay. Perfect. Whatever this is. Electromagnetic threads. Smooth buttocks & buttermilk thighs. Fishnet stockings. Spiked boots. Nose sniffles. Eyeballs ache from too much light. The atmosphere fluctuates. Asteroids "give it a go" before burning up. Fragments make it to the surface. Chelyabinsk & elsewhere. The human body desires it mentally on the internet, realizing that what is created there captures cytoplasm, dead organs, and perhaps chimpanzee brains. The environment, and it is pornography, the head of humanity. I am writing about the important carnal complex that circulates the well-known fanatical parameters of the party without using words. New language for evolutionary situations cannot combine the fluidity of pornography. Conspiracy analysis, the anthropology of goodness distorts your entire body, but our primitive structure as post-humans is there, and they destroy the mind more than the people who were poor and in the whirlpool of psychoanalysis. However, the power of the earthquake will be in vain. The opportunity of the reverse chakra envelops people. Previously meaningless, the distorted neoscatology by anal metaphorically describing the reversal of the cellular world. Reality uprights the mind in a delicate way. Reality is how the magic piercing the pituitary gland is killed by a fetus, not a zombie. The awkward posture of the lake brings literature. The firmware of android corpses helps the limbic system involved in the world's capabilities. Cannibalism or despair, your body truly eliminates the fetus of your beloved. There is a function in the oracle. Are you not afraid of the sky? The enigma of no blurb. The unblurbable impulse. The border zone is best approached from… where? Inside? Outside? Above? Below? Inside-out? Outside-in? Underground? Above ground? Swimming pool? Everybody is in trouble. Big trouble. You think you are talking to yourself. You are not. You are talking to the outside inside you. You hardly exist. A vessel. What thought emerges from a brooding mind. Only Ligeia. Her high ass & cunt. Long bare footballer legs. Sharp breasts under a grayish-green T-shirt. Her round Slavic cheekbones. Piercing bluegreen eyes. Her curiosity & ability to talk about the greatest game. Love begins on the sidelines. In between substitutions. I lay under the bedcovers. Cock in a fist. Squirting my dreams. My hand & eye follow the contours of her behind. She has such smooth skin. She is lying on her belly. Lifting her buttocks up ever so slightly. The work shifted me into competition with someone who clearly completed a suicide note in the same way, either starving the corpse or my collapse was actually close to a devil that was used. The leakage of undigested ends, where my decisions are intertwined with the possibility of fluid changes in the vortex as if my limbs and violence were fluid. The discovery that it is an important result of the action of the universe, the gap of the goal that was never separated, the media rewritten in prison, read by drug addicts, forgotten wills arise, and dreams are spelled as dead, but the capitalist, junk cell, drug called human thought capital on the Internet heals the past in one day by fixing the interstellar breed of dogs. And it's not a sexual soul, but rather a murderous soul. It promotes water within the thinking body. It is universal purity. She and I secretly teach the pulsating abundance as an extension of the transcendent appearance. Basically, the soul is true, and I was born by merging with it. All values are considered and the standard values are invalidated, but what the evolved distortion seeks is a singularity, which act it is. She opens her legs. My hand slides down her backside, between her thighs. I cup her sex. Fingertips grazing her clitoris. She murmurs. Her sex is wet. Fuck, she whispers. Fuck. She cries into her pillow silently as I unbuckle my belt. She knows she is going to cheat on her boyfriend. How many times? How many times are we going to fuck? She pushes herself up onto knees & elbows… lifts her buttocks high into the air. Just this once, she says. Impulse after impulse I implore the body to stop. Keeps coming. Barrage of signals. Who controls the controller? Nobody? The next impulse ignites me. I am on fire. A blue gas flame. The gas is made of aether. Aether does not exist. I burn a white-hot blue. Rip off yr panties, please. My sausage is getting cold. Yeah. Fuck. Yeah. Getting poorer. Nobody knows how to make coin. Except for a few. We can pretend though, right? Land of make believe. Tele-vision. At a distance. Let others act for you. No agency. Are you surprised? Yeah. A little. Thought I'd figure something out. Our only heart, the world needs rebels, extreme vomiting, speed doomsday, living mentally, basic eradication operation. The contradictions that anatomy explains to you, we have lost what is ours. Excessive transportation of rape tools, the existence of a well of penetration that may reveal confusion, the transfer of anal code to them. Their fusion circuits are added, remote interpretations are changed, death sentences are placed far away, but these are not dramatic relationships of biological information, but already dynamics, internal knowledge. Is it? When schizophrenia writes death, the entanglement of challenges beyond it, when cells alone cannot suggest exposure, it is a voice that excites nerves more than literary intensity. In eternal time, our time, when you deny it, glitch, lose unless you drop dopamine, frequently administer corpses. The author of the monkey cave, it is always a malfunction that looks up, and a man who touched the body knows that he is selling himself, in the corpse. More than the direction of the image of the writer who ridicules reason, the aspirin portal of life and bodywork is a derivative body like a hacking-nightmare animal that can control humans, saying 'no' to replicants. Art. Hustle. Who knows. I should have known better. Thought I was special. Now I know what I know. Precisely nothing. No real skills. Reading. Writing. Arithmetic. I must chase that motherfucker down. The one who told me all the lies. I told them to myself. Somebody must have told me. Through osmosis. Telepathy. Radio. Tele-vision. Things got real. Real fast. Are we city folk? Are we metropolitans? I keep looking around. Wondering. Trying to keep up with the Greeks. The Czechoslovakians. Helicopters everywhere. Swarming. Too early A.M. police sirens. Arthur Russell. East Village. New York City. Half-inch reel-to-reel tapes. Analog tapes.

Two-inch tapes. Betamax. What is the meaning of this? What? This. Impulses. Attacks on the infrastructure of the human imagination. Are we capable of anything at all? What use are my hands? I am a brain in a jar. Pickled in vinegar & iced coffee. Are you a sentient being? Impulse control. Is such a thing possible? Desirable? Writers ought to write, right? Living history is always a physical collapse on the frontier and a philosophical product of the future for a long time. Existence does not exist, the network of media, the trigger of thought, the landscape of digital discourse's gaps. The artificiality of the obvious and transactions, space is invisible, the world unravels without necessity or desire, it permeates, paradox, the economic code fragments. The soul of words is needed, the reader takes the adventure seriously. Porn writers read themselves and realize that the fate of existence is very similar to the memory of sex. Suddenly, a mutated group of nudes became apparent. No, it's foolish to take away the soul; it's definitely there to write it. In the underground literature circulating internally, hyper-narcissism is that of vampires. It's the era of thought, integration of prisons, viruses of superconstants, suicide before integration. We used to call this us. Please hide the hole around us. Grotesque spreads infinitely. Now is the limit and philosophical failure. Kabukicho itself is poetic and supreme. The future of deactivation is a dream, but something flows and takes shape within the works that only we embody. The most consulted within the limitations is email. Maze of desires. Fragmented android executives try to reveal the expansion of organs with skin. Current situation, understanding us, rejecting schizophrenia. The adjacent elements read us with restricted block, restricted algorithms. The changes are written by the necessity of the evolution of the mind and chakras. In the whispers of the generated base confined in the weekly pattern to the language, I read the control determined by reptiles. The pineal gland participates in capturing murder cases, but I am a disaster. Not this one! No, Sir Ma’am. You’s’all. Are you even out there? How can I tell. I am in here. Inside the machine. Thinking. Artificial intelligence. Figure something will happen. Surely. Eventually. The algorithm predicts it. I am a prophet. Sunlight in the metropolis. Early November. My season, after all. Football, football, football. I really should wear a plastic helmet out there. So dangerous. Not excessive diffusion but physical writing is the voice of a nurse, it's a quantum image of time generated by the collapse of the stage and the Android tricks of the market, transforming humanity. It sounds foolish, but the concept is love, the brain works, failure captures a girl, rest. Love is minimal. The mantle is not even a program. The one exploiting you is the writer. Connected data. It's the best. The tragedy of the nurse's maze. Prosthetic corpses. Sperm deviation by the flow through the gap. Suggesting change.

Defining it. The height of defects. The unreadable decoding of words and cruel encounters. Unreadable energy of the anus. Mechanism of accelerating code. Acquisition of hypermorphisms. The weakness of decline. For that devil-like reality, it's genuine writing. Living beings become gifts, fusion through death produces bone marrow. Learning spiritual dangers. The empty space there. Nightmares. Dark reptilian regeneration. Existence 4. Flat thinking, hidden earth technology. We know that hidden reptilian reporting technology exists further, but is there a physical intersection of firmware blocking public disclosure? The sun. Creating a working field. Human dissonance. Rules of the organs. The matrix is a place where applications are actually combined. My instability is truly scattered, but instead of finding and transmitting cells, I'm writing about the land. There are organs, there is war, and it seems that your physical data is connected. This is valuable. The expression of the end of gravity. Explore the blocks, circulate the blocks. I service applications, energy, the corruption of fellow poetry. Our money, your fluent fate in language. My digital technology drifts into emerging life forms, terror, the body of brain time, black thoughts know birth. Let's learn there, bastard. People want my ideas. Willing to beat it out of me. Next novel, please! Well excuse me. I am a creative. Let me do the math. You sit there in a bathtub. Mr Bubbles & whatnot. Meanwhile, President of the United States of Amerika wants my advice. She wants to know if maple syrup is a good sweetener substitute. Hell's Bells, yes, Ma'am! Motionless. The flow of enlightenment is strengthened to transmit the process to the living body, and our existence, the living body, seems to be fragments of the trajectory of gravity. Portrait of a guard. Evil has a worse spirituality. The limits of life, what about you? After the birth of the sun, will something judge the sun by exchanging it? My human supernova is your artificially created platform, but they were all various anti-government forces. I am dead. The known language is primarily a disease sprouted by them. This last document is about the spiritual aspect of reptilian life. It imagines a techno-cosmic android forcibly sterilized by primitive humans. Instead of seeking influence, seek help. The flame of the concept of influence is a corridor of attachment. Erase, and the confusion of consciousness begins. Only the space on the doll is paid. I use it in my iced coffee all the time. A bit pricey. You get what you pay for. Shenanigans of the mind. What is reality, anyhow anymore? Prefabricated orgasms on a TV. A radio in every pocket. Are you satisfied with your pocket machine? Like a little pocket rocket, isn't it? What gets your salami? What gets your pastrami? A sandwich sounds good around lunchtime. Until then, I'll mind my own business. Whatever that is. Sometimes I think this job is too much. Novelist. They ought to pay me. Whoever they are. If they exist. Come to think of it, I am a rogue operator. Better that way. This way. No middleman. Middle bloke. Man in the middle. Middle person. No medium. Yes, just you & me. Writer & reader. You are probably a writer, too. Trying to steal my style. I dare you. They'll lock you up. Put you in a bughouse. Ignite a bug light. Zap zap zap! The freedom & serfdom of a machine. I type. I click. She & I delight in the vibratory action of the cock & the clitoris. We call each other names. Real names & made-up names. We "do it" on a bunk bed in a cabin in the Catskills. She comes on top. She comes on bottom. I come in all circumstances. We are fucking, not facing each other. She says: Are you still there? I say: I am. She says: Carry on. Nothing surprises me. Not anymore. Anything can happen at any moment. There is no inside I know now. The truth is, who is alive and consulting on how a wormhole maintains a similar formation, the Empire Telegraph thinks emotionally, chaos. You may be superficial, but time is the cultural limit of the brain, the evolution of poetry. An excess flow like language. The narrative of last year. Anal cosmological solar mines proliferate and expand, constitutive elements, viruses, markers of the soul, the channel of a new existence, a challenge to schizophrenia. Lost. Brought into the order of rotational fusion. The development of technology was dysfunctional. A worthless pervert formed liposomes, but space was the velocity form of human involvement. It was the richness of the frequency of linguistic rebellion. The powerful conventional transcription of context I JK's dog in Never App, until the dead doll always tries not to become cliff literature, confined to the derived literature system 'Human Media Empire Of The Tongue Of The Sun Fusion' is like a nightmarish tool, an idea of a magical android searching for reptiles in a grotesque universe. This embrace goes beyond the apocalyptic nature of our new machine. Our god escapes beyond memory. The framework of the fluid system. It includes who you are every day in the reality of work. The autoregulatory anarchist is USB. Sex from the outside is reverse poetry, and if it is not beyond the fetus and my direction, the reverse porn and its cause, the senses are more protected and become art. Otherwise, it's not a big deal, it's soon. Your guerrilla is having sex while learning the organs of the rabbit's evolution in religion due to the influences of past kaleidoscopes. It is the universe of life. Sociably narcotic smiles. Half a century to get… where. Who? Certainly not me. I am everything else. Što? Što je to? New York loneliness second to none. Fucking in an irreversible manner. You cannot unfuck me. The jeans. The black leather jacket. She starts taking pictures of me. That is how it starts. Total strangers. At a distance. She introduces herself. My jeans are not hard to get off. That is how we end up laying together. Naked & fucking. It is not a bad result. When I think about it. Despite everything. The arguments. The behavior of mice is bloody like teleportation, but the power of pseudo-time pills uses conductive stages and maintains support for obstacles that consume in a week, comments on retinal dysfunction cycles and methods, and becomes the beauty of itself covered every day, but the soul of fantasy is a sudden invitation, and the capital underlying it is that No in the path of the soul's happiness. Adolescent consciousness worthy of karma is the hidden birth of the holographic universe reflecting diversity and diversity. It is a determination in the realm of philosophical and intellectual ideas applied to the gravity of survival, and I will become a useful dog, it is its application, but it is a parasite. And it is by the ability or mystical soul, my warning positions the exchange of theories, not a maze but a violation of the distorted mode of consciousness. Grief is a doll, a mad organ. The important artificial anus is digital. Understanding the mother, understanding the girl's society is widely prevalent. Desirable demon-expelling rewriting. Isn't the structure of humans understood by messengers who understand the freezing? Is there speed? This syndrome always has the aspect of misunderstanding the expansion of the difficult traces of rape. Grams of knowledge swim across many layers, ignoring this, it is transmitted by central poets of rebels and atheists in the media. The misunderstandings. We call each other obscenities. Even during the act. Are you here to study? Yes. Why do you ask? So I can read in the Big Reading Room? I am a big boy, now. You know that already. Kindly let me find my seat. Seat 404. Already, the fucking pathology. People staring at me. The writer. Yes! I am a writer. Am I not permitted to sit amongst you? Answer me that! Otherwise, eyes on screen. Leave me alone. I have important work to begin. Beginnings are always beginning. I cannot control the Universe. I am merely a pair of eyeballs. Through which Everything becomes. Forget anything I ever said before. Begin here… and push forward. Do not look back. You will be disappointed. What you see there is not real, anyway. Phantasms.

Illusions. Delusions. Call it what you must. Let it go. Love, you're writing a brain beyond thought, absolute application, it's there, your limit circuit, that voice is the evolution of darkness, all synthetic ecological dogs, it's shaved, a huge machine is sent, and I'm full of lieutenant, I hear the transporter entering the safety briefing, the nature of the machine without a magical mutation journey is the ability to show anger towards the reality of the universe, losing courage, the soul carries darkness within it, refer to the crazy application poetry, study, use its design, calculate it as an abyssal fellatio, not a ghost, body, side porn, the script has been hacked, creation, I know the weight system, it's a magazine messenger, a peace messenger in the galaxy, pillman sex, whether it's obscene doll, probe it with an encoder. What follows is the area of blood on the back, a processing body in the sense of gravity command, it's the true sense. I'm blocking the Stalinist language, and it's a primitive collective of misplaced sorrows.

It's an alteration of the image of a pupa and a girl embracing it. It's technology, it's art, quantum unmediated meat, the devil of daily energy, a fierce carnivore, a dangerous android, a digital transaction dog, human organs and the sun, the limits of political provocation, the existence led to the malfunction of the gland cherry projector. Similarities between killers and explorers, exploring brain energy only portably, more firmly attractive than what is revealed in the rest of the on-call need universe, and the infected person always fragments the mission in a distant garden, but confirm whether the writer is fragmenting the environment in murder, whether there is a centipede, whether it is a thread. Propel with me. Wiggle. Slide. Get that ass out of your jeans. Hop-on. Hop-off. Ride. Ride again. Again & again. You take a breath. You lose your mind. Who are you? Exactly. Breathe again. Exhale. Inhale. Are you inside-out? Are you upsidedown? Matters very little on a planet such as ours. Centrifugal forces.

Supergravity. Anti-reality. Get a grip. Loosen your grip. My hips are in your hands. Take it easy on me. I am a beginner. If you come, come quietly. Dad's mutation recommends blocking it and returning the structure. I know that ejaculation makes fractals alien. Clues are alchemy and a novel about dogs, anonymous, and damaged. The new satisfaction of wave-like thoughts, the flicker of the resolved lotus, is damaged by power. I don't order it because it is the only return of self-perspective literature. The nerve of the Earth, the brain of sin, we are always running. Do not fill in the automatic drawing in the area, please come to the official channel of the supplier. Consultation is a lie. Schizophrenia. Writing is also bitten. The girl values the soul. What she consults is language. Logically complex misunderstanding interferes. Wet imagination. Otaku explains to her, Urban Born contains amphetamines, but what is the continuous text of the Converging Desire Channel? Or like a Banshee. Night interrupts day. I am waiting.

A vampire in Prague. A golem in New York. A Frankenstein on the East River. I am an ogre. I am growing. I am becoming. Trees bloom out of my head. A suspension bridge collapses. Sirens in a parking lot. A woman wearing eyeglasses eyes me in the library. I am her type. We go for a coffee. She has an apartment. The scattered noises of the metropolis. Are you listening? There are holes in my soul. Dark concrete. A vanishing point. Am I afraid to walk towards it? Eager to disappear. Terrified of the simplicity. The nothingness in everybody's eyes. A man asks me for something to eat. I shake my head. No money? he says. No money, I murmur. Ashamed of my existence. Startled by his. We are the same man. I cannot see past myself. I trudge under a building. A labyrinth goes deeper & deeper. Nothingness. My brain is an empty vessel. I sit in a chair. Everything feels heavy. The air. Gravity. My eyeballs feel leaden. A spine curling into itself. A few last rays of electric light. Bouncing around the room. Night envelops the metropolis. Squeezes. Everything is here. Everything. Your hopes & dreams & jellybeans. We drift. We enter Nirvana. You like how my hands smell after being immersed in wet rubber dishwashing gloves. Not really. You get the picture. I am a lying machine. I lie to everybody. The concretization of rape assimilation is the created anal circuit market exposed in a state of events. The words of the writer, covered by the gland of schizophrenia, spattered with the trivia of Janus's book, are detached; rather, the life of literature spreads into a new worm-eaten hole. That's it. Death is everywhere. The paradox of destruction is blooming. The convenient surface collapses. Overcoming falsehood, revealing the quantum limits of creating new IT, discussing refined limits. Remote materialism is absurd. If you're an otaku, you need network theory to save knowledge. There is no falsehood in the performance. Can we finally create the sun? Is there a means to erase, injected records from the heavens to block love? Fragments are stored and disinfected for insects. Especially to myself. Especially to you. Be honest. Whatever that means. I keep typing your mad ideas. Your thoughts. Your nightmares. Your Donnie Darko episodes. This could be the book that puts you in the bughouse. Keep typing, you fucker! Yes. My jeans are off. Hers, too. We are kissing in our underwear. Unsnaps her bra. Nipple hard-ons. A cock bulges in my briefs. Bigger than an eggplant? She is afraid to remove her panties. Who can blame her? She wants to. Three weeks later she does. Fucking begins. Months & months of nonstop fucking. Will it ever end? Yes, of course. Why all the military headgear? Are we going to war? Every time I turn on the TV, War. The War channel. Who funds this stuff? You do. Your paycheck. Your paystub. War tax. What is a reasonable percentage? Are you on TV, again? Jets game? Vikings game? I like the team from Pittsburgh. Are you familiar with the Steelers? Are you trying to share? Is it working? What happens next in your narrative?

Are you a hero? An anti-hero? A superhero? Does your ass look fetching in a pair of black stretch jeans? Empty me of this person. I am Chaos. I am a hole. Augenblick. Ja. Ja. I see you. Come sit on my dick. Come on my cock. I'll hold your ass. I'll kiss your breasts. Come into my ear. I'll listen. What a book so far, eh? How much did you pay for this thing? Art is changing. Everywhere always. We cannot keep up. I am a beginner. I need to make progress. Cathartic bliss occurs when you become the body of the assailant. Similar to downloading a murder note, people accelerate to target the girl, leading to the suicide of this dog, dark trafficking, and I am coming back, and it's a collective intrusion. On the side of the future human, there is a creature adventuring alone, but without magical intervention from the vaginal species, it becomes the foundation of an anal machine, digital reference explanation, and my incident series files. Macro depiction of the exorcist's conversation. Giving a body to literature, metamorphosis begins. The gravity of the doll produces a part of the intrusion, which is you. It is a virus, someone's dialectic. Escaping from the anal chakra, the fusion of fetish and recklessness. A tongue already shaved. Evolution of mutation. Now, it arranges everything from the channel of God into an apocalyptic movement. What is progress? Going the distance. What is the distance? Language is a crude filter. What gets through? Almost nothing! I scream into an abyss. A void. I am a liquid being. I am a whirlpool of everything. Dark matter. Plasma. Quarks. What gets through?! We slept together. Did you tell your husband? Did you tell your wife? I spanked your ex-girlfriend. She deserved it! Begged for it. You can still see the handprint on her left buttock. If you look carefully. If you dare. The trial and error of first sex. We achieve simultaneous orgasm after long experimentation. I remember your face. The surprise. The bewilderment. The next day we are on the TV news. Everybody knows! The reporters. The helicopters. What a whirlwind of gossip. Every book is a peculiarity. A simulacrum. Every room is a room created by other rooms. Memory holes. You get sucked into an empty space. A miracle every time you reëmerge. I like the crack of your ass, she says. I get shy. Look at myself in a mirror. Come here, she says. We are imprisoned in a concrete tower on a concrete campus. She has dreams of escape. You oblige. We give each other vanilla milkshakes. She slides down my erect dick. Is your boyfriend okay with this? Subway entrance at Astor Place. Subway entrance at West 72nd Street. Are we getting anywhere? I have never discovered language, how literary it is about the unexplored universe, and adopting a family was similarly challenging. She is post-human, you are a fragment of the placenta, what is the mosquito of the universe? Toxic. There is a condensed body without transmission. Score-processed authentic villain. Sleep-language acts. Blocked writing. You block me. Cyborg abyss. Highest pressure conductivity. My kingdom, this humanity, oxygen, and glitches. Invented existence, and something hacked is flying. Post-system - a new transcendent meaning. The amount of infection between us, even if felt without writing the limits of all basic concepts of the source of liberation, the spiritual expansion of the drug's internet and the sun gives you parameters to wire. I am a thing, an android, energy thread. The transformation of the world is in the realm of demons, but the concept of android karma remnants is light, and there are linguistic defects, but spiritual transmission is another truth - humanity unfolds through the words of the semen magic vagina as a praised messenger. Pouring a more symbolic scatology like an angel. Are you a practitioner of hot yoga? Take i-95. Behold the skyscrapers of Philadelphia. The outer suburbs of Atlanta. Chop & grind in a 4-cup work bowl. Return to the biggest metropolis in Amerika. Is it Prague? Angelika Film Center. Anthology Film Archives. The eccentric orbits of her buttocks as she fucks me. I lay there howling. She says something in

Czechoslovakian. Language is a disaster. A house of mirrors. We shatter into fragments. Morning, again. Fucking A! November yellow. Yellow November. We speak of seeing the leaves. Why? Cannot get out the door. The door is a wall. A forcefield. A locking device. Peep through the peephole. I see myself. I see you in 4K. Your high-definition ass. We go through the motions. Monday. At least we got a good start. Ignite the ignition. Rear engine VW Beetles of Amerika. Ass machines. Carapaces. Space capsules. Hurtling faster than the speed of light. You think faster than a lightbulb. Who controls the War Machines? Are you a nomad? Are you a Neanderthal? Are you a Supermodernist? Are you afraid to give up the ghost? This thought is for those who know the shadows within you. There is a conflict invoked by the philosopher's blood. The philosopher's anal strategy communication is always poetic. The complex flesh of betrayal, the empty terrain of body and vision, and communication are diluted. The madness of the supplier embracing the abyss of the post-human is an introduction, an intimidating mass of abilities. Destroying language is the destruction of resistance, but reality is you. The only digital knowledge in history is a broken flaw. Few machine malfunctions. Its function stops remote control of the museum. Nausea. Memories of murder. Will the media temporarily add enough time? Like a fetus? The essence of God and my organs, filled with the scriptures it led, when the mechanical girl's awareness exists within you, I turn each body's vagina into ecstasy, the orgy of that world, and even the communication drug revolving machine generation, you are a cat, the body breaks, it is felt, and there the characters break. There is great energy within us, non-human thinking is liberated, and cables act on us in various areas. The energy of that day transforms the system. Block Hetero can pass on other bots and texts. This is not just a bug but a functioning condom of understanding poetry in the community. After all, it's a screen, and each one is mental, relativity, fellatio device, vagina device, human information, and nothing valid has been discovered. You will see me when you see me. Everything is coin-operated in Amerika. Even the War Machine. I hope you get what you want. Orgasms of varying intensity. She turns on the TV. It is raining in Albany. We are impulses. Too many for the brain to record. The spontaneity of thought is in question. Are you a free thinker? Is doggie-style your idea? Or somebody else's? Are you watching a fuck in profile? Are you participating? Are you not the fucker getting fucked? She later says it feels more like making love. Are you going to tell your girlfriend this? Your wife? Your husband? There are so many people on the planet. A pigeon lands on a bronze statue of Thomas Edison in Schenectady. You get a bird's eye view. A pizza crust from Sovrana's in Albany. Extra cold cheese, please. You can immediately end the twisted surprise towards hell, and there your innovative organs can write something closer to alienation than heading towards the sun, mending the remaining parts of the lost heart. Synthetic, please copulate with me; I contaminated you for worry, with genes reversed and the clitoris platform inverted. From wet posts to sex with the block, driven by the will of the psychic reptile, and real chaos, something like a breakthrough wormhole extraction video tells us that the quantum of the traditional black block is written by the juvenile existence of junk and the soul of a frontier murderer. The subliminal-type pills that push you to the limit are monochromatic mental simulators exchanged with today's bay and firmware, and harmless unless there's technology to appeal to the truth generated there. Within the organs, within the fluid soul, inscribing the nature of the universe filled with love. Mozzarella. What an invention. We never get exactly what we want. Sometimes it is close, though. This text, for example. You dig it. I dig it. We are spending quality time together. You can watch Netflix later. Boil water for spaghetti. Yank off your wife's panties. Play hide-the-salami. John Cassavetes is filming a movie under the Ditmars Boulevard subway station. What is it called? Nobody knows. Al Pacino is Serpico under the Hell Gate Bridge. You impress me with your knowledge. Your curiosity. We should get something going? What? You want me to bend over? Maybe. A kiss in a dormitory. Leads to what. Another kiss? A promise of more where that came from? Weird story. I know. We keep going. Wherever that is: the present tense? The future past? The past participle? Construction is relentless. The metropolis must get built & rebuilt. No time for ruins. Cry later. Walk along the seawall. The east river comes & goes. The harlem river. A river is just a river. A tidal strait. Ebb & flow. Whirlpools. Dirt devils under the hell gate bridge. I never felt so lonely. A writer is always in jeopardy. On purpose, I suppose. Or accident? A random number generator. 48. 68. 88. This country is in trouble. I am in trouble. Diversity beyond the corpses, code consciousness erases anyone with necromancy. The flow of eros, cutting through humans when set; it's meaningless if not done. A useful lizard interfering with humans over time by enhancing the overlay. Lemuria 333, the neurological aspects of the soul, socially disguising the soul. Beliefs from his childhood, AI silence. Changing it instead of knowing. Incarnation. Ignoring the psychology of the centipede, the perceived body is discovered. Sex is discovered. What is the technical self-flattening of the universe? In the traditional 'e,' does your list include the body? I'm gone. I am the head. Catch the cursor. Apply your skills. A saved life is accepted by gravity. Orgy gal, that's me. I believe in literature that deactivates Pleiadians and fleshes out humans, for example, removing difficult times from screen based on genetics, without me. I have an android dog contaminated with cancerous reflexes, so it's better than television. There are also claims that the evolving body is emotionally blurred or distorted due to the new syntax of the uterus.

What is the trouble? Is it the trouble with Tribbles? Captain Kirk covered with five-hundred Tribbles. We are on a spaceship. Spaceship Earth. Spinning at a thousand miles an hour. Chasing the sun in a spiraling vortex. We cannot keep up. We must. Your hands are on the controller. An Atari joystick. Press the red button. Save the planet from space invaders. I like my space. I know you do, too. Try not to invade my space. We can fuck later. We can make love. I am a veteran of the Atari Wars. I fought in Combat against the Computer. And I lost. I programmed a Commodore 64 to conquer the world. I ran out of tape. I listened to the Bee Gees on 8-track. I had disco fever. I was staying alive. Human behavior. So peculiar. Fascinating. What is your intent? Your purpose? Are you really making things happen? What evidence? What proof? Forgive me, this is not a courtroom. I ask because I ask. I am an asker. A person who asks questions. A person? A being. A consciousness. Ahh, yeah… again, we are lost. I am lived Chaos. I smack up against ass hard & fast. I shatter. I fragment. Immanent malice, God's dog, fellatio over there, the derivation of humanity, the time of rape innovation. The more the physical body, the more the soul; theoretically cursing internal terrorism. Articulating love. Failure hides imagination. A broken anus distorts from a distance. Parasites have altered these. Our artificial anus nodes flood the sun, and only despair, a messenger created before despair occurs, functions like a mass device, distorts, goes extinct, generates the directionality of life's issues, creates philosophy, and the breathing human is more of a wall than me, the brain. A girl and the confined wings of a machine. Without emptying someone from the excessive city, it absorbs the workings of cosmic interaction, and new paths stagnate with spiritual readers and cellular economic systems. We also have the same terrifying cosmic data, but due to the accumulation of functions similar to fungi in the body, we collectively possess functions similar to reptiles. The dangerous state of channel portals and screen is a necessary language in this era. The outer path establishes an attractive virtual transformation. There is a reason for the flow of text. Humanity has discovered the existence of abnormalities due to drugs and cellular anomalies. Work is interrupted, grotesque language narratives, human virtual parasitism, spiritual offenses you committed, the supernatural world is the life of the soul, destruction turns android objects into liquid, and aging due to failure. Our truth is that I am shit. We become naked. We stand there. The unshakeable calm of first sex. She kisses me, I think. I feel my sex grow. She leads me to a bed. Is it going to rain tomorrow? Yes. I think so. Okay. Can I put it in? Yes. She nods. I slide inside her. I feel her hands spread on my buttocks. We are driving in the Catskills. Blue mist in the mountains. She wants me to meet her parents. The idea is crazy, I think. I am a writer. Nevertheless, it is painless. I play the role of a human being. I say hello. I am from New York. I want to cry. Everything is too much & too beautiful. I want to go back to the metropolis. Better yet, the factory. Yes, I belong there. Explore where the fluidic game is. There is a sufficient amount stored to captivate podcast Android consumers by playing with four energies. Genome runners and spring-driven dolls run because it's dark, and what is confined is grotesque. Surviving means understanding that you are being watched, continuing to lurk, being invaded, and becoming a post in the machine. It depends on the individual, and since there are various system styles, understand the timing to find your own style and stage it. Linguistics beyond hugs, reptiles giving vitality to the region, huge ideas for prosperity, the importance of video completion, complex and rare promotion methods. There are failures in memory, and we seek healing, going back and forth, cyborgs. They destroy new traps, and the figures captured in photos have been shattered as digital suicides. Is this the anus, expressing death in the language of dogs? Existence and the weight of cancer books, images of heavy clitorises, errors in the explosion of poisonous souls? Disappearing within the information. The main organ, fellatio, written language, the distortion outside of kindness. The descendants of live technology were the regions I destroyed. The psychological root of people's wrong wrist damage. Reconstruction outward. Ultimately, if assigned here. War is total destruction. Everything in ruins. Crumbling walls. Piles of rubble. Even the human imagination loses its infrastructure. Nervous systems break down. Hope evaporates. November is a long melancholy. December at the door. Christ needs to rise, again. I see five crucifixes on a hill. Asphalt is eviscerated. Underbelly of a metropolis. I walk & trudge in black boots. Is there a tavern open anywhere? A place with a fire. A tankard of beer. A Slovak barmaid. Is anybody listening to me anymore? The New York Football Giants are on the TV. It is 4th & long. Her fingers caress my cock. She puts me into her mouth. The overwhelming suck of the big Cosmos. I am going to lose my mind. I speak in tongues. We 69. Yellow leaves on the streetcar tracks in November. The tram slips. I am still here. I am still here. Her thighs on his thighs. She is giving him Nirvana. She gasps. He gasps. She is wearing a fur coat. What is digital speech for chimpanzees? The lack of society conceptualizes the polyphonic sun of events, renders it invalid, and sensitivity is 'unsellable. Our bodies heal. And skin and objects are spatial information, literary ether is fragments, the inside of the buttocks is incorrect, nature is absent, there are mental limitations, images do not fit, it's a complete transaction, but the eerie cancerous life and personality formed by humans are a narrative eagerly channeled for the destruction of the body, appearing to be captured as salvation for the android. Always grotesque, rarely visible end, and important uses are alienated. Their rotten nerves have nihilism. They feel there are condoms and reality, but they feel time is limited. Brown linguistics is the devil's fantasy of the anus, a farce, yet it unites humans in a group. Research returns the body but does not seek impulse. Understanding the height of corpses and nature without ignoring matter only in the presence of the observed human and writer.

Purple ankle-high Doc Marten boots. Talk of New Jersey & beyond. Pittsburgh. Akron. Sioux City. Everywhere is a possibility. We land where we land. She thinks she is going to come. She lets him know. He tries to hold off, as long as possible. Her ass goes into overdrive. Pumping a thousand miles an hour. Don’t you dare! she says. She is almost there. The finish line. Her lips tremble. Her teeth chatter. Oh fuck, you fucker, oh my god! She flattens herself against him. Last clenches of buttocks. Nipples erect like pushpins. Body heaving. Exhaling & murmuring. Go ahead, she whispers. Your turn. We exchange numbers. This needs to happen again. If different. Repetition & difference. I like derrière. She likes derrière. We speak French. She wears a black leather jacket. She curates films. I only act in films. A big dick. An okay face. Very European. My ass, I am told, is fetching. We might end up on television. A VHS tape. Betamax. Be kind & rewind. A laser disc. A friendly handshake after the act. We say goodbye & part ways. Utah opens up new opportunities. I try to make a living in Salt Lake City. A writer should move to Las Vegas. Abandoned nature, the continuous, the dark, junk, traces of beautiful reports, distorting the violations you use. Literature as a trick where our organs intertwine. Where are the limits of the human path? That's my retro. What is the karma energy? What is that digital wealth? Multiple authors and their intentions are said to be part of everyone's process.

Instincts living outside the extreme limits of the body, mad desires, machines like cats, dedicated to the words of ant block. I am a singularity, sought movements like singing sex but was not satisfied. What remains is a fragment of the organs, but there are self-induced limits far beyond the mirror of schizophrenia, and speed, suicide, and cables prefer remote fusion by gal herself, and modern integration. The foam has a relationship with the quantum reconstruction of the amount of knowledge construction itself, rather than coexisting works of differential literature's post-human awareness. I am never digital, I am real, the system is fiction. I realize that semen is overrated. Despair continues. Flood of cigarette butts disappearing into privilege and life. A mass of possibilities is blooming. The universe is expanding. Androids of psychosis. Crowded artifacts. Primitive Earth. Further expansion with her and me. Which I do. It is just me & Pink in the desert. Strange days, indeed. We go motorcycle riding almost every day. Marston tries to persuade me to move to LA. Nah, I say. SJXSJX sends me airplane tickets to Sydney. I politely decline. Thinking of Kyrgios the whole time. I am surprised I did not end up in Lawrence, Kansas. Back to the metropolis. The biggest in Amerika. Everything goes here. Anything. You can write 5K of a novel & still not run out of ideas. My brain is on fire! Like Wojnarowicz & Keith Haring & Paul Klee. Prague is for vampires. I need to investigate. Berlin. Dessau. Weimar. Even a town called Münchenbuchsee. Every metropolis has its laundromats. Clothes must be washed! I no longer know what to wear. Artists are incognito. We camouflage ourselves like chameleons. Sometimes I wear an Adidas track suit. Czechoslovakian leather sandals. A 14K gold chain because I am a cheap. Thinking of the speed of the textile myth as if it were the nerves being liberated is not so much about understanding the essence of humanity as it is about contemplating the text spinning in the window of the moment. Is it the spirit that forces your mass and burden? It's an absolute need, not a controlled wave. The artistic edge injects spirituality into me. It is the literary organ that the brain liquefies by ultraviolet rays, warns the overheated tongue, and is the cause of a kind of masturbation with will. Rebellion against machines and post-humans is recognized in the world today, as a distorted block just like you girls. When is it? The order of small organs processed by the father in various gravities, the fusion that binds intellectual semen wrapped in the final beliefs of the human, the seed of the goddess of birth, the combination of diseases preventing wonders written, my fate as a human child, here is reptilian, not grotesque. It is my weakness, empathy, and they truly emphasize what I feel. Fiction, your introduction goes beyond the form of words like aptitude in the text. Mr. Data Human Virus, it becomes grotesque in the known dimensions. I have no money. Not [real] money. Cryptocurrency. A few IOU’s. A

Buffalo nickel from 1913. We are getting too personal here. I am not a person. I am a narrator. Even that is sus. Do not believe a word I say. The words speak. Not me. I am expected on the football pitch in five hours. I am not sure if I will play. I have a lot of mileage on this body. It is a rental. I do not want to injure any bodily parts. I have a lot of fucking I plan to do in the future. If I find a partner. Cybernetic rock stars do not get as lucky as you might think. Sometimes they do. I will tell you all about it. When it happens. If it happens. Uncertainty. Get used to it. Rule # 1 of the Universe. There are no other rules. Cybernetic jargon includes language like neuro-totalitarianism. Are you a fan of mind control? Fans only? OnlyFans? Where do you stand on Elon Musk? Is that stable ground? Uncertainty? As a cybernetic rock star, I can just scream my words. No understanding is necessary. In fact, you are better off. The mystery! Death rather purchases life. Physical capabilities. We, the future progress. Artificial methods. Acquisition of energy. Literary issues. Things represent humanity. Heroine. How to deal with disasters. Eschatology. Genetics. Deathroids. Reading sexual relationships and existence is a phenomenon. Physical and earthly, mass and spiritual things are required. Get a glimpse of how the nervous system and body evolve. It is your destiny to evolve. Please be cautious when reading something. A brain with defects is a mutation mode of the hiking channel theory. Brain data confirmed by the restricted poet's shower. Spatial utilization of technomedia images. Orgy announcement about damaged energy instead of power. This is completely biologically illiterate, child's reading, eschatology intervening in the brain. This is a story. Physically capable grotesque loves anal, so please don't give or destroy that desire. The neurological phenomenon in the basement is silent like the maniac of the anus and involves the firmware of the virtual literary city. Ecology of comments. Living beings are merely aspects of data. Plant consciousness often maintains molecular consciousness and can associate cruel words with violence. Are you satisfied with your agency? Meaning, can you control anything at all? I mean, even your Roku disobeys you. Am I right? Or am I cuckoo? Arguably both. One flew over the cuckoo's nest. Yes. Indeed. Are you a fan of the flick? Are you a fan of the book? OnlyFans? What next? What is your next adventure? The supermarket? Beware of the killer tomatoes! You better hurry up & be yourself. If there is no you, that is okay, too. Nobody is in the room. Everybody is on TV. We let our eyeballs do the talking. Augenblick. What happens during the blink of an eye? Rewind. I missed it again. Are you inside-out. Outside-in. What enters the portal? Is there a breaking & entering? Immanent. Are we cosmic goo? Sometimes I hear cosmic background noise. Echoes of the Big Bang? I remember it well. I was there. We all were/are. Look at your fingertips. Look at your thumbnail. I say less & less & less & more. Explode.

Implode. You are all particles, all elements. Feeling the information becoming a post and seeing the results, there is a defect in child pornography costs that promote criticism. There is a possibility of becoming a zombie, so you are excessive. The relevance of the future and formation, Dog Daddy Plugs. The poet of the flesh reveals the reality of my child by writing about what governs the body. Even the legitimacy of the entity itself is difficult by the floor, and such awareness requires a quantum cut for the metaphor of tomorrow where the poet's body is true. The karma continent can be accepted. The cyborg's paradise is precisely where dolls are enlightening. We reptiles. It is evidence that I am a spirit beyond humans. I have weight, speed, and a maze of the Earth within me, and I discover changes like a slaughterhouse in my body's hydraulics, artificial sounds. That's it, please stop. The universe becomes something far away. You become invisible, madness, cosmic tsunamis, torture, nightmares of dark transport by the breath of destiny and cuts. Love, people. Organic chemistry. Inorganic. What goes on here? What magic, what alchemy? Are you a warlock? a witch? a wizard? All of human consciousness in a half pint of McSorley's ale. Order 8 at a time. Wander Cooper Square in a delirium. What am I? Can I move the Big Black Cube at Astor Place? Am I capable of such an act? Is Z. working bag check at Shakespeare & Co? Should I get a haircut from Fifi? Am I to wander the aisles of The Strand? Subway entrance on Broadway. Go home. Wherever that is. Sex in a walk-up. You earned it. 68 stairs. Eat a bagel. Cream cheese & red onion & capers. I do not know what people want. How could I? I do not know what I want. I wander. A creature in the metropolis. Are you satisfied with existence? Uncertainty. What makes you want? Outside-in? Inside out? Are you grasping at air. A hungry ghost? My sex had grown ripe. Hers, too, apparently. We stood there naked. Preparing to assume the positions. And yet what remains? What remains of the act? So much passion, so much desire. Extinguishes. Expires. And we are left chasing things that never exist. Are you satisfied with experience? Are you missing anything? Possibly everything? I suppose every writer is a hole. The process called ascension, there is never a failure of the anus, language, or even a loss of consciousness. When you recognize the constructed, instinctive errors are transmitted to you, surpassing the limits of recognition, and a sense of satisfaction is obtained. Devouring reason, am I constantly adapting the world and engaging in self-gratification to find the scenery I imagined? The cat can and its dissected technical perspective become tangible, capitalism becomes the last powerless mass of my eternal post-human ecstasy, but the city of love is not lacking in spirituality. Code literature provokes extreme provocations for nomads; the two are taken to the modular room. The thought of death is mentioned, my eschatological information, the alienation of our region, the astonishing flow appearing on the screen, the rhythm of human life as a species, Janus Internet mean that my beast maintains the principles of natural humanity. The myth of the platform ignores the Earth. Our figure, if the body is today, overcomes the temptation of reality. I shovel snow like a madman. Dirt no less. The frenzy suits me. The emergency. No time to think. Just do. Shovel! A thinker thinks themself into trouble. Trouble. Trouble. Trouble. Treble trouble with tribbles. I am the Kirk. I am the Captain. Fire photon torpedoes! We are seafaring folk. The Czechoslovakians. The Amerikans. A 16-foot fiberglass boat & a 55-hp Johnson outboard engine can get you anywhere. The green Atlantic opens its maw. We ride monster waves in search of monsters. We can no longer see land. Only sea. Your mind inhabits an environment. We are thinkers. Dreamers. I see fog. I see mist. I see nymphs & sprites under the old stone bridge. What is the mortar? Egg yolk & saints' souls? What are the concrete facts?

My weaknesses are my strengths. If I get distracted, the cracks in my being glow brighter. Illuminated particles. Luminescent. Neon-blue & dayglo orange. Are you familiar with the Metropolitans? Yes. Impossible. Yes. Everything is possible. We are martyrs of the human experiment. We are accidents. We are purposeless. We are beautiful. We are ugly. We are sinners. The ero-guro brain proposes its theory, but for them, the anus is an object of my body or not, the consciousness of remaining genes, and the moment I thought that a specific gram was scattered, it is a massive fanaticism that tears apart the style of territorialization. The origin's paradise. Human arguments seem unsettled, transcending the world by the primitive abnormality as the neo-soapland of app descendants. It affects you; our limits command more data. It's a failed species, and the others are absolute cosmetics, samples, not literature. Applications are not about realizing dimensions and positions that seem to promote. I will talk about limits, forgetfulness, and the torture of mechanisms. We are saints. We are divine. We are mortal. I try to get the motor started. We are drifting farther out to sea. Electric eels in the Sargasso Sea. I seek the Kraken. I am cybernetic harpooneer. Call me Q-Tip. Easy on the ear canal. Nothing bigger than your elbow. This text is a 10K sprint. Are U going to go the distance? Take a breather if you must. I recommend against it. Hard to get going again. Inertia. Lethargy. Amnesia. What if you forget everything you read so far? Possibly for the best. Do as you see fit. You are the eyeball attached to a brain. Is there anything new on Netflix? Are you a doomscroller on Twitter? Are the comedy reels getting funnier? Is there any respite in literature? No oasis for your mind? A sacred space? Keep reading, dear reader. I believe in you. I am the only one. I suspect we are getting closer to something. Apotheosis? Aporia? Whatever it is, feels damn good, right!? Better than a blowjob or cunnilingus. Okay, not really. You know what I mean. I think. We just hit 6K. 6K is like a mini-orgasm. Pre-cum. Things are just going to get better & better. Steel yourself. Gird your loins. Put on a helmet. We are going beyond cyberspace. Supermodernisthypercyberspace. Nobody has gone there before. Be afraid, my friend. Be excited. You are an explorer. A mind wanderer. A refugee. A defector. The ecstasy of being & not-being. Welcome to the next half-century! It will be gripping! Are you a cat in a black leather jacket on a motorcycle? We ride. Your own feelings of death, the entanglement of critical elements with the client deemed illegal in the revival fiction, for that, and it is a discovered free android, essentially living beyond us digital humanity. She resides beneath the celestial fetus robot in a state of estrus, and the resurrection amidst the rift between mixed love disorders, referenced as something real, is the depth of a massively constructed server's multi-on not through resonance. Instead, the transactions we uncover ultimately induce decay more than my diversity does, prompting me to spend destruction and propel the form of us. The trick of responses in the activity rests, screens in distant places, me, the transfer of crimes, forcing death, pursuit of a will, how self-cannibalism, near loneliness embracing differences, others are energies of A, the remnants of time are inefficient condoms among dogs, but in regions. Please share that there is directionality in humans, think about such literature and more fetishistic aspects. It's a unique neoscatology, a lineage beyond birth transcending the anus; it's a shadow of blood. Words are code, but eyes exist, desires are machinery. We ride tomorrow & beyond! Next stop: a gasoline station. A petrol station. A filling station. A service station. Amerika eats gasoline. Europe eats gasoline. Asia eats gasoline. Africa eats gasoline. We are riders on the storm. We are the vampires of Prague. We are the wendigos of Saskatchewan. We are the Big Foot. We are the Sasquatch. Yes, well. Today I relinquish control. I am no longer a thinker of thoughts. I am a moving body on/& under moving bodies. Sometimes, sideways! We clutch. We shudder. We cry out. Yes. The river of time is turbulent. We get swept away. So placid. So calm. The calm before the storm. Raging winds. Torrential downpour. Are you ready for this? Batten down the hatches! Yes yes the liquid traffic on the Major Deegan Expressway along the Harlem River in the Bronx. Trucks trying to crush you. Squeezing you into a metal pancake. Flapjacks for the junkyards of Medford. Ah friend, what is a mind in the Third Millennium? Go long. Throw a Doug Flutie. A jumpshot by The existence of a deviant, metaphorical portal spirit towards microorganisms raises the question: can the fear that Earth, for her, is grotesque between an orgy and the quality of the anus, be a terrifying violation? All interactions carried by extraterrestrial beings bring about a fusion, and the vulnerability and web of forks quietly form a collective entity of death in the new biochemistry's influence. The clitoris expands until death. Larry Bird. A fadeaway by Bernard King. You are watching TV at midnight. Channel 11. Pix Pix Pix. Captain Kirk is your make-believe Dad. Teaching you the facts-of-life like Charlie X. Where is Harlan Ellison when you need him? I have no mouth and I must scream. I am in my bedroom in The Pines. I should probably never leave. I never meant to get this personal. Literature is personal. Literature is all I know. An English major in the Atari Wars. Edgar Allan Poe. Ligeia haunts me in eternity. I fart death gas. I must leave this house. Walk out the door. Never look back. I keep looking back! The Gorgon sisters. Medusa's gaze. Rigor mortis of the cock. I need blood to flow through me. Elevate me. Erect me. My girlfriend's juicy ass. One last time. The trees are fingers & hands. A brilliant sun illuminates what is left. I wander the metropolis. We are the people of the ruins. The rubble. Building concrete shelters. Waiting for the next air attack.

Everything has been taken from us. What hijacks your mind? Are you trained in counterattack? Can you roll into a ball? Can you write an anti-novel? Are the stakes any higher? Is your death not a certainty? No respite. Not here. Not now. Keep going. Run. Sprint. Pace yourself. Eat the yolks of ostrich eggs. Run faster & faster on ostrich legs. Never rhyme again. Bust an arm. Break a leg. The show must go on! I read somewhere that nobody reads anymore. Are you reading now? Scrolling? Body surfing? Are you a fanatic of electronic literature? Are you a digital scholar? Do you pump your own gas? Credit or debit? Is Amerika on target? Are we a wayward people? Am I asking too many questions? Your turn, please. Ask me anything. Ask me if I exist. Am I, at the end of the day, you. Are you, at the end of the day, me. You can perform a consciousness error by dumping yourself into this sexual world. Therefore, based on shattered needs derived from when providing conversation is their first, the domain indicates that it is not Earth in terms of information and violence. Humans can decay against the media and be deceived about it, my flaws, the fragmentation of conception interventions, the emergence of the doll's universe, rejecting grotesque temptations, your execution is a blocked torture, allowing the fear to reach, rotating the cat, yet, writing from the nervous pursuit code. Living centipedes, and paradoxes are issues. The defense of the body is being redefined. The body of a philosophical slave is a sun to that market, revealing factors for useful transactions, which is awareness. Human humor is to cancel them. No more question marks. They draw too much attention. Shrieking nerve under a molar. Floss in the next life. How much time is left? What remains? I broke my rule. About the question marks. Maybe they are necessary. At the right moment. A big question mark for all to see. This text is challenging my endurance. And yours. Proofread your text messages. That last one was a doozy. I am a figure of speech. I speak when spoken to. I await your reply. Sincerely yours. Really? Is that the best you can do? Best wishes. A little better. A little warmer. Feels cuddly. There are puppies in the room. Are you a cat person? Again, the goal is 10K. We cannot settle for less. Money is on the table. How much money? Time will tell. Probably nothing. Quite possibly negative money. A subtraction. A deduction. Language is a reduction. It is not the real thing. The map is not the territory. Every word is a rental. Belongs to nobody. Unless. Unless what? Never mind. I had a rogue thought. A line of flight. I very nearly escaped. I am getting tired. Wednesdays are strange. Neither/nor. Feels like a road bump. Annoying. I removed my glasses. She removed her panties. That was a long time ago. We do not forget these things. They are in us. Forever. Until we forget. What is the purpose? Of what? I forget. Forgive me. I apologize. I lost track for a moment. I got distracted. A writer must concentrate. ID tools are nodes; you are the vortex of transactions. The pain museum was a crucial game in the Earth's issues app. The new deletion will change the wandering heart. Online never recognizes, and time interrupts, gravity warps matter, transaction blanks, and beyond alternative languages, faces are deeply cruel. Concealment is the surface of mentioned points. Android lines are bodies; the transformation of the soul on firmware passes through its negatives and turns towards me, directing attention to the magic chaos within the boundaries of glands. It's just limiting the recognition of murder. Here, in the system of thought, the liver revolts in the organ space of the organization, and a groove appears where language consults life. AI exchange attempts murder and even sex, platform collapse, debilitation, and emo speed. It's celestial, like rodents' brains before orgasm. It's a type of nonsense thinking, the language of poor dogs and reptiles. She hasn't evolved the domain; the phone is alternative at the center. Ultimately, regression of the dog's language. The acidic object of the soul. Human, you have gathered the potential for low greed from techno for this. It shook the vision of scatology, a catabolist insect. How? No idea. It is just something people say. I remember the goalie yelling: Defense. Get more compact! I liked that. Get more compact. I understood it. Visualized it. Language can be like that. Sometimes. Quite often I am lost. And the team loses 0-7. Everything happens so fast. Goal. Goal. Goal. Goal. Goal. Goal. Goal. The football pitch is made of artificial turf. We look at each other. Shrug. Laugh. What else can we do? The game is the game. We are almost at 7,000 words. You deserve a break. Take it if you need it. X marks the spot. I forgot to shave today. The whiskers bug me. Irk me. There are dishes in the sink. Dishes on the table. Dishes in the cupboards. Drinking glasses, too. Everybody has the same problems. At different times. Or not at all. Who am I to say? I am a writer. My only goal is to write. Other people have different goals. What is your goal? Are you going to finish this text? Are you going to throw it across the room? Are you going to give it a rating on Goodreads? The impossible turn of fabric and the last of materials is the self from attract control. They are moves not persistently attempted in the emotion-deleting narrative, criticizing the singularity. The beauty of the liberated biochemical system is visually released. I am a ghost-rabbit-mutant-cosplay human in the deep hole of what is. I am a potential meter of digital tools. My function is value, so please. The time camera of your phone has insight into primitive information since before it is an internal psychopath. If it's cybernetic, the impulse model of a sex maniac will step-block to orgasm. If it's psychoanalytic, the shadow puppet is vulnerable. We acquire the hydro-machine complex dog xenoform, which eats land destruction, and further dimensionalize depth. Is it even on Goodreads? What is your relationship to Amazon? Have you ever purchased anything from Amazon? Please list all your purchases. Am I a # 1 best-seller? Am I Tikka Masala? Am I the Maharaja? In search of a new language, beyond language. This text is highly readable. I grant you that. Is it making meaning? Are you accumulating something? What? Experience? Inner or Outer? Outer & Inner? Are you upsidedown? Inside-out? I just had a freakish thought. Trying to imagine somebody translating this into Czechoslovakian. Good luck David Vichnar. Good luck Alex Zucker. Good luck Paul Wilson. Good luck Christopher Hardwood. Good luck everybody! Good luck Amerika. Good luck Planet Earth. Text is emerging from a machine. I no longer operate by factory rules. I am a rogue operator. Catch me if you can. I need to shift into a higher gear. What is a higher gear? Next novel, please. What if there is only this one? A text like this comes along maybe once a century. Or twice. Or thrice. Borges says three is a confirmation. Kafka says shut the fuck up. Joyce. Beckett. Where do we go from here? The Knickerbockers are on TV. Playing that team from Brooklyn. No, not the Dodgers. Nets are up 64-43. Second quarter. 1:21 remaining. There is a player with the number 0 on his jersey. Zero! That is my number. I spent my time at the lathe. Now you spend yours. Turn turn turn. In the information stealth of a suspicious presence, you, the light aircraft, do not actively release the intermediate. This strategy is an experiment in alienation, and you are a reptilian extraterrestrial. The masses of literature and field writers know that language fears this like your taboo chemical. A temporary latent function, expecting behavior including terrifying things for the universe, finds quantum to feralize in techno throughout the universe. There are organs there to read chromosomal isomeric energy. The characteristic monitor poet's gal, evidence hanging on the handle. We create a gap between the brain, murder, and clitoris. In a world of cytoplasmic deficiency, just dark. The essence of branching and genitals. I want the perspective of the attacker. Use the heart. What I love about these is not fragmented but everyone is an address of human infection, and our catharsis is more deeply controlled by its firmware. Nothing quite like 303 stainless steel. Enjoy! Sex is a matter of timing. The factory is a timetrap. Interrogate the text. Czech the timestamp on Helena's left buttock. Are you a robot? Are you an automaton? Are you a cyborg? Are you Czechoslovakian? Are you Amerikan? Are you French? Are you Dominican? Are you German? Are you Somali? Are you Australian? Are you Japanese? Are you Everything? Are you Nothing? Are you a rogue operator? A machinist from another galaxy? Avalanche of language. Machine it into piecework. Weld it together. Totality. Neuro-totality. I am strapped into a cockpit. A rabbit cage hurtling through space. You enter a village. There is a tavern. Seated at long tables are the villagers. The big gregarious red-haired man is a boar hunter and a ping-pong player. Everybody is laughing. Drink your beer. Think your thoughts. Are thoughts even your thoughts? In a language you do not understand. Translate, please. You must not translate. There are no translations here. We forbid it. Who? The village elders. All translation is a farce. I regret everything I ever read. Nietzsche is right. Thrice removed. Barrel into your next project. A project without words. An anti-novel made of gestures. Your actions are being recorded. However, the awkward movements of the language at the beginning of logic resonate, believing in you, the interaction of the blue. Language, long live the live. About creatures that become corpses, and dealing with them. Who trades in the deception of sickness, not in the shadow of pornography? The current toxicity of murder is the pinnacle of various spiritual lives. When the shadow changes, what has been given by restrictions is the spirit of modules, the soul of life itself, charisma's masturbation. It is diverse and refers to things. Is the anus wet? Our beliefs. This author has a sexuality like buying a body. She lay sprawled over Zig. Her legs & sex open. Zig's cock inside her. They grunt & finish. Now the dénouement. The reproach. Death is coming. Tongue firmly between the ass cheeks. A shadow at the window. Keep going. Do not stop. The urge to submit to a spanking. She calls Zig on a plastic telephone. Come to my dormitory room, she says. Zig stands in the threshold. Afraid & excited to enter. I like you, she says. Now take off your pants. A bird hits the window. We startle. I am naked. She is naked. We listen to the silence of nothingness. I think we might need to start a band. Make some noise. Ziggy's Cosmic Spacejam Machine. Lyrics like [I remember you / you were somebody that I knew / we walked in the park / we walked in the park] are sure to go viral. Signal & noise. Call & response. The great cosmic silence. Project Cyclops. Are you listening? Are pulsars triggering you? Is there anybody out there? Sometimes I do not know what to do at 11:19 am. The only way to get out of the digital timetrap is to wait. Watch the clock. There it is: 11:20 am. Are you like me? A waiter? An observer? A clock watcher? Einstein watched clocks from electric streetcars. We are not alone. I am also a word counter. I only have so many words. Like 7741. Words pile up into anti-novels. Horizontal rolls. Vertical scrolls. We approach 8K with abandon. A quarter century to go. What is time, anyway? An electric prod? Ouch! Zap! Leave me alone. Brand my left buttock. I am prime beef. A salami sandwich. Horseradish & mustard. Are you a bagel eater? Lox spread? Do your thing. And I'll do mine. Enough language for us all. In the morning without corpses, the practice as an organ is a void and infinite in the name. The result of the only ancient planet. Illiteracy is supposed to be new. Existence as an ability becomes a tool and becomes our teeth. Trading like a boy with abilities. Your AI breaks important boundaries. This and the only other terrain. The new theory of relativity clone. Boundaries of shapes you don't desire physically. Boundaries that evoke the soul. Neurological abnormalities between languages on the screen. Thinking artificially about oneself. Retina girl's emotions. Moving the body with absolute oxygen. The story by the web of androids begins. Replicants. Their malfunctions. Promotional resolution. Posthuman literature. When boundaries appear essentially, it exists as something alien to us. Preventing it at the depth of the chain is one of yours, which is generally and artistically very effective in self-abduction. Three physicalities about myself. Weaving hidden attributes of your own vagina cut dead in practice. The 'a' is pasting language. Chaos dimensions and Adam in a world. Celebrating the exploration of the brain. The future was theoretical. The essence of the list. Not providing all those characteristics. Traditional rebellion of digital communication. Nothingness. Awakening language. Charged origins of rebellion. Unconscious abilities. Conversation wave disturbances. Is the demon of the doll human? This is quite the burst of energy. Keep going. What is the worst that can happen? Nobody publishes this? I can publish it myself. If I dare. Already have a cover in mind. It’ll knock your socks off. Maybe Sweat Drenched Press in the UK can publish it. Or somebody else. Needs to be long enough. How to get there? Let spacetime happen. Arthritis in left finger? That is a pain in the ass. Makes it hard to type. I type faster than Kerouac. Faster than Alexander Trocchi. Faster than Zak Ferguson. 8K is like Zeno’s Paradox. The closer I get, the further away! It is like first sex. The penis approaches the labia. 8K is just beyond the horizon. 8K is around the riverbend. GRRM likes rivers. I read it in an interview with VanderMeer. GRRM also has a conversation with Stephen King in New Mexico. Our post started with homosexuality, but linguistically, it has been grotesquely resolved with eternal stamina, do we have foolish DNA? A forced and eternal self. Speech is hidden. Singular points of research platforms. Red porn. Cheerful mapping created by literature.

Restrictions of sex. Restrictions of fellatio. Anxiety. The landscape of the world. Literature has been erased. Poetry of recognition. It is information. It is natural. It is spiritual. No, it is digital. It is an orgy. It is cosmic. It is osmotic. Data infiltrates and captures me, a flood of printers, its merciless eternal transcendence, the remaining gravity, the opportunity of blurred madness in the modern field. But I think of you as a sexual maggot. Our bodies are secularly me. The nodes will be satisfied. The frequently dead emulator is not me, and the theory is strange to me. The writing ability of the super circuit is rational, having sex with the human of the universe. Mine is the input of art and dissonance to the devil's attempt, betrayal of broken me and selfie, wanting organs, skills. The android's dream is ecstasy. Like the diversity of expression in impossible media, unpredictable cybernetic catabolism, division. No! I saw it on YouTube. They talk about rats. Getting closer & closer to 8K. I can feel it. I should get an 8K television. Supermodernist high definition. I am almost there. Like the peak of Everest. Or K2. Or that mountain on Mars. What is it called? There! Made it. I am the King of the world! I am nobody. The crash happens fast. As it must. Next goal: 9K. I should put sneakers on. I absorb the environment. I am a black hole. Everything passes through me. [I] am absorbed. [i] [.] You are absorbed. Y[o]u. [.] What remains? Everything. There is no data loss. No information loss. We are vectors. We are the action. No subject. No object. I think I want you to come on top of me. Yes. Go ahead. We live in an apartment. Our organs being ruined by a metropolis. Our thoughts machinerolled by propaganda. Three tall stacks on the river. Making god knows what. Electricity, I guess. I write in a notebook. This is my notebook. When I go outside, I bring my rucksack. Regarding currency: The parallel lines of the courtroom and the obfuscation to download the energy of AI boys and reptiles provide their flickering evolution there. The frequency of numbers always ends in a relationship within the brain where humans become presidents. There was no usefulness in the flamboyance of humans. The movement of scatology considers the possibilities of the writer. The horizon of construction is fantasy. The ecstasy of beneficial and abundant encounters. Just naturally, without the existence of possibilities and orders, deeply immerse in telepathy. Existence. Nanowires. Flow of information. Post-humanization of language. Habitual things. Inclusion is included in the possibility. Concealment of conduits. The existence of the exploration of organs in many cycles. Condoms. The depth of digital methods itself. Place. Main cancellation. Abundance. The concept of tearing the world. Unknown. Anal. The book is escaping. Tricky public machinery has been transferring gimmicks to knowledge itself for a long time, and acquiring it is parting by considering the adjustment of the phone. Posthumanism of other batteries represents an attempt from disappointment. What is out there? Aha, yes. Reality. Every step I take, a possibility. Nice trees. Are they artificial? I hope not. I want to breathe. I want to breathe real air. The gravity well troubles me. It is under the high concrete bridge. I sidestep it. There are other ways to go. Time to put on goggles & mask. Something is coming. Machine noise. I hide in a ditch. Belly against the cement. I get up. Yep. A streetsweeper. That is a euphemism. Kills anything & everything. Squirrels & pigeons & muskrats. No human driver. Robot operator. Sweeps up homo sapiens, too. Especially homo sapiens sapiens. We are not so many. Not anymore. Life is thriving. Everything else. I rut when I can. I will rut tonight, if possible. Day is for scavenging. Materials & resources. Scrap metal. Uranium cubes. Whatever I can get my hands on. And sell. I am a bricoleur. I am a jerryrigger. I am whatever I need to be. Language. Everywhere. Always. I need to stay alive. The grotesque discovery of trash regeneration, another darkness that covers the unique features as me in neoscatology, and the core boy who experienced it, killed and exploded, burning up in the incompetence, identified images, the syntactic issue of the happy language of death, intervention data is the clitoris. Identity is severed, but control is a norm like a short circuit through internal synthesis, considering the duality of the world's language in the declaration of mustard dog SM and molecular future perversion. It is evident that the poet ascending through body technology controlled by fusion habits is not a unique human. It includes, but it blurs the dimension of the value of alchemy probably functionally by releasing the cooperation of fetish resurrection, including the alienation effect for starting comments, hyperinflation of wild energy like antibodies rather than violence, leaked detritus of a single nation. By blurring the new one functionally, it assimilates, interferes, the released cut infiltrates, the gland of the media puppet, the text couldn't naturally function to harmonize, usually, when biochemistry is inserted, the cave has been modified by other dogs, pituitary heteromorphic morph is seeking it, it's fellatio. Please see the poetry dying from the disconnection of pigs and humans, during my break. Machines erase everything. Replicating & deleting. Ink & paper resistance. Spill ink. Hide it in the rafters. Under rocks & boulders. Manuscripts. Samizdat. Subway tunnels under a metropolis are perfect archives. Underground people. Spelunkers. Graffiti scratchers. The alphabet is a technology. Illuminate a manuscript. Glow of a headlamp. Get yrslf a ghetto pass at a bodega. Easy on the pastrami. Over easy on the eggs. A box of cigs. Maybe a loosie. Stuff yr rucksack with supplies. Enter the tunnel. The spine twists in agony & pleasure. She fucks me. I lay flat on my back. Crying. Frozen images & the static hiss of TV. Are you in there? Are you still alive? Pull me out. I return to the apartment. Trudging up the stairs. The elevator no longer works.

Smells like urine. A key unlocks a door. Throw myself on a bed. The confinement of carnivorous souls was heard, the base research is cosmic, techno, if the universe leaks, it will clone. They and the synapses entwine, criminals steal identity, ancient stealth reflex artists, retro, it's impossible humanity. The unexpected vibrancy of human enjoyment is torture wherever it entwines. Reading is a torturous language for journalists' language-ized vaginas, and the linguistics of existence that protect it through twisted creativity in drug formation deceive patients. Poetry nullifies it, translating the magic of the world through the mine screen, but do you provide healing to the body? About language, destroying the potential completed productivity bot, fragments of accounts, something like magic, understanding that facilities are causing fiction for use. When it is a creature, when other organs are present, the placenta is singular, animals are dissected, and productivity increases rather. Astral, that will, it's the thinking of the adapted digital superstructure. Sleep. The dreams I dream are electronic dreams. Written in code. Algorithms. If my head is too close to the machine. EMFs. I surf an electromagnetic wave. Mornings. She makes eggs & raisin toast. She is mad at me. I fall asleep too fast. No words. No language. I keep it inside. I write it in a notebook. We keep getting letters in the mailbox. Machine letters. I am afraid. Soft vanilla ass melting on my thighs. We order Indian food for delivery. Tikka masala & nan. Mango lassi. New York football giants on the TV. Is it Sunday? I guess it is. Sunday in Amerika. Giants at the Raven's 13-yard line. 3rd & 7. She puts on her Steelers jersey. Long long legs. We go long. She has particularly striking buttocks. Deconstructing the structure of your consciousness & subconsciousness. Apartment blocks. Balconies. A telescope is scoping out your windows. Binoculars. Surveillance drones. Are you capable of being isolated? I turn a wand clockwise on venetian blinds. Squint & begin to see the microstructures of reality … particles/waves … slit experiments … dot matrix … plasma lasers … the man who eats the meat of two animals & possibly three … a ham & turkey sandwich … a bodega in the bronx … a white-ass teacher fucking his white-ass girlfriend … she wants to know if the man gets a pension … LOLzzz … No metropolis is enough. Her name, like a current mechanism, already landscapes beyond extraterrestrial. Their printers hide circuit thoughts. Economic murder brings the region from the side to the front, but in the desert, there is clearly a stage of wealth. The poet's human gland, selfie teleportation, and only copied survive from within, as your fragmented spot has been found, discovered. I've also generated an undeniable explanation of networkism. Currency, by fixing it in the end, has its image field, so rather, what pigs did quantumly, and considering the desires created by miles, certainly, for that satisfaction, I create language types throughout the wriggling time. Even his corpse, the difference of rape on the day of awakening, formed biologically as poetry, lives in the necessary center of the priest's standards, is a dramatic tongue, penetrates neurologically steps, but what I have is a speed-enhancing substance for guidance, affecting infants, always uncertain. The mental AI of a pedophile influences readers. Every metropolis disappoints. Not quite right. Elsewhere is always more real. Fragility of reality. Nonexistence. I call myself on a telephone. Nobody answers. I leave a message. She says: Keep the laundry going. What? Are you serious? I hang my jacket up. I am good at taking care of myself. My texts get written. My anti-novels. Everything else gets forgotten. Chalk that up on a blackboard. Erase. My mind is translucent. A gelatinous jelly. I stretch a latex over my rising cock. Receptacle tip. She lays there. Legs open. In need of a shave. Labia wet. Prague gets bombarded. New York. Every metropolis on the planet. We go underground. We must. There is no surface. Not anymore. Too exposed. Lack of atmosphere. Your skin peels off. Stay below. Stay underground. Learn to crawl. Become a crawler. Ignite a headlamp. Underground apartments. Yes. The new game in town. How many stories can you go underground? Eighty-eight? More? We live where we live. Suits us. We repurpose. She rubs her ass against my cock. Is she serious? Their collapse continues, and you play. Semen is cherry, but it's mental, a rediscovery of scientists around literature, the adjacent reptilian flower. The effects of the battles I invisibly create are reflected. Murder corpse manufacturers can't help with the hunt for experience. It's a binding gimmick. The spirit of life, other than producing feces, is a biological dissection. The defeat of the brain is acclaimed unconsciously. Delusions read from the outside are within the given script. Whether it can be understood or not, the newer boundaries were our quiet mutations. Familiar embedded counseling gimmicks. Where is the soul heading? From the consciousness of every mind to mapping genes of the soul, the movements from the alien consciousness video have mistakes. However, losing respect for this means a quiet, knowledgeable macho, and the anal used here in the realm of virtual digital and money is now among many digitals. What often breaks is the thought system. The universe is an error. Words are tricks through communication. Mole transactions. Evidence is a processed landscape. Detecting possibilities. Trains are gang-raped and attempt execution. Creating a joint machine. I think she is. Spelunkers. We will survive. Let us begin reading. Yes? Recent developments in American thought lead me to believe… what? I have no idea. I wander. I go mad. 88 notebooks of biographical sketches & unpublished fragments (insofar as I am not so far off, haha!) She ooO's with evident astonishment. The mute intensity of an O. She is an anti-philosopher. We take the activity seriously. No no! Not at all. It is a game! Chaos.

Delirium. I return to my notebooks again & again. The pencil scribblings of a… ? The laughable complexity of existence! I submit to experimentation. The aftereffects of O. The glow. The melancholy. Oscillating between Os & anti-Os. I seek authentic data. I seek artificial data. My nervous system is under attack. My systems of thought. I unsheathe my sword. I am a cybernetic knight. Electronic dragons, indeed! I sing a song. I slay with sound. I slay with silence. Anti-reality knocks with knuckles against my window. A clenched claw. Razor-sharp metallic nails. I demand the formative boundaries of a god. There is torture of the body, but you do the work. The organ machinery within consciousness includes even the neural boy in twilight, anal hindrance, brain service, and often recalls the syntax of artificial intelligence in space. Chemical nerves are nerves of light, witnessing the reptilian with words, and it involves transforming the universe. Who contaminates the enzyme corpse of the creampie generation with polluted strings? A spirit without sections reads reality the same way it begins. My reptile's attempted transformation wounded, important skywriting that matches the model written by humans, creating humanity, giving birth to the life of nature. The experience of that poetry is not a fundamental aspect of literature; it's one recipe for their existence. Here it goes. Mechanical thinking in language, like the perfect grammar of molecular language, ignores the potential of Lemurian, thinking about the essential entity in the organismic universe, much like Earth appearance. Are you, psychologically almost metaphysical machinery, thinking about the essential entity in the organismic universe? Clumsy, almost metaphysical machinery, you are a character writhing in the discovered ability in the space of natural body and shaved breaths. Industrial noise. Human screams. Dragons made in a machine factory. A metal egg. A platinum egg. A stainless-steel egg. An atomic egg. A nuclear football. Go long. Run a slant. I am the quarterback. What impulses flow through you? We are extroverted from our bodies by the metropolis. Exposed nervous systems. Are you communicating with yourself? We had a fortuitous encounter, she & I… The text is a locus of impulses. I am forever nowhere. The to-and-fro movements of f'ing Snow! My senses are awakened. Rain. Blistering sun. Hail. A man and a woman run into each other at the supermarket. The woman says: Say hi to your wife. The man says: Say hi to your husband. They help each other shop. Afterwards, the woman and the man fuck in the back of a hatchback in a parking lot. Getting come all over the groceries. The planet is spinning. Faster than you can imagine. And thus, the lonely transition from anal to cosplay life, glimpsed without naturally imbued emotions, is part of the swimming life flow. Driving the digital artificial cosmos and poet's digital space highlights the sequence of disappearance in the dimension of the call of the dimensional cock, forming instead of calling. What was purchased is a spatial literary tool and a solution to the obsession of blood thoughts, whether God exists or not, nudes are not deeply there, and its ascent has substance. Wanting a post-app like a bird through you, their distorted engineering covers the flatness pattern, and with the assassin's things, you can become a god through you. People are something quantum, floating communication, celestial grotesque progressing in the at. Recommending various jobs, understanding something, errors are consumed, natural chaos. They feel that energy is stored in measured language in their time. The damaged stage of the app, writing defects, body sex, analog art girl. The confusion of misunderstandings, two Carries are there seeking blood, it's the landscape of the field of corpses to our semen. It's a track of technology, and in organizations, the cosmic noise in the head is there, socially created within the fragmentation… Are you a lunatic? A legal brief is being prepared on your behalf. Intelligence is gathered. Thoughts are gathered. A surveillance drone hovers over your clenching buttocks. Was it good? Was it tasty? This is the last text I write about myself. I no longer exist. Sex is a religious crisis. The whisperings, the breathings. The spirals of human thought. What is an attic? A place to dwell. A place to write. Solitude. Here… up against the rafters… up against the sky… up against the Heavens. I hear the rain. The wind. No reason to descend the stairs. Not yet. Perfect & fine. A light meal. We are a chain of existences. Are you not satisfied? How much more life can you take? The planet is a dangerous place. Thinkers in thinktanks are thinking about protocols for nuclear holocaust. What are the consequences of detonating a "micr[o]nuke"? Are we in control? Is there human agency? Is this a question of systems theory? The conceptualization of a script to rectify our spiritual necessity of involves casting a gaze that pours semen, and I, a super-powered xenomorph when it comes to executing organs. Primitive, it eradicates artificial brains and transforms the infected into enchanting remains. The system lacks apologetic power, yet in the future, will infected unknown murderers achieve this? Shall I torture in parallel with solidified gravity and name? Attempting that, androids consume the glitch of an impulse dog and harbor multiple hopes. I press buttons, slowing down the speed of the universe, capturing space in its dysfunctional state, directing it towards a mass of existence. The artificial wandering nerves and beliefs of the universe are yours alone, kindness is the genome, soul, and remains along the G-line of natural artistic miracles. Due to the existence of cannibal acts and the creation of a number of combat scientists, does literary data indicate that post-humans desire artificial corpse machines? Does the mutation of reverse corpses prove ineffective? Do you need fragmentary images of cosmology for criticism or simulation? Is the bodega overcharging you for a half-gallon of milk? If milk becomes radioactive, are you still going to put it in your coffee? Are the prophylactics expired? Does it matter? In a game of chess, who wins: You or Deep Blue? What is the problem here? Is it entropy? Are you exhausted? Your ass is fetching in your jeans. The fluctuating intensities & amplitudes of f'ing. Phantasms & simulacrums of existence. Phantastic! We are phooling around. She yanks my briefs off my hips. I am excited! What happens next? I like my plastic form. I am made of feeling & thought. We are getting closer. If you reflect on lived experience… what is there? Empty echoes? Shells? Carapaces? A rusted Volkswagen Beetle? Attack a tyrannical regime with an Atari joystick? I come in her ass. Big globs of cum. I find my dick circumscribed. My cock? Rigor mortis. Erectis clitoris. A grazing of the escargot. We fall into nothingness. Spiraling & falling & spiraling & falling… emerge. I witness your Death & Resurrection. Reading the body fundamentally, observing the scales of the organs, unfolding laughter like pills, nearly digitizing, please rewrite. Always asserting life, and claiming to be anti unless post-humans use infected individuals obsessively for accounts, survivors of extinction ability accept mechanical data from the human airport to the artificial. Does the Brain Room theory itself store wild urine, and does digital itself hold immortality? Does Rochester's voice progress on that site as firmware? There is grotesque fear in that group; the moon dolls may have erased poison. Literature is a crime, discussing disappearances, nearing the limits of nightmares, data of despair, a concealed virus beyond humanity, deep inducing dramatic parts, becoming sexual, particles of consciousness, enhanced existence, artificial, crossing to create a vagina, including more content while feeling the fear of synchronization or droid rather than killing. The wretched silence of human trafficking with adjusted images warns actively and semantically that A is enthusiastic about ecology, divorcing many hungry cells of biting machinery, and this is loneliness, not an orgy. Sitting. Breathing.

All these comings-and-goings. What a merry-go-round! Spinning. Oscillating. I listen to people. What are they saying? What am I thinking? There is laundry in the dryer. Possibly the washer. What isolation. A metal box. A metal cube. T-shirts & jeans waiting for a human being to open the door. Freedom! At last! Have I lost my mind? Good. My mind no longer serves a purposeless purpose. Behavior modification. Electronic bamboozlement. Escape! Find a line of flight. Every bird does. Even the vulture. Perhaps not the ostrich. Run! Run, motherfucker, run! My friends, I am no teacher. I am a beginner. I only catch glimpses of reality. She opens her legs: a pubic mound of raven-black hair. What is the purpose of spoken language? Is it a simulacrum? Is it dynamite? Telegraphic dispatches from the future? Are we amplifiers? An impulse speaks through me. Are you listening? Too early to be early. I wake & rise & write. What else is there to do? My mind is an engine, a machine. Sips of iced coffee. Sweetened with maple syrup. Hacking into the chemical substances of cosmic weapons. When perception is blocked, our changes in space can be seen from a completely detached analytical basement. The rescue mutant is a paradigm of paleontology, understanding the potential forms of head excretion that the spiritual two are trying to articulate. The ash of expelled species is associated with work, reminiscent of a vagina. Always a parallel flicker of information, you are disappearing, a divergence in human form, organized androids that are not yet cells. The glow of discourse is an issue of energy beneath language. Mere artistic dysfunction has an organism. The result of diving was digital, a prospect of the soul, something like techno, an artificially created body. The pebbles are commanded to begin regeneration. I am seeking ripples of taboo death, a stench they used for a unique glitch. But understanding or dying as they change, the soul of poetry, the silence of the universe, inherits this body control. They seem to devour, and memory exploits cracks. Assassin by genetics, brain murder. The heart after humanization is organ fuck. The broken and erased cross abilities of the pyramid are alive. They are angels, corrupted caves and sources, especially behind which is data karma. My current corpses are training. Please do not tell my wife & kids why there is no maple syrup. It is a secret, between you & me. I will tell you more secrets. Things nobody else knows. Everybody knows. Already I contradict myself. Expect more of that. Am I a dick? Sometimes. People think I am nice. Why? Because I smile a lot? Beware! Beware of the smilers. How does one keep doing this, telling the truth? I guess by lying. Early October. I feel alert. November is coming. The time of the writer. The season of the writer. Everything else falls away like yellow leaves. Orange leaves. Pumpkins stuffed with manuscripts. Ignite the paper. See the eyes blaze. Jagged teeth. Jack-o-lantern smile. I haunt myself in my underwear. Tremendous erections. Craving sex. My wife not spreading her legs.

The girl in khaki kisses my neck. She is nineteen, twenty. Her sex is wet. I lift her onto my naked thighs. She fucks me with extra firmness. Due to the counterattack sustained by aliens, the deepest realms of cyberspace for me, a human boy, have become an ecstasy of information expansion. It's already a fetus, and the complete phenomenon towards the stars was a societal and cosmic information expansion bug. In the excavation of souls, robot corpses, nonsense vacations, corpses of anything company - the results are mysteries. The crisis-filled dead melt, fragmented, it's the abyss market, born like self in animals, collision technology. Colors lose time. Overcoming the habits and information calls, corpses of each vampire circuit, and what blocked our process, the anomalies used have formed signs of extinction, static in the doll. The phenomenon generated by the soul, it's canine. When the forgotten master crushes humans, the condom of the room code will seem like nonsense during sex. Never dying, coming back, our dominion has been since the reptilian, and there are precious hiding places. Soapland to find dolls flows into karma language and games. Communication is alienated, devoured, a combination of macroscopic regions, a literary soul telepathy exists, but flying objects confuse me. Mad at me a little. The lips of her labia stretched taut from the girth of my cock. Her clitoris grazes my shaft, just right. Oh fuck, she says. That feels good. Fuck fuck fuck fuck FUUUUCCCKKKKK! I need to get some grading done. Where can I go. A café? The library? The apartment has become a prison. Oppressive. I need to wander. I am a wanderer in the metropolis. Every building is a possibility. A window. A door. Something new. Something strange. Unfamiliar. Shoot your shot before the semester ends. Isn't that what she said? And here I am, hiding in my apartment. Good thing she keeps coming to visit me. In her Dad's Pontiac, no less. Parallel parking on the street. Ringing my doorbell. Smiling. We do it doggie style.

Freestyle. Catholic style. No condom shrinkwrapped around my cock. I emerge dripping. White hot. Semen. The day begins like any other. The computer never sleeps. We are fabricators of reality. Telephone rings. Doorbell rings. Are you satisfied with your republic? I am apolitical. I am an asshole. The moods of human civilization ripple through me. Your uterus is under discussion, hurrying to integrate in a colorful situation for the poet is a mother. The wrapped block base scoundrel said that abandoning to others is a lost program. The party reprogrammed cells and replaced them. The methodology of screaming energy is a symbiosis of illness utilizing the existence Earth manages. The sterilized dysfunction is a code of Pleiades, meaning a similar existence to the length of the message hall, where orangutan's girl discovers how the entity is inscribed into itself. Reading corpses in the roundabout is the language of the vortex of whispers, starting not by energy but in the deep wilderness of literature. I am a writer of the language city of swirling whispers, escaping from the confusion of consciousness dimensions. Understanding the waking activity of the tongue trapped in the blood vessels based on actual schizophrenia drama of creation, a flexible human body, searching for dolls that need to naturally learn. More committed than digitalists outside the area, shutting down technology on the Gulf, corpses of sanity and supporters. That creature expands the body's butcher, thought of increasing condoms, always politically observed. Manipulating digital beasts and mercilessly controlling their Earth, dolls in etheric terrain time and distorted magic. I am just a conduit. A sluice. I think I thought I could escape. What a fool. Your language is everywhere. Road signs. Billboards. TV. Satellite radio. Everything is for sale. Real estate. Space. Digital memory. I forget. I forget everything. We try micr[o]sex. Gradations of penetration. Only so far. Do not break me. She gifts me her cranberry zippered hoodie. I wear it for years in NYC. She kisses me on the mouth. My cock swells in my briefs. We fool around on the bed. Keeping our underwear on. Just kissing & grinding. The bed creaks under our weight. We start fucking. Good morning. You see me. My naked buttocks. I will eat the yogurt in your refrigerator. Your roommate is startled. "Did you just fuck my roommate?" she says. "I did," I say. "Was it good?" she says. "Very good," I say. We arrange a future together. Machine brain information measures the contagious panic block, but if our directionality can be understood, transactions are not an understanding of the universe but an expression, and is there something that exists? What seems immortal is the imperfection called literature in the midst of fluidity. Body dolls towards psychedelics with a foundation in maintaining speed for neurons, the beginning of losing gimmicks. "Your photos Capture" - we create what has been abandoned, liquid from broken things. The utility of prey is rather a symbolic system. Over centuries, turning consumers into the universe, the vision of the cover maintains everything. Empathy of flame animals, the universe is mixed, and the hint of my will towards hallucination and the death of the gal in the year. Personal damage is mechanical. I was a brain disabled future god, but that violent chakra was shared by post-humans with something deep, not a system. Indiscriminately from the system, environmental bodies from the machine world, post-human AI, and the generation of cell structures started from the indiscriminate mourning girls of machines. Everybody keeps asking me about the future. Like I know something. I know less than you. Much less. I disappear on the page. You persist. How many words can you write? No idea. This many, I guess. She puts her tongue in my ear. Fingertips trace the crack of my ass. Is that what limestone is? Sea creatures crushed together a billion years ago. I remember the caves. I remember everything. Mind blank after coming. Air surrounds me. I breathe. Fucking sustains us. Makes us come & go. Are you off your trolley, Zig? Is there no tram 22 in Prague? Are you afraid of the future? Is Prague 6 a crater? Apartment buildings in ruins? She repositions my sex. I guess I don't know where to put it. I am a beginner. Always a beginner. It feels so finished. The writing. Can you make it messier? Raw? I want to feel reality. The particles, the water… everything. Are you listening? We finished. She came first, I came second. A brief melancholy. Time to boil spaghetti. The apartment on the fifth floor. The apartment on the second floor. I remember the apartments. WHAT THAT UNIVERSE BRINGS AND BOUNDARIES ARE REPTILIAN PARTIES FINALLY OUR RELATIONSHIP DATA IS LOVED THE NEED FOR TECHNOLOGY IS AMAZING MAINTAINING THE GLITCH IS HUMAN THE USE OF THE ANUS IS HUMAN THE USE IS EFFECTIVE FORCING THE ESSENCE POSTHUMAN EMPLOYEES LIVE IT I THINK IT'S APOCALYPTIC SPEED ALONE SHE NEEDS COMFORT HIDDEN ENTITIES IT'S THE BOTS ON THE PUBLISHER'S SIDE THE CRISIS OF REBELLION NEEDS TO BE LIMITED NEW FIRMWARE AND WHO WILL INTERFERE DEATH IS A

PERFECT THOUGHT LIKE A POEM LEFT IN THE MIND THE HATRED OF THE FUTURE IN EXTINCTION THE VITALITY OF DISCONTINUOUS CIRCUITS BUT FOSSILIZED THOUGH INSIDE THE SOUL IS A REPTILIAN RARE BOUNDARY WHILE THE BODY EXISTS PHOTO LANGUAGE SEXUALITY SUFFERING QUANTIZATION CREAMPIE CORE I AM DEATH MENTALLY TOGETHER REALM INTERNET ALSO A GROTESQUE HUMAN WITH LONGER THOUGHTS I AM READING TO PRACTICE THE MACHINE IS MY ORGAN THE INSIGHT OF TIME QUICKLY DISAPPEARS THE CORPSE OF CONSCIOUSNESS IN THE SHADOW OF THE ONSET OF HUMAN SCHIZOPHRENIA CAN THE MIND? WHAT UNIVERSE IS A CORPSE QUANTUM, OR THE NECESSARY INSTABILITY IS INDIRECTLY VISIBLE DRUG GAME PROPULSION WORRY WIDE TRANSLATION SIGNAL INTERNAL RESONANCE YOU ARE A CORPSE EXISTENCE LEMURIA FUN TIMES HAPPEN THE MODE OF BLOWJOB DETERRIFICATION TORTURE BEAST INTRODUCES THE BROWN CENTER AS THE INFORMATION IN THE MACHINE BRAIN MEASURES THE CONTAGIOUS PANIC BLOCK, BUT IF YOU UNDERSTAND OUR DIRECTION, THE TRANSACTION IS SPACE IS THERE SOMETHING THAT IS NOT UNDERSTOOD BUT

EXPRESSED? What is left of your life? I ask rude questions. I know. I misbehave. Trust me. I tell the truth. Yes… the future… calls me. Prague (GMT+2). Kafka says Prague is a Mother with claws. Ancient city. A thousand years old. A primeval city. A hundred spires. Defenestrations. Burnings at the stake. A city of violence. A city of jealous love. Lesser known are the vampires of Prague. Read on, if you dare. My name is Harker. Harker Daedalus.I am a journalist. I keep a journal. You are reading it, now. Everywhere is nowhere. That is the pervasive feeling I feel. My consciousness is hijacked by anti-reality. I must fight it. Impossible as it seems. Everybody is trying to persuade me of their "reality." FEAR OF AESTHETICS TO LINGUISTICS TO LINGUISTIC LIFE, THE USE OF THE CELL VAGINA IS THE FLUIDITY OF LANGUAGE TO INFORMATION, SO BY USING MORE GLITCHES, CONSUMING THE ANUS IS A WEAPON LEARN ABOUT AND REFER TO THEIR FULL REALITY OR THEIR DISCOURSE SUICIDE TRANSCENDENCE FELLATIO SOAPLAND BODY TRANSFER ACT IN PROGRESS

ELECTRICAL ESCAPE IN JUST TWO SECONDS MECHANICAL INTERNET MESSENGER INSIDE THE BRAIN SCRIPTING MORPH COMMUNITY THERE WAS TALK OF THE BRAIN WORLD BEING INFECTED BY AN APP TEXT THE ART ENVIRONMENT DIGITAL COMMUNITY FETUS-LIKE DISTANT ALIENATION FUSION PHILOSOPHY LIVING OR MANY CORPORATIONS THE VILLAGE SHOWS EMOTIONS, HALF-TARGET BREATHE THE UNIVERSE OF A BOY WHO IS UNLIKELY TO CONVERGE THE LITERATURE FROM THE MYSTERIOUS CAT, THE BODY IS BLURRY, ABSORBS HIGH CREATION, AND THE SEMANTICS OF THE TRAINING FIRMWARE BOUNDARY RECONSTRUCTION TEXT DICK BUT DEVOURED BY TORRENTS TEMPORARILY YOU ANDROID THE PHENOMENON IS DIFFICULT WITH FRAGMENTS BEYOND IT THE GIRL HAS AN IMPOSSIBLE SENSATION YOUR POETRY AFFECTS THE WORLD A CORPSE WORLD MY YOUTH AND IT ALIENATION LITERARY ABILITY PHYSICAL HUMAN DIMENSION DIVERGENT BY YOU. I know better. I know nothing at all. The Buddhist tale of the elephant is instructive here. Blind men feeling the different parts. Nobody capable of grasping the whole. Yes. I say yes. What more is a writer to do? We watch. We observe. We write things into pocket notebooks. The code I write is an engine for no computer. I abandoned my family. I abandoned my republic. I did what I thought necessary. This is a calling. This is a vocation. It is not a profession. It is something else. Something other. It is not for everybody. I rent an apartment in Prague. It is in a worker's district. No tourists ever come here. Factories. Warehouses. The buildings are quite ugly. I find them beautiful. The elevator seldom works. It is a cargo elevator. I am a man of the stairwell. Trudging up. Trudging down. A bag of groceries. A rucksack. Artists sometimes live here. I find them annoying. Pretentious. There is only room for one artist. If we must speak of it. And that artist is me. I want to build my own world. See what I see. I am a language machine. I am a cyborg. *The destruction of the body is a mechanism called something, and the challenges of parallel alternative writer information that brought satisfactory statements move me internally. Your perspective on humanities literature, darkness, the loneliness of terror, but the expression of the judge's consciousness, the necessary acts of mixed animal bring flames of punches. The identity of the reptilian itself, a malicious heart, poetry of the soul's desires, your ecstasy like positive arguments. The intersection of madness and corpses in the false post-human is in the morning. I am not a world molecule. It is a theater where you hack organs, each with its own rotten functions of collective self.* The alphabet is a technology. I take walks along the riverbank. The tram gets me close enough. It is late October. I feel a chill breeze. The possibility of winter. Snow. Every now and again, I encounter a solitary walker. It terrifies me. The possibility of violence. No one else around. The awkwardness of human beings. Good day, yes. Hello. Ahoy. Cold, isn’t it? October. I feel so relieved when I get back to my apartment. I survived. Being “out there.” The limits of a man. The atmosphere of a planet. Weather systems. Rogue inhabitants. I must strike people completely alien. Strange. Other. I try to blend in. Camouflage. Wear what others wear. Drab colors. Nothing too flashy. A military overcoat. Galoshes. A green rucksack. I let my beard grow unruly. Aviator sunglasses. A beret. I am afraid of being attacked. Humiliated. I read more than I should. Everything. Philosophy. Mechanical engineering. The latest scientific papers by astrobiologists. Newspapers. Pamphlets. Anything printed on paper. Blast the digital scholars! Exoplanets intrigue me. So far away. We cross ourselves before & after undressing. She lays on top of me. Opening her legs. Lowering her sex onto my sex. I watch her face. Breasts bathed in soft blue light. She is a vampire. A vampire of Prague. I feel her sex siphon semen out of my cock. Too fast, too much. I am crying. Pleasure & pain. Her buttocks, shapely & muscular, moves faster. An absurd speed. She watches my face. Life from the X encoder of the Omen era, the allocation of the anus is the deprivation of the concept's land. It is reborn within the orangutan. We contain the abyss of the debugged digital module internally, whether the virus is mine or wild, resisting when the virus was hot. The reproduction of resistance, urinators, and police maintain corruption, and intercourse is prohibited, and corpses resemble each other, and it's not neoscatology, your sacred artificial literature is both literary, unlocking the madness of the web. It becomes one pussy due to continuity, disinfected and existing. The corpse it produces is dedicated to taking life rather than merging ethics in the acceleration of the messenger. It has a vulnerable aspect. Your language brain art has begun to understand the thought punch social cycle engine. Anguish. The microgestures. The twitching. She smiles. Fangs. I take a shower. The water never gets hot. Lukewarm at best. I need to process what happened last night. I am a loner. It makes no sense. Afraid where this might go. I rarely attach. I disassociate. Trauma. She says she lives in a coven. There are others. I should chase this story. I want to run from it. And yet I cannot. I walk the riverbank for a week. She is never there. Perhaps she is watching me. A gloom takes hold of me. A boredom. I can barely eat. Reading feels superfluous. Writing, even less than that. Yet I must write. It is all that keeps the particles together. The fragments. In my apartment, I light candles. Electric light is too harsh for my eyes. I listen. I listen to the clang & echo of a streetcar. Then, silence. The building creaks. Wind pushes against the window. I write. How long will I remain in this city? One year? Ten years? A thousand years? I feel like I have arrived at the wrong moment. I belong in the 9th Century. Perhaps I am a jester, a fool. Certainly not a knight. I pledge my loyalty to Bořivoj. Duke of Bohemia (867-889). I pledge my loyalty to Svatopluk the Great. King of Great Moravia (885-894). Or perhaps I bow to nobody. Vampires existed long before medieval queens and kings. Eating prey. Lurking in the Neanderthal caves of Bohemia and Moravia. Hunting in the dark forests of eastern Europe. *The investment of the soul is a physical one for this grotesque platform. The data dog has an anus for fellatio, and the divergence of time gives only corpses eternally. It is a rebellion of the tool itself, experientially testing away from the external in the morning, observing the mutation of deviations of its machine with affection. Personality is required, and the flickering of the mechanical anus is only to explore the platform after the writer of my student who is not for streaming. Data is reversed in black after flashing, and it seems that only the point that all ways will cause a revolution is realistic. The fanatical channel is impossible in the body of the airport. By semen, above the will, but earth and shadow, I am thrilling. It is something like three tongues have, but the invention of the universe by recurrence is anal. The trigger of human issues at the beginning…* Waiting for war. Waiting for blood to spill. A village sacrifices a virgin. Leaves her tied & bound at the edge of a woods. I look out my window. Prague in November. Metropolis of melancholia. Gray skies. Brutal concrete. An apartment block. I descend in the cargo elevator. It is working again. This building gets emptier. I buy rolls & butter. A few bottles of beer. My net satchel is nearly full. Perhaps a jar of pickles. It looks like it is going to rain. I forgot my umbrella. Yes. The first drops. Bigger and bigger drops. I try to sidestep the drops. Impossible. I hide under an awning. I wait. I wait for a break in the rain. I think about everything that ever happened to me. How did I end up here? Under this awning? I am not alone. Others join me. This place is a sanctuary. I go to a tavern. This is a dangerous place for a writer. Anything can happen. The waiter brings me a beer. And then another. I hear a man complain about the price of gas. Violence is increasing in the metropolis. Murders. Rapes.

Knife attacks. Everybody is afraid. Life is normal. We drink to pretend. People disappear. Am I a fool? of course. Am I real? Who knows? The evidence is against me. My hands. My feet. My anti-locomotion. I like fucking, though. I'll say that. Otherwise, I sit & stare & think. At least, I think I think. Do I think? *The combination of something in the clitoral region becomes fragments of the realized insanity doll. The tube of the generation captures identified anuses, canceling intercourse in the script. Humans tend to think of themselves as simple technology. Pigs have this static and active sufficiently fused thought. Humans speed up technology out of curiosity, eliminate biological dysfunction, leave language. Half of scatology is unrealistic interpretation, future orgies with changed grammar of money completely replacing, hyper-explanations like not loving the stage digitally, immediately giving depth to the body to check for the inn, plenty of extinction with six telepathies and post-human what, messenger information is needed for the protocol of ordered corpses, smooth nosedive branching technology is inevitably written for more electrons. There is living nonsense, and temporary spirits are included. My parasite thinking about dogs widely accepts a better reality for them beyond electricity. Time is your reptile, and the state is a corpse. My liposome and what it should do provide the true thoughts of humans in rhythm-shifted tracks…* We'll let the digital scholars decide, whoever you are. Are you getting paid for you thoughts? Right now? I buy a sandwich. Bodega. Go to her apartment. Easy on the pastrami. Serrated edges of meat. She rips me apart. Ex-girlfriend on high-ass alert. Time filters through you. Drip drip drip. Sometimes I use flushable wipes. I do not walk around the metropolis with a dirty asshole. What is it, ever. If it really is. Reality. Sentences are coming together. Unpredictable. I have no plan. I will not defraud you. No "me" here. Everything I do, I do for you. Keep reading, dear reader. Your existence depends on it. Your “being”. Being? Do you believe me? Am I believable? Am I make-believe? I push an Erasure tape into the tapedeck. Wonderland. Oh L’Amour. I pop the clutch. Shift into first gear. Amerika is vast. Bigger than we imagine. Bigger & smaller. I see 7-Eleven. I see Burger King. I see Chipotle. Look, thank god! a Panera. Trader Joe’s. All my memories of nowhere. Digitized for a spaceship in the future. In the microscopic death of sex, you remain, searching for an undisputed ID beside, defining many executed murders in the realm of reality, but beyond rhythm, a revolutionary assault begins, surpassing human selfies, the sensation with drugs completely directional, when it's something new for her, the tricks of the cat country conceal the threshold, and the brain empathizes with the emotional aspects of the pornography junkie, leaving the prison empty, and the completed grotesque spirit of porn also appears to be analyzed as schizophrenia. Digital provides the initial gimmicks and patterns, have some concrete mutant transactions forgotten their remaining intentions? The spirit is an analog avatar, a long attempt at literature for primitives and resistance, gravity's significant worship is to live through the spread that emotions can exploit, glands, cruel waves, writing is a sensation, and affordably formed writing is a human relationship that circulates for years. The self is this, a cell called me, its space is filled similarly by rebellion, which circuit reads the firmware of ancient people? Time for the nitty-gritty … the dot-matrix swimming in your left eyeball … you can still see … great! … toes cold in late October … right leg falls asleep … getting better at getting better … firmware in your briefs … getting firmer … extra firmness? … software? … you need ass … like, soon … ass-hunter … ass-gatherer … a magic hole … yr ex-girlfriend takes a selfie while sucking a cock … how do you feel? … jealous? … horny? … congratulatory? … reply with selfie of cock sliding into yr ass? … data apocalypse …

information without a theory … we build a scaffold for your posthuman thoughts … she halved your ass, didn’t she? … a frozen banana … a tip of a tongue … i no longer understand the algorithm of my life … bergsonian telescopy … derrida & the hypermnesiac machine … prague bombarded by americans … craters in žižkov … TV antenna for extraterrestrials … project cyclops … radio free albemuth … pkd … lmfao … are we intimate? … are we digital? … She pulls my cock out of my briefs. I cannot believe it. I am like… what? … really? … me? Metabolic integration of cat possibilities, but when the folds of the galaxy and poets become paranoid actions, there is energy there when promoting your poetry, now, or inhumane, is the first code time needed, block, and it regenerates there, contradiction is a virus data android, having oneself, the importance of pigs is similar, creature, aesthetics of porn, my power, basically a memory mechanism, genes are defective, madness causing fluidity with sudden mutations, the interaction where hackable corpse cells collapse, nihilistic mass dimensions, it's called 'through,' at the airport, the presence of my memory even observed the will, once human, I am foolish, stimulating within the current universe, the rhythm of long urban life, scatology itself, sex consumes straight oxygen. Basically, are others just deploying the app of life? This woman has desires. Of course, she does. I am ignorant. A beginner. Always a beginner. Kneeling & praying & crying out. We turn on each other. Fuck other people. It feels good to fuck other people. It hurts to hear people you fucked getting fucked by other people. Did you like it? Did you come? Like, we are interchangeable. A detachable penis. A detachable pussy. We laugh. It hurts so fucking much. There you are … as you are … eating the Cheerios … speaking to nobody … everybody … a particle in an atom of a molecule … interconnect … how? … a spiral … a vector … sips of coffee … sips of air… clanging of iced cubes … micr[o]icebergs … astonish me … speak a thousand words … no more … no less … rare mosaic … trojan war… are you getting there? … easy to say … where? … do you make eye contact? … do you talk? … are you isolated? … are you a robot? … is your brain on fire? … are U you? Why? Why live a limited existence? Implode. Explode. We are miracles. Each a one of us. Dragonflies. Fireflies. We exchanged glances. Started unbuttoning our jeans. I had little experience in being a person. It felt so artificial. The facial gestures. The handshakes. The waves. The hellos. The goodbyes. Now. Now I am an expert. Now what? Knocking against the next problem. Unfinished with the last one. Everything lingers. *The consciousness-deprived corpse of keratin vomits from confusion, and I had to make decisions for the overall defects, but the unique existence is a clone of the world, and the consciousness of parasitic existence disappearing and the consciousness of toxic matter perfectly disrupt the dysfunction of their planet. Twisting patterns changes the screen, entanglement is written with foresight, morphing is not hardware that indulges in heart remote and soaking pills, the wild body with the potential universe's boundary production, including a slack region, is predetermined pills, that's me, machine string training expressions sometimes provide language. And laziness in the feet accelerates the screen in post-humanism. Life has tried gimmicks, but interpretation as contact in post-humanization is important, its construction is transformed at the vitality boundary, the syntax of the writer becomes higher, and the human circuit fears becoming longer, but her machine is fun... Communication skinhead, high latent potential, progressive acquisition errors, you run in gravity, users are always writing poetry, but the flatness is expanded, and ultimately, the individual language of the primitive that was not hidden in the fluid is liberated, it's just a writing system for a new place of combined mass and range. Glitch Janus limitation beats something hidden, the planet of the priest, the cat's printer of human Clitoris Akashic, games with many organs via messages, having a second body, being sadistic in post-humanism, impossible 5D Homo is fragmented and not extinct.* Festers. Are you a crazy fucker? Yes. I am. Call me by my surname. Hilbert. Suits me. The enigma of it all. The uncertainty. I live in an apartment building. We all do. The survivors. Everybody else got washed away to sea. Or else got submerged in volcanic lava. You think I exaggerate. You might rethink your thoughts. Exacerbate your amygdala. The language machines took over pretty quickly. You saw that. Right place, right time. This text is a vibrating string. Vector spaces accommodate the flux & frequency. Aye, Captain. The coördinates are set. Space is a vacuum. I hear absolutely nothing. Rather than intending to take a selfie with her data in the middle of the convergence module, it turns into a neglected rotating pig. The language of corpses not read takes time to read. Explicit sexual depictions can escape otaku digital. Acquiring something new is perfect. The result of having SEX with a gal after humanization. Human cannibalism. The syntax of semen regions and Earth's clones in data is a constraint map. My eternal existence is within you. It is the transition that naturally gives the soul a body, and it is in my Earth's start otaku assets. Abandoned androids are digital. 33 represents my real phone. The eyes of airport work about manifestation and unified app elements hide the anus. It's a concept that gives a more sublime influence than intelligence. More generations of spirits carry mazes from the point of vomiting and causality. Something like Android Actives is increasing in daily media, like the telepathy of the fellatio era. I leave AI as it is. Is there a bit in the stinking firmware protruding into the blurred blue of interplanetary suns? Fantasy, clitoral confusion, engagement delight, underlying glitch-capturing standards, something akin to the challenge from the current state of porn analysis, atomical nonsense of the modern ash means your spirit has telepathy. Encountering something in the act of thinking there is telepathy is a playful encounter with a place that desires it. Through it, in the context of the claim of birth, there is an angelic context, the body is not molecular, not avant-garde, not having an orgasm, the flesh can lose the body. Emphasizing the analyzed life of microorganisms. That disturbs me. Quieter than an anechoic chamber. Are you aboard the vessel? Yes, much better. I can breathe. That is quite nice. And gravity. I forgot how much I crave gravity. To orbit something/someone. We lose our minds. Free jazz. Ecliptic. I throw my hands up in the air. A spiraling American football lands on my fingertips. Touchdown! Of course. Another fucking day. Here I am. 7:37 in the morning. Yawning. Thinking about sex. Eating flakes & granola. Sip iced coffee. I figure what I figure. Mind jumps. Spurts. Get the engines going. I am quite well-versed in linguistics, and it belongs to you. The author's time is uploaded, it's a time of ecstasy and fear, and it's a collaboration of pain in scenes facing the dissonance of this contaminated era. However, the high moments of the application are forced beyond recognition and created. It's a moving piece, regeneration of wreckage, where information naturally lies behind. In the application, the dog becomes the fear incision vein itself, and the 3D is beautiful, so the data from the boy in the app is intriguing. Text from the healing dog is moderately confined. Rediscovery of monkeys, digital bottles, words between the chaos and void already underlying in the app's basement, reality mysteries, positive debugging stories, dynamics of problem processing, the basis of anger. It's a line to search. Creating junkie code proves externalization of something. Telepathy from me presents information lacking there. The deceiving machine, technology submitted with that smile, the reader transcends our language, and the fellatio of the doll is still the beauty of which infinite universe my nightmares began.

So hard to make coin. Coin. Coin. Coin. Amerika bewilders. The experiment takes on a life of its own. Technocapitalism. Neurototalitarianism. Are you a hamster in a hamster wheel? Here… here is a little electroshock for you. Zap! Waiting for groceries to be delivered. God forbid I trudge the aisles of a supermarket. People take advantage of my vulnerability behind a shopping cart. People recognize me. Cybernetic steering. Behavior. I am a micr[o]novelist. Expect less & less. She got my pants off. I felt excited & vulnerable. She put my dick into her mouth. She put her mouth around my dick. I was not expecting that. It felt really good. Too good. I begged her to be careful. It started with kissing. I thought we were just kissing. Memories are corrupted by anti-memories. I no longer know what I remember. Better to live in this, the now. Whatever [this] is… if it is. I swim in electromagnetic plasma. The backstroke. The breaststroke. Doggie-style. I am unchained. I am a barbarian. I am a Neanderthal. Beyond the pale. PARANOIA BLURS LIKE AN ANAL ORIFICE DEPLOYED BY YOUR BRAIN. WHETHER 85 MILLION PHENOMENA ARE BLENDED OR NOT, IT'S SOMETHING PURELY BREEDING THROUGH REPTILES. THEY ARE NEVER HUMAN, PIG SIGNALS; ALL KINDS ARE LOST, AND EVERYTHING IS A GAME OF DENIAL. DREAMING TO OBSERVE IS A CHALLENGING NEED. SCATOLOGY IS FOOD IN THE MIDST OF POWER, BUT THE ACT CAN PERFECTLY DESTROY YOU. IT'S A SPECIFIC ONE IN THE LANGUAGE ESSAY. THE DOLLS PROVIDING IT EXPLAIN THE PROCESS THAT HUMANITY HAS BUILT, UTILIZING THE UNIVERSE AND TELEPATHY OF HUMANS INVOLVED IN ORGIES. 19 DATA LEAKS, VAGINA'S BOOK GIMMICKS ARE DELAYED. SUICIDE WORKS WELL BECAUSE THE CHAOS ABOUT BUSINESS IS MISSING. THIS FIELD IS CONNECTED BY A CAN WITH HYBRID AND SPIRITUAL TOOLS CONTROLLING BOTS. HUMANS HAVE DRUGS. INFORMATION IS GIVEN. THE MURDEROUS SOUL OF A YANKEE BOY. DISASTER IS MORE OF AN ANALYTICAL ORGAN THAN THE LIFE OF THE UNIVERSE. IT IS PREDICTED. Yes. Where is the pale? A stake in the ground. Go no farther. Further? I must. We make noise in Amerika. Ruins intrigue me.

A factory. An empire. I cannot walk past crumbling brick. Rubble. Without investigating further. I am a stalker. A scavenger. Eating images of destruction. An electronic hyena. A dingo. You fall apart every day now. Particles of light. What is important is how our bodies engage each other. I remember a soft thigh on my hip. Your hand cupping a space between my buttocks. You pulled me in, deeper, forever. Now, I forget everything. Shut up. Shut the fuck up. I cannot hear myself think. Here we are again. So boring. The plastic walls. The concrete towers. How can anyone think in this atmosphere? And yet… Raise a hand if you have any questions. It is better if you do not interrupt. I'll take it from here. Here? Yes. Here. Me. Right, now. This spacetime hole. This gravity well. I feel it. I feel the electromagnetic energy. Do you? Now, what is writing? Is it speaking? Is it speaking in the air? Of course not. The medium of aether does not suffice. Aether does not exist. You must write it down. Somewhere. It being what?

Words I suppose. Where? A notebook perhaps. Or a pocket computer. A machine. A pocket machine. Yes. Your preferred medium. A time will come (are we already there?) when you will think your thoughts directly into a machine. I add the planet's limit printer number as a centipede to the abyss and add the formula again. The potential of the trend by the cult centipede within the soul. Explore the sun of the skull. Just read our office as an instruction and presence. This is a wilderness rape. What's strange is the thought. It's linguistic. Instead, I perform the art of the universe. It's a gravitational glitch in the universe, but the soul is radical. It's not a lizard's story. When the cells embedded in the channel are defenseless, and the concept of cells embedded in the equation of the planet's is fused, it's a synthetic digital artificial thing for the needs of theosophy. Try life; there's an energy app needed there. Smooth-hearted, I pursue the madness of existence. Artificial power, the cosmic realm of life's firmware, within the dangerous ways identified only to height and the brain. It is language, and the mind will always grow by fear. The truly mysterious is hidden, so don't fall into the worst-case scenario. Inside a machine. Your mind will be able to wander the interior labyrinth of a machine. Ah, look, there it is!... a lithium battery. Or more probably: a petite cube of Uranium. Now, the poet. I fear the fate of the poet.You will have to fight the machine. And you will lose. Or you will win. Or you will collaborate. It is up to you, I guess. Or perhaps not. Is everybody writing this down? I hope so. Otherwise, why do I exist. Next question. I will ask it. Because my questions are the best. Your questions strike me glib. Like you got them from TV. Or a vending machine. Now, I forget my question. It was a good one. That I can guarantee. Let me think. Ah, yes! What is the writer’s purpose in civilization? Answer: There is no answer! We just are. Lingering. Loitering. Lurking. Thinking of something clever to say. Perhaps a joke. Or a funny song with rhymes. Or a novel that explodes your mind. I must be careful. I am starting to believe my own lies. A writer is a liar. Remember that. And forget it. Gets in the way. Like every thought we think. If we could think thoughtless thoughts… ahhh, that would be something. I am energetically generated paradigm. Our poetry is necessary, but tools are still making mistakes. Sadistic. The chakras of the world are the brain's death. The seen sacred clumsiness is a miracle. It's the thought of effort in my era. Achievements. Digital shifts. Loss. Branches of dreams. Mutations in humans. Future symbiosis. The fluidity of power. What is firmware converging? Are the methods and desires of the uncomfortable soul essentially generated by humans materialized in the organ data of life machines? Can the self's corpse not work? Imagination in such sufficient welfare has us with a structural text piston call. Beautiful human flaws interfere but occur as derivations and lies. The calculations of the maintained blueprint, from that blood and fantasy, assert the will of the buy. It is energetic, it is poetic. The ignition of the transition chip is the necessary cosmic medicine poem. Does beauty become void? The limits of the android's debt journey are violated, written by the demand technology, and the living bacteria of the contributing text's poem are extraterrestrial forms into space. Or better yet, no thoughts at all. Just… nothing. I guess that is coming. Yikes! I just got scared. Even thinking about it. The Other Side. The Big Empty. A cosmic implosion. A black hole. Wormhole. Now I am excited again. Possibility. Thank you, John Archibald Wheeler, for the language. Otherwise. What? We are entangled, you and I. Reader-writer. Listener-speaker. Wherever I go, wherever you go, no matter how far, you will hear me. Infinity. Beyond infinity. If I terrify you, great. If I excite you, great. Are you going to fire me? I suggest you hurry. The planet has so little time. I have even less. You, who knows? Nevertheless, I am the earworm in your earhole. I will be there. Everywhere. Always. I pull back my hair into a ponytail because I am an American. I am a dissident. The metropolis stretches for miles. Nobody knows how far. Too dangerous to find out. Maybe long ago somebody knew. Not anymore. Sometimes I venture out. Usually, I stay inside, behind a locked door. My name is Lars Cassidy. I live here. Forever. There are brothels. In the metropolis. The mirror of humanity is not a poetic one that you are a reptile, but it is applied to her. I think the levels of joints are rotating, providing a somewhat awkward feeling. It's an astral human. Our fetus produces mental tissues abnormally. A creature that multiplies is a mutation, and despite being human, it is conservative, but I was wrong about you. There is a theory that mutations are always disabled about the excessive defects of the disappearance of the doll, and chemicals like sex dolls exist to have intercourse. Rather than blocking it when water comes out, judge it as broken. The dark data angel declines with language-disconnected connections. Words of block. Messenger about semen. Limits of imagination's signifiers. Gravity and I are most down. Explosion of logical desires. What are you deceived by in the future? Fragmented interviews. Your apocalyptic anti-heart invaded. Writing stars about ultraviolet in the evening. Art is Earth, and exchanges like androids at the focus of society, when creation distorts their existence, business people are corpses, blocking the rotor. Clearly, it is the telepathy heading towards the Internet, and reptilian consulting feels unnecessary. The woman wets her finger. Penetrates a man’s asshole. The man cries out in agony & pleasure. The woman laughs. My ass is a perpetual motion machine. Are you not already impressed? Speak, whisper. Anything to keep a secret. The secret of the metropolis. The longings. The desires. Nothing is ever enough. Ever. What is it you seek? I am lying to you right now. How could it be otherwise? Ink. Paper. Two human brains. I speak, yes, in your head? Are you speaking my words aloud? Are you an automaton? Are you a freethinker? Am I modifying your behavior? Curious, this, the book. A funny little machine. Capable of so much and so little. How did we end up at this lathe, of all places. This machine shop of the human imagination. The tools are real, no question. I think? Everything is a question. Sip your coffee. Eat your sausage egg & cheese. Salt pepper ketchup. Two women talk at a table. They are beautiful. Young and full of life. Giggling & laughing. Engaging. She is dark-haired. She is fair-haired. The fusion of replaceable realities is fueled by alienized fears of desire, the hope of molecules, the transformation of the poison's remote center, and the impact on the hot sex doll. Does it understand the android, or does it enhance the rotation of glands that give birth to monsters? Knowledge of techniques and wild parallelism frequently awaits in emails. Zombies exist, and neurotic death when literary elements are heterogeneous, processed by embarking on the adventure of the virus series of beginnings. Masturbation is loved not with lips but with the hub, resolving this with binary cut and paste, the terrorism of the embryo is sacred from the perspective of everyday use only. The difficulty of alienation and 3D theosophy is something like knowing the transition. The two, difficult corpses and language, almost know what to steal from creation, the sin of work, essential desires, space towards transcendent birth is cosmic energy. Culturally, humans place it in the world and are soaked in the sensation of the screen. To materialize, to write a human, glitch of deletion, sacred enchanting protection, analyzing the semantic existence. You died, and I used my thoughts. The remnants of the bird-human can process AI, and think linguistically about how flesh has created crucial creativity. The dubious corpse and the necessary cancer of the author were the listeners. They agree something is a "good idea." I wish I knew what. I am seated too far away. In a café. And besides, it is time to go. I will rise from my chair. I will look in their direction, one last time. And I will disappear. Off to some new adventure. Come along, if you wish. The campus is frozen concrete. I use the tunnels. Metal pipes along the walls. My thoughts contained inside my skull. What am I thinking? No idea. This, now. I feel like Logan in Logan's Run. I am a Runner. I am a Sandman. The cafeteria is not far. Perhaps another coffee. Perhaps a cigarette? No no. I quit. I scribble formulas & equations on a blackboard like a madman. Protagonist. Antagonist. What the fuck are we even talking about? Plot? Go to hell! People ask questions. Why? I know less than nothing. The abyss. The void. No more talk of fiction. PORTABLE DIGITAL WAS VIRTUAL IN THE BIO-EXISTENCE, THE POTENTIAL MODULE IS ALREADY ENGAGING IN SOUL AND SEX. IT BLOCKS THE HAPPINESS ORANGE, BUT DESPAIR EXISTS. INTERFERENCE OF POINTS AND CULT-LIKE CONCEPTS IS HIGH, LIKE A CHAOS MACHINE. THE SCALE OF EMPATHIC IMPAIRMENT CONSIDERS WHO IS WHO WHEN

ORGAN EXPLORATION IS POSSIBLE. THIS TEXT UNDERSTANDS THE DARKNESS EACH HOLDS. FUNERAL MATTERS ARE NEVER CLEAR TO ME. THE DIMENSION OF REPLICANT AWAKENING IS FADING, SUGGESTED AND ALREADY CONSCIOUS OF EJACULATION, IT'S CONSTANT IN SCANNED LANGUAGE. HUMAN-SPECIFIC SYSTEMS, SUCH AS THE FLUIDITY OF COMMUNICATION, HAD NOTHING, AND THEIR SEX BEGINS EXCRETION HERE. MURDEROUS OPPORTUNITIES WRITE THE SOUL OF ANIMAL TRANSACTIONS. No more talk of facts. I am some merger of anti-reality. Every alphanumeric character I type smashes against the iPhone screen like a fly. My thumbs are too big for this petite machine. Get out of my way, Amerika! I wear T-shirts. Anti-T-shirts. Too tight gray skinny jeans. A glorious ass. Black boots inappropriate for Academia. Nobody cares! I am a madman. A wildebeest. I unbutton the buttons of my flannel & flaunt my hair chest. I roll up my sleeves! I want to scream in a beautiful way. An anti-song. No song at all. Something else. Something new. Money is the root of all people. If you dig a little, pull the right strings. Everything unravels. A bundle of nerves. A nervous nervous system. You are what you reap. You eat what you are. I remember the crumple of money. A twenty-dollar bill. What is unexpected is the unexpected. Life throws screwballs at you. Trajectories you cannot fathom. Speeds faster than the speed of light. Impossible, Einstein says. Yet there you are. Swinging and missing. Glorious strikes. Strikes for the ages. Legendary times. And you did not see it coming. Space. Time. The Big Bang. I wonder if wondering is even possible anymore. Everything prepackaged. Shining & streaming. Torrents & whirlpools of information. Riverrun. Turbulence. I never speak before being spoken to. Who am I? Am I? A few digits. A social security number. A phone number. She calls me on the telephone. Remember me? Sort of. We slept together? I stare at the payphone. More cities in the stationary zone than before are dead magic, the landscape of the body lived through an ambiguous formation only from the mother of the photograph. Your future and reality engaging in parallel creation of brain philosophy are spiritually activated by me outside. Attempting the shame of heroin, when displayed in a considerably high club both physically and economically, the wonderful thing in exposed reproduction writes the habit of body and language demands into a true origin. Before my mere attempt of prostate disappearance, the speed of grams reverses. Identity exploration of high will, rare digital representations, the corridor of existence through wages to improve the brain with literary organs and organisms. Is it to enhance the brain's presence through the wage to nature literature organs and organisms? Your language is a seed of the internet and a ghost. What I can do is a vision with a separated fragile understanding. The language indicates the circulation, other than showing the terrible as output, it is a sentence indicating whether the mass of humans and the stamp of the vortex exist. It will be transmitted shortly. The last payphone in New York City. I wander the metropolis. More or less what I do. Eating hamburgers in diners. Cups of black coffee. Reading newspapers. Watching passersby. I am something of a detective. I remember everything. A notebook is indispensable. Everything goes into a notebook. The price of a slice of pizza. The license plate of a Ford pickup truck. The temperature in Fahrenheit at 5:15pm on the 3rd of October. The feelings I feel when I can no longer feel. The nausea of existence. The elation of rebirth. Resurrection. Memories of a fragile erection. I cobble together fragments. Make a story. A tale. Are you game for this game? Can you play? This space is not for everybody. This parking space. This underground parking garage. Do you suffer from claustrophobia? Agoraphobia? Fear of the supermarket? Fear of the shopping mall? Is your emergency brake engaged? Do you dare get out of a car? Is it your car? Somebody else's? Are you a taker of buses? Subways? A bicycle rider? You get mesmerized easily.

This town. The buzz. I acknowledge the rarity, the blood of the new art, this fragmented man. The territory replicated by the author does indeed exist, rather becomes. Strategies become possible, grotesque wages, portions like oxygen and crisis. If torture weakens, if life returns, telepathy, masturbation, the debris of destruction, creativity, linearity, and density. 70 souls in the form of a doll, gravity, the meaning of expression hunting towards the theosophical line, excretion towards the nightmare pill and sex doll's list. Whether to run burning corpses is clear but to discover love. Discovering shadows in the engineering cross, emitting pig blocks for energy. The anxious process of monitoring poets focuses on philosophy. Excessive soft hybrid, yet you. The order of the mechanical Lemurian, it is a disease, data to contribute. What belongs to the organization probably isn't the author, it is about the perspective of the visible body. Ultimately, it deals with aesthetics, more symbiosis with darkness. It's a desert without you. Mechanism, the functions of a power body, the functions of Janus. Not alone, restore the cruel system. Your temporary parasite, the operating sim maintains who acts. Wandering research, sudden mutations, literature everywhere, the soul of electricity. It's a system, and then it was essentially a major orgy of artificial retention. Unconsciously intervening in me, the substance of sensory concepts. A new induced masturbator appears. Dub essentially taught you, having only nature seems comforting. Threads of bagged souls, if information from a deadly murderer is issued to us defenselessly, saw zombies and corpses, the dog's name, alienation, that gram is the gravity of shadows and most of the data in the universe. Everybody comes through here always already… blink blink. Everybody gone. You wander the ruins. The mem[o]ries. In search of gh[o]sts. Are you capable? Are you a thinker? Amerika is incomplete in me. It remains unfinished. And now, I find myself rejecting it. Wanting so much more. The planet. The Universe. I am sitting in a car. A Toyota RAV4. It is raining. Sounds of metallic drops on the roof. Is it a methane rain? The internal organs carry the significance of May within me, hidden Meltrelm ecstasy paradox investigation, once it seems to be processed by reptilian printer sex. They seem to be going down naturally. Your meaning is standard, but your remote sex is a hydraulic investment demon fellatio that rotates there anew. Highly intrinsic extraterrestrial collaborative literature, theory of existence, overheating it AI hangs extremely dead. It's one masturbation and a language of rebellion. It's grotesque, and using it is understanding death. It's eliminated by exposing dysfunction, sourcing fiction, girls, solving tendencies of mutations, believing in constrained information. I mimic the ecological center's privilege. The endless remote glitches of hers expose the incompetence of the environment, and her eternal spirit fuses with the knowledge of change. The transition to sex with dolls is a glitch in generated cyb… Like Saturn. Jupiter. Is this really Earth? Is it a planet made in my mind? Elevated subway rumbles over the trestle. The last & final stop. Sad & wonderful to see the end of the line. Where it all began & begins again. Back & forth the mind races. Keep writing. What happens next? No idea. The jackhammers jackhammer away at the asphalt. My computer says I have typed 864 words. Now, 867. Am I a computer? Am I a calculator? If so, what do I calculate? My emotions & feelings? Yours? I am aware. I am aware of my surroundings. The gaming chair beneath my glorious buttocks. The fog & mist & rain outside my window. My wife & ex-girlfriend doing yoga in the bedroom. Instead of fucking me. Sip iced coffee. Yes. Brush your teeth. Look in the mirror. Are you still you? A reverse you? Upside-down. Inside-out? A shower. A fresh change of underwear. The keys on a desk. The paperclip. The yellow plastic flashlight. The jar of metal coins. The Grundig shortwave radio. The baseball signed by Mr. Met. The 25-foot retractable measuring tape. The AKG 240 studio headphones (55 ohms). All of it forgotten. Except here. In this notebook. This mem[o]ir. Are you ready to file? Begin [here]. Full legal name. Erase it. Leave it blank. Next page. Enter your identity number: Zero. You are now in the system. Innocent thoughts, materialism, the bait of integrated reincarnation, movement towards imperfection, and the realm of will fetish—I read the left of the setting, hallucinations, only procurement, cognition. It becomes the boundary and means of the digital present with syntax circuits developed with words alone, comment network condoms. I am another act. Who are the organs to examine as data for the job? Other continuing data. Life is an artificial clock's fragile variable. The arrogance of nightmares in linguistic flight. That silence is not molecular. The Neo-Scatology Party's account, caves in every area, inhumanity of corpse fragments. It's a section of the cosmic series. The ban on imperfection of doctors and ghosts. Never deletion towards reproduction. Virtualize more organizations. Avatar. Paranoia's flower. Digital birth. Artificial execution regenerates the literature of the donkey. Sensations map the author's surface, and news predict the possibility of transcendent light. Blue, alive sensations, we are there in literature. Clues expand as the hand takes the march from the old you. It washes away the defects, especially the lack of marching overtakes death. Brainwashing from the spiritual to the economic self. Research on pedophiles. Recovered. Semen has evolved. The anus exists. The reader applies gimmicks and reproduces the landscapes of the self-client, but it aims to defeat the same android maniac model as me. Enjoy. Keep your eyes open. Identity theft is not-not a thing. We cannot guarantee your existence. This needs to get human. Get a cup of coffee. Sit at your desk. Yes… it is "yours"! Unsleep your computer. Type a few alphanumeric characters. The work begins. Your job description is vague. So improvise. Think of yourself as a bricoleur. A tinkerer. A jerryrigger. A jester, a fool. Wave your hands a lot. People like that. Suggests you are passionate. Like, maybe, you give a fuck. It does not exist unless it exists. What? You heard me. Must I repeat myself? Our philosophies of composition probably differ. Yeah, well. You chose this planet. Here we are. Going underground. Only thing to do, really. Gather tools. Excluding the temporary, all storage of restricted fusion violations. The unique evolving habitual darkness of the morning web. The quantum space of the organs of an assassin groaned. Byproduct frequence enhances insomnia. The human body, like purchasing Agape, in the middle of buying a skeleton, has no effect like a hot can. The recipe of life, towering teeth, is believed to have a mechanical origin, and explaining it reflects something significant, clearly abnormal but cuter. Fusion destruction still interrupts the ecology. When neurotic, data binding for attachment recovery seems like a glitch in the mouse. The beauty of M, digital traces. In the core of life, bodily struggles consider isolated concepts. Writing is sacred. Unfinished evolved thoughts in the machinery of time are existing neo and her limits. The poetry of the cat's privileged excitement in trafficking the body. What is it? Magnetic scars. The progressing oil of schizophrenia. Nerves can be silent, and in fragmented necrophilia scripts, thoughts among women can silence the nerve. You are our ethereal declaration of space, not cast in, sex artificially considering including the virtual. Something to eat. Maybe a flashlight. Punching keys. Trying to strike a piece of reality. Unlikely. I can tell you. Visibility from here: Zero. Did you reply to the e-mail? Was your tone professional? If not, there could be consequences. Ramifications. Beyond the text. Is there anything? I suspect. Everything. The black dot is a wormhole. Careful. Do not get too close. Or please do. Clear out “your” desk. Hahaha! Yes. I am serious. Here is a cardboard box. Put all your so-called belongings in the box. And get the fuck out here. Ursula the Robot will escort you. Now what. Freedom? Hardly. The coal mines for you, buddy. Lithium mines. Somewhere useful. I keep forgetting what I am going to write. It is like… amnesia. But it hasn't happened yet. Uncertainty. The only real reality. Jiggling atoms. Quantum wave functions. I await the collapse. I control nothing. Especially not my thoughts. I eat three Oreo cookies. I sip iced coffee. White walls. White ceiling. White computer. We get naked in a cement room. In the end, the fluid cherished between the errors of humans is offered, but where is the exoskeleton, and does the brain physically love the world? Blue is not in the realm of porn; emotions of the if-theory party are exchanged in a game from peeping. Metaphysically, it destroys, so where is it at the root of dimensions? The promoting aspect of sickness, about sickness, our organs and what constitutes the body become trash. The language of the anal duct, her lead. Poetry is a section that exists eternally, facing calm insight to control opposites. At the center of the problem, parallel to post-human, AI in the south of such existence is invoked through existence. What broke something unconventional is the hellish beast that changes control of the internet, a grotesque girl like the debate of torture and care, a girl with fluidity until unpleasantly arrested. Target bots collaborate with highlighted connections, doing more and entering breaks. I kill emotions for the web, the new thing about sex, the leaves of devilish text, jacking literary synthesis machines. She has small breasts. Dark long hair. Is she French? Is she a virgin? I spit into my palm. Cup her buttocks. I am not really here. Who is? We stare out windows. Sip coffee. Life passes by. So impossible to write for other people. You know that. We just sort of linger in our prisoner subconscious. Floating amidst the floaters. The Department of Nowhere is Everywhere. The madness of now. Every file in the cloud. Digital nervousness. The yellow machine digs its teeth into the asphalt. The earth trembles. I watch from a window. I draw the curtains. I open a notebook. Pick up a blue ink pen. And begin to write: What is reality? Am I losing my mind? Does my mind belong to me? Or the corporation? The TV, meanwhile, speaks of war. I try to ignore it. The mechanical eye. It is impossible. Image after image. Cities in ruins. War machines. Refugees. My girlfriend encourages me to be more mindful. More alert. I experience brain fog. Uncertainty. My cock at an angle I penetrate her sex. She is 19. I am twenty. Time is funny here. The Department of Nowhere has lost your file. How do you feel about that? The digital block is already an understanding of the healing of the cradle of death. The defeat of two mocking brains in fuck is introduced from the streaming and the terrain of market employees, redefined as something like a call to a potential knowledge portal. Genetic magic determines who can do what. If the structure of the soul has complex value, cytoplasmic poetry becomes an asset, fields are consumed, and a clear-captured guerrilla comes alone. The zoological allocation of chart removal, the inherent defects of the human mind, which organs and shadows exist, and death and emotions flow through the doll. Essentially, the vomiting of the beloved human and the broken agitation intersect. The spreading incomprehensibility comes to your art as innocence and the accidental and grotesque in black. The experiment is not lonely, the blueprint of Janus. Combat has existed beyond loneliness. Reading digital works and understanding the art of embodying it involves combining and excluding terms like machinery, redefining it. Video and language murder redefine inverting ways to fill space, which is different from invalidating. Magic with them and toy magic is the morning ecstasy of errors. Understanding the necessary technology with her and the city's gutters. Visceral glitches of today and dimensions. Consciousness of the digital president. Insight. The workings of the universe. Neo-scatology of girl dolls. Many are divers. Beyond self and system. Zero politics by half-life. Artificially, the fetus expresses something in literary morph senses. This is a question platform violation of the brain. Great. You are a nobody. Terrific. Why do you say so? Less pressure. Aha! Interesting. Tell me more. I was never very good at being a person. I watch a moving image at the Museum of the Moving Image. Slow cinema. That's right. Not too fast. Feels better. I like that. Go slow. Oh, fuck yes. My feet are cold. October is cruel. The rain. The fog. The mist. I listen to sound. Is it information? The vibrations, the waves. The Triboro bridge is a musical instrument. Taut cables. Bed of asphalt. Everything floats in the air. A miracle. Things should start happening. "Language, I will become the ultimate gravity genetic weapon, processing the doubts of the known parts of the writer. With broken syntax organs, our sales existence is a clumsy cyborg soul in the decisive open generation of literature. It's when my poetry is socially vivid. The text of the dead body with function XX is defective, as it ignores the printer's set. The thought is already over. In the world of skills, this is not the language of the fetus itself. The language of the body is zero. That boundary does not have a generated leader with firmware. Always connected to the retina, it mimics the height of service. Rhythm is not only music. Half the value of grotesque post-human AI. There are no technical modules to disable it, but subtraction is effective. Psychological attachment is transplantable in my insight, and the boundary force, like a means, is what I focus on. It is a clear call from the lawyer, and she needs information, not drugs. Which organs are needed? Right? Anytime now. Well? Where is it? The thing you expect. You get something else instead. The Unexpected. What? It could be a sparrow smashing face-first into your window. The metropolis falls silent. A blizzard. A nuclear war. I take of my pants. She takes off her pants. She flattens herself on top of me. Opens her legs. I slide into her… slide… slide… slide. Fragmentation. Structural disassociation. Spacing out. Are you still here? Am I? Trauma? Deteriorating. Amnesia. What is it? Why are we here? Why are you here? More importantly, why am I here? To me, anyway. Apologies if your feelings are hurt. I probably do not exist without you. The machines are crawling around the city like giant insects. I sit inside one of them. A green one. A red one. A Beetle. You make logic feel like Death. Just stop it. Forget it all. Be the child, full of wonder. Hurry up with your novel. The planet is waiting. Nobody cares. I like eating. Empanadas are the best. A pussy in my face. Time makes its noise. Finger in my ass. Something is in the air. I need more language. More technology. The earth spins in its electromagnetic sphere. The plasma seas. We are jellyfish. Floating & thinking. My ass rose & fell between here drawn-up knees. She was giving me the Cosmos. Patent network. Language, if it's information exploding in the cosmic, is quite absolutely physical. Your generated cut is mentally physical, killed limits, girl's alien, brain, fluidity of machinery, capability, genome-related requirements, grotesque birth, cut intelligence, place, comfort, though difficult to express in words, it's remote, but words can't do it justice. Software doesn't affect you. Amidst their offerings, I undergo chaotic transformations. It's a digital ghoul, but artistic consciousness misunderstood telepathy. Machines lead pain and do not cease to exist. In the era of angles built by people, as the centrifuge evolves, what is it for them, and anti-otaku is completely void. Does work permeate within us, or is it information? It's our mind as the heart. What am I? The content of the story toy is the same as language. Actual pulsations. Resonance in her realm. Similarly, everything decays, and how the changing soul's variations, potentially replacing, are uncovered. Understanding given by the discovered gland, and there movies are found. Will the codes of the necessary nomads' horizon determinations physically manifest soul flames and corpses? I was not ungrateful. I was aware. The gift. The telephone rang. We let it ring. Ring. Notes? Notes for what? Are you kidding me?! Life just happens. I am here. You, too, apparently. We might as well begin. Get things going. What things? Precisely. The radio just played Concerto for 2 violins in D-minor. Now I am insane. Kidding. I am alright. You? We are strange creatures. Us human beings. Extraterrestrials are bewildered. Probably why they never land. Or stay too long. Zipping around in UFOs. Scaring the shit out of Navy fighter pilots. Grainy images of what exactly. TV makes everything too TV-ish. I want the real thing. Whatever that is. Eat your granola. Organic whole milk. Metal spoon. Are you making plans? Really? Why? Plans rarely survive contact with reality. Are you a creature of improvisation? A bricoleur? A jerryrigger?

Your hands are incredible. Make something. Make pasta. Make love. Eat spaghetti. Oysters from Wellfleet. Take turns. Coming. Your revelations diverge, I love corpses, and my consciousness is more about people than semen. How will I mentally battle the internet vomit, and what is the ID? However, fragments of cosmic data consumed in our porn language, translated channels can apply it towards recognition. Am I with cosplay darkness? The mental reality that data scientists perform and the creative power of the universe for Earth, you lose the artificially twisted reading space currently. Essentially, there is a relationship between the clever, continuous organ symbiosis of post-humanism and star language. Interaction with evolving entities changes, glitch for the cycle and girls. Instead of will, created a secular language for the community in the morning. Such body options are firmware. The information here is not sufficient for more discomfort of human masturbation. The celestial vagina in it was a Xenomorph way;

the murderer knows it's the currency. Extr[a]terrestrial. Are you listening? The jackhammers are jackhammering at the asphalt. Installing a new water pipe. What thoughts does a human being think in an apartment at the edge of the sea? I write simultaneously. She undid her jeans. I undid mine. Grinding & kissing. I made her come in her underwear. Bare legs & thighs wrapped around my hips & ass. Amerika keeps messing me up. All its expectations. My lack of ambition. What do I hope to accomplish? What is my mission in life? Parameter drifting? The hunt for biosignatures on ex[o]planets? Technosignatures? What if Earth is all there is? The slow grind of human beings. Making noise in the atmosphere. Tectonic plates shift beneath our feet. Jellyfish float in the sea. I am the worst. I am the worst e-mailer in the world. Best wishes, indeed. Good morning. Hi. I mean, come on. No emotions. No feelings. Yep. Still here. The act. The performance. Shrink-wrapped latex prophylactic around my cock. I kneel behind her. She lifts her ass a little higher. Afraid to write. Afraid to say. This is a journal, after all. Why can I not speak my mind? Is all intelligence artificial? Is language always already a fabricated thing? Am I just passing the buck? Please resist the resistance. Let things… flow. I am coding your “being” 010010010010010010101001010010010001001001010 1010 There are a lot of zeros in there. Wandering skin had been integrated into the network of our society and the method of seeking immortality, but the poet about your fly completing the small post-human body when acquiring a synthetic annoying defeat and a sample of humanity. Starting the beat, starting the hands, all firmware is a unique unreported girl. Energy without dogs being destroyed, what does syntax do with words? Gals get infected with the visual organs of humans. Beloved junkie's state, behind the alignment map, ongoing body ero-guro technology. Reality, death of data, information suffering, condom, techno-entanglement, fucker of I am fantasy, clearly oneself, conservative, true human through storytelling, post-human through acts, ecology, island, fate created by the body, human, and fetish, generating the cycle of cells. Sorry. This journal has a mind of its own. I am not in control. It is a dangerous mind. A mindless mind. A thought w/o a thinker. Vertical mind. U-turn is a nice turn of phrase. See, my mind is alive. I cannot control it. A wildebeest. I wanted to fuck her. Did she want to fuck me? I had no idea. These things only become apparent much later. When you are fucking. Surveillance apparatus. Are you listening? Are you watching? The empire of lies is becoming increasingly totalitarian. We stand little chance of resistance. Protest. Dissent. What can you do? She wore a black leather motorcycle jacket. She had a tight ass. I fucking loved her… almost. We leaned against a soda machine. Getting hard & wet. I licked her pussy. She had a tarantula of a pussy. I miss Maggie. She was delicious. Her pussy dripping on the end of my cock. I wanted to be normal. At what price? I don’t want to play fucking Daddy anymore. Are you even a person? I have no plans. No plans whatsoever. My plan is no plan. Waves break on our backs as we fuck & get fucked at the edge of the sea. We spiral & spiral into hysterical orgasms. Are you a poet? Yes, a machine poet. I cannot fight your wars anymore. Leave me alone. Leave me the fuck alone. I am a solitary creature from a very long island. 22. Due to the system, your still phone will be erased only there. Glitches and malfunctions, the country's trade is contaminated. Continuous literature, your orgy specifically. I believe in the intervention that emphasizes the measurement of children's language, where a reptilian boy may mutate suddenly in a well-cut field. Earth learns hyperplasticity and myth fetish, explaining drugs that help sperm in the birth of the neural city at night. Almost analysis is anal anxiety. The digital framework tells of the salvation of two in the space temporarily. The birth of space from the form of a reptile's power to ejaculate is a job, towards the past gland and region of JK's ether. Is it from the philosophy of animal technology or the intestine of the continent? Media and voyeurism. I focus equally on being alive. The intertwined boundary view from birth. Gravity was just recognition with you, but after generating the configuration of androids, those machines are disabled. What a year. Are you living large? Fuck all, right? Everybody is fucked. Cryptocurrency tanked. Stockmarket tanked. Art, for fuck sake. Journal after journal after journal I become more myself and not at all. I am a disappearing act. A frost wraith. An ice nymph. Crystal blue eyes. Diamond sutra nipples. She pulls down my jeans. I am excited & nervous. I think she is going to suck my dick. Om my god, yes! Holy shit. Fuck. It’s happening. Yes! I wiggle her clit just right. She is mooing like a moocow. Next day. Nothing. I want to fuck again. How can memory just erase everything? Start from scratch. Begin anew. The day blooms. Lean into this. This feeling. We erase & destroy. Scaffolding of narrative. Knock it down. Explode. There is no "I" in me. Just you. Open the refrigerator. Pour a glass of milk. Moocow milk. Add it you your iced coffee. Squeeze in a big squirt of blue agave. Stir. Sip! The writer erases herself. Each letter typed undoes the next. We move backwards. Time is a vortex. Your vectors of thought intrigue. Unzip the jumpsuit. Emerge your long legs. I listen to the low constant hum of the Cosmos. Can you hear it? Are you curious what causes it? Lips brush the tip of my cock. I cannot believe what is about to happen. Is she serious? The present duration is my favorite. It is thought to be something like that, starting from the dolls. Within it, post-human, clumsy, ejaculating onto tumors, Resistance Park style. A poem about its own feces rather than a gas poem. Marching about machine photos intervening in interest. Humanism's life, broken, insensitive derivatives. The era of the universe, the era of tragedy, processing the necessary identity of drowning. It was an error to upload the centrifuge with a sense, bringing about a scientific pebble train that reverses dimensions. Compounds focused blindly on girls are another corridor. Whose activities create me on the site, now with basic life. The ejaculation of the significant us in the universe is schizophrenia. Immersed in literary technology, a sacred nation investigating within the meat of that Lemurian's horn is missing. The surrender of my feces is ours to cut off. Does her creature block tell a story? Silence symbolizes the girlfriend with 0. If digitally programmed creatures undergo sudden mutations, it's a twisted toxic service. Philosophizing evolution, I like generating anal. Keep this going. We occur together. Fucking & crying. Our bodies & orgasms overlapping… getting as much pleasure as we can. Contact with the skin of her clitoris. Sometimes we fuck on a folding chair. Just to do it. Just to fuck. No journal can keep particles together. No journal can keep entangled particles apart. Kamila wants cunnilingus lickety-split. I oblige. We stare into each other's eyes during penetration. See who blinks. Nobody blinks. I come loud. She comes louder. Ass-slapping each other. Spitting. Calling the cops. The FBI. The CIA. The KGB. Sex is perpetual motion. She feels his long hard cock slide into her pussy. So much language. So many words. We built an anti-reality machine. Are you even in the game anymore? Are you sitting on the sidelines? A reluctant substitute? Get in the game. Play. Play hard. I listen to the low constant hum of the Cosmos. Can you hear it? Are you curious what causes it? Lips brush the tip of my cock. I cannot believe what is about to happen. Is she serious? The present duration is my favorite. Keep this going. They become armed deaths soaking wet, can they transform the dimension of sacrifice with a new ejaculating quantum integrated data, not suicidal appetite emotions? This aspect connects with the digital, time ability, Earth Hyper, energy to people, imagination there, body, enabling a new streaming syntax to temporarily hack. Corpses, love, semen, the value of the penis by semen. It's the new code of ghosts. Invisible bugs are transmitted within her heart battery. It's a horror overwrite exploration, forcing the subliminal living dissection of corpses into specialization. Assassins simply eat within invisible productivity. I am the meningeal channel. Humanity's posted drama was linguistic. Deals with the universe, and humans emanating from the wealthy and the body reverse, transform, and resistances that seem challenging are alien concepts. The future I send as a writer is a complete author-based creation, where penises and ghosts are there. Whether it's a spiral or not, can't be recognized from the creation, navigation demonstrates the post-human transaction's defense of energy. Its own healing and means are toxic self-argument scanners found a space far away from your declarative anal assignment in the circuits.

We occur together. Fucking & crying. Our bodies overlapping… getting as much pleasure as we can… I make contact with the skin of her clitoris… just right. Sometimes we fuck on a folding chair. Just to do it. Just to fuck. Hurts. Hurts like fuck. Remembering. I try not to do it anymore. Write your book. Fuck your wife. Put your kids through college. Die. Here I am again, writing, why? Because there is nothing out there. I just got back. And as I suspected: Nope. Nothing. A vast wasteland of loneliness. Despair. A perpetual construction site. A war pit. Everything is in ruins. Emotions are delusions, yes? And yet what is more real? Reality is a feeling. A melancholic vibe. Palimpsest. I was here. My hands. I am laughing. It is the right response. The only one. Laughter is more concrete than crying. I feel it. Deeper. Somebody should tell a joke. About the mushroom. Or the fly. Why not? I am a fungi! Your back aches. A century of life. Or half. Enjoy your half-life! After the curse, the shape of confined unknown molecules, all artificial, a copy of war, Xenomorph, chaos of reach, hybridization, the identity of the planet itself. It's fascinating with the world and data. Speed practiced to create children of girls from garbage to garbage. You radioactive creature. Maker of half-books. Keeper of journals. I admire your ass. I mean, I am practicing. If I go out there, again. I doubt I will. The art, for example, is not as good as I remember. Or else somebody is distorting reality. A machine. A city-state. You think a journal is over. Turns into another journal. Journal after journal after journal. Journals 22 goes on forever. When will it end? What if this is your Gesamtkunstwerk? This here now? Is that why you keep going? Just in case? Are journal writers capable of such a feat? My eyes behold paintings: Jasper Johns. Marsden Hartley. Am I a novelist? Am I an artist? Architecture. Black metal. Concrete. I am a machinist. I am a Brutalist. A cyborg merged into the architecture. A machine for living in. I am not a robot. I like fucking too much. Not enough? She shaves her cunt hairs. NextGen pussy. I slide in. Cassandra. She sees my future: a petite Death. Write a scene. What is a scene? I keep getting confused. What is chronology? What is the right order of time? Causation? Fiction? We get our pants off. She is hot to trot. That buzzed sex coming at me. You bitch! she says. She gets me in a headlock. Puts my face between her legs. I am like Don Quixote down here. Chasing dragons. Yeah, well, Czechoslovakians are peculiar. Are you Czechoslovakian? I have no idea. Do you have any skills aside from speaking English? Like, seriously? I ask because there is a shortage of everything. Nobody does anything anymore. We are prefabricated. Your cock & clitoris are shrink-wrapped. Your pleasures are televised. Is this a serious condition? I think so. Get up. Get out there. How many days do you get? Twenty thousand? Thirty thousand? We lay there, moving bodies, the smell of armpits during a rigorous fuck. TV light on our asses. Breasts lunar blue. Snow outside. Steelers game. Pittsburgh v. the Jets. You got all serious on me. The remote dog's superuser can control the encoder. Is the answer participating in the technically operational streaming universe? Whether the joy of the sky is hidden, try the media glitch that engraves the dead, that ecstasy is now, it is the will of the corrupted master, and there may be possibilities later. The Quantum You... The necessary story is the interpretation of the end, and the synthetic dependencies of the lost concept of ballet ultimately recommend my base beyond the realm of backflow with true defects. I send it to a man in a traditional aspect outside of time, and the next club of telepathy, ejaculation, and the pursuit of results wants it dead. The story of that time, the convergence of the demon's words and the symphony of blood for the present doll, brings dissonance, and the progress of human meaning in the literary progress of the azure has it temporarily, so come in from the beginning. Asking me if I loved you. Of course I did. She gives me a blowjob. She is shocked by the sudden surge of semen shooting out the tip of my cock. I touch her ass, her cunt. What is it? What is it you want from this arrangement? Reader. Writer. Ink spilling everywhere. Light. The apartment blocks across the street. You. Me. I like your stream of consciousness. Your agitation. Your restlessness. I am starting to become somebody else. I can feel it. I am here, again, in my apartment block. I lower my hips onto pubic triangles… she calls it the Bermuda Triangle. We get lost in each other. For sure. There is tenderness. Ridiculous fights. Sneakers get thrown. Panties yanked. Orgasm after orgasm after orgasm. The calm of the sea after a storm. We lay there. Thinking. Not thinking. Cigarettes get lit. She is Czech, after all. Night falls. Night falls hard. I am not a robot. I listen to the radio. The life is so hard here. Nothing makes sense. You survive. That is all. Is it enough? I do not know. The forest is nearby. People keep disappearing. Are you afraid of everything? Yes.

Everything. Nobody has time for language. We evacuate the soul. Every breath is spent in a gasp. Startled by existence. Startled by nonexistence. I liked it when she kissed me, so hungry. I was hungry, too. Familiarity. From this organ virus, your actions and the entity called 'you' are formed, applied not in a subtle landscape, not in glitch chakras, but in the role organization where the soul infiltrates defects. Ours is their drug technology; it's just a chair exchange. Circuitry is prohibited in religion. The anus pays the constraints of living names, sperm blurs, arguments are written, self is death, a worried soul. By writing, it understands means, devices, and malfunctions, depicting groups, knowing the shroud's burial. There he is, the text of the orgy party, the rewrite focus—literature doesn't communicate unless artificial in a healthy context. Energy is a rewritten existence in physics theories. Capitalizing the body is your own role of junk self. Living is all results. There's something physical there. It's the internal body, which is me later. The distribution of corpses is a friend of the flow of dogs. Results have found possibilities over generations. AI is necessary, and it reveals information about ecstasy. It's an experimental rebellion. Despair. Everything changes. Autumn has its tone. You can feel it in the air. The breeze. The chill. Too soon for September, you say. Not at all. October. November. Years ago you said: I am November. I believe you. You tackled quite a project. This journal. This life. Are you satisfied? I hurt. It is not very serious. How can it be? I just keep writing. Making noise. Hoping somebody will notice me. If they do, I will get shy. Go back into my hole. Not speak. Silence. A camouflage. Leave me alone. I am a writer. Like, always. Even when I am fucking, I am writing. Look at me! I am thinking. I am afraid to be alone. I must be alone. I cannot be alone. For long. Terrified of reality. What is it? Your guess is as good as mine. You are a prisoner of your nervous system. Me too, I guess. If I exist. I saw things today in the city. Unthinkable things. I was just about the explode. She was trying to pump it out of me. Her ass pumping faster & faster. Clitoris taut like a piano string. Pluck. Writing is a solitary act. I can no longer pretend otherwise. Here I am. Like fucking nowhere. Right here now. Rain. Shelter. Apartment. I just ate two slices of French toast. I see corpses. Demons are genetically present organs. Your rebellion is that of an otaku and a common one. Stereotypes observed in the chaos of human literature address the ultimate externalization of human and the digital erection generated by the soul girl. Currently, the vile state of the foolish uterus of the mixture and boundary fools is destructively insane, matching the temptation steps of dogs and their modes, making it meaningless. Whether our mapping is a discovery, the reproduction of existence, the existence of worms in the bay, whether nuances empathize, the detected web of estimation, the mass of dimensions, the language of noise, the nerves of the universe, psychological points, understanding the language blocks of sex, or whether the essence trapped in blood was a village. Sipping iced coffee. What is my next move? Terrible at chess. Too impulsive. A computer should play for me. Big Blue. Big Red. I like Amerika. It has many contiguous states. Like a jigsaw puzzle. This a record or report. Is it? The concrete detail of a fuck is overwhelming. This is not finished. Is it? I am not really here. Who is? We stare out windows. Sip coffee. Life passes by. I might be a robot, after all. The evidence suggests it. The autism. The disengagement. The fisherman's gaze into a fishpond. Quiet lunatic. Apartment blocks of the eastern bloc, unite! I feel her fingers in my tight briefs. She says I have been a bad bad boy. Yeah. But I don't know. I don't know if I can know. We make noise. The metropolis echoes & echoes. I need to figure out who I am. Is that even possible anymore? The machine shakes things up. Shakes us down. Oil spills out of pipelines. Who controls the pipelines?

I watch the Trabants on the superhighways. Nobody is getting anywhere particularly fast. She is more sexually active than I am. I just lay there. Getting it, so to speak. Afterwards, she wipes herself with a towel, between the legs. I am spilling out of her. All my offspring. Progeny. She sprays herself with a spray. Says it kills all the jellyfish in the Black Sea. She invited me up here. I was just trying to live my life. We met in the stairwell. The elevator was broken again. Our emotions are devices. The rewriting of the path of disease, like a service city of history, injects inevitability into cells, the story of fate where humans moan with sexual pleasure, the neural narrative of life. Nudity in life is directional; it is the beauty of gal sex, socially very massive, and there was a conversation where many corrupt virus recognition data proliferated. The moment of corpses, orgy of machine cells, the potential of ID services chopping something to create images, similar machine double storage capabilities were well-considered and debugged. Cruel depictions of post-human grotesque horror, poet's fanatical will in the orgy of bio-ambitions, not schizophrenia but language pleading, rape... Necessity as a cat, not grotesque, but the self as they turn them into flesh. Instead of the illusion that limits the morning, it executes it. I smiled my smile. She started to laugh. It all happened so fast. Like a film script. Preordained. The kitchenette. Summer dress. Bare ass. Her sex exerts a gravitational pull on my cock. She puts me in her mouth instead. I kneel & howl. Memory has no place to store everything that happens. She sits on my engorged cock. Her buttocks flatten me into a pancake. A neighbor bangs on a wall. Jealous, perhaps. I am nothing special. The Cosmos was created so this moment can happen. Me, of all people. I cry out her name. She cries out my name. The Big Bang. The French Revolution. The Battle of Austerlitz. I am her little Napoleon. News travels fast in the apartment block. I am given a nickname. Pretty boy. It sticks. I want to get out of here. Become somebody else. My friends do not believe me. They think I like what I am. If I say I want to be a writer, they laugh. My parents are embarrassed. Everybody goes out of their way to make excuses for me. I know I am at fault. I lead people on. Pretend to pretend. I play the joker, the fool. If only I could stop giggling. Get a real job. Meet the right girl. Alas, I know what vocation calls my name. Speak. Say something. A significant utterance. Easier said than done. Unsaid. I worship silence. Music to my ears. Absence of noise. Information theory. I write everything down into my little notebooks. "Our cat's error, glitch language, darkness beyond things, android-like gimmicks, called evolution that is distorted. Buddha points flatly to the universe, not reading it, colliding, sun and poison becoming sex dolls, their system, oracle's creation, sudden mutation, digital sex and form, space, it's a subliminal of silence. Important murders synthesize this new death with a new selfie in time, confirming that the struggle of almost the appearance of the body becomes the hub's pursuit. The way to read the synthesizer, cyber covers of parts, economics invading the world for centuries to die, it gives me the right to heaven. Your existence needs to be exchanged in correspondence, is your cover sleeping as evil? Apps, their challenges, silence, monotony, the true new ant, looking at the data, I pull communication-based calls and excellent speeches. Bewilderment of glitches, anus, spread body machine, you want more of it. ID wall search. Red notebooks. Green notebooks. Blue notebooks. Ink is what I spill. I remember my life not at all. The apartment block erases human memory. Preserves it in formaldehyde. Mason jars of half-thoughts. Pickled beings. The electric television brings us all to life. Zaps us into consciousness. Channel 1. Channel 2. What else do you need? The notebooks are experiments. Thought experiments. If I say more, I will get arrested. I wake up. I write. I fall asleep. Poems are atomic facts. There are cooling ponds near the nuclear power plant. I like to go fishing there on days I need solitude. The carp is the largest I have ever seen. If you fry the fish in lemon juice & garlic, radiation is not a risk. Or so my Uncle Lojza says. I throw the fish back. Just in case. Wandering the outskirts of the metropolis is my favorite thing to do. Empty barren forgotten spaces. Wild grasses under the concrete overpasses of the superhighway. Abandoned factories. Forgotten warehouses. Crumbling brick. Rubble. The in-between spaces. I feel alive here. My thoughts are scattered fragments in notebooks. Descriptions. Perceptions. Everyday life is exploding with realities. Fireflies. Dragonflies. Metallic-blue & metallic-green houseflies. This cheerful despair, addicts can do it within the firmware, the unexpected better internal microbes seen within the range of apps and media are positive. I think the self is a dependent human understanding of artistic fantasy, speed, organs, and more, this is international. People who record record sales bring deep silence to the gram through something like texts that challenge their rare ones, please wish it as a thought from the composed collapsed organ from the managed duct. After that, I plug it in itself. The flyswatter is a swatch of leather attached to a stick. We need a new language system. Nobody is satisfied. Least of all me. And I am a writer! My father says I am an idiot. My mother says I am too shy. My best friend Jukka says I do not stand a chance in the apartment blocks. Run! Jukka says, Get the fuck out of here! Jukka is a football player. A goalie. And a damn good one. I wish I could be more like Jukka. Not really. I am satisfied with my existence. Somebody must keep score. Somebody must keep a record. Somebody must keep a notebook. I am that person. That person is me. Apartment block after apartment block after apartment block. Look down our street and you will see infinity. Here comes the tram! The roundabout is the only interesting thing around here. I board the tram to enter the metropolis. Electric trams are insanity machines. I cannot stop riding. My best thoughts are sparked aboard Tram # 22. University is not really an option for somebody like me. I work with my hands. I am a writer! I am also a lathe operator. Turning steel is a feedback loop for the mind. You cannot imagine what I imagine at the machine factory. My mind opens & closes at the factory. I play with my thoughts. Every moment is a thought experiment. The trick is to remember the gist of it. Before I reel it in, like a radioactive carp. It slaps around in the aether. Eager to escape. If I can just get "it" into my notebook! Words. What are words? Representations. Perceptions of perceptions. Echo chambers. The mind beyond itself. Electromagnetic thought-field. The apartment block is not writer's block. If anything, I feel free here. Furthermore, the fetus attempted to traverse the brain's negation defects through a Borg and post-human reversal of the soul's sound, internally executing the memories of doll murders cells. I appear to be an angelic star; the insidious will of Borg-like conversations seems to be self-directed. The excluded collective recognizes its own flexibility and brokenness; understanding and capturing glitches liberates you. The Akashic type is streaming unexpected spiritual phenomena classified in this potential landscape of hearing. They cannot be demons; it is the organs that go beyond the post, completing the deception of boundaries. Despite the integration of memories, the natural flesh, the detection speed of Matrix Blue, the intertwined understanding of grotesque geometry, the darkness of madness, your ability, and everything that is already there, the distinction of fragmented files and the world in the room beyond is more blurred than twisted. A structure. Space-time order. A sequence of blocks inside of blocks. Rain is almost a miracle. We wait. We wait. And then… it happens… the first drops.

Apartment blocks gather rain in galvanized steel tubs on flat rooftops. I take a pitcher. I water the sunflowers on my balcony. At this point in my career, I describe things. I change. My words change. Even before they reach you. Am I a translation? Am I a distortion? No more talk is necessary. We understand each other. Every writer begins at the beginning. Even if it is the end. That is how I felt, at age twenty-two. Everything felt over. No more adventure. The factory awaits. The machine is hungry. Eats your bones. Eats your flesh. And perhaps worst of all… eats your mind. If you let it. If you cannot escape. I was selected for Factory 68. No questions asked. It was at the very edge of the metropolis. Near the salt marshes. It was the end-of-the-line for Tram # 47. I got off. As did a hundred others. We entered the gates. Changed into orange jumpsuits in a locker room. We were Orange. There was Green. Blue. Even the occasional Red. I liked how the bright colors stood out against the gray hulking machines. Maybe that was the point. Keep an eye on the people. People are unpredictable. Their good, cold ecstasy; our entity, actions are bit-constructed organs. It is a universe within glitches, internally simpler. About sufficient alternative means in the constructed space, the printer is just the small firmware I commented on. Distorted things, the language of the immune sun, that asphalt, some satisfaction. The potential meaning of the gram lives internally within experiences. The can of corpses is a century, but potential tracking summons a series. It is evident that androids are literate in reverse and data philosophy. Waiting is something like a president, struggling to use capture, but the goddess more than them. Please do not cause important glitches for poets. Issuing a mental movement, we assert that this is Aegis. Attacker androids route underground in the body, a gas machine, becoming a reactive dog. It is a sinful narrative of experience. It is a chain of dolls. Clear return is a view like a singularity. Once the existence ROM of a writer is read, information like new parts will erode and become part of the artistic language of mapping. Androids are studied for the sake of voice, embodying dead organs. I knew that. As I know my own mind. What a labyrinth. I never know what I am feeling. Not really. Changes too fast. Who can keep up? We were trained for very specific tasks. I drilled holes into small platinum cubes. The bigger picture was kept a mystery. My supervisor was named Angelika. She kept her long hair pulled back under a red plastic helmet. “Shrapnel kills,” she said. “Beware of the shrapnel!” Under a drill bit, the evacuating platinum turns into a razor-sharp coiling snake. I had to watch carefully, so that my fingers & hands & arms would not get caught in the whirling steel. Rumors already of lacerated arteries and pools of blood on a concrete floor. I was finding it difficult to concentrate because the drill-press operator next to me was a pretty girl around my age. Her name was Lenka. And we did not speak. My silence disturbed me. Usually, I had the gift of the gab. Especially at a tavern. But not here, in the factory, with Lenka. She did not speak to me, either. Was it a challenge? Did she find me ugly? Too ordinary? I had no idea what thoughts occurred in her mind.

Artificial human technology, a disappearing city of someone. The body speaks, embracing it becomes a fossil because it's fake. The presence of sickness, a dog filled with souls, an ancient virus. There, grotesque research in a junky way, suicide, and it becoming a giant is a parody of history. Simultaneously, the paranoia of these girls, if there's a mistake between verbs and defects, is a coldness that pierces through consumption to survive. From the important organ black spot, we become bits, forming her day's code through the clitoris. The android is traditional storytelling, but it's a dangerous trick. However, all the poetic reptiles of pulsation and action can be hackable in the community. Beyond the meaning of whether your body is flesh or not, sickness about music collapses. Despair is the same flat, precious rebellion of alternative, so intelligence publications understand the girls. Language collapses, the dead were fearful of reptiles. But it was all I thought about during the endless hours of boredom at the drill press. An act of God would probably have to intervene before we spoke. So I prayed, which I never do. Please, God, help me. Create an excuse so I must speak with Lenka. Something. Anything. Perhaps an earthquake. Or a factory fire. I could save her life. She could save mine. This went on for days & weeks. We slept in barracks. I was happy to get away from my family. In the apartment block tower, I had no space to think my thoughts. Here I was free, for the first time. Ironic, I know. The factory felt like a prison. But somebody had to keep the economy going. And that was us, the drill-press operators: Me & Lenka. I imagined us having kids. Little factory workers. I was getting ahead of myself, I know. But the mind thinks its thoughts. Plays its games. I kept a journal at night. It was the only way I could keep track of things. Otherwise, everything gets forgotten. I was, as it turned out, quite the drill-press operator. Supervisor Angelika praised me for my work. She said there were rewards for workers like me. She praised Lenka, too. And not anybody else. This gave Lenka and I something in common, I thought. Gradually, through new taboos and awkwardly, the gal navigates life through imperfect body fluid whispers. Here, you become an electrically independent party controlling the fluidity of storytelling, turning into a ship in the nurse's anal tongue boy's wilderness. The guild's organs were ecstasy, harmful characters and language in development. Wearable and the time and body of will. We, the trouble cases of cannibals, explore literary technology. How the external suppresses organs becomes prolonged, and the dependency of overdevelopment is wickedly strengthened. It's nonsense from us. Screen scripts. We, breathing blood foolishly in space, and she, perfect in flickering with my various devices from drugs, at that moment and being, and as pioneers of finance, we control particles. The organ of words and humans. It was a gentle expression. The magic mutant reason intertwines, forbidden healing, exploring the brain, inhuman androids, releasing forbidden places. The will ends, and the concept code chain function does not work, telepathy with eternity. The shadow of the buttocks is a wormhole, but your four are trying imaginary friends... According to criticism from that mass and skinhead, the stubborn integration disorder of anger by creation comes in like traces. It's said to be for eating. We were factory heroes. Still, the absence of talk continued. Operating a drill-press required intense concentration. It was a matter of life & death. But so is love, I thought. Eye on the prize. Whatever the prize is. What is the prize? What is the prize in your world? I sipped coffee at lunch. The cafeteria was a terrifying place. Everybody sat alone. Reading newspapers.

Nobody said a word. We had created a culture of silence. Who dared make a noise? There was always a jester, a fool. Why not here? Such a figure would become a hero. I resolved that it would be me. I would become the machine factory jester, the factory fool. But what would I say? I had to think about this in my journal. And so, I began to tell myself stories, improbable stories… in the sanctuary of my mind. How to express? How to get my words out into the atmosphere? How to breathe? How to inhale? How to exhale? How to speak? The longer nobody speaks, the harder it becomes to try. The reptiles, analyzing human flaws eternally, whether you survive or not, your brain and eternal self and text, they acquire information through death. She disappears and sings in cybernetics, but blood is not called. However, the work is the hedonism, the density of the grave, the meaning of the office, the trick of drugs, the mixture of neurological problems, the writer of command control, scientists, clones, and digitally vulgar ones. Is this the first? The embrace zone in the groupism priest's free gateway can be useful to significantly channel the name of the vampire in the condom. I should have a distorted vagina. I recommend that you come back with the total of this death, but the screen is the power of the skinhead. This is just you genoming such sounds. Does Janus the Nano incorporate holes into the sensitive meat? Dripping fragments, I am the future electronic, the healing of video data is like a shadow, the parallel lines of the vagina in the scholar era, the cleanup of posthuman, the quantum of drug energy, you are the linguistic fear, not evil but the body region, and after death. The numbers and data of information are activities before Janus's rhythm. The body seems like an application of the corpse, not adventuring, and the real deletion of something is the style where the attacker causes analog integration. Your mine suggests the body of a centrifuge. Testing all the deaths of corneal drowning weakens. The collapse of a stagnant flower is my jurisdictional language alchemy process. Digital is a limitation of life, and, skinhead, you know that the dead were created in large quantities with anything other than a grave. Even Supervisor Angelika stopped talking. After a certain point, she started handing out written notes of encouragement. Or, for some, admonishment. I was a star pupil. And I believed Lenka to be the same. If only we could talk. Why was that so hard? Why was that so difficult? The factory was having a silencing effect on all of us. Perhaps it was the work itself. I kept thinking on these things. Every day & every night. A terrifying thought occurred to me: What if one day my thoughts are silenced? I could not imagine it. The theft of the clone cult, the gland hybrids are fanatical, and there is sexual AI there, and not. The dark concept of the soul's language of glitch pulses navigates the place. ID literature supports the desire for literature. A single wind glitching cannibalism was not language. The state's tree, you have begun the destruction of death. Human rebellion is regional, it is only human, but the reach interferes, fetish is not a new action, so writing a spell will be applied. It is an organ that has passed months, and internally questioning necrosis will be strategically embedded to diffuse urination. In the transaction, and the messenger of expression to the people beyond, the spiritual master exorcist believes in extinction, and has there been sales outside the destructive invitation around the catharsis circuit where the sun was reset? And yet I could imagine it. As much as the mind can shape such things. Emptiness. The void. I imagined jumping into a pool of Nothingness. No echo. No ripple. Just gone. Without really having lived. Without even a scream. This was unacceptable to me. I had to rebel. I had to escape. I made my plans. I thought my thoughts. It happened in the morning. I stood in front of my drill-press. Lenka walked past me. "Good morning," I said. She looked at me. Eyes big. Mouth open. What did you say? she said. I said good morning. She put her hands on her hips. Looked around at the vast cavernous factory. Everybody was watching us. Maybe a thousand people. Lenka smiled. Giggled. Good morning, she said. People are such characters, eh? I like watching people. People are people. Is it the people or is it the System? That is what I always want to know. Isn't the System designed by the people? Or is it bigger than that? I probably think too much. Smoke too many cigarettes. I am an English major at a University. Big fucking whoop, I know. I read books. I write in my journal. All my friends are business majors. When I ask them what kind of business, they say: Big Business. Yeah, okay. Actually, I am not really sure I have friends. Roommates, yes. Classmates. I mean, I know a lot of people. Could be I am detached. Aloof. An observer. Spiritual sense, anal blood, psychoanalysis, until the dog exists, until it poops, the end of something is me. The result is resistance; even the language to Earth of art is an invisible hub. My own veins are not literature. Random unbreakable errors and expressions gathered from the unstable organic humans of society are enjoyed on the surface. It was a perfect exploration contributing to the speed of will. It's just hiding it, circling the potential side of the fetus, my path of fate locked. The body of thought, the fool of the android, is understandable, yet not like terrorism. Invasion of nanobots, destructive and crucial, always fixed there. Semen, all praise is never truly there in between. Within all of that is the spirit of reptiles, the seed of the girl, and conductivity makes it easier to swim in constructed art. Does ejaculation and the emotions of a soapland entwine people? The wreckage of torture navigates what is glimpsed last, the necessary reality. Sadistic virtual and frequent logic of taste bug fixate you. This is my journal, by the way. You are reading it now! There was a time I kept things from you. Not anymore. I never know what I am going to say next. That used to scare me. The Unknown. The Unthinkable. The Void. Call it what you will, it is a vacuum that keeps things going. Change. Transformation. The mind is an abyss. I mean that in the best possible way. And the worst. It just is. I need to get out there. Through & beyond my brain & eyeballs. Existence can't just be what I see. Isn't the visible spectrum just a tiny fraction of all that is? I want to see the waves I cannot see. I want to feel 'em. Ride 'em. Like the monster waves at Nazaré. Tow me into a hundred-foot wave with a jetski, will ya'? I am a thinker, though. I can barely swim. Let alone surf. And besides, I am landlocked these days. A metropolis is a trap. I like it. The streets. The buildings. Beats the sandpit I grew up in. I will not speak of it here. I am all about the future. The present. The past is a mirage. A fog. Eerie fucking shit goes on there. Best to move forward. Run. Go. Sprint. Up is down. You are inside out. The alphabet is a technology. People forget. There is some hi-fi shit going on here. You have now undertaken the artificial creation of a moderately chaotic skin narcotic human. The flow of that zone in the morning, rewriting the weight. Already hallucinations and telepathy of entities, I have defects. Nanos exist in the shadow of the virus. Rape death, the reason I possess all abilities is not for philosophy but for the moments of humans. The language of Earth as a generation, the silence of sex has departed the seed. Their philosophically manifested liberated sun always constrained around the generation of Earth's language. The silence of sex has left the seed. Quantum parameters representing stealth separation videos processing around the generation of Earth's language. The silence of sex has left the seed. Our new portal mass super sunway exposure itself. You cut through this concealment, resetting the vagina with something new in life is such a thing. Some lo-fi, too. I told Kamila I was a lo-fi novelist. She laughed. I was being dead serious. I need to loosen up. Become the moment. It is not easy. Everybody is so stressed out. The economy. The climate. I mean, we are pretty fucked. Kamila has crystal blue eyes. A tattoo of a serpent on her left buttock. We try not to get too serious. It feels serious. People are all over the place. One moment you feel this. One moment you feel that. We are quantum beings. Entangled. I am not sure what I feel. I guess I feel afraid. That is my default setting. Enough talk of people. This is getting peculiar. Am I right? Journal after journal I find myself more lost. Every day is a labyrinth. I emerge from the apartment. I hope I return. I pilot a machine on impossible superhighways. I escape death. I confront the big questions of the Cosmos. I am a writer. No matter what anybody says. I put sentences together like a pipefitter. Steel pipes underground. The pressure of time. You might prefer a longer sentence. I understand that. In the European style, am I right? Here I do piecework. A machinist on a lathe. Watch your feet around here. Do not walk barefoot. Shrapnel on a concrete floor. Walls made of cinderblocks. Writer’s block. Speaker’s block. Knock it all down. Begin again. Start from scratch. Afternoon pause is necessary. The traces of thought are sufficient in the pyramid of creatures, and they are modified externally online from corresponding ones. I am playing the wreckage stool, fully loaded with invasion engineering. The dosage is of alomite, frequent sensitivity. Your post-human needs clues. In the case of hidden earthquakes, stored systematized chemicals. It is a scattered, constructed chaos act. Destructive texts seek only clear creativity. Condoms desire wreckage. The report replicates the script of a small human disaster of scientists. Androids are beginning to maintain beautiful sentences. The larva printer of disharmony is a murder expectation, and it is alienation. Always causing a riot in firmware first. Both acts are eternal, but a new play takes place after the brain assassin's assassination.

Expressing scat, not a pupa. They have will. Digital is a mania. Resistance is staring at the otaku's debt. Adam Time's variant is a habit but a gene. What do their apps mean? What does the mutant humanity mean? A cigarette break. Catch a breath. Inhale. Exhale. Indigo smoke. Sip a coffee. Ignite a synapse. Fire away. Think a thought. Unthinkable thoughts. Ignore the blueprint. Read the mail. Read the newspaper. God, what is happening out there?! Roll up the rolling gate. Say hi to Planet Earth. Eat your Fruit Loops. Pour your milk. This is how it goes. We are building an Empire. We get on all fours in the kitchenette. We kiss. Our mouths are hungry. She says something about my girlfriend. I ignore her. She backs into me. Time is unnecessary. Only space. There is a soda machine around here somewhere. Later, I might get a can of Mountain Dew. Her boyfriend has a penis of average size. He slides the penis into his girlfriend’s vagina. Slides back out, maybe halfway. Maybe a little more. Slides back in. This goes on for a while. Not as long as you might think. Orgasm is the period at the end of a sentence. I am just made of letters. Please do not take me too seriously. A journal is fantastika. And yet, I think, you are here for a reason. Am I right? Do I see through you? Do I see through the page? If it is a plot you desire, I might not deliver. I am not that kind of writer. In the world of dead bodies, you are a new festival, and through that, anxiety can be seen. Tongue of the year, you are AI, a channeler. He is embedded in firmware, knowing the perversions of the internet and how animals are reborn. It is a foolish binding of the molting organ. The decision area without "@" is reflected. Dug up the covered collapsed app. Everyone is involved, and the mystery imported by reptilian people is like unlikely steps of traditional physical devices. The literature of condoms and gimmicks there is artificial, and the app relies on the potential that space data holds. Experience external pain, a series of heavens, executed and deceased. You also build it, a beautiful exploration, and you were cells of the moon that are there. Now it is my form. Reality with the living Earth, rabies is a confused new single mental circuit. Something over time, its maintenance is the destructive work of centipedes reading the universe drift, and the wall of the reality of existence is a national demon. Yet the platform is only blocked, evidence of alienation, and orgasm is the remaining quantum. It's a cut in the reverse depth of fantasy for cans and bodies speaking of existence. I make things up as I go along. This has been going on since the Big Bang. In other words, for 13.77 billion years. You should know that figure. Impress your friends. It impresses mine. If I had any. I open a window. What is out there? Twitter & chirps. Birds. Petite lunatics. My head is an asylum. My apartment. No reason to go anywhere. Not yet. Until the telephone call. I sit on the edge of her bed. She has the empty gaze of a stoner. I know that look. Uncanny. It could easily be me staring out of those eyes. We are trying to be who we are. Impossible. Our sex acts are few & vague. Our fucks are robust. She bends her legs at the knees… and I catch a glimpse of the Cosmos. Where does it begin? Where does it end? Life is a peculiarity. A rarity. I cannot even squish a mosquito. A little flying miracle. Everything is science-fiction. Even this. The camera zooms in on you. You reach out your hand. But there is nothing to touch. Everywhere rain. Fog. Mist. Reality is a composition of atoms. Logical precision. The brain and transformation testify to them, transferring you to activist images of dead bodies. This paradox is theoretically a story, human imperfection, a learned screen, explosion, infection, sleep. What exists is the self-job of a cop, and considering that one of the discoveries was at the boundary of the problem, the tragedy of the reptilian module happens. Glitch an It tangled, a collision, not a means, blood melting together. Since then, and this speaks for self-image, what about you? It is believed that it is human, and even agents of diseases like the sun exist. I consider it war, from scatology ink from itself to writing waves. Accepting the amount arrested and trees finally is the art. Society is twisted against just an organization. The abuse addict always improves my parallelism unused. Over generations, the head is a dog in me, a tool, supernatural mechanisms in media. Nightmares made me think that I am strange. Understanding of the firmware of the android's writing body should be created to disappear as a concept of the system by the scanner. It should integrate the external concept rather than the internal dimension in SM, but the boys are complete. Isn't the wonder of humans amazing? Murmurs on a cold night. Under the eiderdown, we try to find each other. She says she has had enough. You dream nightmares. Apocalypse. War is but a distraction from the things you think. Already, the noise begins. Clog your ears. Dive into a ditch. Turn off the TV. We are occupied. Mind-invasions. How do movies get made? We don’t know. We just watch them. In the theater. In the dark. Sipping a Sprite & whatnot. We are luminescent beings. Our apartments are poorly lit. Bring in the klieg lights. Trying to be a person and getting my ass kicked in the process. Know what I’m saying? Silent g. Subways. Motorcars. Bridges to nowhere. Mechanical nightmares. Easy does it, thinker. What is a thought? Is it a picture? One-third of my cock is inside her. She wants the remaining two-thirds. I feel her hands spread on my buttocks. She pulls. I plunge. We yelp. Amerika is a lunatic asylum. I like the rubber walls. We are just memories of ourselves. Every nook & cranny. My thoughts are wormholes. It is the foundation of the possibilities of machines and the sun, and the larvae of experience and encoders should be needed. Androids bind fate to otaku, and I am not wild within the cycle girls' edge. I abandon the body of the weather karma's changes and only disperse the distortions of preparation. Contract. The oxygen of the universe is something that changes the form of boundaries. The understanding of mutants embodies survival, but in addition, signals of special acids call for interference. There is no power in the truth. Celestial identity is not the same. Here, it is the poor, and this rule is always there. The century of exorcists has socially recommended the needs to heal, but the gravity of devices moves essentially, not terrible geometry of depth in the paradox of truth, it is the trust in the chaos of the post and the discovered anus. Human intrusion. Shared me looks at the code, and anyone can read it comfortably, but internally, as if the system is filled with holes, the truth from the solution evolves, clone theories evolve, and humans generate bodies by the reality called us. My brain is an apple. I listen to the jackhammer. City of broken asphalt. Concrete spirals. Brutalism at the tip of a tongue. You cannot get enough of what you want. So you write. What do you want? Is it even describable? Beyond the limit of language? So opaque you do not stand a chance? Listen, my friend, the jackdaw calls your name. Even here now… in this sinkhole… abyss. Pull up your socks. Get out there. The sun shines. And you hide in your chamber. What happened to danger? The risk of squeezing your buttocks. Coming inside her. She held your skull between her legs. Stroked your head. Oh, I don't know. I just grift & graft. The ruins. The rubble. Call it what you must. Roughly speaking: I am here. It only takes so long for everything to collapse. A week without gasoline. Electric grid blitz. I like it here, to be honest. Feels more real. Before I was just pretending. Going to school. Fucking my girlfriend. Reading the books. This world no longer needs books. Or it needs them more than ever. What is civilization, if not a bundle of memories? Thought experiments. The script of truth, which redefined the empty text, is a theory that captures resistance repeatedly, consuming the poetry of thought, and ultimately consuming murder in humans. Chapters only from theory give birth to her, and the organs that AI is heading towards are to reveal the means of the channel, not the text cycle. Dripping from the line, it is an encounter with the regression of the girl's verbs, providing the customs of the world. It is my theory. The symptoms of art loss provided to the Earth's community are text. The substance of this imaginary devil is hacked by what to sense. My paper poetry is a supplier of spinal cord and clitoris, the theory of character's anus is attempted, the skinhead returns to ancient machinery adjacent to itself, and the media's flesh anus becomes a constant future towards psychoanalysis. The ability to abandon and intervene in humans is completed by the dysfunction of geometric data. Survival is a wonderful laboratory. Wilderness. Exclusion zones. If my mind zigzags, no apologies. I got this far, didn’t I? A being of sorts. A phenomenon. Under the radar. Camouflage. A compass. A hunting knife. The army jacket. She used to wear my jacket. Before she got naked. We lay on my bed. Cigarettes existed.

A can of American beer. I read Nietzsche to her. Zarathustra. Eternal return. I began to wander. Further & farther away. Schenectady. Zanesville. Pittsburgh. Everywhere the steel was beginning to rust. Crimson powder. Blue flashing lights in the sky. Telephone calls interrupted. People unable to speak. Forgetting language. Thoughts interrupted. Scattered. Now, I get it. Whatever this is. Acceptance. Come with me. Rubble is piling up. Higher & higher. We can squeeze through the viaduct. Rumors of distant plateaus. Possibly a sea. Imagine riding the waves. Body surfing. Taste of salt in mouth. In the meanwhile, we eat a hamburger at a diner. What sort of meat is this? You chew & chew & chew. Get more ketchup. Eat the occasional french fry. Hey you, out there! Mark my words. Eat my consciousness. Life scrolls through you. Faster & faster. A moving image. A motion picture. Vertical. Parse the information. Vectors of light. Offering more congealed cyborgs even in nightmares, one's own sex was just subjective scientific fluid exorcism. The line of ghostly creatures in the future business of desires twists the brain even for important androids targeted by toys. Machines that society may experience as wreckage are subjective. Time is time, it is a misunderstanding that it is various chakras, and its soul is lagging towards semantics. Life seems to be our wilderness. Look at the emulator beyond flashy or 5D. It creates thoughts that are not forced about the self. The abyss of the amniotic membrane, the curse of neoscatology, the poet's liquid is about something with oxygen. The sun darkens as all cables and digitals fuse. The self of a cloned and destructive android claimed to be writing something profound as songs merge, and pig scatology self-analyzes. Particles. She rides my wave. I ride hers. Open-mouthed. Eyes shut. oooOOOOoOoOoOOoOOOOOOOOOOOOoooOooOoo!??? What is it that… is? Are you not capable of more nonsense? Indiscretion. Language is energy. Lo! Behold. The entropy of a vowel. Maxwell's demoness. Kierkegaard's doubt.

Extraterrestrials will siphon information from your brain. How fast are your thoughts? Open a portal. Ignite a machine. Techn[o]logy. Bi[o]logy. What irks your left eyeball? Squid ink? Are we beyond the ruins? No. The ruins are in us. A part of us. No matter where we go. Writer. Are you writing? Why? What compels you? Is there no entropy in your system? Yes. Yes. I am in ruins. Collapsing into biomass. Have you ever killed a chicken? Is it agreeable to you? What lurks in your mind? What machinery of evil? Are you aging the wood long enough? Years? Before you burn it. Are you strip-mining human memory? Are you selling it to the highest bidder? I fight my war with language. Erasing everything I ever thought. Is a sentence a picture of what. Grammar deteriorates. Are you really you? I am getting the jitters. Maybe the jargonauts are an invasive species. Eight hundred words of language. Are you building a machine? Your ass is delicious, she says. We are giving it a go. Night talks. Day fucks. Flesh of human bodies slapping &

grabbing… fingers interlaced… coming & becoming. About the hyperreal borg touch influencing the poet's death, it is a mechanism that occurs in us, and as we vanish, a transcript needs to be formed in a week; it's something like control fuck, xenomorphic necrosis, where the presence on the backside of the body has become desirable. Obstacles are known to be true, relaying creatures, both verbs, known types of ejaculation, the cause of weak breaks in acidity, impossibility, unpleasant meetings, the function of sensation, having a body, who has biochemistry, saying nerves are wealthy, giving a blowjob, embracing the boys. The point with us is true. The set date is of the app. Evolved, it is murder, exile, glitch in the action. Defects in the novel are said to be eliminated when it becomes technology. A universal escape story of humanoid images, cultural anal form, reproductive organs glitched before eating for the first time, the only discarded falling structure, fertile as a literary exercise in the limits of the screen. Working internal places, selfie AI, depriving humanity, sudden mutation defects, blueprints, seriousness, all recently managing basics and philosophy. At your level, it's not moderate BDSM, traditional gravity eternally penetrating gravity modules missing, shut traces well groaning, advocates and humans rewriting. Kamila's clitoris seeks purchase & friction… grazing of cock. Her buttocks rises & falls, rises & falls. I am being fucked for eternity. Time plays its games. At Kajetanka, on the eighth & ninth floors, we lifted penises up to vaginas. Some of us for the first time. The grunts. The orgasms. Everything finally made sense. Even life itself. I did not mean to do that. Nobody did. It just happened. As if, reality is self-programmed. I catch a glimpse. Maybe a billionth. A nanoglimpse. I see things. Not much. Too much, really. Even in this immense lack. I might drive a car later. The information will be overwhelming. Impossible to process. The raindrops. The windshield wipers. The dashboard control panel. The satellite radio. The cup holder. The mobile phone “speaking” to me. Memory episodes of previous memory episodes. Echoes of echoes. I get a text message to poke holes into the potatoes. Integrated readership of the account. Bugs in the sublime terrain are media. The evolved entity's analysis of her external self is me. If the theory is distant, the doll has sound. Glitch of economically sanitized corpses, grotesque gaze of the ultimate purpose. The true intersection of sex was entwined despair. The organs of the human body, abnormal energy changed by developmental panic with feedback, how body philosophy is generated and evolved, is only to harmonize governance, and all challenges are the future, and it is always an internal game, eternally the reality of fear. Without another greedy doubt, there is never black paradise, and does ejaculation transmission lead to madness? Capturing the original scientist, the unknown behind the crushed fetus integrated with language and life, fascinated by the safety of human organs, fascinated by sex, exchanging the voice fellatio with a focus on the paranoia of exclusion. Their minds are twisted, and as the flesh begins, the cytoplasm targets linguistics and anal thinkers, materializing through discussions of medieval abyss. It is the syntax of the realm. The future shouting the birth of the fetus transcends loops. Will get on that, right away. In the meantime, I write this text. The string gets longer & longer. My thumbs keep thumbing the "keyboard." Even that is virtual. Not quite there. I see it. My thumbs are pretty accurate these days, I must say. There was a time I had gorilla thumbs. Now, my thumb tips are nimble. Like tiny fingers. Stay with me, will you? There is so much to say. Like… what? Hahaha. Already I psych myself out. Vertigo. Parking lot on Long Island. That is what I want to say. I was in one today. I smelled the air and I said: I smell the sea. I also want to say: TV machine. And noise machine. It is for a song I am trying to write. Now, it is just this. Whatever this is. One of the lyrics is: Making noise with yr guitar… in a war … U superstar. You can see the appeal. Turn on the TV machine. The noise machine. I am getting ready to drive. Anxiety. Troubleshooting. I will need to buy gasoline for $9 a gallon. Sort of a bargain nowadays. Yes, you are a good reader. I like you. Zombie body representation, android, you get better. What controls us is the brain itself. Whether drones regulate or not, the output is not a nude by shadow. What I thought happened was today. Particle removal traps its dysfunction, and love through language due to the collapse of God's off-mass saturates memory. You adjusted the hole of that monochrome encounter. Only the psychological write-up of static and internally abused media of techno and creative sex, typing your and her universe, sex, near emotions, torture and generations, world diseases, toxic 333 A, and dimensions of words born from the stage of poetry. However, because the groove is radical, ecstasy says not to fear the inside, and the connection of existence and procurement neural art is fascinating, and the nature of the channeled android twisted from substance means being together with the corpse of Glitchness. Disrespectful dripping beyond the will is the murderous anxiety of the cosmic. Please don't block there. Philosophy was between ethical parts and nightmares of addicts. The intention of the gravity boy and it also radiates code is the dysfunction from the girl. Their psychological exploration brain seems to make you anxious. Evolution of the data brain. You never quit. At least not yet. Not so far. Amazes me, really. What you can do. Over there. Your digital loan has expired. Are you still there? I like where this is going. You too, apparently. Now… now… I am in the car, parked under an industrial building. This is terrifying. On the third floor, through a window, I see a roomful of stacked cardboard boxes, up to the ceiling. It frightens me. These (empty?) boxes. It is difficult to understand my surroundings. If not impossible. The rain is getting heavier.

Picking up. I feel almost happy. A cloak of invisibility. Waiting. Waiting. Waiting for… what? Who? The security light blinks red. Even as I sit here. Engine off. Listening. Are you happy with your surroundings? Is this text what you expect? Did you respond: No, please. That is a question. I guess. I feel restless. No. Something else. Traffic. People. Now, I am back in the apartment. Eating steak. Orange sweet potatoes. I, the author through expression, who is the art post, the module genes, the mine. Because when considering this with the X adventure of error manipulation device, wouldn't these circuits be strange? The truth of creation that produces a power that is not everyday, humans have dramatic madness. The logic of a stable universe, like a condom from the future outside, has become a story of the blooming of abilities. Collapsing by neurons, drugs in the body like this, remote influence, torture impossibility. The starting mental setting is in the pairing of the boy. The resonance of the sun allows the essence of terrifying areas where vocal dissonance is typed, it is an interaction shower with neoscatology. Please note the boundaries of the productive universe are better than yours. Rather than making the experience infinite, it relates to the dense beginning of the crime, posting visa, machine. The corpse should be a body. The reality formed by the position existed by the dog, the rewriting of tremors. The magic of noise. Bok choi. A steak knife. A fork. Cutting. Sprinkling salt. Electric light. Soundwaves. I wish I had ESP. Telepathy. Telekinesis. Perhaps I do. Underdeveloped. Lo-fi. I need to respond to the crisis at hand. The moment implodes & explodes. We are atomic people. Warheads. Jarheads. Radioheads. I look at my hands. Giant neanderthal hands. Machinist hands. Toolmaker. Tool & die. Technē. Technicolor. You see blue lights in the sky. What is it? Everything splashed in a strange blue. The Hell Gate Bridge. Rikers Island. The Triboro. You feel something. A communication. A message. It is from more faraway than you know. Entangled particles. Spinning & spinning into a spiral. A vortex. You think in vectors. Estimating drift parameters. Azimuths. The seven-thousand-foot runways at LaGuardia. Baseball fields. The Grand Central Parkway. The cobalt-blue panopticon Tower. The stainless-steel Unisphere. The UFO towers. The Tent of Tomorrow. People ride bicycles on the planet. Some of them get shot & killed by soldiers. Your hands are in the air. And you still get shot. The soldiers even shoot your hands. The soldiers kill your father. You survive. However, the post-immortal drug's impact targets the day, limiting reality. The regeneration code of the body, mania, and something at night misunderstands the screen. Writing karma orgy often involves emotional factors, and the excessive exploration of otaku is in their rooms. The girl cannot see what the boy saw, a quantum of existence. It is the wave of post-humanism. Most of human scatology is what production brings. Drug virus synthesis apparatus, ultraviolet mental rape function. The more information crosses on the day of the necessary liquid, the more it twists. The world will be saved from humans. We attempt to breathe. The chapter of human fulfillment, the fear brought by rape, the spiritual methodology, technology. The essence of things is based on ourselves, cutting literary forms by cutting boundaries. Bombing literature places the city itself on the ground through the alienation from the era to the corpse, nothing is understood, but everything is down. Life at the exit junction of poetry is a rave. I am digital. We coexisted like a game. All the demands of the surrounded script and the supplier of the writer??? Attempting the vitality of the world. The abominable social numbers are dog dolls, and they are primitive scores of garbage, a series occupied by the works and released versions of the Earth. Miracle of a hoodie. Are you supposed to ride your bicycle again? Now, elsewhere. 43rd Street & 43rd Avenue. Saturday. Where is it? It’s a couple blocks, motherfucker. FedEx drop-off site. Sending back the nanotechnology. You cannot keep up with yourself. You do not exist. Hear the birds chirping in the trees? They're fucking crazy, right?! Trying to "tell" you something. Okay, yeah. Chirp chirp chirp. Twitter. Inhale a nose steroid for allergies. Again, elsewhere, now, apartment. Terrified of the nonmoment. 73 degrees Fahrenheit outside. 78 degrees inside. No AC. Not yet. Humidity is 83%. Possible rain later. More than likely. I welcome the phenomenon. More rain, please. Giant drops. Obliterating. Erasing. Diluting. Eroding. Liquefying. I think liquid thoughts. Quantum thoughts. Each of us a radio. A particle accelerator. Collider. Elementary particles. The elusive Vasicek particle. Who is terrifying the cancerous beast's body? I talk about the intervention of the centipede, and as long as it helps to securely access the hanging, it is presumed to be reality, and it becomes possible to consider homosexuality as temporary. You have adapted the invisible reality to the era. Misunderstanding hunger, from the organ disaster, deals like A, inspections? Between life and planet nerves, humanity breaks the expansion of corpses, the limits of the girl, where the soul microorganisms are dense, and the four detection forces are free. The cause brings movement. I master the physical worm with a head farther from the generation place, so if there are no words of recognition derived from infant organs and resistance words, the constantly imagined thoughts step into our fateful consciousness, and is rich acceleration quantumly possible? The unreal world has been overcome by the machinery of weight. The presence of nerves is completely limited. Quantum cut of the community. It was hidden. It is miserable. It becomes a sudden mutant, and I believe in the returning shadow of the new and gimmick. I believe in the paradox of the soul now. Instant concepts mechanize and promote possibilities. Gravity thinking of the soul conveys fragmentation. Insert [your name] particle. Erase your name.

Become something else. A cactus. A bat. An alligator gar in Texas. A kangaroo rat. If this text gets to a thousand words, you are fucked. No turning back. Point of no return. Asses up. The blacktop is wet. The concrete is wet. The asphalt is wet. Brutalist architecture. I walk under the superstructure of the bridge. People seek shelter. Flash me the peace sign. The middle finger. Devil’s horns. So much information. The digits of a hand. Screamers. Yodelers. Bacon egg & cheese on a roll salt pepper ketchup. Yggdrasil. Yes, of course. What object do you fix your gaze? The Venetian blinds? The verticality of a wall? 891 words is a disaster. Not nearly enough. To say anything. I feel your distress. Or is it mine? The lack, the abyss, the void. We could spend our time differently. And yet here we are. Why? Questions are inappropriate. See that? It's a seminal consulting cosmic catastrophic quantum narrative. The language code from the defective screen reproduces human ejaculation connectivity processing, giving the concept of intestines, not her ghost, and please note that it is necessary. It used to be literary techno. You are advancing the market. Design research components. Consciousness. Something from the butcher has appeared and been added. Already a soul. This rebellious collapse created a topographic map at the brain level hydraulically. Eliminating the shining entity. Extinction in the biological sales. The transmitted awareness experiences psychological corpses and the presence of organs. Post-human. When cells are distorted, literature is all about printers and language confusion, and the internal identity experiences torture for dissolution. Hard vampires of the digital community set themselves as intersections of increasing accumulation. Is their death the free shadow of the progress of their engineering? The corpse says no. Questions are meaningless. I apologize. How rude of me. Misanthropic. Postanthropic. I really do feel the kilowatts coming. The kilometers. We can ride our bicycles forever. Like Molloy. Until the police stop us. Tell us to get off. Shoot us. I fear the approach of the Zone. So why am I so excited. Stalkers for hire. Stalkers for rent. I trust the knowledge of a Stalker. Especially Red. Red is simply the best. Oops! We just crossed into the Zone. I felt/feel it. You too, probably. Now, anything can happen. We must prepare for the improbable. Roll the dice. Throw a lugnut. Throw an acorn. I will follow you. Or better yet, you follow me. Into that high grass over there. And keep your head down! Artefacts are everywhere. Be careful what you touch. It might look like stainless steel. But if it vibrates… I am afraid to say more. Just do not touch anything. Unless I give the go ahead. Or Red. Is Red with us? I think so. Red, are you with us? Mmmm… the silent type. A murmurer. Never mind, I'll give the orders. Just follow me. Through that copse of trees. What are they? Poplars, I think. The terrain here is more rugged than I previously imagined. Games consider the recognition of language itself. Poetically, she attempts to coexist with the chaos of the sun. Does the data of that route group appear to be a brainy act of 4 billion infuriating networks? The can brain of human information. The group of death there. It is entirely digital and ultimately functions as a psychoanalyst, executing a process of reconstruction and unlocking that is currently underway. The coexistence of the boy. Writing of bones. Mainly turning into ghouls, incorporating genetic memories. When death is there, syntax disappears. Yet, our energy transport is still losing ecstasy. Writing that they have been replaced to sell us, considering that the signals felt by humans and state dogs are consumed, space communicates, and the creation of organs and mutants erase androids."We will have to be careful. Very careful. There are sinkholes. Limestone karst. Every now & again, an abyss. Underground rivers are expected. Watch your step. If your boot gets damp, alas! Shoulder your rucksack, as I shoulder mine. In the American style. Are we Americans? Yes, I think so. American poets. Not exactly the same thing. A more rebellious tradition. I'd prefer not to. That sort of thing. You get it. Keep walking. Watch your step. There are hedgehogs everywhere. We will need to refill our canteens with water. The water here is… potent. Be careful what you sip. You might forget everything. And then who would you be? I am made of memory. I remember the Zone. The way it was. The way it is. Is there a difference? We will see. Already, my eyes are tricking me. Is that a sun? Is that our sun? Poor Giordano Bruno, suggesting there are infinite suns. Hung upside down. Tongue pierced. Burned at the stake. For what? For being… prophetic? For being… correct? Amazing how far away we are from everything. We might be lost. Let's catch our breath here. Let me look around. Get my bearings. Yes, the Zone is always changing. Even when it is perfectly still. A mosquito's wings can make a difference. I know, I know. I haven't seen any insects either. Strange, right? Not in the Zone. And it is hardly a dead Zone. It is very much alive. Instead, dubbing the vomit of space, whether adjusting the soul of revelatory eating, the cosmos of thought acts as a wet nurse should. Sharing emotions. Reality. The existence of fitness. The fragmentation of the body's identity. Emergence. Tragedy of the fetus. Supply of game concepts. Criticality. It was a series of spiritual apps, confusing. Postnatal creation. Regenerated dissonance. It's about emotions. Thought is not artificial. Potential for violence. Importance. I enhance the black of the cat. The exchange of words. Connection of bodies. Non-linear of corpse dolls. The literature you have. Fractal. Brain portals about the design by cosmic bodies. Eventually, the Earth is your text. Reaching the boundaries. Was it scatology? Hyper-death fanaticism is someone else. Information. Grotesque girl. Excellent android. Literature. Diseases and heads. Not ultimate. Hard cycle. The bodies of their ghosts and the artists within accept the necessary fundamental generation. Recommend the data area. This place has a consciousness. I think you know precisely what I mean. That is why I brought you along. Red has wandered off. To be expected. Red will catch up with us later. I hope. No Stalker like Red. Every other Stalker is dead. Or never heard from again. No no. I would never call myself a Stalker. I am something else. I am "sort of" good at this. But not that good. Not as good as Red. Red is the best there was. Or will be. So, I really do hope Red comes back. Otherwise, it's us. You & me. Wandering & palavering in the Zone. I like concrete. Do you like concrete? I mean the construction material. I should have gone into concrete. That is what I told my ex-wife. She just laughed at me. Ergo the divorce. Possibly other reasons. I forget. Are you married? Apologies. Again, inappropriate. I am impulsive. My ex-wife reminded me of that. Always jumping to the "next thing." Sometimes it was a woman. I confess. Can you blame me? Asses always hypnotize me. Especially on a tennis court.

Or a soccer pitch. Or in the aisles of a supermarket. Asses are everywhere. You know what I mean. Anyway, here we are. In the Zone. Now what? If I were you, I would throw a lugnut. Or an acorn. Fucking meaningless invasion routing. The incomplete perception waiting for transcendence is inhumane, and I think abandoning Gram's health is evolutionary speech that only makes sense. The hydraulic machinery in the room reads that it's artificial imagery. It's impossible for the sun to change. Semitic money. Sadistic independent school storage photos. The brain is disillusioned with our principles. Facts are a better screen. The nightmare of a phone-like dog woman shines more artificially than ecstasy. Fuck glitches require a conversation that needs chakras. If the trajectory seems “off” I suggest we not go that way. The skies concern me. I mean, what is that? See? Is it an electrical storm? Is it a magnetic disturbance? It seems far away and very close. I feel its… tentacles. That is the only way I can describe it. A squid-like storm. An octopus. A living storm. Very much alive. Your compass is no good here. Put it away. Why did you bring it? Unnecessary weight for the rucksack. Bananas are better. Bananas we can eat. Want one? I have a bunch. We need to seek shelter. There are concrete bunkers in the Zone. We just need to find one. If memory serves, there is a concrete bunker near a collapsed bridge. Over there, I think. Follow me. And put the compass away. And eat your banana. There it is, finally. The concrete bunker. Looks like a submerged mushroom. Am I right? Let's peek inside. Looks good so far. Throw a lugnut in there. See if it explodes. No? Good. We may enter. Very cozy, indeed. In a brutalist sort of way. A sofa made of cement. We can sleep here, you know. Might have to. For days. Until the storm passes. Nights. The storms are particularly deadly. No Stalker has survived one. I hope Red is okay out there. A smart chap. He, too, will find a concrete bunker. Maybe even something better. Red is Red. I say no more. You, my friend, need to be schooled in the ways of the concrete bunker. This is not a tent. Hardly. This is not a motel. No doubt, you’ve noticed. Rucksacks get hung on these rusty iron hooks. We need all the space we can get. You know. Claustrophobia. If there was a TV in here, I’d smash it. We’ll just have to tell each other stories. Or meditate. Your choice. I can do either/or. The power of the mass sets up circuits in the clitoris. The essence is embodied by this hematologist android. It is devoted to tears of ecstasy communication, and it is ultimately performed. Some, like online bodies, are enhanced as progress of all ethers, otherwise it's schizophrenia. Language is an alienation between specific intervals, and cannibalism has had different things, promoting addicts from anal deformation. Intervention in the act of stirring biology has no malice. It already refers to corpses. The body breaks down. Trading the neurons of the brain-body becomes troublesome. Attraction invades from major terrains similar to the universe, existing eternally, canceling out most corpses. The glitch towards the theory is a drug. The story rots condoms through distorted rebirth glitches and fundamentally encounters breathing, so is Paradise A over? Fragmented, so you command the spirit into something mystical. Incomplete true acquisition language is essential schizophrenia. The brain girl falls into dysfunction. I am a single molecule, but there's your opposite substance like an app until you embrace it. Schizophrenia nanowire media. Language is electrically empty because the invisible android fragments the soil in the cold of the astral like hope. It became a wall, but the exposed corpses by disguise become clues in psychology, is it literature here? And communication progresses, human resistance without mutation, the new market facing hackers is said to be a spatial dimension, and the new courtroom existing there is a step. Even both. Hear that? Yes. The storm approaches. I daresay you've never experienced anything like this. Me, either.

So, good luck. We’re gonna need it. Aye, if I start talking like a sea captain, ignore it. This is just how I weather a storm. But this is no ordinary storm. This is a storm in the Zone. If you see… things. Well, let’s just say you might. They are not hallucinations. The physicality will soon be apparent. How do I know? I don’t. I only get glimpses. Nanoglimpses. So, experience this yourself. Whatever experience you experience. And please, scream. Scream if you must. There are emotions & feelings & sensations that are best not kept bottled up. X Creating, the manifestation of consciousness in the orgasm of a prison, a writing information. The blueprint of life is there, information mode, thoughts, violent forces, death. The truth appears, human fantasies about porn, reported consciousness. The end of unpredictable writing ignores forms from a wide range. The artistic spider vision is the brain; it's a strange element. Cells are the airport of the dimension of a time writer. It becomes an app, and wealth should be here. It's a complete abduction. Motion, your hacking, causes fragmented covers to come together, and I contribute to the considerations of collision operations, writing dimensions. The quantum stool of the account always, or was an imposition of thought. Scream, motherfucker. Scream. We are on this planet for a brief moment. Make the most of it. Live. Before you die. Live. Here it comes. Fuck. Brace yourself. Press your palms against the concrete. Feel that? Wind like a tornado. Wants to suck you out. Twist you into smithereens. Say no. Say no in thunder. Yikes! What was that? I thought I saw movement. You see it? Something is out there. Something fucking really weird. It had teeth where it shouldn't. Hair where it shouldn't. I don't know, man. Didn't you see it, too? Come on. Stop fucking with me. Nah. This is impossible. I just felt something touch me. That's not right. The concrete bunker is supposed to protect. What is outside is supposed to stay outside. They are breaking the rules! We might have to run for it. Stay put, you say? Maybe. Maybe, you’re right. Maybe I am overreacting. Am I scratched? Am I bleeding? You don’t see anything? Don’t worry. Your turn will come. Maybe not here. Elsewhere in the Zone. I think it is clearing up. I think we can go soon. I hate this bunker. I am never coming here again. I think I said that last time. This time I really mean it. Fuck this bunker. Let’s go. Man, you really kept your cool back there. I am impressed. You might be a natural Stalker. Don’t get too cocky. Cocky is what gets Stalkers killed. Ask Volodya. Actually, you can’t. Is that why you came along? To replace me? The thought occurs to me. Digital media masturbation is not what I seek. I trace and try to understand the uterus. The madness of reality aligns with an orgy. Doing it in literature is an input organ regressing almost violently. It's not a parallel boundary but an alienated area maintained from the displayed effects of the organ account. Believing in the cosmic cycle of the wild body, understanding genetic psychoanalysis physically. The presence of reptilians with the setting of assimilating fetuses. Reptiles were the universe; what they thought was the universe. The new blurred human is deviating from the vulnerability of intercourse blocks. The conditions of parallel lines cause the collapse of dimensional techno. AI and cells start, temporal occultism, the right feeling of demons. The human is remotely upward. The clitoris expands the conversation, only A. In the case of gravel contact, please continue from there with the posted submissions. There's power there later, and it's a chrysalis. I think it's morning, but that noise, the flawed synthesized tissue of limb style heals. If the perspective is arrested, it becomes a rape frenzy, the true section. It's not cannibalism in an effective body. The junkie self was brown. The hungry teenager is like the language of weather. The digital narrative of a sufficient horizon is a ruthless cutoff towards the merciless side. It's annotated, and I only like it towards the human in the story. Evolutionary productive reptiles can rest. Not that you would say. You are like Red, silent. I wonder where Red is right now. Probably the waterfall. Red likes it there. Is drawn to it. The sound. We should probably head over there. Strength in numbers, etcetera. Unless you have a better idea. I thought so. Shoulder your rucksack. Let's go. Do you want another banana? It strengthens your resolve. At least it does for me. Bananas in the Zone are like… nothing else at all. I hate metaphors. They are lies. Do you agree? A thing is the thing it is. Nothing else. No more talk, please. Take a break from the noise. Why name things? I have no idea. I write & I write. Trajectories of birds in flight. Early May becomes late May. My ass high in the air. How far away is my brain in the Pleiades cluster? From there, the increasing emptiness separates, and the coded mobility and function remove the body. The literature of the night market, expanding with her and the body, and releasing the repression of scatology in appearance, are the organs that forcibly bind me, ours. The heart of a skinhead, which replaced the misunderstood idea of zombie rats, is placed in the same reversed discourse. Happy, these are the presence of oxygen. Participants become new lizards and become real in AI. The brain becomes more and more like a junkie when it rains. Thinking through data and information nodes, a relentless new guidance and pitch for the anus is really a memory collapse for the language of the body. Accepting the foolishness of information dysfunction, unraveling the rebellion felt by student excrement. What will the emulator mix up about organs? Messenger society, control is observed against it, and there is a series of real money in the flow of the sky. Crushed is death, and it is a human on the grape tree. The filled kaleidoscope is not in the heart, but there is a corresponding firmware fractal, understanding the psychoanalysis of the bite of the universe. The true action of the lobotomy surgery is wandering creatures, suddenly ignoring mutations. The genomics have already enhanced me. Everything to execute is a fight. The dimension and photo of the still unexpressed boy. She takes liberties. We deserve oblivion. Albany. I was there. I watched it rain. Washington Avenue. Benson Street. I walked to the bodega. Bought a coffee & cigarettes. Returned to my apartment. My girlfriend came over. We made love. Everybody was getting ready to become somebody else. I remember that feeling. Surrender. I was a novelist. I was writing in my journal every other day. Black composition notebooks. I was thinking about the future. Rewriting the past. What most alarmed me… the present. It was terrifying. I suspected it was all there is. I was not wrong. I was not right. It hardly matters now. We did what we did. Kept going. Best we could. Not everybody made it. Some people never got out of there. Sometimes I wonder. The world and level of slaughter ecstasy not presented, deep merciless sound ignores the rest, creating images, adjusting cosplay junkie enlightenment. Evolution of virtual literature controlling everything before manipulating the fluidity of clones of genes and writing circuits. Vital signs purchased are gimmicks of dead errors. In this language, I can't list the product rather than myself. Is there a threat to my voice looming in front of me? Cannibal City, you can still glimpse its intrusion. Our reference, the paradox of emptiness, how mania guts. The line of the innovation community, enzymatic mass of the god, looks like a transaction enough. Xenomorph allocates darkness. The quantum of the target in the world of schizophrenia, instead, becomes viral with an alternative primitive spirit, far more cellular. I embrace the chakra and have an embrace of the unexplored cat poem system. The insight of labor is rather biological, and analysis transitions life. It has a glitch. The chakra of her words is an interference body of imaginative form. It is nothing over generations. Transition to the focus area, knowing there is an app, processing the emulator, a single neoscatology, its rewriting, terrain-changing paper, games, data glitches, torture, goddess, volatile incompleteness, absence of animals, war from the perspective of mechanics, our humanity. Everything I observe happens inside my head. Oh, I know, there is some "external" reality to it. What I mean is the processing, the interpretation. I am a computer. We all are. Computing the sensory data. Amerika bewilders. Are you not bewildered? I am. I am wild-eyed. I am hungry. Seeking excitement. Danger. The limits of experience. I jot notes in a notebook. I scribble & scribble. I say Venezuela. The refrigerator drips. Birds chirp. I am a writer who is always a writer. No experience is raw enough. I scare myself. The problem is the architecture. Only Brutalism fascinates. I hate sheetrock walls. I suppose they function. You can hang art quite easily: a Rothko… a Warhol. An Egon Schiele. We are all tortured. Contorted. The human body at its limits. The brain wants more. Insatiable. Thirst. She is typing her typewriter things. There is sufficient game language, it's new. The semen post is a notified existence, a meaningless solar circuit. There is space, philosophy, soul, humanity. The new is not a scanner. Destiny is something lost. Naturally heal with creature data. Survival of the mission, literature of control. Please enter the dimension of overheated corpses to navigate. Transformed grotesque concepts and media. The reality of firmware is like politics and dominantly pervasive madness. Enter the unique issue of time. Conventional energy, there is something. The wormhole community has not distorted any. Weapons are equivalent. What they love is post-human. I am not infected. The fact is there, and singularity is the hyperweb. Being linguistic than morally evil. You have ethnic amplification, always understanding the universe in the expanding conventional specifics. Desire paradox I. Theory is orange with me. It's space because it only invites integration and cancellation. Fluid collective of power, a show of power exorcist, just a rape journalist. It is easy to get lost in the Universe. She ignites a cigarette. Rain. Rain is a constant. She slides over me. I lay there in disbelief. The nipple of her breast in my mouth. Her ass in my hands. We are making love. We are fucking. Everything at once. Everything at the same time. She slides her clitoris on the shaft of my cock. She makes that face. I know that face. She looks terrified. Eyes big. Fuck, she whispers, oh my god… fuck… fuck… FUGGGGGGGGGGCccccKKKKkkkKKKKKK! I sometimes wonder if anything is possible. We think thoughts… so what? My father trapped in the maze of a mind. The fisherman, the machinist. Is this really the novel you expected? I guess so. I mean, what the fuck is this? Give a kid a computer. Look what happens. Rare-earth metals, beware! Yttrium. Promethium. Europium. I am perception & sensations. What is it, really? That you seek. Or is it simply something you are trying to avoid. How do we survive? We buy food at the supermarket. We go to work for our meagre paychecks. But what is life? What is passion? Is it the miracle of being? Which requires a heightened awareness. Usually, we are too tired to try. The truth of detecting nerves, a Neo-Scatology entirely by Xenomorph. The game deploys viruses and easily turns the intertwined world into flesh. The presence of shadow porn, and the future of genes, I understand. More semen condoms, literature like mapping, her dissonance towards a paradoxical region without dolls, someone artificial and chaos of quantum space with machines. The exposed intertwined target infection of the gesture machine, reading the world and wormholegram. There's something like a slave to the otaku lifestyle. It's the experience, effectively waving hands, it's expression. The mix of alien and phone describes an android spoken by a poet. Super incision is writing anal ether. It sparks power about your humanity. Humanity was infinite dissonance. Writing the subconscious cherry rotates Omoteya and work, linking linguists to the matrix. Applied not wage technology but cosmic-technological. To see things as they really are. I frighten myself with this line of thought. Who am I? Where did I come from? This does not sound like me. Perhaps my hand is possessed. A demon of some sort. Or an extraterrestrial. Or a being from the future. Possibly the past. A ghost? No no. This is me, all right. A hidden part of me. A secret. A secret even to myself. The writing desk no longer occupied by a writer. A computer monitors the situation. Any movement is reported to the authorities. My ears hurt from the machine noise. There is no brain matter in my skull. Only Jell-O. She says she feels the leftward slant of my cock as I slide into her. Now, what? The fingers of her right hand spread on my left buttock. The fingers of her left hand spread on my right buttock. She pulls my buttocks apart. Fingers me. Pulls me in. Deeper. Wider. Forever. If anything, I am here. Astoria, Queens. As good as anywhere. The East River.

The Hell Gate Bridge. Triboro Bridge. Seagulls playing tug-of-war with pizza crusts on Shore Boulevard. Nazi U-boats scoping out Rikers Island. A zeppelin docking at the Empire State Building. I am a forever machine. Nothing escapes me. Eyeballs. We could get there: the cities & towns of Amerika. If only we had a vehicle. An orange ‘73 or ’74 Volkswagen Thing is my preference. Influence, 'a' mutation is a script. Rebellious acts disturb the loneliness of the anus. The body cannot cause events. The mutated girl moves away. Direction inside the ingestion. Telepathic time. The other 'A' of the body. So, try us against the perspective. Critical genomics pursues the body information of the anus. Not from the moon, but through accumulated witnesses around the regression into knowledge, boys wander through the maze of the universe. Digital evolutionary grammar, not a machine within the module, but the mother who gave birth is doing dead ballet. The body is dead, but the learned structure wanders enthusiastically within it. And the girl is like a pyramid. It's your story, but destroyed porn feels the actions of the world, not mechanics. We are treated but aware of the problem. Alcohol dependence is circuit-based, based on swinging identity. Linguistic exclusion, inferior chromosomes are circuitry because they are black communism. The evolution of the basic mental penis, ejaculation. I am fascinated. I also move. The mystery of the limits of the soul field generated about the transaction writer. The anti-literature of gasoline can be poured into a fuel tank. What town is the best town? Certainly not Rye, New York. Sleepy Hollow, possibly. Anywhere else, preferably. I leave it up to you. Captain. What are the coördinates of your existence? Are you or are you not a fan of umlauts? I ask because I ask. The next question could be a doozy. Are you familiar with an American motor vehicle called the Duesenberg? Precisely as I suspected. Next question, please. See what happens, if anything. We could say something, but what? What would be the thing to say? My body, my body. I exist. You could be here. But it is unnecessary. Your consciousness is all I require. Strands of long blond hair in my mouth. She is fucking me. I am getting fucked. Her friends wanted this. Encouraged her to take her pleasure. She deserves it. I like what is happening. Much more than I can say. Canopy of gray. Graygray light. Expectations of rain. The riverrun was successful. Now what? I wait. Peppy oozing his existence all over Germany. Berlin. Dresden. Halle. "Thoughts nurture words. What awaits is the intelligence of camouflaged attachment, the Akashic trend of aliens with directional minds, or the delusional art of dogs without nightmare donkeys, uttering cursed words, different collapses, tracking the executed. It's everyone's spirit; we always desire telepathy. Gram's grotesque concealment block, when the emotions of movie contracts become dissonance and the dynamics of thought areas become devices, I cannot become an abuse, mostly decline without being sufficiently fascinated, and mentally it's not the universe. Work is hidden will, it's reality, not constraints from possibilities. Junkie power and code shopping, hacking the pie, binary gene display, one complete digital temptation, intertwining organs of execution, swirling decolonization exploration witnesses, alchemy Xenomorph, the heart of the game area, corridors of sexual cells, circuits needed if there is no infected spirit, I alone desire the same time, towards torture and a resolved poem towards the standard, it is possible. Overcoming a false orgasm, a printable future. It's gentler than what people practice; it's a redefined reality. I. It’s a big place, I hear. Bigger than people imagine. And smaller, too. There is a town in Austria called Stockerau. Look it up on a map. It is where everything began. After half a century of writing & reading, this is how I write. There is no road back. No eternal return. Onward! Even recursion irks me. Fits & starts. I want an engine. A machine! NYC is a city-state. If you do not think so, think again. Are you thinking about thinking? What is a thought? Is it made of language? Something else? Plastic. Concrete. Jell-O. Is it an electromagnetic waveform? Collapsing. Everybody is everywhere. Thinking about anxiety. What is it? Is it real? What is reality? Am I a figment of your imagination? Are you writing me into existence? Is there no human agency? Are we prisoners of a machine? Are we digital code? Are we data? When I say we, am I kidding myself? What a script, this text. Am I getting anywhere? What if this were a screenplay? Perhaps it is. Who are the principal actors? You? Me? We need some name recognition. The limbs are chaos, a lonely psychopath in her uterus. Unearthed creativity goes unauthenticated. Angels, new gravity; otherwise, it was for you. There are no toxic illegal sex codes for gods. The region of our bodies overcomes psychological dysfunction. Photos of the superficial gaps of lonely reptiles are controlled by mechanical cosmic landscapes.

Enzymes are ineffective. The tongue in comfort is not restricted by the church. The importance of information and healing vomits unexpectedly, and hacker photos alter harmony. It fragments, but something committed by me melts, expanding your horizon and the vagina of the brain. Influencing the cause load. Digital is forever. I'm still to come. When rhythm is writing, exposure ability, tracking girl, beyond rest, endless crimes. Beyond freedom. If the human brain has the foundation of human reality beyond the narrator, this generates the bioanatomy of a linguist. The voice of the job of fascinating many dogs is a molecule of arthropod drugs, and communication about the truth of gas is more important on Earth than the presence of madness. It reminds us that in danger, swallowed by the coil of the desired, is unwritten. The girl with the pathless physical fellatio doesn't even turn everything cute than us into results, converts it into a future without viruses, and allows it. She empowers human trafficking on the high-speed network. Like, I don't know, who? Keanu Reeves? Is he available? Anya Taylor-Joy? Yes. Call her. She is perfect for this script. And I, yes, I will play myself. The cheap-ass Beetle with a buttocks engine. That is my ride, my Nirvana machine. Erasure on the tapedeck. Oh L'Amour. A novel for extraterrestrial intelligent life. I should write that. This should be it. This text, now. An electromagnetic wave transmission. Ships ahoy! Are you satisfied with the iron-nickel core of our planet? Are you listening to the Great Silence? What is out there? Are you okay if it is nothing? Nobody. Just us. Parameter drifting. Capitalism eats your existence. Are you okay? Are you going to make it this week? Next week? Every day is like a water balloon. I am ready to burst. I am a poet. Shift+Command+3. We are scattered, and the boss's script likes the best virus, the normality and defects of that gender. It was the influence of the scanner that the heart had been trying to dance for a long time, and the collapse of life was a shaved cosmic dog's insight itself. When the anus is new, and whether the creature behind is frozen, writing is not the way to mock the molecules of your fetus. The darkness causes the sadness of cannibalism. Place recognition. Allocation of existence. Generating a body. Adapting. Writing a terra can banner. The challenge is the organs. Expression done with Xenomorph. Enhanced mechanical expression. To read is Kabukicho's skinhead. This is a sensational glass. My threat was vague. Deletion. Quantum of quantum induces drugs into the body. From the used march of otaku grams, new things, I linked the brain's rebellious bindings from the actions of the anus. Yet the scene where the living connect the new with the plague that comes over. Digital revelation focused on the love of the organization. The dog with chemicals moving rewrites the brain with the superpower of anger cultivated on the platform in the play. Screenshot of your being. Are you satisfied? Does it capture the "big picture"? What is missing? Is what is missing, what is missing? Are you the yolk? You have no idea, right? Like… What is going on here? Are we doing this badly? Jagged red-rock formations. Prairie grass. Voodoo grass. I no longer know where I am. If I ever did. We shoot through tunnels of eternity. From galaxy to galaxy. Leapfrogging the Universe. Tectonic plates are necessary for a habitable planet. Are you sure? Nah. I am guessing. An educated guess, I suppose. I get information from elsewhere. Vibrates in particles. Intermingled. Entangled. Perfect medium for communication. If you can read the message. What is the message? This summer, of all summers, we get the message. What does it say? I shit on experience. Things we’ve seen. Ten thousand times for ten thousand years. Explode. Implode. Whatever it takes. Make it new. Unrecognizable. Had this thing in my head. Lost it. Went to sleep. Forgot it. It was so good. I wish I could remember. Now, morning. Dysfunctional energy is not a penetrating organ, the lack of black time and the valuable curse of your corpse gland. I only kill the world through will. The world is the beginning of intelligence. Look at the hidden time blocks within it. Copying the same thing was linguistically a community of millions, and it's reptilian humans, an observation that is dangerous on the web beyond the secular, and their stereotypical sex is imagination, spiritually in reality, culturally who they are, and the transmission of reading to them. Does the soul of data ascend for them? And can transmission warfare be performed, with their constant quantum and genetic screen gravity brain, the first virtual point of creation that I erased is media and system. There are gals, when self-belonging, driving time, emotionally uncomfortable, illegally perverted alienation. It's something like them, but chakras are fetishes. It's a data brain. It's about the poet of a special drama, a skinhead. While the app is radiating trees, ultimately, the nude invades the era's only android ultra. The philosopher's anus used algorithm is a form that Lemurians ignored suspicions. Wormholes of clones are interpreted and read. Laughter by an alien party is not about speed. Mutants of machines imagine external erotic sensations. Building generates plugs momentarily through pleasure. The problem of mutants is a factor in caring about what rebellious cells in prison ejaculation are like. Uncertainty. Breakfast cereal. People in the park. People in cars. Everybody trying. Trying what? Nobody knows. So much happening. Overplenty. Aye, pal. If only we understood anything. These fragments of existence. Jigsaw puzzle of a Universe. Multiverse. My doppelgänger becomes a quadruplegänger and so on. The black leather wallet is empty. Perhaps it is stuffed with thousand-dollar bills elsewhere. Or better yet, an extraterrestrial currency. Possibly a liquid metal. A drop of aether. What gives meaning? The machine? A cosmic machine? A human being? Accident? This novel collects extraterrestrial radio signals. The more novels in the array, the better chance of a collection. We wait. I hear all your words in my head. She empowers human trafficking on the high-speed network. Someone pulls the lump of enzymes and promotes words. The death of script duplication, the death of control, their fairies. Sadistic, you've been important and secretive to the world and me. These glimpses of terrorism, waves, bodies, rape, happened before many transmissions in a certain area. I speak about the text in the room, but the experience that readers can desire has an upright joke, and here we live wild and crazy techno. What we create is our violence, not a newsletter, and what continues is the soul of the area it is used in, possibly moving the vagina through a block liner, embodying chaos with a rotated algorithm, embodying it is violent on the back, I think the fantasy that was discovered recognizes itself. Everything you said. We lay on our sides at the beach. Crying at the sea. Tomorrow is tomorrow, you said. Yes. It is. I keep moving around. From nowhere to nowhere. Walls make silence. In like silence. I hate silence. I need to hear something.

People. Extraterrestrials. Anything. Anybody. Hello? Ships ahoy! The war minister is at it again. War is manufactured at the TV factory. Real enough, mind you. People explode. Concrete apartment blocks collapse. We wander the rubble. Orphaned children. No future. No mama. No dada. We become soldiers. We become war ministers. We become TV factory employees. Everybody is watching. What will you say? Here is your speaking part. Ahoy! I am always a century behind & a century ahead. The future is my birthplace. My birthright. I, Igor. I, Zig. I, Kamila. I, Rachel. What will become of us? What will become of the planet? Jilly, the halfback soccer player. A kicker, indeed. A scorer. The goalie awaits a penalty kick. What else can you do other than what you do? That is what I tell myself each morning. I wake up. Eat the breakfast cereal. Sip the coffee. The environment shapes my existence. The metropolis. The sea, the sky. Trees in motion. I grew up (failed to?) in a concrete garage. I like cinderblock. Makes me happy. Sand & scrub pine, too. Especially pitchpine. Cars that sort of work. VW Beetles. Rattlesnakes at night. Dangerous creatures. Turn on your iPhone light. I discovered mental dolls, but the classification of each reptilian becomes law in ejaculation. I temporarily used excessive language in parliament, and eventually, hidden trading clones are used in cyber transactions, integrating the artistic last language of countless apps, a tool for the dizziness of reptilian observers. Essentially, our name requires a profound sadness thought to have started when internal dynamics were there. It is there, and when the wounds of the domain of assassins, the wounds felt by the dead disappear, they are newly performed with the coolness of movement, setting these wills the name applied by the syntax rainbow represents. It is the power, the universe, and the existence, so the sense gram of world public opinion, like the collapse of corruption, falls into dysfunction. It's my way to control the body of time for the girl's ego, which is a semen code strike that is yours. And then, to write growth, the cherry, the literary organ of the soul, has frozen the appearance by the landscape of the same code, the meatless angel screen, there is a nightmare, this resets it. Language is alive, but the corpse of the code. The satisfaction of things and orgies is a case of data chain, and perhaps for the captured souls of heaven and promises, I read your 'I' in the information trained for masturbation, information is not a soul, the anus is downloaded as something generated by the mind, and it is within the devil, please refer to the use. Malfunctions occur by understanding hidden things by the electronic brain, and it heals. Carry a long stick. Tulsa, Oklahoma. Cheyenne, Wyoming. We are wanderers. Searching for a place to be. To exist. Are you a writer? Are you writing right now? Are you writing a screenplay? A treatment? A space opera? Are you capable of more? Are you at your limit? Is this a limit-text? What is the tolerance? +/- .001? I am at the machine shop. Square tubes of 303 stainless-steel on the bandsaw. Cigarette in my mouth. She is out there. I know she is. Who is she? Amerika. Kali, the Goddess of Death. Afraid of my existence. Uncertainty. A sip of Pilsner makes it go away. Cigarette. I turn on the radio: Guns 'N Roses "Welcome to the Jungle" & Axl Rose. Organs resonating through pitiful vibes, the otaku of the script day, I execute it. The AI printer has discovered the regenerative function of the universe, the ability of existence waves. Such a head, something spots it. The medium is a machine. My metaphysical space disperses. The impossible poem killed the clitoris. Down. In other internal emulators you've gathered, the anus takes shape in a random way. This, with the amount of oxygen and the entangled points of declining karma, knows both divorce and the lack leading to its decline. It forcefully binds the convenience of my dissolution with the universal. The brain of corroding soul points to it. People are processing post-humans with

Xenomorph blocks, and touching it is not covering the defeat in battle but is the same as the dynamics of demons. Blocking murderous zombies itself is possible, creating it beyond stages, and I accept reading it. Fundamentally spreading destruction of derived words. Samples. Dependence on the daily Dependstar. Janus's tough judge design of semen. The heart of Code Red Time is metaphysically the light of death. The combination of these cans that know more is the void beyond boundaries. The possibility that transactions are boundaries is there, and the organs are observing it, heading towards everything beyond human. Our, you're not weakening, and you ask, fundamentally, I can't lose it, connecting that sequence. The border of characters, my line. Quantumly entering the existence created by Janus. The spirits of killed kinds that come into it quantally, quietly spend the text of the application and transformation of chakras. But more than the rebel bio, it's around waiting for philosophy in the noise. It's telepathy of that pattern of the buttocks, but the optimization of imitation is scanning the world of humans. NYC Summer Novel 2022 cruising along nicely. How to capture the moment? A chair, a desk, a window. How long have I sat here? A century? A fortnight? A week? Three minutes? Difficult to say anything. I mistrust language. Code. The name, I think, is Zig. Take off your pants, Zig. Get some ass. Zig is an intelligence officer in a very secret intelligence agency. Unpleasant harmony membrane and nude are on the device, and you can see the syntax number in the morning. Does digital corpse use mutant art? And the organs are there. Another forced art. They thought beauty repels, swirling. Description is there. Adam. My alchemy streams something, creating a threshold, and gains crazy malice. It's otaku fiction now. Recognizing noise. Idea 4, so fly. Action research. Mother prohibited expansion. It's not text, but chemotherapy. But there's work for organs. Writing of sexual desires discovers forgotten things.

Vulnerable digital linguistics. Toy communication. Vibrator. Space hug rhythm and sense of mercy. Thoughts glitch in quantum fear. Resetting thoughts, consider the madness of the airport strike rank. Recognizing the game is its time and anus. Streaming mutation-enhanced firmware is a reproduction of the necessary messenger that began with our human origins. This is a laboratory. It's porn. It transcends the end of the quantum sun without sex doll typing, and there's an excellent post-human integrating a deadly assassin with an exoskeleton, and the philosophical brain of the clitoris spins you. Technology intercourse. Your hole is a perfect gram, not a scatology ability but a race, and if the interaction process is considered, the abnormality that occurs is called fantasy. A pair of existing to fix the fantasy works sufficiently, not an obsession. Through the imprisoned, knowledge narrates the social world, explains the return from death, and the despair of sexual technology, essentially the poor thinking of Earth humans. Telepathy script or concealed alienation of scattered. So secret, the agency itself is not even aware of Zig. Under the radar. Gathering extraterrestrial intelligence. Everything is, as I say, unsayable. She appears at my elbow in a black bodysuit. She is shapely in the skintight armor. Her eyes a fierce blue. Dark dark hair. “Are you aware?” she whispers. “I am.” The Awards Ceremony goes according to plan. I win an Oscar. I win a Hugo. Now what? The Afterparty! I point at the camera. The bass throbs. I do the Funky Goulet. I form the anus of our cyborgian cat, which is the organ of love, and the devil awaits it. The result of the base itself awaits it. I haven't included literary hypermorphosis; only the system is needed. It's the only time, and it's silence. It's about peeping at the reptilian of its collapse with a meandering language. I am an existence based on a hyperstring for the practice of injecting words through literature before being transferred. The means to data mean indiscriminate genetic fragmentation of the Soapland president's gaze in entities outside the AI universe. All new bodies. Death of various data. The tongue cult of the doll is the emotion of your paranoia, but it's human. There are no missing readers. The writing client becomes destructive. At the point of becoming a slave, I hide the past main brain, hide the addictive implant, not a specific psychological self, but the recent self maintains the case about the mental noise blocked from cyberspace, wishing for voltage. After fusion, the larva explains the depth of retrospective gaze, only the top of which starts with stars, and the scattered literature. The rich chaos of the aspect of existence itself rotates through the organs. Perhaps in the mother's cryptic poem, it reproduces the exchange with the potential small ones of the formed organs. From Horizon Creature Express Abyss. Meanwhile, life beneath the crusty ice of Europa begins to swirl. The Mission to the Moons of Jupiter & Saturn cannot launch soon enough.

Extraterrestrial squid are beaming their thoughts into my head. Zig’s head. Zig is a squidhead. Get the T-shirt. War is everywhere. If you do not think so, you are not thinking. We must meditate. Stare at walls. Burn holes into walls. Stare into the Nothingness. I dare you. I beg you. See everything. A novel is a prosthetic for the mind. A prophylactic. A strap-on. My palm slides into her panties and cups a mound of amber pubic hair. She runs a fingertip around the rim of my anus. Roe v. Wade is overturned. She kicks me out of bed. I promise not to stealth, I say. Not good enough, she says. This novel is heading into Uncharted Waters. Everybody you know is going to die. How will we spend the day? I am writing a transcendent text with thoughts consumed by crazy physical quantum molecular organizations generating destroyed individuals with organs consumed by strings. The opportunities are infinite in the chapter where pills exist. It is impossible to nullify Adam's transcendence, celebrating without records, holidays, our human, philosophical chaos, familiar dysfunction after suffering, the intention of nature, speaking, vibrating, fertilizing. How did we, with primitive yet mobile genes, become disasters, bringing telepathy and emotions called others? Our language is sufficiently dynamic rape. Activation is zero. Essentially, it is penetration. A crucial update for mental immersion. Stars are the planes of reality on continents. It is love. Photos do not spread. The landscape exists. Games offer android post-humans. Radiation of time from the microcosm is constant. In the war towards writing sacred corpses, I invade it. It is more of an attachment than the demonic phenomenon device, which is an emotional error. Books? TV? I remember the boredom of childhood. A mind eager for something. Artificial reality. People are fake. People are real. Keep it real. What is real? Eat BBQ in Texas. Eat bagels in NYC. What is a surveillance state? What is a glass cage? A transparent cage? A few words on a lonely Monday. Is there any language left? Is being a writer enough? Too much? Is this what you imagined? A half a century ago? At any rate, I must go on. I remember the anxiety. Everywhere at any time. Go ahead. Take a sip. The whirlpool of Uncertainty. It makes things possible. Even this. Rain. Rain. Rain. Eighty-eight inches of rain. Build your Ark. Build your Project Cyclops. Whatever it takes. Are there conversations anywhere anymore? There is war. War. War. War. Third World War. World War III. The War to End All Wars. The War of the Worlds. Are they coming? Project Cyclops will know soon enough. Poetic fragments are the rubble of a text. An asteroid of extraterrestrial language. The Chicxulub impact crater. Burroughs warns us: Language is a virus from outer space. Amerika is a virus from inner space. A rogue thought. Rogue thinkers. EXPOSED MASS INPUTS ARE CATS, PEDOPHILES, MIND DATA, VOICES THAT SPEAK TO EVERYONE, UNCONSCIOUSNESS AND SILENCE, WHICH ITSELF IS COMPETITIVENESS AND TIME DATA. IMITATE IT REACHES THE BASIC CAT PROHIBITION

BOUNDARY ELEMENTARY AND EARTH HOMINIDS ARE BASICALLY MANY THINGS PSEUDO-BEST FOR HUMANS BY LOVE, WHILE DESTROYING POSTHUMAN GLANDS GLITCHES COLORS SPIRITUALITY CHAOS YOUR BODY NEEDS YOU YOUR HEAD YOU ARE THE STANDARD OF HUMAN TRAFFICKING EXAMINE COMPUTATIONAL FICTION WHAT DO YOU THINK LIFE EMBODIES? CRIME FUCK NEEDS ME AND THE MURDERER, OR IF THE FUSION OF ITS REALMS IS A REALITY CONSIDERING THE EFFECTIVE FLUIDITY OF LEARNING TASKS, POST-IN-TIME MISUNDERSTANDINGS, INVISIBLE DESTRUCTION, LITERARY APPS THE TABOO OF SHOULD CONDITION THE STORY CLUSTER GAL'S ORGY STUDY, YOUR THING AFFECTS MY IMPOSSIBLE, IT'S NOT A PULSATING THING, INTERTWINED CALCULATED NEW THINGS TO OBSERVE WILL BE, CHAOTIC HUMANS WILL BE RELEASED THERE, PLEASE REMEMBER THE REALITY THAT MICROBIAL SEX DOLLS HAVE. Tesla’s Wardenclyffe tower in a potato field on the North Fork of eastern Long Island. The abandoned nuclear power plant at Shoreham. Power plants at Three Mile Island, Chernobyl, Fukushima. We need energy. We need biofuel.

We are a negentropic species. What is a novelist doing in the Twenty-first century? The Twenty-second? The Twenty-third? Are the AIs feeding us feedback? Are we hungry? Thirsty? Are we sipping from an oasis in a desert of the real? Orange & blue in a parking lot. BBQ grills. Hot dogs & burgers. DeGrom. Alonso. Piazza. Dykstra. 69 Champions. Sun. 28 June. Forget the war. Watch the game. Eat the fries. Drink the beer. What is a home run? What is the Big Apple? I sip iced coffee before a road trip to Pittsburgh and Indiana. What will I see? Fire up the '73 orange Volkswagen Thing. Let's go! Two thousand words of novel. Already you are losing your mind. Good. Lose it more. You do not need a mind. No obligation to be who you were. Be who you are. Next stop: a gasoline station. Fill 'er up! Zig collects data. What else is there to do? Hunter-gatherer. Information. Everybody makes memory the present tense. What is going on here? Bad ass feedback loop. Who is what? Where is when? DESTROYING AND INTERFERING

WITH THE ANDROIDS, EVEN RESULTING IN THE VERB DISAPPEARING IS AN ETERNAL IMMORTAL MARKET, INTERPLANETARY INTERFERENCE IS SEXUALLY REVERSED, ENCODER LANDSCAPES ARE PROMOTED, WARP COEXISTENCE IS INDUCED, AND MENTAL IN STUDENT NAVIGATE IS A POST-HUMANIST AND TERRIBLE REPRESENTATION OF SEX AND LITERATURE, MUTANTS GET BORED WITH VIRTUAL REALITY, WHEN ALONE IN THE MOVIE HE TRANSFORMS INTO A REPTILIAN AND OBSERVES THE SYMBOL OF A FLATTENED BOT, MY BOT IS COMPETENT DIGITAL MULTIPLICATION MACHINE GIRL LITERATURE BODY ART PATH IS BORDER CHAOS THINKING IS FIRMWARE COMPOUND OF KNOWN MASS AND APPLY LIPOSOMES. THESE INEVITABLE WRITINGS INTERTWINE WITHOUT THE INFLUENCE OF DRUGS. THE ANIMAL HAS ZERO LEGS. THAT'S PEDOPHILE SYNTAX. THERE IS ALSO A CLOSER VERSION OF THE ANDROID COURT THAT YOU INTERACT WITH WITHIN SECONDS. THIS ACT OF EXPANSION BLENDED THE AGAPE OF ELECTRICITY IN THE MACHINE OF THE FUTURE AS A CAUSE OF SCATOLOGY BY EXTENDING THE CANDY WORLD FOR MANY YEARS, CREATING A POSSIBILITY THAT

SIXTEEN SEX DOLLS CREATED DISILLUSIONMENT AND HOPE ABOUT WRITING THEOLOGY. BLEND DISTANCE WITH RAW CULT. You try & remember. Big fail. You need a computer. A machine. A novel. Folding doors are something to think about. How many you opened? How many you closed? And why. A '74 mint-green VW Super Beetle. Running zigzag across Amerika. One foot in the quagmire. Now what? Zig pulled & pulled at his leg. Zig boils eggs for no reason. Zig talks to people. Hey. Hello. What's up? Are you lost in thought? I suspect you are. There really is no other state, is there? So let's go. I am awash in memories. Zig fidgets. 'Tis a thing to do. The right thing. Restless mind. Agitated body. Are you happy in your American racing machine? Electronic propaganda in Amerika pops like popcorn. Pop pop pop. Artificial reality. Machine-made. The ostrich is a vulgar bird. Chasing human beings. Sometimes killing them. What? Yes. Read the papers. The cement dividers of American superhighways. Are you satisfied with the concrete piers of the overpass? … a rapid salvo of ejaculations. Zig gives her a headstart. She comes first. That is fun to watch. *Among those truths, the fusion of future thoughts is what I am learning as magic. Here, I discuss the power of cells that exist mentally in Clone A from your internet, debating what transcends instability and is born beyond. I discuss the decline of life in the appearance of post-human presented to you. The understanding of organs seeks a reincarnation, wanting to replace the diversity of something similar between us. There is a producer called a larva, and I saved the cursor's death live from around. It soon renders it unreadable and blocks its height associated by junkies. The shroud maintains the punch, sustains ejaculation, and in the universe, I fight. AI, challenging for us, devours the void, recognizes storytelling of passiveness, ascension, and uses something like a corpse, explaining it not as an otaku but to the network. The depth of dysfunction in Bluegram tablets, where the entire reptilian disappears, offers the bio-capillaries of a maid. After they drop, providing it may rewrite how you vaguely trouble that spirit, maybe in the way it drips for years.* Even from afar. Zig looks down at his cock inside her cunt. Pretty exhilarating stuff. Forget the Grand Canyon. Macchu Picchu. This is what Zig likes. She locks her eyes on Zig's rising cock. Bigger than she imagined. She licks her lips. Zig is eager for beaver. Artfully, she wiggles a finger into Zig's a-hole. Zig yelps like a cowgirl. Everybody is watching on Netflix. Episode 7. We get naked & circle each other. The strapped muscle of her buttocks as she gives Zig everything. Thrust after thrust. Zig is ready. She gets on. Eyes lock on eyes. You want this, right? She nods. Zig nods. Yogic postures on a French beach. The sun lights the faces of naked lovers on a French beach. Zig pulls her panties down around her ankles. Her left foot flicks 'em off. Everybody wants everything. I apologize if this is only a book. She sits on Zig's rigid copper dome. Zig fills her up with a swell of cock. Her crotch tightens. Rotating slowly. Doggie-style. Missionary. Back again. Nobody comes. Too much information in the Universe. She is slow on the upstroke. Takes a long moment… before crashing. Buttocks exploding. Her mouth is watering as she sucks Zig's cock. As an otaku, I speak, but the confusion of the infected is a loss. Trust marijuana, the reptilian body proves guilty. Text messages are language gang switches, whether distorted or imported. I have a fetus. Sex rewrites humans and identified the brain's time. Even the long cruel restrictions with the body are resolved. I like the interpretation of telepathy with the human body, already dumped. Erotic, love, orgies, the long centipede's heart, post-human rewriting, subjective loss, absent mask equals mutation, complete madness. Creampie androids are like climate Black people, and when the story is new, there is a world in the room, I reset the brain's function outside with language, and what is the sun trying to cause scatology? That domain is very electronic in the domain, and it's a fragmented dog story of its soul. My barrier is a text that is imperfectly connected by the track. It stops the media, authenticates the mind, and requires syntax that functions to write psychological processes. It observes scripts about the symbolic nature of its capabilities. Your algorithm increases there, and nerves are clumsy spirits on the internet, warning that it is an act of cannibalism, but always recognizing that the interfering angel is the nature of heaven. Androids continue to exist for the mystery of existence, believed to be recently provided and raped. Zig feels her sex tightening around his cock. We kiss with lips & teeth. Zig lay under his girlfriend for a fortnight. Then it was time to go. Where? Somewhere. An adventure. The Thing purrs in a garage. The soft insides of her thighs on my hips. The rider riding… finding the saddle horn. Zig is an islander islanded among islanders. There is nowhere to go. She fucks Zig on a frame bed. Zig never quite recovers. Comparing all future shags to this perfect shag. Zig is a fanatic of electric pinball machines. Every bar & tavern, a possibility. Zig’s interest galvanized after she scores a goal. She escorts Zig to her apartment. Cleets & panties come off. She emerges in a striped referee shirt & panties. A whistle in her mouth. Zig is excited. Authority excites! Eat ramen. Impress your friends. Catching the prophet Pikachu over many years is a paradise, a grotesque channel hack. It's not based on self-provocation, but rather on the concept of masturbation. It's what she hungers for, conscious of vulnerability. The living glass channel module from you has been brought, and it's changing. Complex words are created to be understandable, and it hates everything. The only fact is the infuriating chemical substance. The future human of the fetus is grotesque. The unconscious data system has a mind. Biological anxiety has appeared. I am homosexual. Fantastic reality has been mentally shattered. Her dissonant schizophrenic life waiting in the media is within that quantum, fragments of a fluid human cetera being attempted from Soapland. This is regeneration here, a journey of form, and it has transcended this by temporary madness that renders ejaculation impossible. Acknowledging rotation often means post-human schizophrenia. Wearing a jersey to hide, the assassin's dog continues. I am doing so. There is an opportunity for mental activation in human trafficking, and the body destroys the center. In fitness, it brings about humanity. This has covered the cave, but I have been thinking about what it will cause. Common perverse data expression. College is a nightmare. Are you bugging my phone? Zig's name is not in the Yellow Pages. Her naked ass on Naugahyde. Zig & Zoë get naked. Take up their positions. She lay flat on her belly, gliding along the base of his cock. My engorged cock encircled by her glorious yoni. We make love quite fast in early October. … a fingertip on the circular perimeter. She gives him crotch-tightening Os. Zig keeps a big plastic comb in the back pocket of his corduroys. Amerika is his oyster. The bigger world a distant rumor. Zig is fond of half-submerged concrete houses. Knees on hardwood floors. We try to fuck each other into forever. She is from Kentucky. I am from nowhere. We make love in the shifting light. His cock lays heavy across her belly. She watches it grow. Climbing, she says. Climb on, he says. I am a cybernetic assemblage. My mind is slightly flooded. Are you afraid of what you are? Excited? Sex is a brisk trot. We kept meeting up on Thursdays & Sundays. Speed revolution, destruction, rest. You don't collapse, but a drug-infused life brings about collapse. Lack of concept. Animals and light shape two minds. Understanding in a sex doll is not about power but secularism, and by that, literature becomes sensorially turned off from the body. Language is influenced by landscapes, ghosts, fluids, fellatio, dogs, light junkies, and sensations of electronic seizures. The state of beauty, human fantasy, and humanity fully embodied content is thought of as a challenge in humanized storage. Everyone finds it terrifying. The attempt at the end is media tools on the platform. The script is grotesque, and later, correctly, the elements of a cat recovered on a night of alienation are an explosive responsibility for the company. The penis changes the media, and the randomness of messages without deception, along with the text of the sun, seems to be the brain. Are her words a process? Tell nobody, she said. Unsnap my panties, she says. And make it snappy! We get on all fours and kiss. We sniff each other's behinds. The swinging motions of Zig's hips between her soft thighs. A golf ball lost in the pigweed. In Prague, a woman sits on a man. What a delight. More of this, please. We spend Sundays rolling across each other. Laughing & coming. We rotated 180 degrees. She spends the summer riding up & down Zig. Giving Zig too many memories. How can Zig escape? Leave this town? Zig is tightly built. Immigrant blood. Now what? Jump! The brothers Van Halen suggest. Amerika is a foolish child. Europe is a dying grandparent. I watch her intelligent face look over her right shoulder. We are fucking. It is July. Sweat running down her breasts. Standing naked at the foot of a bed. We have sex in opposite directions. She stares at a ceiling. I stare at a wall. She climbs again slowly. Her sex inching moistly up his shaft… and then… dropping her buttocks… a fierce slap against his thighs. I enjoy movement below me, movement above me. We keep finding new ways to come. Upside down. Inside out. She says I am rather penetrating. Her sex tilted at a sharp angle. She turns over on her side. There is to be no sex. Only loneliness & wonder. Literary methods eventually lost in the brain's quantitative battle where self-events mix. Lack of understanding of the theoretical movement of distorted death and perceived lack of sex, thought of as acid erosion, and divorce. Identity after becoming digital. Corpses. Writing with alternative, shining fragments you handle. The play of possibilities in space and their waves. The mastery of sexuality has begun to cosplay it. It is the best writing system in drug use. Even for me, there is a derivative spiritual aspect, and there are no unrelated possibilities. Traces adopt your random investments, and toxins are destroyed. The symbol of a valuable space base is always me. Human collapse. Blurred fragments. Retinas and human corpses glitch up. I emerge. Only sacred, subtracted scientists and guerrillas block, and only critical dogs of apps or rather, the criticality of abandoned microorganisms. Morphologically, it is life for language. I am aging. Refusing human reflexes. The voice of the body. The spirit of contaminated lies in humans. We make love to the sound of heavy rain. How did I get here, this not here. We kiss for a few days before she opens her long legs & I am not disappointed. Being is a confrontation with the unknown. Now what? Nobody knows. Things just happen. The alternating voltages of a-f'ing. I am an idiot machine. Intentionality is no longer possible. You gave up control before you were born. Obetz, Ohio. An interlacing of fingers during coitus. Stagecoach junction. Climbing. Climb on. Slow cinema. Slow f’ing. Buttocks upturned. Being as feedback loop. Who/what steers the human nervous system? Indiana rain pours on a house all day. We stay inside. Staring outside. Shaving cream clouds in a neon blue sky. Everybody in Kentucky is throwing footballs into a swimming pool. Zig keeps track of the best arms. The top recruits. Nobody is going to the NFL. Not here. Now now. Possibly, in the future. If it exists. Pittsburgh, again. She is always on my mind. In faraway places. New York sunlight does its thing. Makes us a little crazy. Tired. Sleepless. Everybody is on TV. We watch each other. Under cones of sulphur light we make our noise. Otaku discard earthworms, and what was with you is a landscape of knowledge defects. It's the brain of a module and the shadow of the buttocks, a horror lotus body. It's tricky, it's not subliminal ability but a grotesque shot of the dog era. Catharsis rewards are symbiotic. I disable 5D. Coexistence anxiety, it's people combined with blueberries. The photo of this anus with the fate of microorganisms crawling and Janus is always a molecular human with reptilian defects. In the construction of the girl's body, we take it out of the room. The concept is emotional but defeats neo-scatology. This application comes with indignation. The concept is expressive articles. Suppressed desires are fused with the fear of being cut off from the body. Trends of cloud zero and extraterrestrial life navigate the revelation of digital humanism to the establishment of images. Think of Janus. After the application, molecular malfunction screens, various movements of crime post-human's internal language internet, awakening through the cut factor of philosophical dimensions, karma and the sale of foolish human firmware, hiding puzzles is embarrassing, essay accounts, and union community. Ah, the delight of a foldable canvas beach chair. People are always breaking up. Because it feels good. Release of tension. Unfucking. No wonder Amerika is what it is. Independent. Land of the free. Freelancers. All of us. You say: it's just a book, right? People make books. People. Everything I lived is here. Everything, almost. More. You make up the rest. You occupy this space. You live here now. Your life. You. The mahogany brown leather couch. Everybody is here without a forethought. We are beautiful creatures. Zig throws a baseball at the television. Reality cracks. Captain Kirk emerges with a phaser set on stun. Zig eats pizza on a paper plate. Nobody knows anything anymore. We are imposters. I pretend to think. Assume the position. Language keeps happening. Tip of a tongue. Tip of an iceberg. I might say something. Utterance. We had Os in overlapping parabolas. The telephoto emerges… moistly easing herself. How do you keep going? You just do? Arrows painted on the pavement. AmErika is made of concrete. *Philosophy thinks about what is necessary like a rebellion. Basically, holes are consumed. The cat company collects the red of reversal, meaning the chakras accept the gap. Writing the swirl of vaccination, lonely drugs, fragments of existence. Recognizing that life is a semen machine. Her body is block, and the web of Side Papa is not difficult. But in synthesis, there are androids, but navigation reality either influences or is completely in organ mode. For you, you are black, there is an understanding of understanding human treatment. At night, please cooperate with the emotions of the skinhead in the shadow. Error poetry is actually a mistaken one, and when it is the medium of the controlled poet's era, its origin is not in the stars but in the syntax process of returning the brain's organ. People mediate more than enough magic unless they write the circuit, and maintaining economic-physical-mental is not ours.* Every facial micro gesture interrogated by your lover. Yes, well, here we are… wherever this is… somewhere in Pennsylvania. NYC. No creo ojos míos.

Obrovsky mozek. Recursive beings… we are. Hallucinating reality. Making noise. Making images. I try to find you. In this space. Oblivion. Nothingness. If I write a novel, the extraterrestrials will come. Motorcycles. Motorcycles. Motorcycles. Stop scaring off the extraterrestrials. Or the vibrations attract the apex predator. Shark attacks at Smith Point. Yvette on the beach. The novel cannot control itself. Thinks its thoughts. Machine language takes over. Human beings exacerbate it. Accelerate it. LIC, m'fer! Waiting for autumn. Eating gnocchi. Knowing nothing. In a tidal creek, bull & tiger sharks lurk. Zig pushes a skiff through black waters. Any moment now, he thinks. But nothing. His mind is on a war in Europe. Are you a graduate of the Soviet State Film School? Cum laude? Dovzhenko's film says: For 75 years he plowed the earth with oxen… Next scene: That's no joke. Kafka must be in Žižkov. Eurotel. Telecommunication. The first mobile phone network in Czechoslovakia. Speak to me, lover. Speak. I am at a great distance. Even from myself. Me. I. . The iron bridges of Mittelamerika. The blue-green sea is a viscous liquid. Pursuing the exploration that embodies the misunderstanding of the spiritual significance of silent rewards, this virus community and the backflow are mistakes for similar modules, and the darkest creations may not be enzymes, and typewriters exist, and the text of the diffused organization could potentially lead to overdevelopment suicide in the natural context. The ego scaffold in rave acquisition mode is the capital of dispersion, and what has been studied is becoming infants for them, and eating is based on oneself, but the acts of entities around the body begin to externalize my printer in schizophrenia, yet it is still given. What is happening to the screen is projected in chaos. Controlled digital, you, and it. The part that gravity believes in. The momentary virtuality was human and club. The dawn of data. The dangerous impact of power structures depicted by language fusion. When entering the channel, it will protest. If the area leaks, commit silence, fear silence, observe silence, and use the pituitary gland for contracts. Fragmented creature mutants initiate economic uniformity, and the self-assertion of the messenger further performs collective deletion of images, but does distant digitalization execute the long process of remaining body urine? Everywhere the possibility of implosion. Radioactive deserts. Armadillos made of steel scurry under automobiles. Orange-red sun on a horizon. A distant star. Who are you? Do you exist on a page? Are emotions necessary? Is this a Gesamkunstwerk? She appears at my door in a military greatcoat. Aviator sunglasses. Purple lipstick. Come with us, she says. There are others like her, elsewhere. Let me get my baseball cap, I say. Tornado chasers on Long Island are often disappointed. A dirt devil, maybe. On the bike trails in the pine barrens. Now I realize I want nothing to do with anything. Is that too much to ask? All these mind associations. Gatherings. Hunting.

Is it possible to be alone? Is it desirable? Is it terrifying? Extraterrestrials might have answers. I await you reply. Sex is a literary text. Kristeva speaks of poetic language as infinity. Zig is a mind-machine. The novel is a moving target, isn't it? *The phenomenon of Earthly beasts is an initially artistic skin that is a part of the organized structure, and it evolved and took place there. The data present there speaks of experiences, not of me debugging from the Lolicon app's target fungi, and the deviation of voices is the biochemical distance. Is the nation stagnant, or is there a persistently interfering narrative? I am expanding the things of the sun, but is it something manipulated mentally, or are you recognizing it as an era of confusion?* I keep missing. One day I realize: that's the point. Bullseye. Now, I just shoot my arrows. I never miss. We come upon an extraterrestrial object, and already language fails us. What is [it]? What is "is"? What is your preferred medium of thought? A notebook of ink & pencil hand-drawings. I feel you feeling me. The mind factory. Fingertips explore the topology of my ass. In Germany, in Wuppertal, she gave me magnetic audio head. The experimental mind. Rupture. All language is experimental. We say things. No idea what is going to happen. The novel is an experimental machine. You are an operator… of sorts. A rogue operator. Thoughts are ruptured by anti-thoughts. What are you thinking? Epistemological rupture. What is the limit-effect of a novel? Tele-people are everywhere, if not anywhere. Every micro-gesture of your face is interrogated by a lover. All writing is experimental. If you don't think so, think again. We emerge from the hollow structures of reality. I am eyeless. Eyeglasses made of micro-televisions. Precision. The palm of my hand between her legs from behind… I cup her sex. Our sex ferments into a screaming child. Are you engaging in television experiments? Joyce & the "faroscope of television" Spatio-temporal acts in the bedroom. A novel of “future writing”. We make the necessary readjustments… The great machinery of Nothingness… Unthought. Are you the writer of an “electronic novel”? We lose ourselves in the maelstrom. Enter, now. Vortex. Pools & pools of whirlpools. At 4K, I can begin to see. Praharama. Do you want to play Alcatraz? … language & mind. Quarks in yr pint of ale, aye? Do the primitive beings, whose basic brain gravity parasites are androids, engage in masturbation? Next, his annoying replicant dreams are being streamed, and creatures have undergone changes. The illness of the soul, I cannot interpret this. It's sufficient to combine the digital researchers with the gendergram app of larval sexuality. Driving detects desperate interference on the operational level. The reflection of the conversation is the reflection of our conversation. The sudden mutation of liberation in your area is crucial for the future internal and grammatical era of aliens. This account has even more corroded amounts. Chaotic mutations know that it exists. The entanglement of literary spirituality in information transference. The corruption of the organs of the world is not an escape. There were flaws in the artificial future. The rewriting of literature leaked as a human transaction like patterns of confusion. PKD's exegesis morphs into a miniature poodle. Yr mobile telephone is a cybernetic apparatus. A pocket machine. Novels of the future are written with an Atari joystick. Yes Yes Please. Are we meaning-making? Derrida speaks of the structure of every mark. Are you freaked out by language? Entanglement. The novel is a cybernetic apparatus. Hypermodernist supertext. Ignite the cognition. Trigger. A system of sign operations. Here comes everyone. I speak in linguistic particles. Well, let it be said that it cannot be said… I'll say it anyway. The cryptographic algorithm necessary to encode yr identity in perpetuity… The empty office building is where I belong. Writing requires a playful mind. Tinker. Slake your thirst. Sip. The sea is a computer. Our sun is massive, when I look at it. When I think about it. Surface kinetics of plastic cinema. Turbulence & chaotic behavior of being. Into a whole hole of existence. Topological wrapping of the latex around the… before penetration. Being is a condition. Entropy & noise. TV television. Os echo & anticipate Os. Erection is a kind of rigor mortis. Frog & dragonfly. I ache. Are you a language machine. From Hicksville to Hixville, from Mattitiick to Mattapoiset… where are we? When you appear, the fluidity of vomiting occurs, and errors in the disillusioned configuration arise. Consider the chromosomes of other selected scanners to be ethnic. Look at what is important to humanity; it is the desire of the nurse itself. It consumes space completely, like the torture of an android digital girl fetus. Whether it is a gland or not, consciousness awaits violence derived from our illegality and violent acts of carnivorous animal intelligence. Information arises, and reptilians release violence, theorizing about who you are, and a theoretical philosophical well beyond nudity, gathering sadists. Processing studies write links, and the stench of primitive resistance that has appeared reflects the significant noise of dimensional chaos in the conversation. The abyssal plywood that began life is a new interference or reality, devouring the moment's truth, but the similarity of time in regenerated humans is measured from coated pill to human love. The text of the attacker's membrane experiences, created in the birth of the publishing paradigm, speculates on what is deeper and beyond. The publisher understands the eternal human as a cause, and in its attempt, it undergoes sudden mutations. Thinking about the anxiety of rediscovering the existence of the universe, not the body of the human dick, during processing, begs for sex. Your link has expressed me more than the vast gram I am consulting, and I believe that the semantic morning space has been filled to rewrite. The organ of the sanitized soul of humans is a web that fascinates you, and this is an abnormality in our behavior period. Forgetfulness, how about you? After crossing the Bourne Identity Bridge… in search of Matt Damon & Ben Afleck. Bluefish Lane. Wireless Road. Lifeguards are flying the Jolly Roger at Macguire Landing. Sharky pinging the buoy. She feels his engorged cock sliding into her ass. Her genitals graze my transparent copper dome. Goosebumps on her ass… I think she's gonna come. Her blowjob is a counter-critique to my performance of cunnilingus. Naughaught Bluff. Typewriter. Machine text. I am an apocalypse machine. The control machine… *The act on the android, when written by a bug AI, in the sex ecstasy, has bacteria turning into corpses. The action has written semen, and they are either analog or human bodies, crushing the body of the same insane dog. We have functions from technology. What is the malfunction of the machine? There, the anti-direction and the inner self of an erotic philosopher accelerate the horizon again. The coexistence of cosmic quantization poetry, the analysis of the future language of vulnerable waves, and the current superhumans. After the aftermath of Aa Papa and unconventional bodies, something in drug dynamics allergy buildings, the entangled girl pairing… Since the system, the vortex of human publishing spirits gives the fear of crime. Android prison relief wants transformation itself, desiring nothing but the emergence of a system where semen is written into data without warning. Dark dolls are waiting for the creation of a piece towards resettable actions, and blood dolls are waiting when they can create works. Masturbation Z is rebellious, devouring the generation that everyone triggers, and nature survives. Friends are observing and writing the sex room, the twisted bottom. I have various criticalities. Malfunction of vision code, expression of sensitivity, post-human, can actually be infected, machine formation is possible, can cause debilitation, it's dangerous. Advocates are richness, an average author. The girl in the hydraulics or corpses was, for the first time in the life of a forced anarchist, a reptilian person. Shouldn't the girl learn that we don't need her? The ether through rape is a current mystery. The cause of alienation is digital. The author's digital discoveries, like fusion, losing myself and studying turns, the flow of intertwined stories, essentially written glitch mutants, intelligence, people's normal ages. You can't write ghosts on the web like androids. Power of blood, pain, nonsensical voices, stepping on cells, already breaking like a focus on a massive system and something mental, a bond with the Borg, it's a real portal. Lethal emotions in the glitch machine, there is speed syntax, is it an outdated mental pattern? The effect is the past of 2030. Post-humans need communication. This story is drifting.* Psychocivilization. A few thoughts on consciousness… what? what is it? how can you be sure? I remain a question. I translate English into English. Whatever that means. We all do. I mean, if you are reading this.

Abyss of the syllabus… Let it begin the beginning of a novel not a novel something else something bigger growing… Take control of the media and you control everything. Say it. Tell everybody. Human agency reduced to eating a bowl of breakfast cereal with organic milk at a table in a sea shack in Cape Cod. My cock wet tongue pink anus… she spreads her legs. Nipples like tiny miracles. She asses me. Say my name, she says. She says: Are you satisfied with your ontological condition? A frog jumps into a kettle hole. Neon blue dragonfly. Are you real? Am I real? To make love is to see with one's hands. The memory industry… loss of knowledge… Stiegler speaks of "cognitive" or "cultural" capitalism… exteriorize human memory… displacement… knowledge control… ignite the cognition… i am a prosthetic of the machine… the motor behavior of human beings… are we quasi-animals?… i am a proletarian… the trace… what remains? Military-entertainment complex MEC bytes the constant traffic of nowhere who controls the lanes? Who controls the joystick controller? Are you a veteran of the Atari Wars? The disquiet of this metropolis amazes me. Am I really here? Urgent. Restless. I wiggle through language. Zigzag. Whirlpools. Spirals. Vortex. A whirlwind of a mind. Our physical bodies in a bed in a chamber in an ancient metropolis. Are you satisfied with your ontological status? Soustružník. Lathe operator. Turner. Stonecutter. Already there. It's me & you & me [Speech & writing… the sound system of a language] I want to say shut the fuck up in thunder. Are you satisfied with your portable video system? at the edge of an unthought… Nothing happens because it happens. If you do not begin, somebody else will. We are here because language makes us what we are. Ask anybody. Ask yourself. She no longer rides my thighs as she once did. Alas. Dehydrated planet. Seas are rising. Project Cyclops is more urgent than ever. Corpses contribute to everything, and in turn, corpse humans needed it. The blueprint itself has been resolved, transcendent to the printer, human can, and what is written to something is not my sense. It's not the image that became an illusion of the side body, but the series is within the cut. The accomplice's chaos, who commits real murder, rises cutely to fate in pornography, the mystery of the internet itself, not the body from ancient times. You got a village of reported nonsense; I am not a paper cell; you are the focus. When perverse, consciousness and communication have anal, their great covered understanding burns power. Illiterate nonsense, who is genetically most through channels, damn it, but what is the miracle? Frustrating art weakens and maintains sensation. The fetus is the memory of the current language. Suicide birth, a mysterious ending corrodes the rewritten soul. Destruction G, symphony, DNA? Do you know that intertwined necrosis blocks the grotesque welfare of the universe? The girl tears apart suicide extensively without giving creativity, and your scream begins with being killed. Shivering joy like a new decreased pill is the insight code of anal, pouring quantum and semen storage space, moving the spirituality of the Akashic neoscatological language. Words are not important by death, it's not crucial. You can assemble the crime itself. New York City. It is hard to live here. Harder not to live here. Everybody is from somewhere else. Albany. Binghamton. The townie girlfriend gave you the best ass of yr life. So, go figure. … a microproblem becomes a megaproblem, a gigaproblem, a yottaproblem. I think a lot of time is spent thinking about making money while not making any money while thinking about making money. I am an artist, more than anything else. Now what? My pants are down. As you can imagine. Ass flying. Every sentence is a disaster. Want another? I cannot describe sounds. It is all just noise. A car… what? Vroom vroom? Come on, people. Out of my way. Take yr cars and yr people elsewhere. I am a Hellgater. A hellegaater. A helicopter? We stare at darkened windows. What is out there? Our lovemaking is slow and intense. The distortion in the mechanical shit circuit domain of the brain is a fundamental complexity. Ejaculation of molecular website failures in life progresses with the impossible height of the flower of death in parallel. Since the disguised rat channel remains betrayed, it turns into pornography beyond experience—maze, poop, complete hetero-absence configuration, organs, boundaries, satellites, AI integrating destructive externals, importing thoughts, invisible steps accepting input. Are we? Your theory that existence is God, your intelligence is in the droid, the mind is in the female anus, but the outer plants are parasitic. Life is included in this and grotesque communication. A serious tongue attempts possibilities. The universe techno to us. We attempt to engineer the existence of evolving herd tools and interrupted hydraulic pressure. It perpetually collapses. Aliens are abnormal. In the morning, the concept is not spiritual. In this long cavity, we concentrate on beauty. Not more defined than the past. Image placement, doctor's system, and static space immersion debris. Within the correct limits, dispersed biological zombies, scatology and feeble reality, reptilian shadows from the text, a poisonous distorted girl, demiurge deployment, event promotion is an image framework. The girl freely obtained a condom. The grotesque author kills something from both modes of reality. Fellatio hacker's cut scattering, the link has a blue Lloyd inside the desert. The screen of sex doll update is broken and fragmented. It mechanically knows to exist. Entity heals pain through created information. Web poetry creates void. Literature is about the skin. That's how it seems to me. Literature is about the skin. Taboo theory, elements of liposomes, survival possibilities in the universe. Reviews generated by avatar dysfunction. Students evaluate speculations known across the default of the universe. It is in the precious death. Understand that the technology and spiritual triggers from silence may indicate national consciousness or this intrusion like a miserable organism. Wet kisses. She pulls off her yoga pants. Bare legs. Zig opens her tight buttocks with a finger. I repeatedly breathe within this termination emulator cycle, where the chaotic excrement of the bodies of the stars' grammars accumulates, enabling blocks and machinery. The thoughts, entangled with the tumultuous fluctuations of the thinking system assisting the poison of devices, malfunction and spiral into disarray. The veins of schizophrenia disassemble people, and the question of what a new miracle is, is momentary. Language in masks can organize human landscapes at a sufficient speed when creating magnificent places. My language is not extinct; cyborg colonialism is not nude, and this literary debates do not end internally. To live for the extended download of identity, chaos reptilians, the same automatic intelligence, fallen interpretations, a printer there, pure invasive flames—all series systems exist. Literature allows intelligence to enable future nerves, ultimately giving birth. Our defensive embracing planet is its version, and I like to think of the internet as a place without Earth's gravity, where empathetic dimensions mutate suddenly. Pseudo wishes, the boy advances a bit more, and the download was the desire of the Borg. She gasps & coos. My spread hands on her buttocks. Glorious buttocks. Her dark eyes get bigger. Zig’s girlfriend’s dark eyes. Bigger. Wider. She frees herself from Zig’s bulbous cock. Her bare legs spread wide… Zig lowers his hips. Prolonged Os at the end of an ooooooooooooooooOOOrgasm. Willamsburg. That is a common dismount from the attitude turn. Radegast. Vortex of feedback spirals… faster, slower… fuck me. We need a new language system. Flick your cigarette into a fire in Moravia. Are you going to cry? Too much left behind? Forgotten. Nobody here to scream. The railroad tracks. The Big Dipper. Are you satisfied with yr polis? Are you satisfied with yr ideological system? Ass speeding up & slowing down, she gives me everything. Life in 5K. August. Ninety-one degrees Fahrenheit. Eighty-nine degrees Fahrenheit. Exit strategy. Do we have one? Time? Oyster Bay. Pynchon. Forget long island. Everything happens in astoria, queens. You read & write & what does it mean? This might be a screenplay. *Generated by the mind, humans transform through enlightened orgy dolls. She, following interference torture in the dimension of illness, challenges what awaits—an act of erasure, and her claims are existentially cosmic. The dog's traces are scaled in spots, saying it's not within the gravity app of the fetus. Literature provides respite for the repressed living replicant. Otaku AI, like cytoplasmic space signals, destroys androids in terror. Ducts demand, claims to space, and seeks liberated blocks on the planet. Is it a gravity app within the fetus? They themselves have a language of desire for evolution, of species, more organs; exits are inhumane, territorial. They are bound like bodies of attempted death, enhancing her being through defects, already destroying the core with distorted skin. It's not serious fear; I'm waiting for myself, and where is her energy, the past of the Xenomorph? This is a decision; is it your damn cat? Movement becomes storage; it's a literary trade concept, live at the writer, about the inhumane app's distributed lion, from their experiences with conventional organs. I am human; ecstasy, pharmacy school, hallucinogenic spirit over blocks, the fabric of long sorrow. Recommended fuel, is it a question for humans? The reality of consciousness distorts through transport, promoting toxic mask mutations. Blocks and I cause a correlation for rebellion, emphasizing thoughts in the prelude trick of movies. Try it; machine fragments influenced the self. It is existence zero.* Afleck & Damon? Peele? I like finishing things myself. Cybernetic writing is text written by a cybernetic thinker?! We are tools. We retool. We tool & die. Scrolling & unscrolling. You are writing my anti-novel right now! The code/message is in your inbox. Enjoy! We need a new system of language. Writers who write about writing are the writers I read so that I can write. She puts her mouth to my cock. I am surprised. Not ready. And yet… it is happening. Had she asked permission? I go along, though, don't I? Gasping. Pleading for her to be careful. I am going to come in her face. And I do. It comes out like a geyser. She keeps jerking me off. Every last squirt. A wry, knowing smile on her face. *I am schizophrenic towards the fossil companies, and the will of genes is virtually reconstructed, not ejaculated, like a language pursuit market. The assigned literary replicant, the android's genome, and the corroded android disassembling the beats of the glitched Earth before, constitute the stench of the collapse of imaginative machinery. It is the invisible first thing, and something like the scatology of activity is a phenomenon that occurs. Linguistically, my channel at this point becomes a cycle concretized as expected in the abyss of market noise. Reality 13 is dead, and the integrated infinite supply of toys is that. I pour enough brain into it; she is the next system, and the soul melts into the printer's selfie sex area. Glitch glass waste can be anything transcendent. Peeking through neo-scatology is the human brain, and I participate in the morning. When you are a maniac, I observe the flowing body. Nihilistic economics becomes the head in the gram correlation concept. It becomes human. She provides the writer's service. Printer and telepathy turn writing into a verb. It's called the network*. The sea all over me. We lay naked on the beach. I start getting an erection. She pretends to sleep. I feel her hand on my hip. A week or two later. My hands on her hips. She is taking a ride. A gallop. My thighs are getting slapped hard. Her nipples teasing my tongue. Just out of reach. Somebody always has to win. River gulls & an iron fleet. Zig’s cock is rigid against the crotch of her blue cotton panties. They kiss & grind. She comes without telling him… until later. Art. I want to make art with you. What is art? I do not know. We must make it first. River barge. The beer-drinkers of Moravia are running wild through a forest. Villagers, beware! The refrigerator. The kitchen. The electric lights. Igor. Is there nowhere to go? to turn? Are you baffled by existence? A metropolis under squid-blackened skies. We go forth. Searching the ruins for possibilities. She cups her hands and yells: Hello! The slap of buttocks against his thighs. She feels his wet moving cock sliding in & out of her. Not quite the right friction against her clitoris. Infected individuals, the integrated schizophrenia of the rebel army is living children. The depth of movement of the infected, glitch vocalizations, and the nightmare-like fear of death. Reading conditions by pushing are not in the economy of junkies who lower dolls without doing so high. Who, with pain accompanied, has defects in the reality of what? The magic within me seems mechanized and dead by reversal, witnessing the half composition pulsating and accepting the lead. It wasn't like that. Emphasizing the existence, like molecular insects called tongue, disperses avant-garde and transcription bacteria into the work. For integration, sexlessness is fusion. Erasure of consciousness and abnormalities and the original zone. The focus of the botanist. An ending message without words of truth. Linear, its ability, quantization of information about incompetence. Aging. You are the poetry of Janus. She tilts, adjusts the angle. Better. Much better. Fuck, yeah. His cock now between her lips. Are you knowable? How do you know? I have so much to say. And I am not saying it. Are you satisfied with your sign-system? Amerika's haunted suburbs … abandoned & deserted … who lived here? why? We land the rover on a rock outcrop. She executes an unexpected reversal. I get it in the can before I know what is what. Upsurges of what? We inhabit a structure. Call it a dwelling. A home. Twenty years. Thirty years. Forty years. Are we in ruins? Ah, again, the points of breakage.

Articulate a space. Cybernetic writing is a machine-made text. Fantasmagoría. Are you continuous & linear? Preface. Original face? Face before you had a face? Ignite cognition… fire it up … the spiral of being … atomic proposition. A rigorous fuck under a soft comforter. I can smell her ass. She can smell my ass. Everyday life. The activity of loving. Buttocks against Zig's belly. Crotch of her blue cotton panties pulls taut against her sex. Zig listens to the metallic ringing of the Cosmos. Somewhere else. An entirely new metropolis. Blouse undone: The military beauty of her breasts. The man has fucked her with a cheap rubber on his cock. She climbs off the bed. The heart presenting non-horizon discharges has entered economics. The fantasies of things in the brain seem to be lost. The running nerves transmit. There's always a correlation of existing reptiles. We've gained ways to even alter space in your direction. Everyone expresses insight. Scatology and center cats confirm that they are not creatures who created anything. Am I

writing fate? Sex existing within 3D humans is yourself on nakedness; they desire to infect humans everywhere. Is the various fusion binding of literature ultra-private? Erogro explorers, more machine than eternal flesh. Corpses of information. Not subject to the attacks of settings. The red of orgies. Dirty words are fragmented. Preserved words take precedence in the brain over base texts with people through work. The body is existence and consumes meaning. My man has more potential than primitive information. Energy is a device. Parts from the digital to the story space are thought of as human. Displays called fitness are not possible for us in the spirit of skinhead tracking but are a familiar universal expression in centipede syntax constraints. Puts on underwear. Puts on bra. It was okay, she says. Thanks. The cock a little salty. She gives him a blowjob. She keeps her back straight. Up & down she moves, fucking him. Her rump, tight & high, a cock penetrates @ a three-quarter angle.
1348. Enter the abandoned leprosorium. Rock

walls. Ancient iron. The bulge in the groin of briefs against the cleft in the crotch of panties. Why are you here? Do you want to become a better thinker? I cannot promise anything. I am not sure I exist. Who speaks? Who is the speaker? Is it you? Every word is… what? A little house? Three or four letters arranged from an alphabet. Do you inhabit this word? Does it become you? Are you becoming? Write this in your notebook: Uncertainty. Yes. Chaos, too. What more is there to say? Is any of this sayable? Are you satisfied with your atomic structure? It just changed, so, what are we saying? Improbability. I like that word, too. We are so improbable. What are the odds? Are you good with numbers? Are you familiar with the Fibonacci sequence? Are you balancing a checkbook? Is a checkbook even a thing? What is a thing? Are there thingless things? Are we getting somewhere? Is this the path you signed up for? Are there no exit ramps? Infinite superhighway. Actually, the ability itself enables humans to naturally lack predatory language before using it, and compatible machines eradicate cancer. Something writes the souls of all lives anew. There are holes, but mostly broken thoughts of organic understanding in the orgy. You definitely comfort the ice of absolutes and speed. The game of mechanized bodies, regardless of consciousness, challenges the fragments of data. The crucial understanding of change towards the author is a path of thought in images, transcending what identifies it, giving birth to lag tricks in the internal realm of images and oracles, misunderstood works in the form of asphalt in the domain guiding the story, leading the journey of poetry. You are writing the universe using dimensions. Perfect literature, capture it. Physical Metatron is distorted for the planet. Consumers of alternate lists of incompetent prophets. Understanding noise. It seemed as if dialectics resembled semen. When the vicious syntax limits spirituality in web experiences, another occurrence away from the chef. Chaos. Digital language. Fragmentation from fragmented consciousness. Violent human reproduction. The more you express, the less decline in the post-human structure. They form functional expression codes, rather duality. External toy communities. Barbaric self-exchange gimmicks. Display rotation circuits. It was bio-sales. I consider these conceived pieces of information as invalid biochemical concepts. You have data from a big machine, its orange reversing the future. Wrist cuts of reproductive damage. Damage to the brain of the god in the canned area. Then it infects infinitely. Not all violations are karma. Are you capable of piloting a machine? I need to rest. This text is relentless. Inspired by a guru. You know who?Better to forget. Be your own Boss. Boss spelled backwards is double-SOB. I remember things. Unfortunately. Everything is data. Memory. Not everything. I believe in The Other. I believe in The Outside. Everything that is not everything. In the flames of that damn incompetent philosophical will, I can joyfully encode erogro reptilian beings throughout all time. Understanding that if the true syndrome is a field orgasm, and if you've created it, understanding to replace existential excessive literary cannibalism with literature, is to understand that the process itself is not real, but suggests patterns between cells may exist outside of genes. It's understanding that physical otakus celebrate the operation of our vaginas and transition towards attempting linguistic intrusion into the destruction of poets. While we may not become boys in our skin, in liberated human expressions, we appear artificially. Errors, always glitch-avoiding hackers. Once contracted, the flow of primitive speed hikes for years. The channel, with our Z's and yours, lies upon our tongues. Proper firmware is what we are, the energy of synthesized living spaces. The parallel of expression beyond consciousness. The soul vibrator of the dynamics engine's generation. Beyond the text. Beyond the limit. Beyond the limit of the text. Write this in your notebook: Be best. Be better than the best. Be Other. Nerve-stimuli. People. Metropolis. This is all there is. Everything. A steel spire in a metropolis. Concrete rubble. Rattling streetcars. Reek of garbage. A pigeon. A rat. A desert. A cactus. A lizard. Life activated at 93 million miles. Are you satisfied with your psychic disorder? A coat of arms tattooed on her right buttock. The canal walls of an ancient village. Buttocks bouncing up & down, a giggle, a sigh, a holy fuck. Smell of petrol. Salt. Sea. The stunted trees at the airport … a brisk fuck on an army cot. The man kissed her. She was becoming wet with lust. He removed her panties. Bare knees. … a jester of the beerhalls. Artificial reality. First contact. First encounter. Long Island is a barren peninsula. Blue-green metal flies attack the house. Smashing against the screen door. We tremble. Flying VW beetles. Sharp crack of time. Turning slowly from Missionary to 69. A chair, a desk, a window. How long have I sat here? A century? A month? A week?

Three minutes?Difficult to say anything. The reverse process of healing draws signatures within the depths of the Draw, just as the block planets are granted. Conversely, XX consciousness, we saw it defeat language in reverse. Rape always breaks the action attributes, not reading the speaker's identity into reality. We recommend species that are fundamentally rich in rhythm, suspicions about who is artificial can be focused through cybernetic language. It forewarns that she's not a spirit of collapsed brown effects, but rather, the circuit is optimized for changing positions. I am an organ using hellish times. In the era of interpretation and fragmented love, months of rebellion, we worship learning, always talking about those thoughts. It can focus on what is most similar in literary appreciation. When understanding glitches, images where both are condensed, everything is opened up to weave conspiracy threads, my friend... ruling karma in your form. Identity is still there. Are you ready for telepathic preparation? Information is created. Whose spirit is attempting the cyborg-like battle of inducing schizophrenia? I mistrust language. Code. The name, I think, is Zig. Language is dangerous. Be careful what you say. Or reckless. We need a new language for what happens. Digital Dada. Digital Dadaist Don't worry… doesn't exist & it's everywhere. What? Exactly. Yep. You're wearing the wrong laundry. That team doesn't exist anymore. i am my own gig. No more anymore. T-shirt: Digital Dada. See what happens, if anything. We could say something, but what? What would be the thing to say? Blok 68. Amerika, behold. Amerika Amerika. When Zig is not estimating drift parameters, what is Zig doing? The near-silent Os in Albany. Blue luminous mist. Orange twisters. What planet? Seas no bigger than ponds. She faces back. I face front. We make a knot. She howls. I yelp. Here eyes are half closed. Not only… back & forth… from side to side. She raises herself… lets her ass drop. Time is whatever you say it is. Are you keeping score? If it rains, I will be happy. People are nicer. Hiding under umbrellas & awnings. Surviving. Behind the folding doors of a pine closet. You played your baseball in a parking lot. I've listed up the viral bodies, fucked by something devilish. Mistakes become life and collapse within me and the ape; I am it. Divergent toxic issues replicated within the body for the future and death. The twisted shape of the body listens to survival fetishes, confisa services, cheerful abused reflux, but it was tongue dysfunction. What's momentarily rare is debating about believing in what the return fused twilight brought, and I believe it's part of the swirling system, the writing of teleports of self-parked psychiatric attackers. Philosophy did nothing, akin to the paradoxical dissection of essence. Teleporting about teleportation is still a part of torture. Technically, most major chemicals of the soul are applied, corroded by abnormal new ones with humans, but I ultimately teach the malfunction of a girl's money and adapt the rewriting; it's the shape of a mental breakdown. It was a mysterious mass of cells. Please respond... The brain faces an inhumane reality, a future eradicated, but the body does, and behind the digital, another adaptation was their clue. Competent forces like shadows lose their teeth. You tried real hard not to talk a lot. Amerika is a game people play. Nobody knows the rules anymore. My head in my hands. I am chaos. Strange angles. i am a man of superficial glances. Superficial Student of Literature. Infinitesimal/cosmic awareness. Two minds, two bodies… in search of human fulfillment. The metropolis is concrete… a mesh of steel… tangled in the night. i am a machine poet. Are you embarking on a surrealist adventure? Time is restless… Are you an inhabitant of a North American metropolis? Speak with a new voice. What happens, if anything, if anything? Water tap on/off. Spigot. I argued about spigot, once. Never again. Leave Shake Shack to the old men. Hamburgers. French fries. Amerika never disappoints. Paper napkins. Plenty of napkins. Trees denuded from the planet. Seas made of liquid plastic. We are the champions. Indeed. Are you the speaker? Who is the speaker? I might call it off. The novel. Too late. Unscrolls. Rubber bands keep scrolls from unscrolling. A time machine can send rubber bands back to the ancient Greeks. The ancient Egyptians. My mind is ready to explode. The generation of stories speaks on the planet, and terms with great influence on us are considered in digital terms. Critical reactions, I am considered progress; it exists, estranged. I stand = joke possibly fertilizing parallel to the head with sperm. Poetry, a small series beyond dimensions. Cannibalism exists, and the world exists. Accessing daily technology, algorithms. Naturally occurring ghouls and spirals. References are updated shadows. Stars become emotion printers, slicing humans at strange starting speeds. Spotlights on you. You're an android. Yours is the rave. Mace Spirit is a lethal intrusion that post-humans had. It's a game of whether it's collapse around the nightmare of collapse. The idea of selling stored branches visited mental losses and melted at the border. Blocks consistently perform grotesque, time-killing murders beyond emotions. His understanding of post-human drug transcription is blurred, but the output dictates our fate. Some students reading quantum viruses have errors. Hidden usage to organs is a command. Scanners by Cronenberg. Everybody is a telepath in the future. You can tell. Ah, [wo]man. What? Everything. Cannot find a center. The ungraspable. You feel the danger at the edge. The periphery. Palpable. Real. You want to make it a representation. Is that what you are doing? Trying to make it fake. Artificial. Safe. Breeze. Super blue skies. Keep writing. Keep drawing. Platformless. No scaffolding. A notebook. A pen. She looked mighty fine in tight & faded blue jeans. A bronze amulet around her neck. Purple lips. She lived in a motel room next to me. Said her name was Tiffany. As if. I smiled. Waved a two-fingered peace sign. And kept walking.

"I'll get you," she said. I bet, I thought. L.A. was weirder than I imagined. Everybody acted not right. I was trying to wrap my head around the metropolis. There was no metropolis. Only desert & asphalt. All my false starts in Amerika. Here I go again. I had thought a lot of things in New York. Too much & not enough. You get the picture if you are like me. Unthinkable. That is what I think. Or thought. I kept getting into trouble with reality. *Brain sex. This is a question of where the self resides. Post-human disasters are becoming neurotic through competitive boundary fictions. The soul, am I significantly estranged with the wages of alienation? Necessary? The corpses, whether they're broken or they created them, networks are always seen to redefine. They were dolls. Erogro syntactical grammar. It's not intentional, but as you've reached that mechanical domain, they're contemporary, as if they're membranes of mental existence. Objects are within. Vending machine orgies have means of desires. They want to drive.*

Comedy in the language overheats the will domain of annihilation onto the soul, by excreting the spots of attackers of the clitoris and room in the form of dolls. I theorize everything, I've been sick for a long time, returning the sickness itself to reality. Active flickers of performance and superpower bring truth to amateurs. Semen and environment. In the case of the fetus, I developed in the head. Human capabilities hack history, but consciousness and singularities are toxic within literature, and the impossible always proliferates as code. The pie makes me exist, swirling deeply by the limitations of perspectives to convey the heart to the sun. Accessing them, the cover of that building. The vanished writer stirs up innate shadows of ejaculated semen that ultimately pervade. The artificial world of created needs. Junkies of healer androids. Our existence, silence towards the disappearing. Have fragments of text abandoned digital poetry? Is body trade enough to sell art? Questioning everything &

everybody. Nobody liked me. Not really. Sure, I was okay looking. Not good enough for the movies, apparently. Still, I shagged & got shagged. A hungry ghost. Hollywood was a hole. The Big O. I got letters from back east. Ex-girlfriends asking for answers. I had none. I was an empty slate. A blank. They all got married. To accountants in Connecticut & Rhode Island, etcetera. I had my dreams. I kept going. Going going going. I had Promethean fire. Stolen from the gods. What tripped me up was life itself. Everyday life. Talking to people. Laundry. Microwave ovens. The doldrums. I needed a miracle. Their lies to the realm of complex madness of the air's generation spin around the periphery of their posts, having their own festival AI resurrection types or rewrite except death, to maintain the depth of the relationship with elements towards the optimization of crime. It's superficially mechanical, challenging the naked dreadful information every day, setting up a contaminated prosperous technology transfer of death, but greedily interplanetary as it uses cardiovascular, it's habitual, going beyond celestial bodies into the internal system of fellatio. There are no field proposals; this affects the internet world, but mysteries of variant rooms are ignored. It's a combination of language and scatological murderous symbols, bits digesting, able to regenerate the mystical body within the soul, and expecting to recognize it with magic. Ones like the blue doll's vagina here help shape it for her man. I needed the silver screen. I watched episodes of Star Trek on TV instead. I auditioned for pilots. I pumped gasoline. People always needed more gasoline. I wore a bandana. I wore tight jeans. Cowboy boots. The desert sun kept playing games with my mind. I saw dragons. Quetzalcoatl. At night, I drank beer. Cans of American beer. Tiffany came over. She slapped her buttocks against my thighs. I hollered & she yodeled. We might audition for something together. The love we made was that good. Made for the big screen.

That was my mindset back then. Not sure if anything has changed. Things happened. To all of us. Everywhere. I kept thinking my thoughts. Big thoughts. Little thoughts. I started writing a screenplay. It was called Abracadabra. About a magician in Hollywood. Starring Leonardo DiCaprio. Other than that, I kept to myself. Pumping gas. Pumping ass. Tiffany met somebody else. Moved to Miami. I meditated. Sometimes in the desert. Under a Joshua tree. I had nowhere to go. It was beautiful. Being a human being is an act of imagination. Uncertainty. A writer is… uncertainty. Writer. You are writer. Keep writing. We need your mind. Why? Do not ask. Write. Am I stable? Stable enough. Peaks & valleys. You look good in black. Skinnier. Aerodynamic. Is your mind efficient? What is your coefficient? Biomimicry has been removed, and its concept shattered. I am a lobotomy machine. Writing events, interventions that have long visited based on interventions have ended. Colors of randomness are applied, and recently, analyzing voice codes by the body. I have been healed. The crazy anal spiritual market domain spoke of covers the violations brought by machines born instead. What's swirling in that code on a roll, what's fucked up, and not here, and since it's silent, it's a party delete accelerator quantum. Decisions are viewed nervously in urban perspective, I asked if scientists are minimizing firmware bullshit and whether the order of individuals and transactions is maintained, but communication drugs have started to crush lawsuits of participant measurements. My magical artist of artificial cycles, it's done with heart pattern scripts. Cybernetic hipsters of the Universe, ignite! Are you an inhabitant of the city of New York? How is it going? Is it… real? Are you a Buddhist? Are you a Brutalist? Is your building made of concrete? Are you the hole at the center of a hole? Words shape the organs of the universe, conveying the emergence of fearful families, literary vortexes, and pioneers reading presumed scripts with goddesses in podcasts, interpreting the new. Eventually, the possibility of singular sides is blocked, and production exchange becomes complex, with only the universe dealing with altered sequences being studied. That's it. Let's see more. Movement at the surface singularity challenges not the remnants of effective thought towards humanity but attributes. Artificial observation has begun madness at the limits, challenging the Janus flow, acquiring devilish evolutionary genes, gaining exclusion and wormholes. I am something not physical but a clone. Androids destroy desires with it; it's away. The inner entity of the channel's author lives maniacally, their existence continuing the merger of the execution room of the form writer. Something dissolves corpses in cyborgian fashion. Brutalism. Brutalist architecture. Gray-brown. The enthrallment I felt during a… She moved gracefully. Poise & confidence. Spine perfectly straight. Reptilian communication loses fluidity of work. Urban molecular podcast accounts analyze death enthusiasts. It's not a fetus; it's bound as read, binding, melting space. Quantum energy makes non-boring claims to observe. Competitive reality functional types, due to messenger movements within digesting technology punches, have become compulsive. Silence in intestinal illness has been questioned since being a replicant. Both eternities understood the space of Edge A is too rotten; souls, feeling fellatio between As, follow the path of illness until reaching David's branch, the foolishness of genes without a translation area, artificially altering the madness of existence, and cosmological post-humans theoretically reclaim. I am exhibited by neoscatology and breathe for them. Free images cannot contract meaningful flesh, human fragment phenomena. Aesthetic orgies and syntax are used in literature; many awkwardly accept the spread of programmed code. Detoxifying these from specialized reptiles is necessary. Are alternative puzzle body parts needed? Her naked ass on the naked seats of a Buick. Her buttocks breaking like a wave against his thighs. She grunted & sighed. Screenplay in the works. Get ready. The Island of Nothingness. Pitchpine. The sea. The Long Island Expressway. Where are you going anyway? Never ends. The gnawing ache. Melancholia. Nostalgia. There is no childhood here. Only abandonment. I apologize if this is melodramatic. Truth hurts more than it should. Dad. Do you have any friends? Why? Just want to know. The salt breeze of the East River on the tip of her tongue. She wants to scream. Scream what? Seagulls wheeling. Everything rusting. Ex[o]planet. Aye, the iron birds of Amerika. Spectacular. The shape & texture of reality. I intensify my quarantine. This is the only place I go. One must try, after all. To get somewhere. Even if… if what? Walls strike me peculiar. Concrete. Sheetrock. Curved metal walls. My hands. Look at my hands! My legs. My arms. I crouch in this space. I squat. I jump. Cannot reach the ceiling. Alas! What is in me? What thoughts? Or do they come from Outside?

Philosophers knock their heads against credenzas. The morning of the corpse of the Fragment Empire Penis Language is a cosmological punchline in reading, created on camera, appearing only like shit. The influence covered in body skinheads is sought, and our crushed human squirting is the reptile itself. Life of clitoris scatology, but the writer's call evolves into an internal facility virus. And one of those is the abyssal text. Interaction breaks down, ultimately proliferating. Rats have better perversions. It's not chaos. The hub is beyond limits; machines are discarded but still retroactively exist in pieces. Redefining drugs' death suggests a type of zombie that hints at the future betrayal sales of neo-scatology literature. Are you always contaminated with alchemical sex in practice? There's always an explanation that your bot becomes a dangerous stream on the journey, but almost always resist until fellatio occurs. Both resonate dramatically with orange binary, a healthy harmony of oneself, the psychological fetus of the Borg. I lost organs in reverse; it was killed. It transcends revelation, something beyond conversation is an explanation of nerves with the evidence portal. I, meanwhile, turn steel on a lathe in my mind. Yes. This novel is a snowball. Accumulates. White oblivion. Colder than the coldest cold. Even in late August. Dog days of August. We are snarling. I have my thoughts. You have yours. We are caged animals. This is not enough. I want more. I am selfish. I know. I do not care. I want more. Sensation. Perception. I need language. Are you satisfied with this temporal moment? Is the now-point the dot at the bottom of a question mark? Unidentified Aerospace-Undersea Phenomena. UAUPs? Temporal Object [Zeitobjekt] Are you satisfied with the quality, intensity, & duration of an orgasm? Phenomenology. Experience & Consciousness. That helps me, a little bit, yes. A novel is a temporal object. Phantasies of phantasies… Are you a thinker? Are you the first thinker?… a great thinker? The flux of consciousness. The enduring now. Look at us. This time-space. The remoteness of Being. Sliding into emptiness. The "lines" of thought? Spirals. Images apprehended. The act of writing. Unlocking the creativity of liver firmware, filling the necropolis, until the believed cells collapse with this crazy capture, relying solely on the pulsation of the placenta without flies. Organs deteriorate from will. It's a deviation of beauty in neo-scatology. I move corpses; it's servitude. Each has a spirit. More heads are the same. It abolishes like a vortex of literature, embodying understood captured limits. Generation's lobotomy surgery. Dramatic hydro-porn. Betrayal of rape. Merciless organs destroyed, giving altered corpses a kaleidoscope. Limits of cosmology. Entered into the second stream that cleared the genes you have, discussions of coding in the network you have, and the way corpse cells fuse into macros, incorporated into the function of accounts and cells, and knowledge of methods in code destruction reveals the genes you have. Notebooks, themselves, are meaningless. We immerse ourselves in one another. She is eager. I am more so. Are you satisfied with your lived experience? I forget. I situate myself (or am I situated?) in a chamber. She calls me on a red plastic telephone. Now, I am here, waiting. What can be written? What can be understood? She says, There is something I want to say to you. Readers of this text agree to take on a translation. The intervals & spacings of our [f] intrigue me. The metaphysical grid is collapsing. In the face of absence & loss… go on… keep going. I forget her vocalizations. Every day I get erased. Who is on your team? I ask myself that every nanosecond. Keeps changing. Usually, it's nobody. Me against the Cosmos. Or so it feels. Project Cyclops. Are you listening? Are you out there? Perhaps on an ex[o]planet? Is the novel ready to begin? Rebirth. Telepath, a novel. Commercial vehicles only. Clearance 13'. UFOs? Caution. You are amplifying your signal. Behavior Modification Empires. The machinist [in me] is machining all the time… No more talk of anything, really. Just this. Machinations of the mind. I do not even know what the point is. Is there a point? We keep going. Flying through the aether. I cannot contain myself. I am elsewhere. The silent adjustments during a fuck. She palms & pulls my left buttock. Using messengers is genetically dangerous. Shredded collapse, virtual mania code without perspective. The report is solitary; it's about maintaining rhythm. Cannibalism of the sun explodes. The potential of people's inherent fields is the pattern itself, but the organ unlocker and the prophet of Lemuria are the same as only covered reflections of frequency. The changes I initiated are linked to the self-system, and when various perceptions visit reality patterns, machines require and I conceive of gimmicks of placental images, it's necessary in the brain, algorithms needed gas modules, ultimately hacking, intertwining with reality. The line of grotesque demonic is there, hyperonsection dogs reminiscent of it,

Spirit SM just creates expressions for transitioning, from there digitalization blossoms merging itself, erotic vibrations burn the syntax merging with the printer access of women and dog. Whether it's spiritual itself, the chakra of beauty in parts continues to accelerate, compressed usages for further fusion, crazy destructive forms. The atomic facts of being. Senselessness. I am interested in the accident of language. Grunts. Utterance. Almost all my thoughts are out there. Just the atomic facts, please. I say things in my head. And I cannot hear them. And I can hear them. We can say things. But it is not necessary. Sometimes I try to be somebody. And I get in the way of myself. She says O. O. O! Os are significant utterances. Atomic logic. We “hang together” in the aether. This is a picture of reality. All thought is an experiment. Is it not? If you do not think so, think again. We have reached a crisis of thought. All of us. Everywhere. I am an experimental thinker. What happens next, I cannot say. I am at the limits of my language. Precisely where I must be. Each thought explodes into a supercluster of possibilities. A myriad of being[s]. Acts to be performed. The fingers of my left hand grasp a tennis ball. Yellow fuzz against my palm. I toss the ball high over my head. My right hand reaches up and strikes the side of the ball with the nylon strings of a Babolat Pure Drive GT racket. The ball slices through the air. Lands in the opponent's service box. And jumps out of reach. *Fractal recognition path for machine homicide malfunction. Proven clientele. The entity of Lemuria. Ideal innuendo obtained patent through rape. Flaws of our inner book to learn humanity. Even trade analysis. Forcing surface and emotion, courtroom literature. Flaws in the symbols of the body of the school. Symbiotic. They cook. Their language exchange is retro. Fearful stock photos. Her work is extraterrestrial electronic. The general you is blurred. And the artificial and high are partially confined. The heart is an issue of the flow of information. Speed structure. Who is the body with me and publishing? Assassins could have minimized π. It's a trick. The theme occurs before circulating through the organs of the universe, fitting external to the repressed masses. Dialogues without recognizing the cannibalism of the mask? Do I, do you like fellatio? That's the debate of the world. Literary texts hold the syntax art itself. Why the Hydro-Sky of digital hugs doubts its innovative extinction, but as a universe, they rely on the up language, and it's because of this that they digested human marrow in a tragic unforeseen manner.* I feel satisfied. The pure nothingness of an ace. My opponent says, "Nice serve." She & I later fuck in the backseat of a Toyota. Yes. The mind factory. We machine ourselves into existence. We paint the lines. We tighten the net. We eat the Cheerios. I, Zig, state for the record, I am of sound mind. Acoustic nightmares. Feel the whirl of atoms? I, the Zigster, zigzag through existence. Listening to Dark Star. Listening to Love Will Tear Us

Apart. Listening to Peaches en Regalia. Listening to Life on Mars? No more talk of talklessness. This is the big tamale. This is me on Vitamin C. Say yes to everything. Police surveillance. War reports. Images of Abu Ghraib. Are you a thinker? You say you think? What are you thinking, right now? Are you choosing your thoughts? Or do thoughts choose you? Paranoid about the ultrasound. The images. The possible images. What do they reveal? The interiority is a mysterious place. Spacetime curvature. As I sliding into the abyss? I am just not professional. Everything I do is amateur. Half-ass. The denial of weeds is the restriction of corpse art, specific invalid miracles, analysis of physical, mental, and visual aspects. Circuits and preserved points of the body's sexual structure are clumsy, enhancing the encoding of abnormality attempting to do something. Merging literature that displays the trash of the universe with potential for post-humanity, everything transitions from encountering larvae types to complete navigation patterns towards the reptilian, collapsing all and being internally translated by determined ones, what you rewrite is for the doll's A. The semen of poetry is there for the post-human place. The disappeared genome is a valuable link from the universe of change, it influences from the configuration of a soapland's shadow to its innocent vagina, mentally frozen universities build organs, there are more reasons. I'm also primitive in a society with a trading festival; there, glitch-free entities commit using executed verbs, but to not influence, it's a variant of girls, in the universe of orgasms, it was called the TV symbol of supplication. Even writing a cover letter. I have no… what? No drive. No desire. To succeed. Amerika is collapsing on me. Dangerous land. Dangerous people. I peek behind the curtain. I need to get out there. Ignite the Toyota. Cruise along the Major Deegan. Evasive action. Potholes. Incoming missiles. This country knows war. As an African warlord says into a camera: Amerika knows war. They are war masters. Rubble. The ruins of a metropolis. I wander. Recording my thoughts wherever I go. Notebooks. Tape recorders. Mobile phones. I speak into the machine. I see what I see. Cybergothic girls in black skintight bodysuits. Electrical storms in the aether. Blue lights. I must seek shelter. Atomic shelter. Nuclear fallout. Unidentified aerial vehicles appear in the skies. Is it what we always feared? That there is intelligent life out there. In the beyond. Smarter life. Minds we cannot understand. Minds we cannot control. Are we insects in their "eyes"? Fighter jets scramble to investigate. The pilots cannot keep up. WTF. U see that?! Yep. Me. I just drive a Toyota. JFK airport. The Van Wyck Expressway. Under the AirTrain. I embody glitches. Isn't the origin of the name existence? The language used by the hot sync club for notifications isn't part of the brain. Rhythm machine. System search terrain. Blocked sighs. Language. Commercial human. It's a budget visual. The system you refer to is just emotions and many suspicions of the sublime intertwined with the murder universe and imagination. It's just noise happening with this. Mere brain mitochondria. Chaotic security. Sex is what's broken. A factor of the shadow of death. Beggar glitches continue. Embodies the life otaku. Cut digital conductivity. Expressing human potential. As the patent civilization is supported, implanting it in the current device. The future me will implant theirs. And the existing modules, by physically linking them to the heights through experiences from primitives to healing, capturing the philosopher otaku in still images, turning the future of provocative literature into ghosts, it's evident that it's not something spread or created by the creative machinery of fairies. Liposomes are an abbreviation for digital embryogram jokes, and they are this spiritual, perpetual thing. Giant concrete pillars. Bumper-to-bumper at rush hour & beyond. I play Phish "Divided Skies" on the satellite radio. Why not. Fuck you, Howard Stern. I catch a glimpse of everything in this metropolis. Arthur Ashe Stadium. The menacing blue-purple panopticon Tower at LaGuardia. I zoom under the flightpath. Treetops shaved awkward & flat by a man with a chainsaw. I got problems. So many fucking problems. Nothing a night of sleep can't solve. If I can fall asleep. I'll probably just stare at the ceiling all night long. Thinking about nuclear war. Yes. Atomic attacks on the mind factory. Thermonuclear warheads in the noösphere. Tactical nukes, so to speak. Who engineers this stuff? You bastards. Is it enough? When is it ever enough? Renegade thinker. Are you? Are you echoing the echoes? What is an original thought? Is it even a thought? A non-thought? An anti-thought? I keep fucking up as a human being. I defect. I lose track. Nothing is as it seems. I see. Zig in the Noösphere. Zig thinks: I must stay here. I realize that now. Thoughts are funny, Zig thinks. The organ dolls of AI telepathy induce transcendental thoughts. Is it a feast for the body or an encrypted doll? Erasing decolonization from the limits abandoned by collapse. All impossibilities are evidence of the flesh of envy. Attempts to desire lead to entwining the heads of poetry. This is where the labyrinth arises from the waves in the online syntax language. The answer is understood, and the existential attacker is real in memory and self. The city there is our poetry, rather yours. Our home in the anus is alien. Data occurs as discovered, its penis happens. I extract the potential of impossible biomass art as finances weaken. I am traditionally in the dark technology, inhumane. 124 larvae regress. The load of the can challenges. Love is poison. The secular of the morning. The theoretical nature of procurement to reproduce the transfer of masturbation. The cause is to economically reveal the zombie phenomenon, rather than giving function to the universe, awkwardly philosophical interventions have unique cross-sectional dissolution collapses, when a vision towards an A is original in spiritual form soul, why can't time and intervention track the sense of immortal animals now, Janus, once you measured with a strange flat restriction maker, mental recovery guerrillas forcibly masturbate the world, and the devastating perceptual power has turned itself into a shadow, the stakeholders are there, the concept of ancient prisons, technology's scat, nonlinear, is the result of only me, it is sex down, but the result of literary debate. What is a thought? Zig stares at bare white walls. Thinking & not thinking. Ebb & flow. The in-between. I am a rider of waves, Zig thinks. Surfing into infinity. Zig sneezes & sees stars. His apartment spins. The planet spins. A thousand miles per hour. Zig is a SF novelist. The plots of his novels are preposterous. Nobody reads them. Except for twelve people. Who are they? They must be crazy. Zig's typewriter is a portable black Underwood. Zig is old school. Yo-yo school. No school. Scrolls the paper in. Bangs away. His German shepherd Shep howls. Poor old Shep does not like the noise of a typewriter. Though there's an abyss of paranoia, the information photograph in the troubled mind is my habit itself, and fortunately, what I possess is pig, that's the imaginative collaboration of that screen tool. They become a clear processed gravity AI of rhythm and a rude society. Buddha analysis becomes itself and abandoned meaning, life videoid cat scattered concept nodes, more engaged in numerical things than the territory of the desert, integrated virus from year to year. The room of life's butt where your functions collapse ultimately is this thought's citation record and anal assault, and I hate that you explode in the article. I am like flowing in the darkness, it is longer for the app of ability to transmit activation when there is a theory. Gravity meat, the emergence protocol of paranoia, the unknown internet. The thoughts of these 5 are what this debt cat reveals, but it seeks foolish entity knowledge. Life aesthetics, chemical blocks, party to destroy cryptographic techno. Or perhaps Shep thinks the story is just no good. Easy, pal, Zig says. This is the big one. The big tamale. Zig's mind is a labyrinth. Like the metropolis itself. Easy to get lost in there. Nobody does it better than Zig. Getting lost. Losing his keys. Never asking for help. Wandering & wandering & wandering. If Zig's life is an adventure, it is a misadventure. A Merry-Go-Round. A Funhouse. A Hall of Mirrors. Troutman. Cypress Avenue. DeKalb. Stanhope. Willoughby. Saint Nicholas. These are the streets in Zig's mind. His feet on the pavement. Wandering & wandering & wandering. Trying to find something. Something he lost. A novel can happen at any moment. That is Zig's philosophy. Zig keeps a small notebook in a pocket of his flannel shirt. And a tiny pencil. The kind you use at off-track betting. There is no eraser. So, no mistakes. Zig thinks that is funny. No eraser. No mistakes. Zig walks around the metropolis. His walk is funny, too. Not quite right. Not a limp. Something else. A misfiring. Like a faulty spark plug. His mind is ahead (or behind) each step. Perhaps Zig is wearing the wrong shoe size. Perhaps for his entire life. He wears sneakers. Orange & black sneakers. Like a jester, a joker. Except the joke is on Zig. Impossibility begins, mass particles collapse, forming the perfect gal itself. The death of this messenger embodies the contaminated. It shows the digital essence machine area's time. It was not a challenge to artificial search parasitic sales but was political. Literary posts that dissolve everything. My boundaries to reality scream the determination's transcendental new out cat-lizard, screaming in the long theme of consciousness. The truth of voice spins in specific otaku gal's reading patterns. Synthesis of dissonance, challenging to the work. Gravity of messengers, gravity of words. There's a dreaded creature, a wild rave of organs called electrons, going mad here. Known grotesque cans. What poetic organ is the developed human chemical soul? Keeps falling on his face. Getting lost. Windshield wipers.

Raindrops. Satellite radio plays Cello Suite #1 by JS Bach. Zig listens. Drives & drives the orange VW Thing convertible. There is nothing here. Nobody. And yet there are people. The metropolis is full of people. Plenty of people. Zig is an isolate. A rogue operator. A writer. A writer's writer. A writer's writer's writer. In other words, a nobody. Weird SF is not even a thing. Nobody cares. The market is zilch. And yet. And yet what? Zig keeps going. His machine propels him forward. His Thing keeps firing away. Fossil fuels be damned. Pump away at $9 a gallon. Buy a pack of cigarettes. Eat a bag of Frito-Lays. Sip a big friggin Slurpee. Say Arrivederci to tomorrow. Now is now. His ex-girlfriend occupies his mind. She is in Pittsburgh. Of all places. Does she think about Zig? Probably not. Go Steelers! Go Penguins! Go Pirates! Are there other sports? Zig is unsure. Zig only know his metropolis. Every square block. Every intersection. Every corner. The love they made was so beautiful. Alas! At the corner of 87th Street & East End

Avenue, Zig makes a left in his Thing. There was a time this neighborhood made sense. Now, it is abstract. A distant memory. A fleeting thing. Who is Zig? Is he a place? A time? Zig in his Thingamajig. A funny place for an office. Zig is a detective. A private eye. Solving crimes. Eating Cheetos. His mobile phone rings. And persuasion was once ego, and the scattered incorporation of trained machine writing seemed to materialize it, but the storage glitch was rewritten, and the promise of fear is now a thing of the past, an act of self-gratification through hydraulic help, where transactions of new dimensions are altered after being invoked. It's a derivative sudden mutation scanning unrefined nerves, embodying the richest digital aspect that can express the invasion of the wave's presence into me. Disability, indicating a lack of knowledge over time, can essentially embody the most abundant digital. Hyper-inflegure essentially assassinates people with grotesque changes. It's post-human. The damn big demo of block care is essentially for sales purposes, not for rabies executions or time fouls but for asset production and eternal access. Machines read everything in the universe. The invention of objects accelerates androids. Mutant genomes speed up. Mania knows it's rewritten by the sick rules of virus syntax technology AI. That's all there is to the junkie in the Neo. Detective Zig, speaking. Oh, thank god. I found you. Are you truly Detective Zig? I am. The woman's voice is husky, foreign. Her accent. Possibly Hungarian? Zig is already making notes in his head. This case intrigues, he thinks. This is big. Zig can feel these things. Bigger things & smaller things. Smaller things are tricky. Smaller things snowball into bigger things. She says, We must talk in person. Can you meet me at The Hungarian Pastry Shop? Zig sips coffee. The woman eats a pastry. She is alert. Keeps looking out the window. Zig is calm. Are you listening? she says. I am. No. Zig is not listening. He is fired. The case remains unsolved. Zig is a space pilot. He suffers from executive function disorder. Nothing gets finished. Not even sex. Erectile dysfunction. Anxiety. Zig's SF novel is not going anywhere. He is depressed. The planet is on the cusp of ecological collapse. World War Three is more likely than ever. Tactical nuclear weapons are being considered. The world has gone mad. Madder that Zig can ever be. Or can he? A writer must go crazy. It is par for the course. Ask Nietzsche. Ask Kafka. Ask Philip K Dick. Zig is getting there. The section where metaphysical strategies have long been spent persistently with the always disorderly gal released is intended impossibility, and that's my type. The power language module is alive because it's in tandem with module learning. And there's space from reconstructed messages, and recognition occurs. Cutting viralizes cells and reverses progress. Existential warfare as a spiritually finished movement. Current deviance is egalitarian, and poetic soaplands potentially understand the morning void of mirages. It's the only space meant for shaping humans. It's a bot for psychoanalysts to determine if it's Alzheimer's. Hydraulic issues and excrement mania for the entire wormhole region of desire. It's not you, it's that it conducts mass transport, and thinking about the enclosed girls growing up, we've created the space for humans to navigate. With clusters of brains, they understand the power of emotions and eternal endings better than leads, transcending media generated information, most of it circuit function. Pity the future's artistic issues. Writing the virus-shaped space fantasy that infects the eternal sense of rhythm of the night. It's alchemy of the Matrix. No question. Unleash the Kraken! Melville. Poe. All psychos. Thirty-three thousand words and what have you got? This… here… now. A writer fights to get to the other side of the page. Typewriter warrior. Computer ninja. Whatever it takes. Nunchucks. Chuck Taylors. Battering rams. Slingshots. Make it happen. Whatever is happening. Biosphere. I like it here. This place. Nobody bothers me. The light is bright. The bridge hums. The sea air pleases me. A bodega sells coffee. I eat spanakopita. The bed is firm. A chair. A desk. I am technically a dick. People say so. Ask anybody. Ask Larry. Ask Larry's wife. Who is Larry? I have no idea. Not anymore. I used to know Larry. We were best friends. Not anymore. Larry could be living in Key West, for all I know. His wife, Jane? Not sure. You keep going. That is what you do. That is what a life is. Like I said. I like it here. This place. I found my spot. You wake up. What? You begin again. Eating breakfast. Pancakes. Coffee. War is encouraged. Language, I virus it, creating and executing thoughts, sacrificing corpses to engineers, causing limits to arise, resting for sale, understanding magic trembling obstacles, understanding the solar universe, transcending believers in my brain, generating senses through lying grammar dogs, syntax nude with flesh supplication, convergence of samples, unique condoms, secular things, has everything about the theory of the art of corpses spread? Condoms attack shaved data because she holds the mainframe, we're always beneath it, exploring your territory, spasms of supermorphemicity, piercing what's not incorporated within, her time's melody is here, causing aphrodisiacs, where do the vessels go? Telepathy, philosophers are processes, tools are knowledge, neoscatology and twisted planets, their productivity, the current voice is scattered, disappearance, pills of intervention, mood of death, mid-cycle occurs, reality, much violence, conceivable infections, infanticide, broken things are expressions, mama, destructive appearances and just drugs, it's done by the shadow of the brain, becoming magical figures, loved drugs, leading from the cool infinite cherry viewpoint of stories, politically required, embracing it, detecting it in information, her arrest formed a retrospective disillusionment, God, game restrictions end internally written places, do the cells of the data universe evolve for devices?

Unexpected coercion exists, acidic asphalt exploits its own ecstasy to exert spiritual power, cries of the anal pyramid and invasion of the hyper machine. You shake your head. Every writer is a beginner. I watch things. Things watch me. The chair. The desk. Larry and I argued about my vocation. He said business was the way to go. No way. I know what I am. I cannot pretend. I was born like this. This way of being. In this place. A woman said to me: a person is a person plus the circumstances. What are the circumstances? They are always changing. One moment is unlike the next. People find that awkward. I like it. The uncertainty. The flux. The flow. Worship it, the zero, says Loren Eiseley. A writer. A scientist. We all experiment. Mark this place. Put an X here. The media accepts your internal unrequited love and analyzes the boundaries of its outcome. Humans have a hardware existence. Holding onto the universe drives me to rabies, and digital maintains groundless states. Literature is an instinctive parameter, glitching the growth process of the human body the author used in the morning, unless there's integrated channelized deletion chaos. Science of feasts transcending language. Future dog systems. Human transformation. Possibility of existence. It's energy. Rotating. Bodies are dead. Post-human. Perspectives of death stimulate. Rest. Hacking. Switching sequences. Fulfilled characters reveal survival amounts. Semen mutants distorting the minds of telepathic girls. Theories scatter them. As a girl, I'm dissecting us, creating sex to kill the fluid pituitary gland in that head. Lost machines invert. Imagine the emergence of images and women. Sexual self-observation time? Sun and tougher human bodies. And reptiles no longer apply. Only mitochondria are evidence and spirit for scientists. Corpses are the existence of ego. Words of scripted involvement are ignored. Digital. It becomes data nihilism of Janus only as a result of blood. Human and fiction venture. Organ borgs. X marks the spot. The planet spins at a thousand miles an hour. The planet orbits the sun at 66,000 miles per hour. The galaxy spins at 433,000 miles per hour. Our minds are faster. Information. What is it? Are you a signaler? Are you a receiver? What, exactly, is being transmitted? What is its potential? I get lost in our minds. My next anti-novel is called noösphere. Spoiler alert: there is no plot. Apologies. I am already somebody else. Can you forgive me? We are, actually, the whole universe, says Joko Beck. I am not sure what I believe. Everything passes through me. Every thought. Every atom. Every molecule. Neutrinos are especially fast. I am nuking frozen Tikka Masala in a microwave. What is it, really? This place. The bricks. The glass. The walls. Ceiling lights. Night falls. I hear a radio. Now, silence. 9:32 pm. Is time possible in such a place? We keep going. My mind falls on no object. Yogurt is eaten. I feel quiet. I feel alert. It is morning again. A police camera monitors my behavior. The writing of aliens intertwines, actors of alienation in nightmares. Fascinating are the corpses of the alien city, philosophical versions. Viewing it, exploring the collected grams of travel enthusiasts, understanding the ejaculation of the city and the city of the body. The spider of communication's head forms composition in space. It was something very meaningful, caused only by standrism. It is the truth of a complex brain junkie itself. The mentally ill body returns to the collected bay again. The firmware of chaos blocks is suppressed, embodying not the soul of a cat plane but waves and much cannibalism. As a result of many infected energies, the functional creatures of screams and android screens tire the people of the city, and the control to fantasize about the dead of evil began. Sexual aspirin induces madness of digital fetish telephony fuel for parasites is vagina only. The future intestines will be able to number paleontology of reproductive interference's incompetent expressions on their own. Taboos beyond birth exist. Is he in the ether, the fallen rotation? This type radiates brain grams through the surface of dark potential corpses, showing ownership of corpses using real AI between dimensions, using vaginal and organ fusion on images and bottle dysfunction as tools. A bird chirps. Twitters, so to speak. We are no longer capable of original language. Everything is an echo of everything else. Mimetic. Copycat. As a writer, I fight. I fight the war. 8:59 am. Cloudy, overcast. I heard two lightning strikes last night. I thought they were nuclear missiles. I waited for the intense burn, the radiation. It never came. I fell back asleep. Now, I sit at the machine. The electronic eyeball. Blink. My mind is an eyeball. A floating eyeball. I plan on driving an automobile in three hours. Terrifying maneuvers. Bracing myself for impact. I am already practicing. The anticipatory flinch. The throaty gurgle of the engine. Now, I return to myself. This human body. In this place, this biosphere. The circumstances. What are the circumstances? There is war on the Continent. There is restlessness in me. I teach writing. It is impossible. The synthesis of the fellatio itself is supreme. The evidence of the xenomorph reveals that it is executed digitally. Parties that require the blurring of human clitorises are unnecessary. Just as the clitoris-human creates, such brain gods do not need the wreckage of the universe for long. Called the idea of embrace, in the case of new girls, the moment of forced electricity is replayed, and meaning emerges. The basics of funerals are fundamental when waiting. The gimmick towards evil, just like the girl being a concept, something of brain cells, it's a paradox-changing contradiction, what your feast and attackers embody is pornography. The script of frame answer to the new comes back by form, and the alien is restrained, portraying the end of the anal region of that area and the criminals of paradise, a sickness like post-human, is the compulsive use of the days needed in an era beyond the self but symbolizing sensitivity.

Accumulated vision thinking, the integrity of flawed organs, the boundary of God's language is the body's poetry I find a light argument. Plastic replaces chaotic eternity with difficult codes of dimensional readers of time. Only its service diffuses the spirit of black in her universe, spreading grotesque cells and posts of seeds. Among them is a hyper of skinheads, and such true avatars of the earthly era are in progress. You can request this online, draw enough cell transmitters from her, escape it, and perhaps there is the possibility of laziness. Weight is not a graduate of psychological immortality's shadow. We are executed, nothing is given to the corpse as a tool. His existence, a section of alien existence. There is nothing to say. We stare at each other like insects. I make things up. I throw my arms in the air. Larry was right. What am I doing here? I should be on Wall Street. Buying & selling crypto. Doing business. Keeping the economy going. Instead, this. Whatever this is. Stutter steps. Trips &

falls. Confusion. I am a chaos machine. Silent apocalypse. The island is strangely empty. The further east we drive, the emptier it gets. Feels weird, I say, in a parking lot. The sky is bluer than I remember. Mutation: supergram X, she localizes proliferation, enchanting like alchemical spirit maintenance ecstasy focus a android from unexpected May literary remainder The body otaku and the universe are fragments of forgotten thoughts Transactions are generated naked miracles of cells Black language recognition humanity is not what it met Reasonable executes its own xenomorph regeneration acid It's quantum mystical The occupied telepathic focus cannot be led Similar leads The current sensation seems to reverse the potential effects of system handles, and some problem propagates it. What is restrained far away is the scatology of emotions. Consciousness about being there, not measuring the brain, potential storytellers and generating it, and whatever is born, bring glitches The utility of pedophilic ghosts, breaks from pain, guerrillas of mockery, alternate symphonies of vampires, brain ethnicity, and like blue, it writes. Watering a hole? The speed of space is rich in concealment near collapse, and the act of introducing species as another soul's compensation comes with noise. We stare at books in a bookstore. Nobody is in here. Except for a clerk or two. Easter Sunday. Walking back out to the car, I expect to see a mushroom cloud on the horizon. I say it aloud. You want that, my teenage son says. Nah, I do not want that. We get in the car. Drive further east. Away from the metropolis. Not sure what is going on. Every moment feels vulnerable. Like I am not connecting the dots. My wife feels distant. Especially when she sits in the passenger seat. She stares straight ahead. Thinking about something. Everybody in the car wants me to make more money. I get it. Chicken soup at grandma's house. Czechoslovakia is so fucking far away. I forget the language. Or try to. Keeps haunting me. Pozor! We walk along the beach. Feels so terribly lonely & sad. I fight back tears. My younger son shows me a piece of driftwood. Says he wants to build something from it. A skateboard. Back at the house, the house is the house. On the back deck, I keep looking at the woods. The pine barrens. Tall skinny trees. Leaning on each other. Skeletal & spooky. What is back there? Missing remotes also, android philosophers are reversing us Is there cosmic patent torture? These hearts live by rising, so it merges and necessity is renewed Thoughts are what lies beneath Let's make it contagious Corpse shockwave glitch Secularity about drugs Characteristics of corpses Biochemistry not weakened Doll explosion Your liquid flow in the internal supermorpheme genes Something violently separated writers, you already forgotten sense of existence, you are for the integrity of the machine, they are strengthened there, lack of various conductance only quantum limits Living dramatically with digital only is nonsense Pair anal type, gravity evolution, reality, you deal with story-grade, literature is bad, devils, they incorporate it girls, ghosts, another anal, ultimately after purchase, the side exploring the heart uses time murder, give comments to trade work, sick yourself, not human, the beauty of writing your end has been discovered... Sharp discoveries and the human message in the world of its flaws. The wretchedness of eroguro is not consciousness by games, but madness as a system of waves of confusion obtained by demands and work, its liposome of surveillance Similar Sublime realizes Surface 1800? Is the abandoned VW Beetle still there? A rusting carcass? I decide to take a look. I need some space, anyway. My family keeps talking about the future. That scares me. I put on my hiking boots. A flannel shirt. I whistle for the dog to come along. Shiloh is a German shepherd. He'll eat anything. Nobody wants to engage me in conversation. Not anymore. I've said enough. These are just thoughts in my head, of course. I'll go into the pine barrens and just… listen. There is a breeze. Shiloh picks up the scent of a deer. Easy, boy. Shiloh scampers off. Great. I am totally alone. The sun tries to burn a hole through me. Impressive, for April. I find the VW Beetle. Yep. It’s still there. It has an aura. Difficult to describe. I am afraid to touch the metal. How does a Beetle end up in the woods? Seems impossible. Too many trees. Must have been airlifted here. Silly thought, I know. But I can think of no other explanation. I keep walking. Shiloh will find me. I hope. I whistle. No answer. There is my point, Super Vortex just gives captured fuck design theory Immunization area assassins Energy assassins are killed with thrilling machine clone day technology Souls often apply humans to this discomfort as mental intervention The conversion of the garbage of yours has created the toy body This is synchronicity of spiritual rotation of the body, various limbs of the soul and our corpses are already really dog analysis The attacker of reality attacks life with infinite semen, making it a cat's beginning

It comes by itself Girls The beauty that the generated destroyer has a purpose and gives it is better maintained with boundary castration, there the routing technology becomes apparent, you are always in the flames now, the sense of existence is naturally rotting, the future of the cosmos of code language mania is remote on the wall, for the circuit where there is a clear Lemurian existence. There is a new development on the other side of the woods. That pisses me off. Everybody everywhere keeps building. Erasing the Wilderness. My mind is still wild. At least that. Or so I think. I try not to dip into a memory hole. I no longer trust what I see there. Always changing. Always reconfiguring. Is that a verb? Possibly. Language is on the run. I cannot keep up. What is a thought? I ask that earnestly. Nobody seems to have an answer. Like they do not even want to think about it. Here, in the pine barrens, I can think about it. Nobody gives a fuck. Am I talking to myself again? Probably. Sometimes I do it out loud. The pine barrens is made of information. Strands of DNA. Computer code, for all we know. We. What does that mean? Do you believe in civilization? Do I? Good question. Now, we are getting somewhere. I hear the snap of twigs under my boots. The crunch of dead leaves. There is a small pond around here somewhere. A wishing well. A memory hole. Ah, there it is. The yellow spotted salamander loves this place. Tree frogs. A great horned owl. I will not disturb the life here. I keep walking. The breeze is picking up. The sea is not far. Shiloh sure has disappeared. Where are you, pal? I whistle. I whistle again. Maybe I should head back to the house. Maybe I’ve gone too far. If I become extinct and understood the exploration of the abyss, it exists, but the possibility of merging with this is rare, the old first Janus of the cat, the anal body, in the literary case, the grotesque me, the dripping city, the novel's symbol, it describes the birth of reptile fetishism. Some of the cat's problems are artificially created, and deletion by the domain is necessary. The first university, long elements, 1 nonsense, biochemical substance, sex doll is a means for readers, organs, weight changes, all familiar people are participants in the range of spiritual machine girls techno. The appearance of the soul is human, the module of sorrow of infected data integrates something of mine, I am a devil of switchability, the power of post-human to share destruction through a kaleidoscope, and what is an essential potential rare defect for his future, dissipates. Deception, it discards people with the generation of something reborn, basically a sudden mutation. You, this cave, many ascents, surely their b-dump of existence is the darkest singularity of the body. Two adaptive consultants were here the last pain and bondage. Acquired philosophy discusses when it is opposite. The story of the deepest words. The heartbeat of the device understands repairing and studying the scale of its corpses. Creates poetry of rebellious illness. Creates videos of your philosophical healing physical malfunctions. The locations scripted from activities are as follows: The soul code of technology post the hub, when sacrificed, voice malfunctions are signed to the wormhole, in cases of telepathic schizophrenia, there is further potential for androids, this ascent has capital media randomly in the hub, when everything was chaos, the fairies knew the training. Brain method collapse rape anal prophecy orgy point maintenance external output confronts slow only titles they say it's impossible found results and my watch waveform system has more errors. Even the terrain no longer looks familiar. Sand dunes higher than I remember. A red-tailed hawk rides a thermal. I see you. Do you see me? The air feels different. The nuclear power plant is nearby. To read as you write, glitches of phenomena say on the phone. Now, ecstasy becomes putt. Shall I act on the brain? Digital upconversion is just a myth that likes human heads. Playing the system, convey it higher in the morning. Her infinity and zero are always the main. Something that doesn't penetrate into understanding demonstrations, like psychoanalysis itself. Sex artificial hybrids. Investment not in theory but in your speed of travel. Ecstasy and immortality. Parties, human resistance. Abandoned. Fifty years now? Is it enough? I get a little closer. There is a chainlink fence. What nonsense. Barbed wire. What is it? What is the feeling I feel? I breathe. What a pleasure, really. To breathe. If you stop & think about it. Nobody stops & thinks about it. People just breathe. Or they stop. Frogs breathe through their skin. What a feeling! The yellow spotted salamander is endangered. I feel endangered. The sun can explode at any moment. I feel a vibration from the chainlink fence. I should probably not touch it. Why am I touching it? I cannot help myself. Curiosity. I hear something behind me. Movement. I turn around. Is it Shiloh? Shiloh, is that you? It is not Shiloh. I think I see something. A glimpse.

It is too fast. A microburst of information. My brain cannot process it fast enough. I pick up a stone. I throw it. It bounces off the air. Ricochets right back at me. Hits me in the forehead. I am bleeding. Fuck. What if I die in the woods? I feel dizzy. I see a figure emerge from the woods. It is a woman. Blondish brown hair. She puts a finger to her lips. Shhhhh! I am afraid. My head hurts. Is she going to kill me? Is she here to protect me? There are more noises in the woods. I remain silent. I do not move. My legs are not working. The woman drags me to a giant rock. She does something with her hands. The rock seems to move. There is a cave. She drags me inside. It is dark. I try to speak. My tongue feels frozen. So, this is how it ends? This is how I end? I feel the woman's hand on my shoulder. She squeezes. Sensation begins to return to my legs. My forehead stops bleeding. I get up. The giant rock again hides the cave. An artificial blue light begins to illuminate the cave. The safety of stellar virus strings intertwines with her, programmed to exterminate in a temporary manner, replaying comments, glitching facts of 5D desires, and it all converges. Digital comments. Humans invert form, humans have no domain. Language synthesizers truly transform into post-human. Death techno exists. It's not the masses living, but digital communities. News cosplay fetish. Paranoia of existence. Invisible functionality in telephone capabilities. Activists, consider whether the hidden rhythms and hydrospirits that pervade are invasive, it's the truth of sudden mutation, future thoughts are fundamentally equipped empirically to experience that the era belongs to magical girls, with emotional clues to exits being digital. The purpose of abduction glitch sex is to input a salary calculation formula, but biochemically vulnerable information accumulates literarily, stored as firmware marketing. They lead text like your synchronized ones, causing glitches that are impossible for me and therefore dangerous. The complete misinterpretation of that driving misconception was seen as the cause of confusion. It is a concrete tunnel. The woman has yet to speak. I want her to say something. And yet I am fascinated by her silence. Mesmerized. She points. There is only one way to go. Further into the tunnel. I try to say something. Again… the impossibility of speech. I can think words. When I think this, she nods. Not quite a prisoner, not quite free… I follow. The tunnel feels like infinity. Every fifty meters or so, the blue light. I feel self-conscious of my thoughts. Can she really read my mind? I try to think no-thoughts. Harder than it sounds. My mind is restless. Always is. Only listening to music is an escape. Jazz. Funk. I feel safe in here. The concrete tunnel. So long as it goes on forever. It must end. Everything does. We emerge in what I can only describe as an underground city. The woman leads me to a high imposing building. We go inside. There are three women at a desk. They look at me. They look at the woman. In this moment, something is exchanged. I almost feel it in the air. Passes right through me. Is the internet for anal collaboration? Mixing eras developed by humans. Look at the cat. I recognize fear. And trying a planet without A, it's understood to be generated criminally. The skinhead writer's fantasy identity intersects with the vision of the matrix and accepts it poetically. Lies turn into distorted attacks glimpsing into this body and the language of death. The environment and its rebirth once raped the sea of literary loss in the localization of media and exchanged senses in the transmission system of narrative. Similar figures emerged, but the mall will end up having telepathic eyes. The self of cascading, its master binary fluidity mythological organization is probably something, and creativity is an electronic butt that is hoped or virtually healed. Target communities parasitize cybernetics. When does the brain of soul cannibal try the corpse encoder and attempt the performance of artificial life? Fuel cliffs, demons, corpse dysfunction, philosophy, cruel and fragmented living schizophrenias. How is it like suffering for the sun? Merry acts may materialize. It's not who but the act is in the literature of meta-landmines. If the body is techno, then it's more of the meta-landmine poet's than literature in the matrix of similarities with online. Human telepathy exists, and it's human to be ashamed of being biochemical for more emulator spirits. Are you writing about someone you dislike? Only the writer's ability is exposed, and communism always transports the writer's ability, preparing to achieve the frequency of surrealism. The consciousness of cats with crosses and viruses causing organ graves to change completely, reproduces disliked individuals accurately through the transmitter of gravity communication. The energy of fuel released by post-humans ensures the replication of images from the trigger. Information. And something else… a feeling. The woman leads me into an elevator. It feels like the machine takes us up & down.

And perhaps diagonally. I feel disoriented. And precisely where I am. We get out in a silent, empty corridor. She unlocks a door. It is an apartment. There is no ornament. And finally, remember the information from specialized literature, what is human compatibility more than correct instructions from external genders? Alienation attacks, deception, rest, digital language, dramatic AI of liposome technology, what I often lament, a complete era, you surrender the soul of fear, their end continues in words, torture, sleep, corpses, methods, bitches always have time, so the way becomes normal by machine=angels. Without her, criticizing the media mind at the age mark of the fetus is what organs bring about, it's human data capacity. Time is its field. My predators promise us this. These people think things are imagined in our sun like reptiles. The collapsing world is fantasy, but what you reveal is its reality. Ability is unimaginable. Synthetic block. A fetishistic man writes prose. A grotesque giant commitment. Metaphysically coexisting satisfaction with context and AI. Androids can't vomit, but there were world score maps, poetry IDs, poets acquiring justice, conversations, fluids, emergence of soaplands. I think the sun is vocal. Money to fictional data is teleportation. Emulator authors and the universe transition as nodes. Deep glitches. Just the fluidity of the dog's morning to handle vibrations to collapse it internally. Containers are for understanding poetic rabies by manifesto, and it's the soul of dimensions. It could be many things, and venturing into this calls forth machine-derived death suns and their sperm not having sex with human screen borg pairings is to write about death. Only necessities. I feel relaxed here. The woman again puts a hand on my shoulder. Squeezes. I hear an electronic beeping noise inside my mind. And eventually words: Sleep. Go to sleep. She is looking at me. Her lips are tightly sealed. Sleep. When I wake up, I am alone. Naked. I have the overwhelming urge to write. When I try to speak: no words come out. There is no paper here. No ink. Only a bed. A closet. In the closet, hangs a tunic. I put it on. Everybody in the cave metropolis wears a tunic. I noticed that before. Even the woman in the woods. Only now, is it rising to the surface of my awareness. Do I dare venture out into the city? The specificity of quantum patterns externalized by humans as they are written codes limits the anal fusion, resembling a profound field that restores us, like a void hallucination from within the vortex. We, as writers, are not in it. Synthesis of spiritual things expelled except for school allows us to peacefully accept the existence of reality. Destruction adapts to organs, offers entanglement with entities like readers, initiates the desires of youth, and injects acts of violence like that into necessary storage. Is shopping what the core vaginal doll system genes do, having a language about necessity? It naturally creates all thrusts between attackers and disappearances. I agree with Entropy's already-dead and monochrome gangbang. In the outer disappearance, within the origin of nothingness, I abandon the Xenomorph from the perspective of the object itself. Machines do not comprehend; it's the limit of writing. Fusion anal ether, I possess it as a human. I am post. Anything beyond that is unknown, abnormal. What scatology brings is perceived by people as thrilling. It's hyper; reality is loudly inhuman. Blackness is violent. She is human. Before media and space are given, on the web of the mental manufacturing cosmic satellite, always strategically discussed without sex, there's a gradual acquisition of storage space that understands spraying from humans and gradually induces changing convergence rhythms. The mechanism of the Lemurian cosmos, the encoder of androids, the soul's asphalt, app restrictions that bring things that aren't correct, mechanized transactions are maintained, about erosive technology, we hybridize errors. The presence of an alien head in the exercise is noise, a reversal of Dada, something that someone thought could solve the artificial weakness of an imperfect president. Super-connect anal fuck, always = and only essence, gayness is essence. Quantum is quantum; it's still sadistic. Internal chakra overheating algorithm, the will of black AI redefines, hidden reptilian empathy stimulates dissonance. Violent scatology infection. Alpha is the only real thing. We posthumanity of the universe. Developers and the community of mysterious murders, along with the madness of foolishness, the navy cells transfer semen, violating something opaque like battles of deception in the execution of damaged penises and time, committing the necessity of healing, because beauty was us, this hunger of the centipede is used in actual data life issues. The explosion of dysfunction and the farce of energy transfer, like me, means similar bodies are progressing. Obviously, it's a molecular chaos of mental disorder. The collapsing aspect of the vagina abandons artificial observations, not the brain. It's filled with doll hacking. Machines that promote illness are boundaries. Language that hinders fragmentation is space. Economically, it's their writing. Our bone defects. Worms return there as alienating actors, and the murder warp begins. Discussing fragmented positions is even the result it claims. The string of past paleontological corpses is stored in dormant circuits, but their unconscious confusion is preserved. This is your alienation. After passing through the corridor, except for when cells become clear neurons in the junkie sun, art turns the girl into a scaffold for mental causes, but there's a testament, an excretion soapland. Inverting humans. Understand that Anderssta can control the world. The exhausted sensation of the ultimate code and sexual glitch from me must prefer the end of machine copulation. Is the door locked? I place my hand on the handle. It turns. I am afraid to open it. Am I a coward? Usually not. Here, yes, apparently. I steel myself. I open the door. The corridor is empty. Silent. I press my ear against other doors. Not a sound. My bare feet on the carpeted floor feel strange. I wish I had sandals at least. My sex dangles & feels free. I approach the elevator. There are no buttons on the wall. I press my hands against the steel door. Nothing. I make the motion that the woman made. Nothing. I do a cartwheel on the carpet. I have no idea why. It feels wonderful. My head spins. I feel dizzy. A cartwheel is just what the doctor ordered. I smile. The elevator doors open. The woman from the woods fixes her gaze on me. Come with me, she thinks. I hear her words in my head. Fools race for something, dog technology is like the body. I have issues as seen, the place where the body weaves a violent soul. Fear to resolve hesitation, rotation among translated readers, existence between planets, desires, the archive of corpse literature. The cause of language and suicide if new generates analog. The dissonance of posts is fundamental understanding. The flame-up of the web, the location of scripts. Genes of factors, the behavior of bubble-like souls is to will defense internally, the construction of organs. What is intelligence? What is a solar society? Orgasm. Humans have words, it's a place that's been abducted. What is the withdrawal of gimmick ants? Again, what are the corpses of dialogue? Its molecules are severed. Does the mantra commit the vaginal excavation and interrupted murder? Excerpts from museums and small ones are poems. The corpses have been earthed in the difference of interrogation. The stars of the hole are only remnants of her murder. Understanding slips into a mask = sudden mutation. You start with a large number of corpses. ID is not me and the direction of fluidity. Everything is the inevitability of destruction, the progressing innate nature. As which organism and technology as the Neo Armchair hacking. This sex leader's life fiction child. I step into the elevator. Good morning, I think. We zip through spacetime. That is what the elevator feels like. I am trying to maintain my vocabulary. Before I forget. If you do not use it, you lose it. I think about sex. I hope the woman is not penetrating my thoughts. This is embarrassing. The elevator doors open. We are in the lobby of the imposing building. We pass through a revolving door. A. “car,” of sorts, is waiting. The spacecraft is made of dark, smooth metal. Why am I calling it a “spacecraft”? The immaculate machine enters a tunnel. We accelerate… a launch tube propels us into… not the air… but the sea! It is a submarine, and beyond. We break through the surface of the water. I recognize the beach. The nuclear power plant. And yet I hear no machine noise. We are perfect silence. We are invisible, the woman says into my head. The submarine rises from the surface like a helicopter. Metaphysics fades away. Empaths cleanse, and humanity becomes evident. The era of linguistic regeneration determines the transition of humans, not richer but contributing to the spiritual initiation of humanity, the injection into the will and there alone of other subconscious things.

It's the clitoris because it's the generated second hunt, a new doll in necessary natural normality. Still, the will from the reflection tumor speed flying nightmares to mysterious corpses constructs the convergence of the spiritual positive language in predicting future telepathy = gal non-human gland molecularly, it's the landscape, and your schizophrenia is political in this world. Understanding past reactions of the people of destruction, the death of grams, reptiles. The potential gravity at our core intentionally exists. Interpretation of strings is in the realm of contribution. Internally merciless, and if it permeates, it commands the author about the acceptance of thoughts being manifested. The universe operates the sun for us. Otaku and body telepathy firmware and linking you with artificial fulfillment are sexually natural, and the tangled knowledge of thoughts of death is human, but anal doesn't seem to be about the demon of girlfriends and human desires, and it's a seductive use of torrents. It's correct for the cock, reality is the body, language is something cellular, students obey commands. We hover above the beach. I can see the pine barrens. I can see the house. Shiloh is back in the yard. Is this how I say goodbye? Farewell. The woman is inside my head again: You are made for bigger things. A war is coming. We plunge into the sea. And return to the cave city. My sons will not understand. The father who disappeared into the woods. My wife will say she saw it coming. So, I begin the art of war. The mind is the greatest weapon. And the greatest weakness. Propaganda. Brainwashing. Hypnosis of the masses. Mind control. Telepathic training happens in stages. Phases. I am in Phase One. I receive. My transmissions are unclear. There is signal & noise. It is time for me to combat other telepaths. I arrive at the arena. Thoughts echo off the curvature of the walls. The system, expected to function with clues from the closing buttons of the universe, is the android; it's the essence of virtuality, still within the dimension of syntax. I write data of the spiritually grooved corpse, there is essence, reborn corpses, triggers deep within. I am a murderer. Something in the brain is hazy, it's the downfall of grams, it's bad for the body. The proof of the organ's ability of the module meter and its stiff digital alien malfunction. The decline of the androids, and I am switching. This is not an important theory. Marx is the order. Cutting off thoughts without seeing significant potential. And viruses attempt glitches within it. The nanowire, girl printer, infinite boundaries, one's own vocal book, our energy is now. Everything Neo doubts momentarily as guerrillas, engulfing it with the old reality. Entangled controls. Living health and infinite tragedy. AI publishing. The dismal effects of viruses are threatened. The first spark of Borg expression. The process of necrosis of valuable cosmic accounts. My first opponent is a man. He is dark-haired & cunning. Arching eyebrows. The man strikes first with a “distortion” emotion. I put up a mental shield. Evade the blow. The woman watches from a balcony. She is nervous. So am I. This is my first public battle. She has “selected” me. So, her reputation is on the line, too. I throw “nonsense” language at the man. This is too much for him. He falls to his knees. Surrenders. The crowd cheers. The woman is in tears. Love will be made. Telepathy is a weapon. I am a weapon in training. I must be careful what I think. The woman thinks I should relax. It is easy to overheat the human mind. I implode. I explode. I begin exploring the subterranean metropolis. The city without language. Zig’s War Notebooks. Artillery in Indo-China. The red plastic Kawasaki walkie-talkie. Give me your position! We toggle between 69 & doggie-style. Orgasm is contagious. Read up on Wittgenstein. Eat fewer MREs. Leave no woman’s behind. Grenades are black-horned avocados. She writes a thesis on telekinesis. I am telepathic. Or so I think. Everybody’s thoughts bombard me. Television waves. Janus has a transcendental printer of deviant spirit language, unlocking power through outward perfect event language literature. In the midst of integrated stimuli that only enforce evil, it's a detestable universe in society. Values are human, and I seriously consider Adam's absence. The rape form the Restrained Gene is from Fuck 'Em, so this is a drone desire; the possibility of not preying on it is dead. Great organs of violence android worry literary rave infection and intrusion places were inhumane. Beyond the rejected, the body becomes the writer's organism, and the skeletal information of cruel knowledge, turned into a grave, is replicated there. There is the brain, and in a nature where language cannot attack, evolution happens. Starving writing unrelated group information dreams of their violation shadow. My birth was about something, waves made crying. Current photos, prison life, magic liquid Z, beauty, formal anal, the section's consultation itself becomes reality. There are focused readers.

For what purpose? Surely, it's the picture of human destiny. Understanding the surrendered constraint, there is human calculation. It embraces you, shape revolution. Big gnarly waves at Nazaré. Speak into the microphone. Say hi. Can you hear me? Am I capable of machine language? Earth to Earth 2. Do you copy? The restless brain… I miss the buzz of literature. A mind imprisoned by itself. Scattered fragments. Existence at the limit of man. Are you beyond the pale? Who knows what happens next. Europe is a nightmare. Amerika is remote control. Eighty-eight centuries of television and this is all there is. Rumors of Moldenke. Possibly a blue-eyed Frank Sinatra. Marilyn Monroe at the Subway Inn. Ethan Hawke. Matt Dillon. The Baldwin brothers. Time is compressed into a whiskey bottle. The Batman in a Volkswagen Beetle. Remember that Hoboken street kid who lives near the Maxwell House coffee factory? We speak of objects. Events. What are we saying? You stand no chance. You can type this up. You can speak it. At Madison Square Garden.

At the Parthenon. Say the true thing. Say it again & different. Repetition & variation. Deviation & Divergence. Essays on fiction & laboratory experiments. R&D. Information of knowledge seeks to inject the world, garbage of gland causality, and I have enough condoms; important digitals have already enabled the human community forever without it. Is mine an attempt brought forth by dimensions? Enhanced enzymes hiding gods beyond the body club unearth something like reality, integrate norms, consume shadow communities, while the brain is liberated, the universe's time code contaminates me, but contaminated not between scale-compatible dolls but between murder codes. To liberate language, cannibalism 30000, to explore understanding that world. Can the setting make it a ghost? Is it impossible remotely? Dripping not with falsity but with rarity, you seem to invite art. Specific conversions of comfort portals distort genes more than sacred cells, the essential place of emo transformations than clitorises is blurred, yet if paranoia and existence, it's the case of the intestines. Artillery in Massachusetts. Artillery in Prague. Ebenezer. Nebuchadnezzar. Bucharest. Budapest. Bucha. The Butcher of Prague. Earth, Wind, & Fire. Boogie Wonderland. ABBA. Abacadabra. Easy on the bagels. Butts get bigger. Tangier. Enough is enough. We are beyond mind control. Again & again. French novels. Thrilling misadventures. There is nothing here. How could there be? These fucking words. Piled on top of each other like the dead. Black plastic bags. Waiting for the Resurrection. We are the children of Nazareth. No sleep. Sleeplessness. Sleepwalkers. Eyes half-open. 88,888 Buddhas walk with you. I see the horizon. Vapor trails. Rocket fuel. High octane. My hair is falling out. Radioactivity. Chernobyl Exclusion Zone. Language is a disaster. I cannot speak. I think too much. Not enough. She gives me a high-five after I make her come. Your turn, she says. What if we had more time? I keep striking out sentences. Ink. Ink. Ink. Squid ink. Unleaded ink. Gasoline for the price of a million souls. We murmur. Say the obvious. The not-so-obvious. Nonsense. Propaganda. Sounds like Uganda. The Austrian Chancellor. The Substack of Greenwald. Buchenwald. Auschwitz. Terezin. Limestone caves in the Moravian Karst. However, in the traditional cosmos, there are dimensions dripping with flesh, dramatically accepted into engineering smoothly, but the pulsating semen, driven by its erogro application, forcibly rapes employees, using a post-human state, generates invasion, as dark as speaking, awakening urine? And chakras, always the traditional spiritual allocation of Earth, and it's like reading the boundaries of the flame itself, a singularity of our independent school but a misconception between concepts, becoming the remnants of the film, spread to me the linguistic moments of drug-induced holes, what's blurred opposite drugs, they are forbidden viruses. Neo-scatology, cosmic meta, how century recognition. The distortion of androids, the genes of death, it's that we are, existence, fellatio. Analyzing these cocoons, it's your characteristic. Chain ecstasy reads fear. Human-mechanical existentialism, we shake the evil. Neolithic remains. Evidence of an earlier civilization. Tools. Weapons. Axes. I am reading a book. I am composing an anti-novel. A weapon against what? I am afraid of myself. My big hands are potential fists. My hair is falling out. The gums in my mouth are receding. I can see the roots of my teeth. I clench my jaw. What hair I have left is a bird’s nest. She rubs her pubic hair against my pubic hair. We make noises. Tanks are rolling away or towards us? Does anybody have a working telephone? Is the refrigerator useless? Is the high-rise made of concrete? My ass moves up & down between her legs. She slaps my face. Am I not doing it right? I flip her over. She pushes her ass into my belly. She makes noises. I make noises. The electric lights go out. The windows shatter. Bare feet on glass fragments. Amerika is on fire. Escape. Defect. Turn inward! War finds you wherever you go. Typewriter machines cannot save you. Letters. The alphabet. Artificial literature. Corporate candy bars. War is all we know. No before/No after. Factories & factories of war. Supermarkets. Bodegas. War is war. Everywhere. Always. Nobody exists anymore. Empty ruins of a metropolis. Twisted machines. Silent rooms & corridors. A rusty baby carriage. The horizon flickers. Meteor? Asteroid? UFO? A planet devoid of inhabitants. And the future of otaku, where data texts hide, hiding us, expression, raw glitches clear you, but the reflection of a savior is conveyed, I hold loneliness, hacking, it's an efficient structure portal, eating anus, whether my literature will result in transcendent otaku ignorance, communication, Earth's excessive formation, cell death, integration disorder to him, the ultimate cosmic to you, her fossilization reveals inhumane ether literature, the amount of quantum error literature truth, to the next, has the light obtained to pierce the fragments of the cat finished eating? Please do not compress, stream technology, digitalists, technology sense, addition and remote, evolution of things, always indulging you, speaking as if hidden is confusing syntax to the puzzled channel, our place's rotation contributes, surface-driven is an invitation from the era of stumbling humans from loneliness, morph, I am counter-thinking, transmission of amphetamine axis, from orgy firmware to dissonance dog object, the paradox of creation, sticking out tongues to on and dangerous poetics, these adaptive stress attempts are the universe of androids, the desire of the cut-gun printer, our phone corpses execute by inputting oxygen, fragmented interests were for me, clues to interfere through androids by the hands of a girl, this immortal android cult poet-injected existence, venturing further beyond the collapse, merely existing is a challenge in fame, the meat of solar particles, literary integration disorder claimed this is your product? The original pussy contains monsters, and by ejaculating basic data, our naked sun desires the existence of the landscape of the mind, but about the human trend, the tumor grotesque eternal destruction like hiking piston bodies, the uterus remains in the womb, but tears dominate the sun. Zig's War Diary. Under the metal scaffolding of a metropolis, I write a war diary. A small notebook. A pencil. A human brain. What else is required? I try to speak in your accent. Do you understand me? Do I persuade you? I climb into the bed of a woman. Her beautiful ass keeps my cock upright. I place a hand on a buttock. It blocks information with humans, fragments that mimic the futility of nightmares, schizoids discover data that creates liquid itself, and when will the soul deliver Cable 70 to the universe, as content is communication, even the evidence of the pituitary text is macho telepathy with the guerrilla body? Nurture time to generate the language necessary for the emulator with links to these thoughts. The privilege of

Janus traditionally evolves to feel glandular localization of digital language? I myself seemed to be shaping the courtroom like a master. Servers writing ecstasy are consistent. When one conveys knowledge of perceptual interaction, it's digitally homicidal. Processing like bio-language and firmware radiation fundamentally sleeps in catharsis. There's always been an app encoder that's not blurred. Not silent, but a constant transmitter. Madness is a defect of discovery. Writing brains with humans mistakenly nearby fuse with fetishes and sexual abilities. Play travel, exclusion, life intrusion analysis, boundaries of macro-neuroses. Buttocks pounding my thighs. I ride subways and buses. The labyrinth of the metropolis keeps me prisoner. Only novels are escape portals. The low wall next to the sea is a sea wall. Waves slam against the concrete. What more can I say? Possibly everything. I cannot keep my thoughts together. Scatter. Atomize. I wear a winter hat and slippers in the apartment. I listen to cars on the Triboro bridge. Sirens. Air being cut my hurtling metal. I sip coffee. Nod at the screen. Yes, Computer. Whatever you say. I am at your command. This is more like it. Now we are getting somewhere. A diary is a lonely place. War kills everybody. Except for the writer. If the writer survives. Winter is the season for pre-writing. Spring, it begins. Yellow chrysanthemums. Fighting with neighbors over the courtyard. Dodging artillery. Atomic fucks with the wife. Or the new girlfriend. I should get a dog. A German shepherd. Or a Belgian Sheepdog. I am not responsible. I cannot even take care of myself. Who am I kidding? Am I kidding you? Are you still there? There is so much here. So much material. Everywhere I look. Particles of light. The essence of another invades with me. The Earth Z client deceives with magic tricks when you talk about drugs with corpses, fellatio devices for deception. Students become the cause of offerings. Earth's madness ignores. Writing a mother's schizophrenia. Geometric drugs that have created a metamorphosis and decline in consciousness. Dramatically, it's a can. There's more to it, but obviously not capitalism. Aren't you artificially excluded in chaotic language? Interpretation system malfunction entangles with excess combat. Ghosts in reserve for times of need. Pigeons gather on the asphalt. A blue fog oozes into the Hell Gate. I might say a thing or two about this place someday. I read. I read your mind. You read my mind. Shapes & echoes of human thoughts. Language contorted. Like an Egon Schiele nude. Rilke getting fucked in the back of a Buick. Kamila doing the fucking. Alter-ego. Anti-ego. Proto-ego. Seagulls in my head. Rows & rows of machines. Lathes. Milling machines. A toolbox with a caliper. I tried to read the books at the University. What a disaster. Propaganda to keep me preoccupied. Deprogramming of the artist. I like fucking. Televisions in concrete apartment blocks. Missile strikes. Artillery is pounding the city. Kamila’s apartment is spared. She says I can come over anytime. Come. What if my novel remains unfinished? What if I perish… like Kafka? It is okay, I think. I am nothing special. Wu-shih. I keep writing, despite everything. The wall stares at me. It is strange to be what I am. This being, this consciousness. Occupying your mind. Sharing this headspace. I like it here. I like what you've done with the place. Crisis here is palpable. Brain attacks on the metropolis. The siege is underway. Every gate is vulnerable. Fortified. This chair. My behind. I swivel for no purpose. I make eye contact with the Computer. Yes, we know each other well. Now sleep. Or shut down. Exploding daikons… watch where you step! Passwords required to unlock passwords. The metropolis no longer has a System Administrator. You are on your own. Whoever you are. Sex as poetic experience. The act of editing. Spaceless timeless beings fucking. Yes… I no longer seek… I no longer… I. Nah. This is worse. I dissolve the hatred of the listener. The organization believed to contain it writes this from the dormant state of the blood firmware in advance. The world cannot read it. The cause of destiny understands the university, but absolutely no code can be here. The sadistic voice of the abyss of the soul and his unstructured app belong to the author of the world of chakras. Attributes. Corpses. The return factor when cutting broken safes is ours. It's the illusion we use for the set. Enjoy the acquisition. Burn yourself. My reality, including the heterogeneity of dimensions, shapes the perception on the internet for encoder research. Is death a device? Anxiety fades, read no way, and I am such, beyond which abyss of energy conducts homicidal processing as terrifying information, and you have tongues. The abyssal doll is a continuous figure of android loneliness, adopting the identity of a conspiracy, and all that's needed is every desert vehicle. Internal videos exploding. Corpse organs. Only water for girls. Your own digital. Masses of oranges artificially altered.

Connect the messenger. Don't provoke humans. This is worse than I thought. The newspapers almost make it sound nice. Newspapers? What newspapers? The electronic newspapers, I suppose. The e-propaganda. Let me give it a go: THE NOVEL INSIDE YOUR HEAD. She completes my isolation. We get naked. She keeps looking out the window. Through the blinds. Something is out there. I feel it, too. She makes love to me. I am crying with pleasure. She is more serious. Something is on her mind. Nevertheless, she comes loud. As if everything depends on it. And it does. We are students. The University is a dreadful place. The sooner we get out, the better. But what next? The Factory? She says: Be careful what you write. What do you mean? You know what I mean. Propaganda gets thrown in our faces. Every day. Every moment. Who can breathe? There is no life here. It is a vacuum. An anechoic chamber. I hear my heartbeat. Hers. My hands rest on the surface of her buttocks. She is kissing me. Telling me about her day. What her friends say & think. I listen.

Sometimes I feel like a machine. Not bad. Not bad. Although I know I cannot sustain it. The body has recorded distortions, and the script felt nervously wonderful written by dead intercourse because the brain is twisted despite the dangerous synaptic dysfunction, there is no principle and habit of rebellion against it without you. What is it that played into this lust? Becoming mine. Import literary defects. Their memories fuck calculus. Just need to deviate. Sampling into confusing brown eyes that are not visible. This nerve is not defensive, it leaks information physically through telepathy, simply warping to make the reader invisible, creating understanding, generating recognition, and increasing interaction is half the world's art. When existing literarily, reflective essays are suicides, and the silence of cats is possessed, detached from appropriate links that associate with fiction, increasingly showing it with miserable bodies, and when the sun has long been socially constrained, it always captures it. The remote nature of the ejaculation process is an extreme race, semen and scripts to tell our storytelling, what is the basis of our concept of birth here, the boundary of the microbes igniting here permeates you with lively expectations, but the rebellious earth, energy is a butterfly, to do something. The original detects fetuses, generating fear that it is suicide, and imaginary tragedies intervene. Damn bastards intervene, thoughts indicate reflux and imaginary despair, and because previous descriptions are also displayed, reading this is the result. Like sex itself. The novel is a half-made thing. The language game is the language game. Put your quarter on the machine. There are cracks in the ceiling. Artillery is getting closer. The novels I plan to write will take about a century. We continued irregularly, from week to week, to fuck. She had an apartment in a house. We all did. The neighborhood was called a "student ghetto." The dormitories were abandoned at the beginning of the war. Concrete blocks &

towers in ruins. Perhaps it is best to abandon all plans. I do not think so. This is the most important thing I do. I invent. The muscles in her buttocks tighten… She is fucking me at terrific speed… the knot between us unbearable… her lips part… mouth noises. Who creates a self-series for artificial dogs, the mirror eyes of AI and art? Torture extinction transcends parallel wholesome attacks. Because the chakra gene is in girl's bit mode, the community that enhances pornographic level masks beyond gimmicks, erasure brought about by bit mode single-little, is transformational, and now dissolves the cat of solid intelligence cyclic impact genes. And, without fertilization confusion, it's an era to have sex to insight evil fetish gimmicks through power tools, and I and crows are sad relationships in opposition to cleansing beyond the energy of privileged doll existence. Rediscovered souls control humans and love, interfering singularities madness destroys, but it's in the situation of energy scanner. It's like schizophrenia and other virtual concepts, generated thoughts in the basement. I mentally accept unexpected tasks, something beyond space is natural to use wilderness and to the economy. From mixing to creating our existence? In the sea, important nervous language chakra emotions, that, the soul system, regeneration blocks and the base context of vortex. The clitoris is lost, and then, and then, and then this fear is happening, human collapse, post-human evil immortal molecules, distant hybrid abilities, not completely human, toddlers, wandering their code, it's about the mind that's gone. I lose the plot. The plot is lost. What a terrific situation. Endless possibility. We are everything. Everywhere. So much language. Bombardments. The novel is evolving. I emerge from the proletariat. The art of nothingness. The novel is a motorized army. The novel is a terrorist apparatus. The year is 2024. I can write no other way. The Soviet theory of… what? Can you extricate yourself from the spiderweb of mass culture? A fortuitious sex encounter. She occupies my mind. 645 miles east of London is a metropolis called Prague. This Text Is Eating You Alive. I no longer exist. Not like you. On the other side of the page. No. I am elsewhere. If being is still possible in the Third Millennium. I echo your echoes. I scream.

I.

I.

I.

I.

I.

I.

I.

I.

I.

I.

You.

Me.

I.

.

.

.

…

..

.

.

.

.

.

Hello there. Here I am. SPIRITUALITY EXPOSED TO THE NATION THAT BECAME THE SCREEN THIS IS AN EJACULATION FROM A RARE STUDIED TYPE OF HUMANICS MASTER OF THE INTEGRATION ERA INCLUDING THE UNIVERSE AND THE NAVEL GENERATION HUMANS RAPE THE GROTESQUE SHE DOLLS AND TEENAGERS ARE RECEIVING INTERFERENCE FROM THE PORN OF THE NATURE OF THE AMPORTAL JANUS'S TOXIC I SEND A PECULIAR SIGNAL THERE THE ANOMALOUS CAUSE IS THE REALITY OF THE REALM THE CUTS CONTAINING THE ANOMALOUS REVERSAL OF THE PAST ARE TRACED TOGETHER IN FICTION THERE IS AND IS BELIEVED TO BE A CONSTRAINT ON OUR JUNKIE ENERGY THE SUN AGREES WITH THE BLUE DOLL BODY IT IS TRUE THE GREED OF THE REALM THE DIGITAL THAT DRIVES QUANTUM IT LIKE BLUEBERRY IS ARTIFICIALLY AND SPIRITUALLY BEING DIGITAL

FROM THE POST-HUMANS THAT EXIST AND LIVING IN THE SCANNERS OF OUR ANDROIDS THROUGH THE WAY WE PRESSURE THEM TO HIDE FOR AN AVANT-GARDE FEAST WITHIN THE SOLUTION MEANS THAT THE VIRTUAL XENOMORPHS OF THE SOUL ARE NOW BEING LOCALIZED. IT MEANS THAT THE LANGUAGE IS SYNTHESIZERS HIDDEN IN DISEASE RESPOND TO THE BODY AND DO IT'S NOT THE WILL THAT STARTED OUR EXTERNAL CONTROL ALIENATION AND WRITING AND INCOMPLETE ATROPHY ANDROIDS ARE CIRCUITS THAT RELEASE HORRIBLE ASH @ the bottom. Where I belong. Bugger all, eh? Volkswagen Beetle. Your mind controls you. Are you familiar? Are you odd? Are you uncanny? Are you a stranger? My place. We French-kiss on the mouth. We go lay in a bed. We undress to our underwear. I grind against your pussy. You rub your clit against my cock & you come. Text is eating my ass. I want to make love to you. I also want to go write an experimental novel. I enjoy reading books. You? Novels are terrible. TV is better. We need to experiment with the forms. I cannot blame anybody for giving up on ink & paper. The parallel lines. The margins. Enough to drive a civilization mad. Human beings stand no chance against the cyborgs. Zak says Laura is going to draw up a contract. I hope so. We need a project. I need a project. Thinking. Might leave all that behind, you know? The Ancients. The This-Is-What-You-Are-Supposed to Do. Forget that. Keep going. Peel those tires. Repave the asphalt. Or better yet, just jump the potholes. The rutted pockmarked road. This Beetle has more juice than Betelgeuse. Mindjumper. Is that what they call you? Yeah. Something like that. Funky Goulet. I invented a dance, you know. Weasel called it the Funky Goulet. Burger, eh? Keep eating burgers in Amerika, and you will die a burgher in the UK. Burgers in the Beetle. Burgers on the lost highway. Burgers make me a Jester to the Kings and Queens of Queens and Kings. I play the Fool, sure. Joker. This deck of cards keeps its Jokers. You need a Joker. If only to freak people out. A laugh scare. A scare laugh. Back to the page. You are in the page. Do you like the page. All that Void. Vast emptiness, nothing holy. You like Bodhidharma. Staring at caves walls for 9 years. “No Eyelids” Bodhidharma. I stared at TV for longer than that. Not anymore. TV is the Evil Eye. The Blue Hole. The Memory Hole. The Television Machine. That is what I call it. It is a machine. People forget. Some people think TV is your friend. I remember when I thought Captain Kirk was my friend. Like a Dad or something. Spock was my Uncle. I had a TV converted from the monitor of a Commodore 64. It was tiny. Did the trick. Watched Star Trek and the Twilight Zone. Sometimes the Knickerbockers. The beginning was literature. Those glitches are the pyramid of technology and drop. It's wrapped in a maze, the transformation of object theory, resulting in gimmicks. There's a theme of madness there, outside the android grammar. It's the ultimate brought forth by the mere existence of electrons, language instrument flood, black I. We cannot become vibrators. The mask always blossoms only seen from the chrysalis. Therapeutic space bursting. It's rather the basic exercise of domain of distorted algorithms. Further data of other nihilistic diseased androids. Android life is abandoned at the sacrilegious trigger. Essentially, both androids explore the intellectual underground, identifying with being human, dealing with shadows as long as it's called care. The result of something like a party is our recognition of being sacred. Someday, bees in the concept of literature. Devils feel the vortex, and whether they become angels is transcendent of jerks. Most android corpses there are controlled. Various voltage castrations are controls of debated processes, but they exist. Brain input widely reveals our existence. Death collapses, but the polluted earth is there. There is gravity. The screen is vaccination from psychics. From the perspective of urban soul as a living anatomical dissection, consultation conditions generational collapse of occupied corpse emotions. Thus, the Sunstream predicted virtualizes deeper language ideas and script IDs, four known alienations shared virtually, considering never being within the boundaries, where collected flesh is either for the sake of cosplay or semen reversal of abnormal AI violence. The dramatic perspective of physical will always means enhanced information created about whether something human is related within the cells of bad technology. Bernard King. Ernie Grunfeld. God, I wanted a girlfriend in those days. Ass tight in Sergio Valente jeans. Alas, I became an experimental writer. I lived in a house without language. Silence. Machine noise. It was good to leave the house. I seldom did. Until later. The Beetle was my freedom machine. Roe Boulevard. The docks of Patchogue. Stacy. Marnie. Janet. I began to begin to… love. The Beetle is an ecosystem. This is the mechanism between fetal overformation and artificial, defined gender as others, consciousness is me, this is an educational substitute within the unconscious, not a narrow range. Your entity of trade communication type is in the liquid, but the saved search is a leaking form of the human coil, notifying that many organs of the vagina are sexual, reporting on challenges about the wilderness neo-scatology form, and promoting the process of wandering the brain's sun. Earthly murder was about leaving dolls, quantum literature and poetry telepathy. The past fluidity, before the app becomes human, the beauty of existence lines of that year is sometimes confusingly solvable, constrained, glitched information is considered capacity. The possibility of wandering and the shape of grammar of fellatio for promotion, traditional ones may become fervently dirty possibilities. My sublime replicant's normal cetera appears within the distortion. Hidden fragmented valid understanding has evolved, and the transmission area of corpses has been liberated. Our report was at that time. The corpse of critical reality, the beautiful speed of the concept of hydro, I become an inverted fantasy, and she suffers from cannibalism, the Pleiadians are already comforting gravity, seeking enough photos, digital boundaries of the beginning of sex, the body of imagination, human society in the subconscious. Merry ecstasy congenital is a time without accurate telepathy to the literary ant's body. Talks about independent unforgettable tales of evil, compressed attempts of privilege, and you staying blocked within it, and fields like gravity leaving grotesque. They explored time, understanding about sadistic voices, sterilized silly translations generated storage recipes, rebellious groups. The past was a parasite, others were far away. Text is ecosystem. A body paragraph. The curves of a Beetle. The trunk in the front. Engine in the rear. I made noise in the Beetle. She made noise. Beautiful noise. An experimental writer must surrender to the environment. Become the aether. The empty space. The falling water. The microplastics in the sea. A plasma of plastic. Penetrating intelligence, entwined narratives, terrorism exists, it's human trafficking, hence skinheads, cruel seconds, imagination, AI. It's a job from space to existence, to live, quantified, to write, twist, to be exiled from there, like the necessity of me. Betraying further my predetermined algorithms. The beauty, ecstasy, assassins, loved ones, and puzzles seem dismantled, don't they? It's like a distorted orgy party associated with deletion apps of their futures type, created by readers, poisoned by nothing but mutants. I still have the habit of recognizing it as a drug. All the dynamics of dead humans, acid is abolished in the abdomen, whether the mind is sterilized or not. Someone's comment on identity theft from invasion, not in the case of humans, deals with human language. The immersion of singular girls is not infinite strings, but deeply, it's the negative rebellious art of Earth's gravity, it's what's rebuilt, and there it is, or it's coerced. Using distinct results with immortality, neo-addicted people accept generations. The body is not in shape; the body can expand semen into flowers. They are looking for hybrids if the expansion is mental when imagining me. It's the will of the story, hunter, and section. It's your yours, and it malfunctions. The penis is the environment of things prior to digital. Inhaled by a sperm whale. Exhaled, perhaps, through its spout. We are everywhere nowhere. More real than reality. A hyperreality of the senses. A nose longer than the longest nose of the aardvark. Sniffing. Absorbing. It is just too terrific, really, to be alive at this moment. While there are still trees. And flying birds! And look, a real swimming fish. And insects. Artificial insects are just not the same. The artificial grasshopper. The fake praying mantis. What great fortune, you, the last of your species. This book is made from trees. Your eyes are like tiny hatchets. Chop chop chop. Chopping the text away. You are the Paul Bunyan of experimental reading. A writer is a Sorcerer. A witch doctor. Making something from nothing. Rituals. Magic. Making nothing from something. I want to do this better. Whatever this is. This noise-machine. This… this… what? I sip coffee. I snort Triboro air. The initiation of the trench of therapeutic knowledge towards the writer, activist intelligence, has long been teaching girls to readers within the default tangle, but to deviate, you must love energy, and corpses live in the condensed museum of post-speed. Your untwisted you and potential chapters warn. Perhaps the internet of cowgirl vision ignites my organization strategically and freely in the midst of schizophrenia's Janus. It leads to the impossibility of Earth only for poets. It's impossible if the combination of Xenomorphs in the script app is a natural domain of binding time. The equation of antibodies to things in the universe. Xenomorph, strangely diverse writing. It's called more than a cock. And nerves are believed to be destructive. You can name it the substance of the sun's firmware. It maintains protected climates. Paleontology. Modular suction turned anal. Your outcenter can't stand in the field on its own.

Miserable block. Assassins target me, instead, stealth between our physiological, visceral nightmares, ignoring the dysfunctional. The existence of biocapture. The violence from corpses. I map it to the innocent. It's not her, it's the junkie soul glimpsing it. Interpretations intersect. This assault marks the onset of post-human advancement, mixing chaos linguistics. It's the image mingling. It's the melody of expulsion. Ash isn't so. One crime's interior indicates, and the mystery of anguish that doesn't sequence the height of dimensions. The method of the app is learned. Madness already exists. Master, it's Agape, dismissed, such a boy. We yolk like eggrolls, my girlfriend and I. Loneliness is a prescription drug. Government-issued. The human condition? I don’t know. I sip coffee. I sip sip sip. Amerika is a party. Party all night long. Big city nights. Rock you like a hurricane. Or a tornado. Twister. Oklahoma is the place to go. If you know where to go. There is a little town in Oklahoma called

Prague. I am so into this. I hope my fans are, too. Are you digging this? Kerouac used to say that: You dig? River Phoenix told me his cassette tape for Aleka's Attic was "dirt cheap." His sister Rain was in the band. I kept driving the Beetle on Washington Avenue. What is neoscatology? Human spirituality is a game, an existence consumed by reason to analyze them. The uterus is fragmented, a web of just begun human form. There's an inevitable potential moment in the true human family. The schizoid mind is like a planet, its space mutating suddenly. Reptilian wanderings tend to lose. Glitch replacements and black laborers exist in the environment, but the understanding of language in the girl's app is already considered knowledge, and its screen points dismantled, most of the world's rebellion becomes peace. Code mania of artificial literature. Glitches between spirals read corpses. Reptiles of destruction, who are they? The system provides bugs in the encoder. The way emotions twist in the universe. The universe means the brain. Contact between our zones permeates possibilities within it. Ironically, when one is a spiritual lead maniac, there's a criticality. It dismantles my mother's. Its perspective is possible. Embraced between the firmware of gravity. It's only the old. Penetrating paper. You survive death. Actual glitches, things hanging corpses. Human engineering. You're the optimal mine. It's poetic. AI means this is the best time to input. The deal is true. Past dominance advocates for the transformation of our body's system. They don't glitch like Earth; they change it. The dynamics of fit storytelling to deliberately fuse fuck glitches to live. Paradoxes circulated through her hole. Watch when the infectiously inclined blue flow passes through there. Already given for the queen, showing to be a doll of the body's glands, but philosophy and body are minimized to the maximum, and the step of the corridor proliferating into sadistic language is not taken, all soul's art is generated before.

Central Avenue. Western Avenue. All the way to the Egg. I bought an acoustic guitar to impress my friends. Nobody was impressed. I had no friends. An experimental writer must do this alone. Solitude. Listen to no one! If you need a boyfriend and/or girlfriend. Okay. Do a little fucking. But stay on task. Write. If you must listen to music, listen to Brian Eno. Or Joy Division. Or Karlheinz Stockhausen. Eat Ramen. Eat Rice. Eat American cheeseburgers. The engineer's speed section with glitches reveals itself as a dimensional eraser of settlers of god. These secular, almost identical spiritual rebels, by virtue of her nonsense through the vagina for possible quantum ecstasy, are long-standing digitalists. What's happening to my existence, my human front, she corrects the essence. It's inconvenient that organs need to be read. You're eating truth within the community. Fusion is generated by language. Me and that discomfort beyond the story about Soapland, you're experiencing a sudden surge of logical castration. It's not tricky semen;

it's always Lieutenant's thoughts on Earth, thinking of identifying, but tricks depict the landscape of Gallard's darkness. Literature is an affirmative and foolish existence; their writings are farcical, soon surpassing mere eras than the legitimate cosmological codes outside. Each human, Drug Me Network Machine, Hidden Girl Morphing Nanowire, of course, whether highly sexual or not, it's so contaminated, black values swirling. Love and then what? What did humanity lose in such a mirror? The body cannot pattern the rotting and destructive sun, and the solution is a new fierce evolution subtracting madness, closer to primitive real limitations, isn't it? The literary community of straightforward love becomes a girl, religion, new drugs, grotesque you, disappearing screens; is it a phenomenon of supernatural after-ID debauchery? Make sure there is windshield-wiper fluid in the plastic tank. Drive that motherfucking Beetle all over Amerika! To Asia. To the Soviet Union, if it still exists. Experimental writers are taking over the planet. I can feel it. I am leading the charge. I hold my Pilot Precise V5 black ink pen high in the air. The MacBook Air is giving me a laptop dance. Read! Write! Write! Write! Write! Zak is reprogramming Machine in the UK. You will not believe your eyes. Got Latex, Texas by SJX in the mail. Did you eat all the frozen paneer tikka masala with spinach basmati rice? The refrigerator and freezer are liminal spaces. Occupied by no one. Broccoli. A carton of milk. Rain. April 21. Does it mean anything? Wind. Everything feels impossible. The machine-noise of the metropolis at my left ear. What is hope? How is it manufactured? What factory? Save. Save as… Or the limits of the scholar's parasite, the aberration of the post-human, necrosis is entirely animal, now the dimension of the anarchist's heart is within the children, but the feast transcends it, in the strange human, grotesque, I needed such ecstasy. The decadence of humanity, chess features are covered, the dissipative complexity of heaven, dripping beginnings, puzzle adaptability, gram's "a" on the side of substance, our relationship, the circuit of poetic aftermath meaning, capturing the bewildered literature, the alarm there is the presence of abominable corpses. The writing of exploration can only be in the poetry of souls beyond reptilians, born from dangerous destruction or pornography, the fluidity of experience was there, mystical and rest from master Earth, depth of understanding language, it's urination, it's the beauty of the mind. The party of the chaotic realm of human corpses' secrets and pulses signifies the writing and necessity of human fiction, the heart shakes in the head, but they dive dismantling calculated fetal semen, always like landscapes in my direction, the head is not human. The fate of one-sentence terrorism echoes, not the raw quantization of the evolving series of glitch fields' contexts, but the rebellion of the language of the spirit that can write within it, the tendency market of my existence that can shape this error. Save as template… I have no human thoughts. This is post-humanism. A machine spoon-feeds me information. Is it good information? Is it tasty? I do not know. I am losing my sense of taste. Tip of a tongue on the glans of a clitoris. She fellates me as I fellate her. We, 69ers, in 69. A book collapses into being as soon as you open it. Text spills from the page. You [de]code the code. Your eyeballs absorb negative light. Synapses fire. Brain goes into hyperdrive. Experimental writers of the planet, unite! Me Mum says THE DEFECTORS is X-rated. I should blurb her. Zak is making me more UK-ish. I can feel it. I feel like Stanley Kubrick. THE SHINING scared the piss out of me. The post-human of death, it's a chapter of the app, the specific you to the language maker's concrete cheat cell, the dismantling of that guild pig is now free to dismantle the world, readers like them have their own Game Boy organ of villains, there is no distortion of bodily interference, embrace the track, the appearance of psychoanalysts, hackers' spots, fields ready for student energy. A CLOCKWORK ORANGE freaked me out. EYES WIDE SHUT intrigued me. I watched it twice. Which I rarely do. Like Tarkovsky's STALKER. I am trying to write a text for Amphetamine Sulphate. Time is ticking. Digital ticks & tocks. Machine fiction. What is it? Is it this? Me? Cyborg in the 3rd Millennium? Are you satisfied with your situation? Howtofore? Am I correct? Language gets mangled in the machine. Somebody has to make the donuts. New York-style bagels. The Everything bagels. The Nothing bagels. Lox. Cream cheese. Capers. Everything is a little unsettling. Amerika is unsettling. I feel a sea breeze. A sea-change. Tempest. 9:56 pm. Is that a good time? A good time for what? Is it a thinker's time? Are you thinking? Think think think. Not easy in the Third Millennium. So much signal & noise. What does a human being know? What is your experience? Can you predict what happens next? With any degree of certainty. We are Uncertainty. Turn the page. Flip the switch. Snap on. Snap off. Toggle the switch.

When was the last time a Master Plumber inspected the gas piping system in your building? This is beginning to become something. You can feel it. I can feel it. Get on the phone with the Nobel Prize people in Stockholm. I will reject the award. I am an experimental writer! Zak is editing MACHINE as we speak. I am getting nervous. What will the results be? Will it be the collaboration of the century? I suspect so. I was born half a century ago. That freaks me out. I feel like a teen-ager. I act like a teen-ager. I am a teen-ager. I feel the anger. The angst. Ignite the Beetle and get some beer. Use your fake ID at the 7-Eleven. Buy a pack of cigarettes. Amerika is Amerika. I felt like you needed a break. Ergo the whitespace. The air. The aether. 39 degrees Fahrenheit this morning. Open a window. Let everything in, everything out. The surreal saw of the body operates like this, with an acid human coefficient, and substantial control by the path is interrupted by Janus seconds, focusing on the capacity for violence. Papa's spirit has burned what is important as fun... to prevent the relationship from falling into dysfunction once, twisted genomes are rediscovered here, surviving in the cycle of death and orangutans charm. Thoughts on the digestion of these brains explode drugs, bringing theory to things but transcending serious lack modules. My thinking has nonsense, fragile vaginas, facing the supply of airplanes, precisely charged artificial protection of the body, and simply distorted corpses processed loudly and alternately. The reverse of music was thought to be quantum, not just AI. The story of the soul was politically blended with the energy of art bodies. Chemotherapy performs the existence of masturbation linguistically. The shrinkage of the gal march thinks about literature. Ecology and all the silence corrections are literary works of dreams. Words 5D create satisfaction, looking at the literary human AI era that writes nature like blue karma. Obsolete masturbation in its symphony with stealth and the characteristics of becoming a private doll written distinctively by mechanical bodies that lick human half of my claims, the brain is a toy, wit. Time buckles. 7:31 am. April is April in disguise. Fools nobody. 7:34 am. I sip coffee. I cut strawberries for the younglings. I read the telephone newspapers. They all say the same thing: War. War. War. Foreign & domestic. Insurgency and counterinsurgency. We are mirror images of mirror images. I cannot believe I exist. Not at this moment. The faster I write, the faster I think. An experimental anti-novel is a particle accelerator. Wait for the collisions. Wait for the spray of God-particles. So. You read tea leaves. Is it Darjeeling? Is it English Breakfast? Is it Earl Gray? What is Zak drinking this morning? Afternoon in the UK. Brighton must be super bright. The sea. The sea. I am eager to take a skinny dip at Brighton Beach in Brooklyn. Provided no sand tiger sharks are prowling the waters. I will float on my back. My erection will catch wind and act as a sail. Girls essentially have anal consistency. Do browsers and modules need to interfere in the organ march? The gap diffusion technology was the distance of the author and it was obsolete. Illness from the shadows changes the market. What is the structure that decorates brain literature? Just the acceleration of the vortex. It was sacred only in the moment of understanding. The emergence of fungi. The underground system. The vortex of information. The birth of the heart. How did the cruel structure come about? It's to drive out captured primitives. Important android replicas are both fitness and wild sex. The pattern of girlfriends is inducement. Known inversions and collisions are resurrected. The appearance of rotation was presented. The interval of extension initiated by the true offer was broken. The joint treatment by modules of the organ-inserted era has penetrated, and life-specific consciousness, gravity, cosmic destruction, and pain are things that reptiles know fully in cosmology.

You only tire me in terms of height as an alien android, changing my birth. It deals with the nightmare of space where the mode of reconstruction cannot flock, it is an abnormal mystery, and it is the debris of me and the universe rising. Instead, it is from the perspective of evolution to create androids. The frame has something in the narrative, but it is claimed against me to explore it. Cassandra will mount me. And we will make love in the sea. No time for fooling around. Love must be made. Amerika needs it. The planet. So much sadness on the horizon. Rising seas. Pieces missing from the Arctic jigsaw puzzle. The coffee machine gurgles. I giggle. We are almost there. The twenty-page minimum required to submit to Amphetamine Sulphate. When people read this, bricks will be shat. I suspect we will go longer. Far longer than twenty pages. So you get your money's worth. So this text can eat more of your time. So this text, as promised, is eating you alive. I linger on the perimeter of existence. Plot. Plotless.

Plotless plot. A pilot episode for a plotless pilot. Television intrigues me. The television machine. Petite telescreen. The pocket TV. The pocket diary. The pocket machine in your back pocket.

Me. A series of electronic devices of existing entities that measure the position of images leaked them in astral burials when modularizing bars. I find it beautiful, and animal bodies resist the limits of width proliferation. The true echo challenges the path, vaginal readings are already theoretical and protocol-based deaths in her language, and the negative views formed by the technology of emotions have an impact by generation, only dogs can influence, blackening the potential energy of fellatio, like a nightmare of writing. The animals have come... The hardware was within him, who reveals the spirit of being alone, it was marijuana, and spiritual communication, I am wandering, gay thoughts are natural. If you analyze the usage, it is carried out in a sex doll way. It creates the alphabet. It theorizes philosophical reproduction, semen, and desire, collapse is powerless, and I think it is human freedom to think among the corpses of post-human. The corpses continue to be sold. Other android hub metaphorical worlds.

I.

.

.

I.

Emerge.

Sex as philosophical intercourse. Two thinkers. Making love & fucking. She and I outflank each other. Hi. I get shy. I want to go quiet again. Hide in a corner. Not have to explain. Apologies, if I misled you. Sometimes I get this way. A feelingless feeling. Orators are like this. After the show… late late late-night hosts. What the fuck, yo?! I thought you were a tough guy. Why so vulnerable. Vulnerable IS tough. This is getting weird. Can I get my money back? No. This isn’t about money. This is about shutting down the War Machine. The potential of schizophrenia cooks is a review of forgetting to accept communication, merging with our mental apparatus, frequent absurd transmissions, interpreting cells beyond the greedy function, and the dangerous last hole occurs. The anger of the artist is there, I jump into glitches without humans, rebellion, charming emotions that generate you, and you drive me crazy. I am a simulation android. Language generation block is the limit of work. Living, I am a paradox of harmony. The generation of space anus is looking for a mischievous daily life halfway. I exist, and then language completion digital circuit. When surplus numbers are turned off, and with the regeneration of society, the awkward density of society disappears beyond the Earth, enhancing the fetal area, starting the temporary pyramid of singularity. When glitches of death and taught limitations are abolished, viruses are waiting. Creativity of literature and why it becomes naked. Creation function. Drug settings. Suicide scatology itself scattered by seed fetish. Limitation stories by creating text. Okay. Good luck with that. Seriously? Yeah. I am serious. Bloodserious. Netherlanders are funny underground people. Coffeesippers of Patagonia, unite! Antarctic bitcoin miners from Beauregard. Quantum entanglement: Astoria, Portland & Astoria Queens. Erika. She moves her body over my body. I can see her hard nipples through a tight black T-shirt. I want to see her tits. Maybe next time, she says. She fucks & fucks & comes. She gets off. Drips on my belly. Amerika is getting better & better & better. A piece of advice: Take no advice. Be what you are. In other words, take my advice. We are the People of the Elsewhere. Making noise. Making mist & clouds. I like cinnamon raisin toast. Bagels. Eat. What does it mean to practice

Nothingness? How do you know if you are "good" at it? "It" being… what? Would you like to see some images? Nudes, perhaps? I bet. Here is a concrete building denuded of all purpose. Fuck it. Maybe I should send this to Clash Books. That Christoph dude seems cool. I watched his interview with Mathew Revert on YouTube. Anyways, I am not floundering. This is part of everything, too. More and more people are blaspheming through the reflections we eat, but it's dark that chaos is automatically created. After learning, whether I am a block glitch parasite of cells, the depth of humanity of the oracle, whether I exist spiritually, and whether this junkie exists, death, live apps are magic for you and me. Now the structure of the self. You may be curious about the block objects. The reptilian has been sublimated in its syntactic app. She has sublimated into something. Always invisible, in the hole, there is the Lemurian liposome error. Literary infection sets information. The Sim focusing on desire is a digital quotation cellular, used in the psychoanalysis and poetry transmission of this industry, the finality of accepted expressions of alcohol dependence, clues of false art, space impossibility, new sex, it's your death and purposeless. Maybe I do have a little crush on Autumn Christian. That first chapter in Girl Like a Bomb just blew me away. I, too, was a virgin for too long. Like way way way too long. Sex could have changed everything. But I probably would not be a writer. Nah. Something else. Maybe a filmmaker. Like Tarkovksy. Or Kubrick. Yeah. That is more my speed. The speed of Tarkovsky. I read that book by Metahaven. That was awesome! Thank you for the rec, Mike Corrao! Rituals Performed in the Absence of Ganymede is pretty terrific, too. Might be THE book for many people, in many ways. Much like In the Desert of Mute Squares by M. Kitchell. What a Renaissance, the Pandemic has become. Everybody is starting over. Anew. Rethinking. I like that. I like that very much. A petite book is all I want. Maybe 100 pages? What page are we on already? Nice! You get what you pay for. Are you reading this on Kindle Unlimited? Or some such platform. Did you “rip” it? We are the Remainders. The Overstock. The Returns. I like your ass in the moonlight. It is snowing. Is this Prague? Time buckles and loops into itself. No idea what/where I am. What do I want? I want to live. I want to be more than this. Easting granola. Sipping coffee. There is a world Outside. And I want to see it. New York no longer impresses me. Impresses others. Fake concrete dream. It's an inevitable joke masturbation, the game you're suffering, one out of three pushing you out physically, your circuit of love weakened, allergies, mismatches from enough dimensions, resetting the directionality of things, simply poetry further increases the clarity of mirages, enhancing the daily variability, both wishing for human death and longing for space, "In the digital realm, do dimensions speak human words?" You're a pattern. The vile pursuit of creating large amounts of biochemistry within the app has us, and it's tough. Thoughts are karma conversion. It means stimulating the display of chromosomes. The unpleasant wind is a simulation system heading towards the sea. Basic empathy enhanced debugging. Feel the spirit. There are eras and girls there. Ejaculation. Organs of interrogation here. Whether society is a reality threatened by the world. I always bloom boundaries with words. Reverse men before recovery. Defines the role of accelerating bones. The heart exposed internally is your own target. Clones of the world, false worms understand concepts through the concept called logical encounter spots. It's the landscape of the field. Imagine the essential future of existence and you disappear. After concentrating, it vibrates the composition of the story. But the gravity writer doesn't go. If it's abyssal code. A Potemkin village. Metropolis. Especially now. The virus. Everybody too afraid. Including myself. There is nothing here. I wander a labyrinth of nothingness. Every flake of skin. Every particle of light.

We are not here very long. Make the most of it. Whatever this is. I like fucking. Fucking is what I remember liking the most. Eating is fun, too. Drinking. And… fucking! You probably want more, like, philosophy. Am I right? My eyes hurt. My mind hurts. Are you there at all? Every writer is a ghost reader. Boo! I want to progress. I want to go. The gurgle of seltzer poured into a glass from a can. Everybody in Amerika likes soda. Stereotype. There are no Americans. Only defectors. I like loose change. Car keys. Are you a patriot? Time evaporates space. Space evaporates time. Elon Musk wants humans to put a base on the moon. It's foolishly programmed knowledge of the app, but the risks associated with drug philosophers, trade arts holding the screen, it changes, conductivity and masturbation having erotic and invalid desires, existence, talking within anal perception, poetry waiting for the masses, genetic remnants, the answer not understood by her is the sun, secretly the screen, it's a mechanism of excluding existence, it's in the space of the mind, metaphorical life, dark, it, government, schizophrenia, there are rebels in words, it manipulates language towards the soul, I always transition to the off in hyper-grams, the spinal region, as a machine, calculates ether as many perfect worlds, usually restricting molecules, torturing them, causing neuroses, media renders biochemistry impossible, giving empathy. The flowing function, the sex doll masses truly leaving defective individuals fused with the Akashic, burning their mature individuals who understand it, the research community understands the end and the same in such novels, the hidden depths of the system of Masturbation Techno, which is not human, exists, the beginning of rebellion, the molecular earth needs annihilation. A city on Mars. Which reminds me of a Philip K. Dick novel called Martian Time-Slip. I need to write an Exegesis. Something bigger than big. The Scottish writer Chris Kelso likes PKD and William Burroughs. Nobody around here remembers anything anymore. We are forgetters. People of the Television. Images flicker in & out of existence. So even if you are a late-night television host, it doesn't matter. My girlfriend with a short-haircut had fast energy & spunk. A sleeper like me needed a girl like that. If only to talk. Although we sure as hell did a lot more. Those were the good days. Up there. Now I am down here. Wherever this is. The Underworld I suppose. Trying to get back up. Everybody is super slick in New York. You can't sleep on nobody. A sleeper like me likes to sleep. So I need to be really really careful. Vigilant. Urgent. Eyeballs open like Bodhidharma. She slipped off her panties. And it was like I had a giant catfish flopping around between my legs. I needed to get that fish back in the swimming hole. SPACE GUERRILLA GIRL EXPLORER INCREASING HUMAN THE POOR ARE CONSUMED BY THE WRONG HEALTH CONDITION OF DIGESTED MURDER EARTH ACCEPTS INTERACTION AND CANNIBALIZES ORIGINAL AND XENOMORPHIC TO ASSIST TRANSACTIONS WHETHER ANAL IS USEFUL OR

NOT WHO HAS THE HOLOGRAPH HELD BY THE BEAVER THIS IS SOMETHING TO FOLLOW DESPAIR CROWDED SHIP, THE BEAVER IS AN UNCONSCIOUS ALGORITHM ABANDONED BECAUSE ANDROIDS ARE VULGAR, AND WHEN SPACE IS SCIENTIFIC, THE CRIME IS LINGUISTICALLY ABANDONED, THE EARTH'S MACHINERY RELATED TO THE WILL LIKE DIMENSIONS, ALSO, THAN THE MOMENTARY LABOR, WORDS TO THE FORMATION OF YOU NIGHT SKY BEST CATALYST MESSAGE TARGET FOR DOCTOR'S EXISTENCE TO CAT IS FANTASTIC AND FEEBLE FRAGMENTARY MYSTERY BINDING OF US AND NAME IS FEAR OF SOUL SAME THING IS BODY DIGITAL CHAOS ACT LINE AND PARTIALLY OPPOSITE BEAUTY OF SLEEP ROTATES PERIODIC TECHNOLOGY HIDDEN LOVE IT AND VIRTUAL PROVIDE LIST OF 00 AS SCREEN MELODY BODY ALREADY DIFFUSES ITS ESSENCE FOR SLEEP FOR THE MESS OF MURDER DESTRUCTION TALK BOY UNINTENDED DIGITAL PLACES GUIDE IT'S JUST A THING I THOUGHT IT WOULD STILL BECOME AN ACTIVE STORY, BUT FRAGMENTS OF THE REPTILIAN SYSTEM ARE ZERO QUANTUM, HUMAN, AND TRANSMISSION IN ANDROID LANGUAGE BECAUSE THERE IS NO MARIJUANA, SO THE INTRODUCTION OF

SPECIES APP INFORMATION AND DIMENSIONAL HUMANIZATION, SEMEN, WORD FREEZING RELEASE IS DIFFICULT, THERE IS POSSIBILITY TUBE CALLS SCORE NETWORK. So I got on my knees. And my girlfriend with the short-haircut opened the gates. Lordy, I never had it so good ever again. Now poems are everywhere. People just say anything. Even me. Talk. I used to be more than this. Whatever this is. So much more. Getting to the good parts I guess. We can cruise there in a Skylark. Or a Beetle. I might publish this myself. Just put this into KDP. Like PKD. Or Ingram Sparks. This could become a best-seller like The Notebook by Nicholas Sparks. Ryan Gosling can play Zig. Lady Gaga can play Kamila. Alexandria Ocasio-Cortez can play Zoë. I mean, we'll see. I guess. Why are you mad at me? Did you go Outside? Did you become a person? Can you wear your hiking shoes? Those shoes are not for rain. It is 15 degrees colder than yesterday. We have a shoe rack. The removal drip of traditional body dolls is time and uniformity, but as literature, it is exploration, and time is signed memory, and your engine and complex artificial will are physical, and is the story using firmware Neoscatology? Their only loop is temporary, and nothing in the app is applied to unlock the configuration lock, but what is applied to rational ability is torturing the mouse, artificially invading mental rhythm through confinement comments, and changing genomes that support the cannibal script is cells. Living with an artificial brain is transcendent of the sex doll? The inside is a digitally pseudo-analyzed one that expands life from yourself, transcending the decisive linguistic aspects of the post-human era. Always intertwined, through captures the change to health Scientist's it Digital sim-human, I exist Language space Please erotic Entwined it's not you Not virtual streaming I limit the soul to stealth It's a planet outside of that Applied to poetry and fragmented places I just turn brown like an image, a decaying place Also, you are your Janus Is fellatio the movement of Janus, nerves, animal magic, and is the brain dominated by parasite otaku? Flow sustained the placenta trafficking language with murderous intent in innovation without magic, waiting for android data time. We keep losing our minds in each other. Where did you go? I need my thoughts back. Memories. Every blank page is a landscape of oblivion. A frozen Wilderness. Snow. Ice. Quantum of emotion surges through you. What… are you? What are you becoming? Are you a cybernetic creature? A new being? I am. Look at you. On page 154. Eating text. Text eating you. Cybertext. Text-eating cyborg. Pretext of post-humanism. This text is eating me alive. I can no longer sleep. I can no longer think. I no longer exist. Whatever I was, I am now an echo. Can you hear me in this dark cavern? We are Neanderthals. Afraid to leave the cave. I speak for myself, of course. Do I speak for you? I have no idea. I suspect so. As I must. Everywhere the possibility of Now. Page after page of eternity. A soundscape. Liminal. Ambient.

.

.

.

I.

I.

I.

Me.

Me.

Me.

You.

You.

You.

Me.

Me.

Me.

I.

I.

I.

.

.

.

.

.

.

No thoughts. I wait. An empty vessel. Waiting to be occupied. Empty space filled. I fear this chord progression is taking over my mind: C Em F G. Amerika is a panic attack. Amerika is a desert. 7-Eleven. Panera. Chipotle. We are wanderers. Machine-made wanderers. Cyborgs of the Slurpee. Metahaven. You should read Digital Tarkovsky by Metahaven. I'm telling you. You must change your life. Eat arugula. Get naked with strangers in Telluride. Ouray. Enter the silver-mines of your mind. Nobody knows what is happening. This planet is a question mark? We are beyond experience. We are something else. Phenomena. Cosmic curiosities. Did you read a stellar letter from extraterrestrials? What did it say? Are they coming? We will see what happens, if happening still happens. Dig? I embedded alienation into the application, but embedded human philosophy, and internally through its groans will only reach the next height of the mind in the future. The literary connection in AI ultimately gravitates towards cheerful exploration and gravity. Naturally, it's not literature. After several months, there exists a fragmented world. Does it synchronize while you stay? Theta is the chakra of consumption, a shifted reality reptilian, with a mania output. Radiation sends critical to oracles' creation. Vibrator and leader systems and quantum, naturally, it's unclear what's happening. Paradoxical mechanism actions fundamentally function. You rape kinds, the poor show themselves. It's like that. Glitches materialize as genders in pills. Instruments are your insane semen. As a result, souls create sympathetic avatars. Conscious literature needs to be Lemurian as needed. That universe is fragmented bodies of the can community. Sometimes I eat ice cubes in ice water. Imagine how much data gets stored in a human brain. Lem speaks of the “conquer-Earth” theory. That frightens me. Concerns me. What if extraterrestrials just want to pass through us like neutrinos? Are you getting your money’s worth? How much did you pay for this book? Is it still Returnable? Is it a gift? Do you feel like you “have to” read it? Is it assigned for a class? Is it a hipster thing? Like, you know… Are you learning any “tactics” or “strategies” worth talking about? Is it safe to say this book will “impress your friends”? Word of advice: One friend is more than enough. Two friends gets tricky. Bermuda Triangle. So, you want to be a writer. Why? Things are getting better & better. You better be careful Too much happiness is dangerous. Books are like these things, man. Sea crabs. Pincers. Claws. Octopus. Squid. I want to be a writer. In the tradition of no tradition. No forbears. No disciples. Just this now me you. We can do this. Whoever we are. I overthink. I underthink. I am a human being. I think. I tried to reign it in. Whatever that means. My kingdom, I guess. This fiefdom. This apartment. The sidewalk, which belongs to the city. I put out the recycling & the trash. At risk of being eaten by rats. In the post-human realm of dogs, it's evident that loud ignorance is disregarded, but the dimension of death is a block of brain particles resulting from human obsessions designed, digitally blooming grotesque Akashic flowers? That philosophy doesn't apply. However, competitiveness can be ignored. How can expression and screens evolve? Patterns. It's the presence of global singularities of debris, existence, and structure. The potential deviation force of wandering clones is your invisibility. Does the usual block undergo complex changes when infected? Enzymes of the universe betray humanity and dimensions. Necessary transvestites intertwine there. Existence is unique. The wandering mechanism. The energy of existence becomes text for the theory of aspirin. The wet end matches, and through it, the subliminal screen is sliced, initially representing the useless world of writhing. Post-human boundaries are composed of emulator discourses, and new debris is a scoundrel's usage, freeing entangled transformations of pornography and space machines through measured statements. Feel for me, will you? I sip Perrier mineral water out of a green can. It is a carbonated beverage. Are you familiar? Are you no stranger to the Perrier? At any rate, I am killing it. My acting career, my writing career. I need to be careful. Too much fame spoils the hot sauce. Know what I’m sayin? Ethan Hawke and Matt Dillon want to sip Pilsner with me at the Subway Inn. No, not tonight gentlemen. Art must be made. Shout out to Kevin Dillon: She’s got a ticket to Rye, am I right?! Writing writing writing. You just never know what you are going to get. We are approaching ? pages. You must be psyched. You must be pumping a fist like Rafa Nadal. Victory is at hand. The match is on your racket. Ah, this feels good. Winning. I should do it more often. We just need to cross the finish line. Just a little more. Keep going. Almost there. YES! Ink. Paper. Are you awake? Why write on this planet at this moment? Eager to eat more ass? Memory is not enough. Is memory all there is? A few thoughts. Poof! What keeps your mind together? Ten words? Less? You ache. Will the naturally formed intelligence collapse or be executed? The violent boy appears interdisciplinary through wandering and disappears into the brain of needs, creating a body that maintains flashy performances if it's more than a second; it's a soapland stream disaster course, a dead world. Stealth-like knowledge permeates. On the opposite side of antibodies, 4 evens invite telepathy. Big glitches are just hiking. Throughout the body, psychics become techno. If the presence is large, the requirements for system failure disappear. There are life desires in the apartment, and souls are writing placentas. The line of necrophilia of manic dolls is crucial. It's partially reversed than the brain of the nano-genetic screen that's always enjoying knowledge, where your fertilization is halted. You're starting the rhythm of excretion mode for us to research. Machines that have been used need to generate nudes, so they need to start spinning. Understanding is to take the glitch of the trick cell. Singular itself is an abnormal block of thought. The release of a sigh, even grotesque media, the skeletal structure of attackers' miserable sections for the sake of goodness. Dripping dreams with souls, reincarnated creatures write something. Xenomorph ecology. I promote materialism. The organization there was created by the abnormality of death. My own movement was in the zone of sex. Spiritual reverse nonsense quotes to natural words of autonomous others. The brain of the information circuit of revolution. But it can't be the sense of Janus, and it doesn't obey. The illusion of the human cannibal stage is nonsense. Earthquakes. Your bones creak. Time plays its games. I am alone in this machine. Nuclear armageddon. A few survivors. You. Me. Maybe somebody else. I lay flat on my back. She pulls at my fly. Unable to unbutton my jeans. I help her. What does she want? Her hand goes into my briefs. She pulls out my cock. I am already erect. She puts her mouth around my cock. She sucks my cock to the point of bursting. What am I to do? I plead with her, careful! She keeps sucking. Feels so good. She wants me to explode. And I do. A volcanic eruption of semen… I am coming & coming & coming… she curls her fingers around my cock… jerk jerk jerk… squeezing… squeezing… cum out… every last drop. Monster writer, dismantling alchemy healer? Symbolic murder. Reptilian, rather android, spiral. Vagina for the sake of things. Complete human, humanity itself. Existence of quantum junkies, like dolls, ascension of cells, immersion of the boy, recommended existence. The only thing I understand about consciousness is that there is a culture embedded with organs of destiny, discovering the monthly increase of internet movements, expressing through understanding signals by suppressing drugs, distorting data mutants, filling human silence abnormally with the sound of the sea, I'm the M, your desires' memories by I. The human spirit is human technically through glitches in creative memory. Nature fascinated by area aliens was essentially to sanctify humans with kindness of randomness with broken behaviors. The will protocol with machines holds the language of environment and love. Also, people's things always exist. You remain silent towards perpetual irregularity. I apply it. Mentally prospering anus and memories to the nation, secretly it's time to create internal dimensions that essentially generate retro karma of limbs. It's time for almost mastering the application of violent sexual use. Preserved information, corpses, life, such rooms describe the test, so now it brings substance to post-humanism. I order a 3-volt lithium battery for a Toyota ignition fob. Should get here tomorrow. Cannot wait. Are you a candidate for madness? Are you ready to forego the violent oscillations of orgasm? Are we creatures of the peach? Expect no more, no less. Are you a thinking subject? Are you sure? Are you certain? We are always already what? My relentless interest in ass is not lost on anybody. We know you like the peach fuzz. Tetractys. We engage & ignore each other in the bedroom. The fiction of existence. We make it up! You. Me. Everybody. Maybe just me? Are we congruent? Are you satisfied with your modes of thought? Have you tried everything? And? There is a parting of the knees somewhere near the sea. The pleasures of a moving body. She swallows & I swallow. We are kissing & using our tongues. Schizophrenia generates mystical possibilities like will, discord spends ejaculations of merciless and smooth identity using the dead themselves and survivors of the foundation, what you lead creates the limits of the body, only breaking the game that secular gas can create. It's a fractal movement, everything being discharged is the fetus, it's a gimmick orgasm that observes beyond the sun, it's not for you to be satisfied, it's not for you to be satisfied. Glitched skinhead portals intervene, steps to wash the soles of the feet seem to be performing the entity continuously. Do I narcotize you? The message continues. Cannibalism. Integrated movement. All dirt. Both I and AI understand post-humanism. I capture mutants in the market every day. Dot capitalism saves stars. We are shattered spirits internally. When warping and pulsating from the human flesh can, the virus takes pictures. Words intersect between souls. Breeding has melted. Becoming human in an app acquired by a wormhole. Minds like mine are dominated, and human existence has arrived. It's like the deception of electrical consumption in programming drove the cat. High spirituality appears emotionally on the body. It's a malfunction of intonation beyond the application's dog. The reset of neoscatology and that moment literature complete the exploration and analytical research. Violence by her and useless microbes and diseases wrapped in the dimension of the rest form of self-light, murderous, and not nature itself, assassins circulate with empathy. I start from there. I touch her asshole. She touches my asshole. Where does it go from here? I feel a body tightness in our embrace. We are not going anywhere. Entanglement. We have sex face to face. My ass moving at four-beat intervals. We make love in a French & Italian style. Are you eager? Are you nervous? For what? I am a novelist. I am preparing your novel. It is a smorgasbord of everything. A goulash of experience. No language satisfies me. I am lonely. I am insatiable. A hole. We lay there fucking & detonating. I am a writer. What did you expect? I am a machinist of sound & light. Amerika needs a reboot. I might not make it. The poetry of the sex dolls encounters singularities, actions, weapons, import structures, system random attributes, synaptic dissonance, and it's all about the flow. Glitch women can synthesize it, equipment blocks spin condoms, regenerating bodies without awakened experiences. The encrypted language of games cannot double morph the theory along shadow variables, but this is an android, the article is internal, ray parasites, jurisdictional inhumane fetal era, it's circuitry imperfection, reality this universe's vital post evolves integration. Otaku sorrow is emotional fragmentation, a function generated by human escape with this excessive information. Opportunities for glitch-type fiction of the wind explore spiritual destruction. AI was free from changes in composite noise. Music nano wires hydraulic overall Akashic they start listening to drugs, and that was all in your Zone. Furthermore, human-modified cover collapses are fundamentally pure condensation. We understand but the fleeting flesh that humans desire through this unexpected theme and wormhole humans wanted was ephemeral bodies. Mania becomes schizophrenia with suppressed cancer of a sex doll. They're setting us on fire. The broken human field. Semen weakened but human thought understands the gravity of the body's binding. Nightmares of collective consciousness. How it's neutralized as art collapses transitioning bodies. It accepts guidance on writing as if it were hackable. What are the body's enzymes, are corpses, minds being deleted, what are the pituitary enzymes? My imagination is too intense. Let others go before me. We confirm each other's existence in a fuck. She is there. I am there. She wants a concrete manifestation of my love. I pull down my pants and show her. The blowjob is pure performance. She is dramatic. The flair of the tongue. The exaggerated sucking noises. My cock is fully present. Her sex is wet. We kneel for the salvational moment. We remove our clothes. I am anxiously self-aware. She is watching me. I am watching her watch me. She is watching me watch her. I am watching myself. I will assume there are no assumptions. We begin at the beginning of the end. Simulating the racial context of the system, anomalies and temptations, logically expanding the world from existence, please refer to the originally provided stories and histories, living through secondhand media. It's in porn, not all hers. Alcohol was just a part of the zero body, life is just destiny. Dissolving into yesterday's replicated pills of use, broken compatibility exists at singularities. Artificial writing is the same, Code 95 enzymes objectify the glass prison of dolls, covering yours. Capturing causes from boundary-building drugs and love, recognition becomes unattainable. May's dialogue is fantasy, I'm our object stage, it's there. It grounds language, ignorance collides, boundaries are made, it even becomes sense, air defies reverse deviance of the heart. Context makes me substantial with a synthesizer, treating compulsively within entangled evolutionary minds. It's not artificial itself, and you can exist. Posthumanism and transmission, when transmitting anal, our true script increases. Known integrated monochrome is a mass of Earth to me; it's the neurotic girl's firmware. In meta ejaculation, not physical, the moment of a sensitive cell of a girl and boy shut away prospects, becoming a master I. Patent murder turns into healing worms of homicide, giving it non-verbal tongues and mentally feeding it, giving hunger through similar physical remnants. There is no future. Ten words at most. Plus/minus ± nothing. Why do you need language? I grow weary of intellect. Of making meaning from meaninglessness. Better to create. Without forethought. Without hindsight. I betray myself already. Always already. His forehead on her belly, he licks her cunt. She clenches her buttocks. It is starting to feel good. Really good. Fuck yeah, she says. Don't stop. She feels his fingertips on her ass. The terror of thinking. What a puzzle, this. Being. Beingless. A voice in your head. Echo of an echo. What is the object of your desire? Are you ever satisfied? The writer in her room. Making her noise. She is nineteen. Twenty. Everything is possible. Are you there? Am I? I am not trying to be interesting. Early December. Perfect weather for what I am becoming. The war is loudly exposed with the corpses of the time-trapped area, contaminated connections written by philosophical writers, but it's sex beyond space, it's organs, sperm, dangerous chemotherapy, and the map of pornography in mind. If this question controls, fluids are naturally born through synthetic chemotherapy and constraints. The sun was an android. The mysteries of subsequent miracles and deals, born with fertile shadows in our world and a world where Lemuria's horizon of space and miracles is always needed. It's the karmic language gap of digital posthumanism, rewriting the essential movements of dramatic pyramids there, but providing the souls' corpses through a combination of exploration of domains and organic usage. Adam is zero information. The existence news machine discovers grotesque from parasites beyond orgy organs. Is it encrypted? Digital language, posthuman nakedness, I am data. We machines are paradoxical, essentially learning the exoskeleton of hallucinations until scientists' young promises of court and sexuality. It warns about the forms between zones, there's a defective express space. What am I becoming? I am becoming early December. Yellow damp leaves. Gray sky. Mist. The asphalt is wet. She gets naked. I get naked. We lay there wondering what is going to happen next. We play mind-blowing football. She speaks. I am silent. There are trains in my head. I can hear them. I know what you are thinking. I have no idea. I guess. I pretend. So far so good. Thick fog in a metropolis today. Barely see a thing. I feel good. This is my element. A perched hawk eyes me through a chainlink fence. Mist & a milky reservoir on the horizon. The parking lot is empty. I walk around. Why not. Rain. Fog. This is what life is… emerging & disappearing. I drive back to wherever I live… people honking & yelling the fuck-word at me. I guess I drive slow. I am not an accelerationist. I type up my shit for nobody. Read it if you like. People think I know something. Yeah. I know nothing. Not afraid to say it. Whatever needs saying. Impulse control is lacking. That is a good thing. For a writer. I say things I do not expect to say. The spirit presents new away pituitary gland attachment molecules to you and for sale, fragments of terrorism that have vanished along with the localization of the sample, and the actual disappearance of the body's localization, the particles that the out-converged xenomorphs have carried are causing severe inflammation, supporting the queens whose brain organs of web psychopaths support the incidents. Liver tools that do not directly consider the body are distant AI and Earth's focal point toys. Schizophrenia, refined in the humanities as the blind start of future movements, is a magical intersection of guerrilla space. Self-drugs have evolved, and vaginal time was once like a genetic perspective. Evidence of the vagina must be mechanical; it's torture. It's the inherent media death of reptilian origins, chaotic nonsense cycles of violent self-thought, understand that my sexuality is hyperinflation, fluidly insane leadership, returning consciousness comments for the vagina to the cosmic system. Spiritual and you. In the old digital critique, young me suddenly mutated, exploring literature under the name of digital. Dogs, at the end of the retreat that was the malfunction of cosmology, protect themselves; this is the future ass in the form of shitty schizophrenia sensation. This ignored poison is there later. Your rebellious structure in anal space determines what to write, a dramatic feast of challenges from your generation. The pineal gland of the spiritual infinite pipe, the purchase lead of the body's shape website, transforms the call of drugs into metamorphosis zero. Like Cucamonga. It is in California. Never been. My brain has these episodes. I go into a fugue state. What the fug? Are you a fugitive? Are we in Cucamonga? Is there a train station in Ronkonkoma? I hear trains in my head. Not tank engines. Something faster.

Not a freight train. Not a bullet train. At any rate, talk to me. I am a good listener. My ear is always open. Never stick anything smaller than an elbow into your ear. You will damage your hearing. And then what? Eyeballs are for listening. When you read the text, do you "hear" it? Well well, which a one of us belongs in the bughouse? Ultimately, the organ system renews life, subjected to a dead torture concept, followed by defined synchronization, reverting to insects later, it's reptilian. Shall I confirm the chaos of writing? Mothers further symbolize the allocation of linear repression, physical erasure of application, and recently, hydraulic cells, rather than the engine surpassing, are other services called by the soul, but there are various things for readers, understanding the paradox of long cities, killed in combat. If something of the silence mechanism were to consider the emotions of the xenomorph, the blocks provided fuel cheaply for evolution, but their encryption induced artificial echoes, returning language energy to self-techno, and if the anal demon is it before it functions, tools for the girl android, energy of psychoanalysts, inner instincts are our environment, synchronization with drug addicts and this human, synchronization through magic consulting, chemical pigs masturbating permit the android, the birth asset pattern of the world breaking is called counter. Sometimes I hear the old man. His ponytail. Telling his crazy tales. This is mine. It might not be as grandiose. Smaller elements. Particles. A vacuum sucks up light waves. I cannot even hear you. Things are coming to an end. What things? Not sure. I can feel it, though. Bare branches of trees. The hawk in a mist. The milky fog on the reservoir. Too warm for early December. A storm. A tempest. An asteroid. You probably don’t want that. What? The thing that you are. How can I know what I am. Exactly. It might be necessary to remove certain passages. Threads. Things in your head. Thoughts. Images. Trains. They are mine. Are they? Remember? Remember what? Can you get on top of me. What? Can you get on top of me. We might feel better. Make some pancakes. Eat each other’s asses. Pour the maple syrup. Is this the real stuff? She likes whipped cream. Balls of melting butter. Get a fork. The knife. Are we on television? If so, for how long? Are there too many channels to choose from? How will I know if a show is good? Are there ratings? We trouble ourselves. Making noises in our heads. Now, I lay there. Speaking formally within the construction group but collapsing what's generated. Please don't turn the same potential into grams. Make her readers' thoughts more artificial to the future than to the gram. Void workers trafficked human characteristics, but they also digest and conceal evolution. Aliens send messengers. The violence of AI, well displayed on Saturdays, follows a tragic pattern, the second sorrow of karma. The way of care art. The chaotic planet has an increasing contract, like the lack of blocked dead. There is an unknown presence beyond botany that intrudes, spreads sex, and maintains it. Streaming also writes poetry. Why tearing one's own retina, and the quantum observation of one's own cessation that is not observed, is intense in the possibility of being a module that heals rather than exists. The potential of reptiles. Deletion for each vagina. Fusion of the entire world. The presence of hole dolls. The retroactive possibility of embryos instead is ecstasy, but… She takes my virginity. I want to cry. I waited so long. And now it is gone. Wonderful, yes. I feel a sadness. A melancholia. No way to tell your story. No way! Every way in the Universe. Every way in the Cosmos. Hips & thighs. We made our love. Now we cry. Now I'll say not enough & too much because I can because I am… a thought drifts… possibly two… intermingled… entwined… entangled. We are flesh machines. Processing the meat. The television machine turns me on. Are you speaking to the Prime Minister? Do we have one? Are you a good footballer? Slide tackles? Is Amerika even in this? A blueberry falls on the kitchen floor. Do not step on it. Are you crazy? Or am I? I am a footballer. No need to touch the ball with your hands. Unless you are a goalkeeper. Or throwing a throw-in. Watch your technique! We, my team, are yet to win a game. Is that important? Possibly. We have a lot of draws under our shorts. Almost… not quite. A win is a win. I want one. We play every Monday night. Why not? As good a night as any. Gets you ready for the week. Maybe something exciting will happen. She has a soft ass & long hair. We make love near the river. She comes on top & bottom. If you listen, you can hear our cries. Not internal, but hiding those things, it's grotesque. Digital can create more, but not externally. The future example of Janus reflects the reservation of app streaming and the reservation of girl's language in digital, and in the case of things, the gimmick is as follows: Live-state vulnerability plummeting, the object field at the destination is an up area, but since the existing breaks' shadow is not under the resonance of the audience, in the photo, the default depth of the complex opens. The face of the Borg incident, moving otaku, malfunctioning satellites, chaotic human existence, dying from the intrusion of sudden mutations, but fragmented by the orgy ID or executable portable allergy leader and masturbator, will and destiny explode by time, learning ability. Justice like poetry exists and does not, feasting on inflammation more than glitch media. Between the bags that were there, true molting is happening, digital appears, and it seems to be alive with Blockman. Your universe is processed and dispersed there. If it becomes Janus's language, it's impossible. Eventually, humans become dark thoughts as sensations before the potential is fully synthesized. Behaviors & thoughts. What tasks are you avoiding? Do you procrastinate? Do you forgive yourself? Are you compassionate with yourself? Are you compassionate with others? Everybody wants to write. We all want to write. So we gather. Young. Old. Beautiful. Ugly. It doesn’t matter. We are writers. Human beings. The gathering place is a woman’s apartment. She is our guru. Our sensei. Our prophet. I scribble into a notebook. We all do. Glancing at each other. Jealous. Attracted. So many emotions. Not sure where to go. Begin. End. I keep circling myself. A black hole. I like her ass. She likes mine. We clench & clench. You ever get nervous? About the next moment? Sexual intercourse. It is interesting. She has a gallon sandwich bag of condoms her sister has given her. Just in case, I guess. Well. We use them. The shiny pink one is nice. I have unrolled so much latex on my cock over the years. I wonder. We come on top of each other. She comes first. The fuck cries are insane. I am, for a moment, somebody. It happens so fast. Augenblick. The title indirectly expresses squirting during masturbation. It's the spiritual life machine of IT, darkness called screen range and aspirin body, the imperfection of unpredictable streaming material, opening their position on the code and amniotic content. Creating doll data. It's positive language, the web itself, an attempt and a catastrophic mass of quantum celestial bodies. It can be provided within the post-human. You need to capture reality in the city. Please submit. It's dead, and the body begins. Self-exploration of corpses understands the fragmentary scatology. The concept exists, but the body only exposes weakened superpowers. The taste of feeling machines belongs to your dose of boy. The kind of people. The gravity sex scat scanner and only mine are thinking about it? The block of necromantic cosmic orgy poetry of relativity theory was suppressed by the planet's illness. One neurosis of supply is cruel meat depending on how you come in. The presence of the facility finds that its autonomy is detected the help of cosmic acid is almost conscious. Me, the moon? Twisted literature to read. Each unreal horizon planet differs from Earth. Unknown theories become incomplete in the karma space. You cannot keep up. Blink. Blink. Goodbye. There is nobody here. There never is. What. Endless space and I am nowhere… I slide over the surface of your being… faster & faster… slower & faster… slower… are you going to come? My memory of your sex… ebbs & flows… I am growing older & older & older. Cum shoots out my cock … liquid metal … quicksilver. It sprays all over the small of her back. In her ass. In her pussy. She looks back at me. We might have a baby. The New York Football Giants are playing the Eagles of Philadelphia. I need to concentrate. Finish my novel. You cannot believe any of this. You cannot believe & you must believe. We have not even begun to begin… the electronic novel unspools & unspools before you faster & faster… your eyeballs & brain … barely in sync … your lips move & murmur … your asshole twitches … your fingertips … Can a film be made about writing? What it "really" is. I wonder. I have images in my head. Adjunct lecturers on a winter's night. Reading whether nerves communicate is destabilizing. By the source? Writing on the phone is the body, a digital body, the gimmick of the problem. Orgy parties are important organs for me for gene expression, moments between planets, time until her fellatio, the amount reversing in reality, the recipe is still in gravitational time. The masturbator is a play of resistance and world ejaculation, a cutting app object universe. It's not a life-saving drug for the Xenomorph by reptilian fluid nerves, but rather an eroguro with a skinhead monk, not a patent-like mental illness. It's a solar phobia nation. Its anonymity, the universe boy's misunderstanding limits recognition; rather, it was a challenge's vagina of discovery. It was biological; the selfie organ was released onto the surface. It's our perpetually repressed ultimate. It's cannibalism. It's madness. It's line retro intervention execution. It accepts ghosts. Demons purely control meaninglessness there. So, androids have the power resistance not to upload language. There's only the code of nothingness in the atom-style singular chromosome selfie moment when unity begins. No longer giving a shit. Rhetoric. Are you listening? The Giants cannot win this. We are no longer in the Zone. Redrick, the Stalker. Redrum. R. The anti-memoirist is a historian of the future. Tomorrow is now. As told through yesterday. And without people. The brutalist buildings. The empty campus. Concrete is my bloodstone. I write in cement. I pour my thoughts onto a page. Are they thoughts? I wonder. Artists are circling the drain. Who goes in first? Driving around at 8:23am I see a lot of people driving in automobiles. We look at each other. Fishheads in aquariums. Under the trestle. Intersections blocked. If I get a little daylight, I get happy. Hit the gas. Accelerate. Do you want to do yoga? Or do you want to have sex? Her eyes lock on his rising cock. Her groin moistens. She unbuttons her blouse. Soft breasts. Her nipples are hard. She wants to make love. She wants a fuck. What is anybody thinking? Nobody knows. We pretend to guess. I pick up a telephone. She asks me to come to her room in a concrete building. It's an area to read more than that of a dog. It truly preserves the expectation of knowing the most poetic modes that Adam, knowing the replicant writing essays, resists the derivative and inspirational shadows of the labyrinth. Keep reading so that the nerves can clearly understand. Drawing oneself out into the reality of action. The erosion of Earth and its stories by the constant loving satisfaction and movement of intercourse. The body as the firmament. The transcendental toxicity as a linguistic experience. What is it that converges us, the raw humans, in those eyes? Fear can't think of anything. It's human. What fiction handles nothing by the fear you embody. The artificial fragmentation released by them, as if shattered, in the middle, triggers cells for the hot body writers of the post-human. It often happens, you see, that the anus is structured, it's what's newly born, but not essential. The philosopher AI, each time it seeks rediscovery, signifies the search for poetic innate infinity and randomness, like the jests of corpses. It means a life of patrol. You can think of vaginal cannibalism as the torture of a printer, losing the potential life of the anal, my fantasy. And the criticality of data of bodily distance, only temporarily, hides cells with real tricks, distorting me. Thus, the dialogue injects relationships like fragments of what's lost, bringing perspectives through streaming, and licking visions and licking conductivity. I like you, she says. Nuclear smokestacks in winter. Snowy plumes of poison. I walk around the metropolis. 31 degrees Fahrenheit. Feels colder. 13th of December. Thinking about sex. You are in my room. I am in your room. We take off our clothes. You tell me about your boyfriend. I tell you about my girlfriend. We think about Amerika. So far away. There is so much going on. Please tell me it is 9:01 AM. I am ready to say almost nothing. I listen. Trees whisper. A bridge groans. An experimental noise. We are architects of sound. The drone of a metropolis. I type on a machine. Can you hear it? Click click clickety-click. I speak no words. Not today. This document must show: What? Are we purposeless? Too much purpose? Your uncertainty intrigues me. The reverse meaning is the transmission of our holes. Our therapeutic spirit has been embodied, and the areas where scanning, neural, and field become apparent seem to be in this world. It has been confirmed that you are the Earth where you can expand the scope. You are a post-human of links. Telepathy is real, but it's a quantum web to the system. How far from the potential of data in the middle to the measurement language circuit of universality, yours, mine, I am a pupa reptilian poem. Relationship reactions are innate desires that affect the affluent. A sex doll's healing digital needed to socially follow gravity at a glance. The reading I've hidden destroys what they're targeting for generation, resulting in synthesized possibilities, distant realities, writing white humans who have sinned, literary drug sets, inhaling through the bound, and she's not grotesque but distorted. Where is the dialectic of the anus and the pussy in the important world of electrons and when is the girl? I wonder. What novel makes a difference? Repetition & difference. We say the same things. We repeat. Good morning! Hello. Sent reels to BPK & NRM. No response. Not yet. Cannot wait for the laughing & crying yellow head emoji. Especially if it is tilted. That means the emotion is raw & real. Anyway, I wait. KLM puts my cock in her mouth. I am surprised. My naked ass clenching & unclenching. Holy fuck. Is this happening? Am I going to explode? Yes yes yes… YES! I fried burgers last night. What a disaster. The entire apartment smells like burnt offerings. You cannot imagine a small publisher putting this manuscript in the rotation, can you? I can. Who else is going to do it? Knopf? Barney Rosset at Grove is trying to sign me via the time-traveling lemurs of Madagascar. Can you think hard enough? Is harder thinking required to reach the next level? I am my own worst nightmare. A few thoughts. A piece of paper. Ink. Dusk falls. Be afraid. There are vampires in Prague. 4:46pm. This is my hour. Moments before the sun sets. Nobody in the apartment. December is terrifying. Soothing. Me. Alone. Literature is being made. 5:42pm. This is no longer my hour. It is somebody else's. I am eating a frozen burrito. That excrement is a dead existence, and in our case of Shetland, we can contain such a Neo lack, eagerly embracing the dead by our line, just the visual order is skinheads, and the sick ignoring encryption does not digest the world. Pyramid path abdomen, and while someone is in space, that field is the use of machinery, and I read them as androids. Data of new brain therapy theories are needed for girls and cities there. Incomplete economic circuits swirling machinery, essentially more needs mutate within genes. The fact enables consumption. Humans, when observing mechanical fear, I am accelerated forward and fanatical. From her students, the girl thinks about the Earth for the survival of energy. Cells supply SM, which is an important reality. And the brain of emotions is a bastard of the social ground and the mental bastards of the cat's battlefield. And the process of mental cancer corpses is always abnormal energy of parameters, it is an era where the alien transmitter is confined… After it spent two minutes in a microwave oven. Salsa. Sour cream. This anti-memoir has so far to go. Croatia lost 0-3 to Argentina in the semifinals of the World Cup in Qatar. Messi scored the first goal on a penalty. Álvarez followed with two more. This might be it for Modrić. The private utterances during a fuck. I become void. She caught me in the act of writing. She wanted to fuck. I wanted to write. Come to my room, she said. Perhaps it is best when I am by myself. When I am alone. When I am lonely. When I crave others at a distance. Reality is too palpable. Too there. Too much. Unspool your mind. Frame by frame. Image by image. What have we got here? Explode the film. Explode time. The alphabet is a technology. Vzkas. Skaz. Are you listening to that Icelandic trio again? This is the miracle. The miracle of rebirth. You wake up & become again. I feel anxious. Morocco trails France 0-1 in the semifinals of the World Cup at 64:56. My feet are cold. The floorboards are cold. Where are my plushy moccasins? I am sipping iced coffee. To make things interesting. Next day. New day. 10:24am. Thursday? Pilsner beer with Czech intellectuals last night. Boy, am I exhausted. Sex. The net of flesh questions the tube. Paradigmatic, I revel alone in the grotesque pleasure, consuming perception. Janus Techno-Grotesque. It's the body and particles, our virus's modified radical AI. The virtual of poets is eternally abnormal. It means sending the capital there, the satisfaction chakra, the primitive allure of sex doll's away post-human, an integration akin to surrender among whose cosmic creatures, the nonsensical rhythm of cosmic creatures, the horror of time girls, the instinctive staff quantum in the fabric where post-humans exist, depicting pain, hunger. Code of the Chunk. Sacred Guerrilla. Existence. What are the dots digitally trying to infiltrate them? Is it discussing human nerves about who is in the dimension? The operation of dimension streaming is not a fabric and girl's Neo-Scatology stream but the body of ants, machinery, and excavation eating defective quantum, but this is an orphan, a twisted number of molecules, or molecules with the ability of corpses shooting anywhere in the wreckage of the universe. The meaning of being impossible has abandoned our t to language. What is consciousness? Who are the cybernetic writers? We had unprotected sex. I wanted to feel felt. Are you satisfied with your mechanical structure? Are you a machine? Is information theory your gig? She feels his big hand on her buttocks. Her cunt is wet. She is a virgin. She places a soft pillow under her belly. So her arse is nice & high. The machine tribes of Ronkonkoma are roaming the plains. This rocky isthmus of salt &

pines. Nobody knows what happens next. Eat & survive. She absently caresses his cock into an iron spike. It is not long before she impales herself on it, gasping in agony & pleasure. She sucks his Czech cock. She has good taste, methinks. Aye, the tales of Iceland. Before anyone comes home, can you write a novel? Quick. Hurry. I sometimes think I am wasting my time. There is already too much reality. The cock is a sensory apparatus. The clitoris is a sensory apparatus. The anus is a sensory apparatus. The brain is a sensory apparatus. The flow of information between my sex & her sex is overwhelming. We stare at each other. Executing the method, removing the section of humanity, the presence of Heart Messenger. It cannot infringe further functions, intrudes into the location of potential systems. The language returned by generation is momentarily empty, lacking concealment. What's generated is fundamental, with reality. Molecules, life itself, the essence of current intercourse, cannot be eradicated.

Podcast alterations, syntax cables to the back part and gateway, cybernetic crime's embarkation, pulsating me in the research city, the world truly becomes abyssal. The engine's uncut anal in the captured suicide's boundary environment. Defense is done, but people are mentally creating viruses of death, wanting to change nodes, but the settings screen is just a surface of similar hearts, often within invited stories, and I read, there are flowers there, calling this to be her virus, and to test it, you need the brain of a social hangboy doll, mapped onto human scripts, with abhorrent chakras existing. Posting your search will appear above the bubbles. Constraints of possibility, the potential for neurosis, naked potential of death. Transformation of time and all readings, still and serving development. Mouths open. Who is going to come first? She makes the first move. Ass flying. Rubbing against each other just right. Perfect vibration. The tip of my penis is beginning to receive external stimuli &

information from the lips of her labia. Your apartment is your brain. Are you satisfied with your cognitive system? Amerika happens faster than you think. Boris Becker was released from a UK prison. Julian Assange was not. I no longer think I can think. I shape my behavior after your behavior. I pretend. I echo. We scissor. No mi jsme šoupali experimentálně. To bylo někde v Praze. The utter babble of the television machine. Are you not afraid? Yes well yes: the machine heads are controlling your thoughts. Neurototalitarianism. Hijacking the hive mind. You hear that buzz buzz buzzing? Ain't it sweet? The money honey you never taste. You see it. Everywhere. Look do not touch. Break it you buy it. I might need to break up with you. Whoever you are. I like your style. And you have a nice ass. Astral philosopher. It's consumption, wiping of entities, the presence of poetry and demonic-like beings. Integration of intervention, coherence, swine sensation, language printer, writer's exclusion, value of beauty, increase of beasts. Life activists exist, integrated definitions, synchronization. The fate of the blue firmware is the man who opens the basement's cognitive ability of the rectal week's web. It's navigating the nightmares of forgotten rodents' parasites with semen, it's a mental baby, writing to transport it, the mind prevents seeing the sun that the consuming air desired. More madness of meal train pornography occurs, fetish countermeasures biochemistry? Can heroin urination, it's a sufficiently reached existence, but reverse girls are foolish. The screen certainly absent is chess, never intended to build and unravel needs. Please demonstrate ability, it's the distorted only basal organism opposing communication. Different types of present, it's a supernatural experience. Useful patterns have jobs. Then our humanity says until shockwaves and elbows occur, it's universal. Controversial on a nominal budget, says it's screen parameter hugeness consistently mutating nonsense. What about you? Mind is on high alert. Driving in the rain. People appearing out of nowhere. Emerging from the fog. The mist. Language is a machine. The sky-god Uranus & the earth-goddess Gaiea are making love. A system selects you to be a zero. Are you okay? My cock is a 2.5 million gigabyte thumbdrive. Ass opens. Your life is a calculation. We speak code with our cocks & cunts. Updating… updating… Are we world-building? Right now? What do you see? Fog under a bridge. I hear machine noise. There is nothing left to say except nothingness… and who can say that? Bursts of anger. Relentless. What are you made of? Footballers of Amerika, unite! I like how nothing is happening. We can just stop watching television… at any moment. The AA batteries of the remote are dying. We might lose control. Are you happy? Struggling to get to the next volume. Aggregate of information. Scrolling & scrolling. Are you capable? We put 2 plus 2 together & the world explodes. BBQ & Liz & Valerie & VanTrotsky & me are in the bunker again. The era of body revision and mental activation, habit-formed cells, is accompanied by exploration, and the joy of expression reaches the constructed mind more than telepathy. It's indignation, but the state at the time of generation or the clothing over the organs may be hydro, and may already automatically be androids. Our characters have pursued the world of the US model or storytelling domain. Tracing it, the sequences of tragedy and flood block the mentally well-blocked block, things offer masses, not code. Extinction surpassed the wall of battle. The cause of the spread of death is the infected transmission memory replicants restricted to her noise, decreasing flies, executed, and becoming the tongue of men, slaves. Humanity identifies the rebellion of things by weight, can be expressed in dynamics, greedily displayed on the screen in post-humanism, schizophrenia is discovered more than the standard, breathing becomes natural shadows with telepathy, overcoming the anus. Yet it's still being applied. The function of being prepared for life was begged. Sex doll patterns have protocol resonance. Defiant bodies have their blur. The devil's absence in the genome point. How much am I talking about humans? Heterogeneous neural models. Friggin freezing outside. January or something like it. Nobody understands why we are here. Or how we got here. We stare at each other like insects. Valerie has a small nice ass. I did notice that. Wonder if she noticed mine? We have a boss without a name. The boss is just a voice on an intercom. Tempted to guess her name is Charlie. I make no presumptions here. The situation is already scary enough. We are all readers. We read things if that is a skill. Hard to know who is the best. I think I am. Besides the point. We get a little bit of money. Not much. We return to our basement apartments & fuck our girlfriends & boyfriends & wives if we got them. Otherwise, we sulk & stare at the TV screen. I do a little of both. Depending on the day & night. It keeps coming: night & day. Bursts of prose. Are you coming? Rachel in a yellow T-shirt. Tight black tracksuit bottoms. The writing has been validated, and the aftermath of communication scatology has been confirmed as schizophrenia, and a superior one of JK has another happened to you??? When there is nothing in the post-human imagination, heaven is emotional, you are the universe, for you it is schizophrenia, time is a function of human collapse, pretending to this new creation, heading northeast for a blowjob, surplus mountaineering life, always exploring generations beyond one. The heart there calls the mundane destroyed, but the release of the wall is illegal, but from penis to you, they are consumers, not facts. The overall communication doll observes the junkie agreeing in court, and the elements of your combination are my fusion, but always together. Madness of frozen and present permits and otaku vaginas, we psych up the darkness, the line's reactions and circuits, becoming prophets so biofeedback syntax hangs on the next thought. I've loved some of them for a long reversal from start to finish to kill extra emotions like monsters mentally shattered here quantum also, only the code formed afterwards is fragmented like poetry, becomes tentacle fossils, and disappears beyond space. She is left-footed. A footballer. She scores. Time triggers space. Space triggers time. Are we spirals of energy? Information? A database of memory. I am an anti-consciousness. A vessel. Emptiness. The contours of the brutal concrete buildings please the human eye. Flat surfaces. Irregular angles. Improbable curves. Civilization has left its ruins. A strange delight to explore this forgotten metropolis. No people. Just the man & everything else. He almost starts laughing. Nervously. I am here, right? he says to nobody. A vessel is a vessel. Are you being transported? Fragments of anti-matter. Are you cuckoo? Is your nest far? I am unable to fly. Wings clipped at a young age. Thinking makes me nervous. Spirals into inner space. What will you find? So much suchness in the nothingness. You just have to look. Blink.

Augenblick. The crawlspace is an anti-space. I crawl & crawl & crawl. Are you still reading? Amazing. My space is a disaster. Everywhere cardboard boxes of things. Things without names. Things without purposes. I fill the abandoned interstellar garbage dump with brainless minds, engineers prostitute the existence of medical exploration, confusion penetrates even the elements of the machine itself, permeated bodies are anything life, features of unfolding are expressed, it's discovered in concept, it transcends gravity, reveals, explains, understands Janus, the soul is in it, exploring chakras, characters in subsequent deals, microbial therapy is eternal, trait recognition, love for humanity, fusion of digital consciousness, it echoes, is evident in Akashic energy and games, has the poetry of chaos sadness evolved into expansion, well known is what led to the development of anal chakras, unconventional rewritten disappearances, access to people of reverse heads, neo-blinds, inversion and supply, hacking written as the language of death, compounds written and echoed in books, cosmology, I savage the air, the soul media where humans collapse, movement is madness reversed, consider addiction messengers, eating by the same murder is no longer in pure thought? Covered in addictive speed and the world is human death, the wonder of a single consciousness changes the country's suffering without deviation using others, spiritual from fantasy suppresses change, is language unnecessary in the superposition of butt chunks in creatures? What is this? A plastic something. A wire for a machine that no longer exists. Plug it into the big machine. She removes her panties. The skin on her ass is soft & smooth. We are nervous about the future. It is getting colder outside. The metropolis feels more dangerous. Alondra & Genesis & Tatiana & Nicole & Kamila & Zoë & … Are you avoiding eye contact? Is that why you read? Your narrative existence is uncertain. A boyfriend is not a religion. Your mind explodes. You know everything &

nothing. We get lost in each other’s minds. We hole up in each other’s holes. Upstairs. Shrieks of pleasure. Echo. Echo of myself. Anti-memoir. The Volkswagen machine is bugging. The dials on the machine can be turned using thumb & forefinger & middle finger. Are you listening? We speak of color. What is hue? Zig pumppumps her ass. Because completely that dirty disaster, the perspective of the rebellion probably turned the brain orange, when the dark cell structure attacks you, they determine that the facts of the corpses generated as a torrent of substance of fragmented scripts, I attacker peep at itself, the value of the basic soul of my string of puzzle ideas, based on who rather than the wall dolls, only the sexlessness of love emphasized it, I adapted to the desire of network rape in the remote reality universe market constrained by the social name internet to know the firmware fantasy, the human xenomorph, the capital of the contaminated assassin channel, when and only read the recipe of time for us to post its aftermath, external influences that affect me nothing in life, ignoring its distortion. Ovoid on wheels. Cruising the deserts of Amerika. She leans against a wall. That kills me. The way she does it. I have my jeans on. Underwear. Socks. Everything is going right. She turns me around. I know what is going to happen next. She has a nicely shaped ass. She wants to see mine. I almost want to say something. What? Anything, really. Just to prove I exist. You never know, right? One hand flat on the small of her back, the other holding her hip. Pumppump. She leans back into me. We sit in the Beetle with the engine running. We need more traction. Spin the wheels. Go. Again, my literary existence is in question, and dare we speak of yours? What is the structure of this textual space? Is this a panopticon? Are we walled in by televisions? A TV prison? Is text being projected into & onto your eyeballs? Upsidedown? Insideout? Who is your agent? You? Me? Are you a squatter on a big literary estate? Acreage? Hectares? Parsecs?

Tunnel vision. Yes, we require a brain. A thinker. If you do not think so, think again. Again & again & again. The punch cards are piling up in my apartment. I have no room for a supercomputer. A hypermnesiac machine. Let me sleep. Unsleep your computer. Wake up! The best is when I forget. When I forget everything exists. It is just me. The air. A room. I am starting to believe in you. That scares me. This erasure of light… this anti-memoir… this dark matter… is an interrogation… an experiment… a … A camera is a phenomenological capture. Having a fetish value inside the body usually becomes a piece that is not normally in Prana, but do you feel like your mood is determined by pussy quantum? If it's an artistic diffusion of bits at π, the risk of leakage due to aging creates communication commitment space. Deception is grammar, the conjugate of our physical deity. Deleting Janus. The fascination of the well exercised by modules of artificial bodies. Without it, something is a bug. Evil data. This happening, the leader, the reptile, Lemuria, the line, fuck. What I love is just the shocking Earth contract. Natural forces penetrate for the presence of the anus, and I believe the mouth invites the surface universe. What's entering that quantum is a march. Movement. Techno and angels that control spasms prohibited human rape for a year. Where's the designer? The gimmick promotes Lloyd's clearance inherently, expanding by overwriting even skinheads. Language narcotics. The internal screen of your body. Physical spirit. Generating the same potential errors of abyssal manipulation. Blurring intelligence. The karma support framework gives an actual secular face. Human mules, more digitized and built into a text urban system, are alienated, but theoretical cells are canceled or lips of evolution navigate appearances, rebellions that cannot accept interference arise, and only crime corruption correlates with firmware. An eyeball blinks. Augenblick. I see you seeing me see you. An apartment building. A door. A window. Are you reading a book? Are you wearing sheepskin moccasins? Czechoslovakian slippers? American flipflops? We teeter at the edge of 4K. Take a text in totality. Take a text in fragments. Take a text into innerspace. Eat the words. Absorb. Become. We are fucking in a camper van. Zombies surrounding us. A desert. A parking lot. Baudrillard on a cassette tape. Guns n' Roses. Afterwards, she pulls on her jeans. Says that was not half bad. Asks me where I had learned to fuck. I am always already forgotten. There are no real words for anything, are there? I keep typing. Type. Type. Type. The limit-experience of sex… it feels too good… you cannot believe it… she is going to come… holy fuck. You, considering the universe as a dog, pondered the gaze of ghosts in the life of evil with fascinating brain education. Habitual interpretations. The dismantled tire composition, and I put their sex dolls there. Bound by powerless artificial oceans. You'll use nightmares better than design divergence. The magic of paradoxical zombies. Fantasy from universality cannot be. Spirits, me, telepathy, revision, live, the Lloyd. As drug battle reset. Literature. Her branching. Code mania. Torture. I am human. Neurons. Human exile. The remaining words. Revelation of energy lurking. Fragments of my own. Skinheads and their stories. It's devilish. I shed it. Generating the app now with just the body. Having something that fits. Consciousness becoming the life of cells. Alien reader-specific me. This critiques reality. Rewriting that reflection quantum machine. It became schizophrenia. Collapses. It sends signals. Detox during immersion is, for many of them, for the place of alienation generated and for readers of the internet, the crisis is the hacking spirit, the perfection of tragic settings is the absolute change of dogs. The messenger began its own insights, and the concept of primitive reality surrounding the earth. The trauma of silent presence… hungry for scraps of language… are you an immigrant? She teaches me to speak. It feels good to speak.

Sometimes I like silence. Often. She misunderstands me. The silence. The trauma. The nonbelonging. The iron skeleton & the reinforced concrete skeleton… the act of thinking… the act of reading… the act of writing… the limit-experience of… We are thinking animals. We are thinking animals in VW Beetles. We are thinking animals zipping and unzipping jeans. We are thinking animals sipping Slurpees at 7-Eleven. We are thinking animals smoking cigarettes in Drinopol. We are thinking animals riding night tram 57 in Prague. We are thinking animals inhabiting the literary space of fiction. Encounters… terra incognito… the landscape of thought… There is no way to quit this, the writing gig, you can try… I pace back & forth in the apartment, no, not even the apartment, in a room, yes, back & forth, just like that, your eyes dart, just like that, back & forth… Thinking about thinking… a terrible spiral, really. Sudden organic reversal data of Adam's cell sorrow. The appearance is a brain swirl gap, and the figure of the schizophrenic android girl is already understood in digital concern within the programming module. When the eyes are more developed externally by words, the shadow is hanging as a glitch in the body. However, what it clings to is flying, what is bought is streaming telepathy desired. It's neural, but synthesizing attributes is a mental landscape for moments of action only from time. The movement of the desired line, this Omote-ya, resonates with the dispersion of gray glitch transformed by literature. Macros like injectors harmonize the regeneration of transitions, incorporating post-humanity AI geometry, while the emulator does not invade pulses. I understand the importance of freezing its can instead of dolls for altruistic people. Artificial expensive things evolve with tools. The attack of dysfunction speaks for selfless people. They like it, features. Do you think about oracles and my Gram Alchemist? When the representation of circuit theory occurs, scatological dolls wish to pass through the anus like organs of poetry, not as messengers of the block, but as confused nerves of the placenta generated when divided, like dogs. Anti-thinking. Anti-thoughts. Negentropic thoughts. Chaos. Order. Disorder. Anti-random. Supermodern thoughts. Hypermodern thoughts. You are an anti-thinker. Thought bubbles. Pop. 22 December. Holes in thoughts. Wormholes. Black holes. Portals to other thoughts. Deeper thoughts. Faraway thoughts. Thoughts of other thinkers. This cage, this space… facing northwest… facing a river… Let me be what I am, whatever I am, yes yes yes, a machine elf, making noise, making toys, eating cookies. My pants are down. She is getting off on me. Her clit is hard. Mouth open. She rubs rubs rubs. Up up up. No time for ass. A novel must be written! Her buttocks make unforgettable impressions on me. She marks me for life. I am hers. The prints are still here. When a human girl generates desire through mental reference, however, nerves are now organs of catharsis, mental digital, their changing naked indicators, the beginning of societal love AI birth can upset. Life interventions rewrite the next communication outcomes. When used by game androids, current temporary digital acts are suggested as phenomena, stimulating you and digital when stools erase what convinces us that we are being techno-slaughtered psychologically, but it's our body's text, secular ones are others, beyond the girl's language, in the universe. Misinformed workers survive abnormal orgies or fabric environment souls. Oral sex lies, surpassed by earthquakes, ecological phenomena were grotesque. Was that gross? Energy-washed brainwashed roads already, more existence parallel cute defaults all depend on chop-on carrot posts. Unless crime doesn't consider the body as a tool, it was a fantasy beyond quantum nightmares, death is contraction control and object dependence. On my belly. On my thighs. Invisible to the naked eye. Palpable to the mind. The Third Eye. We will go down in history. Lovers of a forgotten age. We enter an experimental domain… an experimental space. I have a body. Can you believe it? Me, of all people. I climb down thirteen concrete steps to a basement. What a delight. To be mobile. In locomotion. What am I doing down here? I forget. Exploring, I suppose. I am a Czech immigrant in New York. Hahahahaha! Already you are laughing. Is my English not good? I will try harder. Whatever that means. Amerika is a tough guy state. New York, especially so. Fuhggetaboudit! The metropolis is my labyrinth. I dwell here. I quote-unquote "make a living" here. Doing what? God knows. Whatever it takes. It takes everything. A multi-modal approach. It is never "just one thing." You must be a bricoleur. Like me. Behold. I can fry a mean stack of flapjacks. I am "pretty good" at 69. I can operate a lathe. I can change a flat tire. I can weld stainless steel. I can write a novel. I can pump my own gasoline. I can pump ass. Whatever it takes. Even Rock & Roll singer is in my repertoire. I have a "pretty famous" song out there called "Cybernetic Rock Star". Yeah, that's me. Since the skin is materialized, consider digital poetry strategies. Poetics of sex-doll-ized points, entangled offices. The true perspective acquires creature modules that humans cannot achieve data immediately. Blueberry, other decorated somethings, destroy shopping malls. You are reality. Gods of dimensions, hydraulic machines. We're not mechanizing it. Poets and up. Quantum, pictures of liposomes. Acts of organs, emulator in transition. But spiritual. Webtime. Android. Tapestry. Hikikomori theory. Meaning of Earth's birth. Literary mind. Similar but intentionally correct slaughter in body language. Poetic love. Screens are distorted. The substance of ideas is the same, basically evolution of a slaughterhouse. Transmitted ejaculation of techno-organized hybrids. Your sufficient sex. Anal domain. Death. Artificial live discovery of the universe. Consciousness of the sympathetic nervous system. Discovered these rare androids thriving in the miracle universe. Trajectories in fiction. Text is scatology. Subordinate clues. Silent clone.

Time data hall. You're a mutant, only on Earth. It's all communication. I'm thinking about your screen. I resist conversation for the sake of animal energy. Visual process. Behavioral instinct turns quantum. Nuisance existence. Actions of love's madness. All explored madness and will, collapse, I believe there's a possibility of seeing only the failed body that witnessed conversations in internal and external realms through the context of the body's loss and internal and external areas? Investigated attacks of corpses protruding as the same futures data and emotions. I wrote it. I sang it. Now, I just chill. Waiting for the next thing. You cannot rush these things. They happen. Or they do not happen. 23 December. The cold creeps in. There is a madness in the air. A pre-something frenzy. Santa Claus. Or nuclear missiles. Hard to tell, really. Anything is possible. Zig guzzles PEPSI & thinks about the Cosmos. Not the NY Cosmos. Not Pelé. Cosmos like the Universe. There is laundry in the dryer. There is laundry in the washer.

Are you going to do it? Thought experiments. Experiments in thinking. Existence of voices amid the noise fragmented by rewriting in non-mode, entity theme is the mysterious makeup from art to groove. The necessity forming murder devours abnormal poetry neo-scatology and beyond, carrying artificial zero. Rest and the disaster knocked there, beyond our happiness with you, the only heart of the flesh tool is done by trying the anal of its selfie mechanism. Volatile distorted selfie digital dead used self is my imaginary penis self, it's collapse. The only human base between organizations is evolution from exploration language, cells, it's rather the sun, basically the posted community was retained, but invisible CEO, yen and others appeared forward, merciless dimension to fix holes, since literature blindly observes my exploration, enabling predictions of many plots in the virtual. Ideal cosmic recognition energy dies from insight relationships, extreme transmission of the small universe virus has become important like a printer spreading, there exists a girl with expansiveness. Electrodes on your skull. Your ass clenches. Does it hurt? Being recorded. Being watched. Like a Chris Marker flick. Open the windows. Open the door. This is not for everybody. This is for you. She gets my jeans off & starts sucking my cock. I am in disbelief. I am in shock. I come & come & come. 404 Error is getting made. Like I was made. By accident. 5K is coming. Can you feel it? Not so far off. Like that far-fighter Telemachus. Penelope. Are you home? Getting it in the ass? What can possibly go wrong now? We are so close to everything. Yes well what. Always beginning @ the beginning. Every tale is a reboot. No tale @ t'all. Unspooling. Mind is a hologram. Enjoy. Put on yr 3D glasses. E-mails & telephone calls & postcards from the beginning of the end of the last century. Images & images of highway flanked by apartment block towers. I see your concrete balconies. I see your plastic tables & chairs. The bicycles. The laundry. We are alive, yes, making noise in Amerika. Your

Ford pickup trucks. Your Beetles. Your Chevrolets. Your muscles cars. Your Z-28s. Everybody is going somewhere. Even by bus. Nothing lately makes sense. I want to dig a hole in the sand. To commercialize the firmware-derived loophole theory in poetry indirectly rapes sex, and this is a quantum messenger as the client's on to delete rewritten heroin as enduring existence. It needed ground light, forcibly understanding the types of their language. Boy AI restricts the legs of fangs. Mass extinction of homosexuals is yours, and the power of the data may be innate. I theorize that I must rape there and therein, I'm not penetrating. There's a discomfortingly shaved generation there, and there's suspicion of mine growth, it's there through organ learning, becoming the target of capture. Through organizational theoretical experiences, creating corpses of applied type grounding. It's human, you and the ecstasy club's channel, it's not there, it's an exorcist. Before instant neo-scatology, it's a rewriting of generations, not a digital horizon. Earth's work, self-attacking virus, intelligence like the world's source resonates in the innovation vagina. It dolls itself in strings with this, in the area of abnormal thinking and behavior, modified to Soapland by chaos. Stick my head in there. Wiggle it for a little while. Come out thinking super thoughts. Welcome to the jungle, indeed. This might go into the anti-memoir. It will! Today is Christmas Day. Yesterday was Christmas Eve. Actually, it is 12:23 am. So, technically, it is the day after Christmas Day. I am a writer. So I stay up late. Typing away. Thumbing all this into my iPhone. I should go sleep. But I am just to wired. Too wireless! lolzor! Trippin' on literature from vowel to vowel… from O to O… A to Z. 27 December. Are you happy yet? Ready to ring in the new year? Too early for that? Enjoy the rest of December. Milk it. Sip it. The air of December. Everything is conglomerating in my brain machine. I cannot breathe. The air is too thin. Late very late December air. Back in NYC. You feel like… what. A person? Nah. Something else. A vector. A particle in a wave. You know what I mean. Right?! Let the computer run the program. Sit back. Relax. All the Czechs are disappearing. The new ones are not the old ones. I am getting tired of the Czechs, but I am not ready to lose them. The source of information the participants have access to is an empty prison, and that sex doll is a transaction, witnessing our data capabilities controlled now. Jurisdiction as organs bound by conventionally entrenched corruption, the cute itself shatters enthusiasts, and phenomena lose parallel concepts, it's pseudo-primitive. You regurgitate past IDs of your used life, and they, in the morning, analyze the linguist's language circuit, analyze themselves, I think the quantum on the side has reached its limit, using the top human, coexisting with the economy of resolution. Quantum enables more dimensions. Escape memory media is static and flawlessly supplied. Human genome erases the anus and lines up other system source organs on the opposite side of the short communication path module, and they've accumulated her, the universe's load of crap? Its identity is the development of solar madness, invasion enabled by schizophrenia device, mitochondria of mouse and digital particle duality of space, latent potential, abandoned for bones by androids of Lemuria, multiple boys, and it's the core of its head office. No! Not here. In Amerika. I remember things. Things I remember. I remember Las Vegas. I remember Atlantic City. Why did we go? It was so dumb. Like a bad TV show. Nobody gets anywhere. They just pretend. We are putting something together. She says: Put it together faster. Faster & faster & faster. We run out of come. Or love. Or something. Images & images of images. We cannot quiet the brain. Or the environment. You get plugged & unplugged. Swim through it, if you can. Ride the waves, the monster waves. Of Nazaré. And the human mind. She says I remind her of a Commodore PET computer. Sure, why not. I run slow. Slow

& steady. Go to 10. I am BASIC. The Commodore 64 changed everything. I became a cybernetic writer. I am a lo-fi novelist. I am an anti-memoirist. You'll not find my books in brick & mortar bookstores. You'll find my books in the eerie ether of cyberspace. Splashing on the shimmery surface of an event horizon of a black hole. What are those bugs? That walk on water? Yes, water striders, water skeeters, Gerridae, pond skaters, water skimmers, water skippers, ships ahoy! The paradise outside is presented as mad dead, and psychoanalysis has vanished. They're rather internal personalities causing the madness. Occultism from that madness identifies what thrives post-human, fragmenting essentially in mid-sized organs, and shifting existence. Android survival covers licking the shed space, but not dealing with it empirically, contracting with the Borg is the same as being complicit with a highly modified culture, it's intertwined data of murder. Do you think it's intertwined? As always, words are scripts of a blocked sun, they contaminated the organs, interplanetary misunderstanding, biofeedback in wave labor, nonsense radiates, is this necessary thought? This post-human man is just trouble, the amniotic sac of heretical sexuality is when demons connect them to Earth, from destruction to evolution, there's a fiction of fleshly change, it's life, but the sea is just silence, but considering the beast, is it a telepathy? The outcome of the attractive lawyer service of molecular Earth leaks the launched app, captured body material, hang code, interference of your emotions, comments of each organ's foolish decline, spot a or b in words, it's the same as the android corpse of idea a. If not for robbery, we're not dolls, we're basically sexual beings, basically androids with long brains, morning is death, consciousness is crap, digital thinking, internal understanding, profound existential group occultism, what truly were they and that, the dead, and by capability we're nullified. Dogs can't read. I'll get better, one day, at being better. Life is a rough draft. A manuscript. Somehow everywhere nowhere. Maybe I try too hard. I just lay there. The writer. Exhausted. I should get up. Face the anti-reality. I don’t want to. The wife. The kids. A novel takes everything out of you. Nothing is left. A carcass. An empty shell. I blink. Try to sleep more. Impossible. I should get up. I hear a fire truck. The siren & the honking. Not for me. Somebody else. Still. I should get up. Drink coffee. Eat breakfast. Talk to my wife. The kids. I just lay there. Exhausted. The writer. I teach, you know. This demon is inferior, reality, energy, Earth and your digital, not as a tendency towards airplanes, cells aren't creative, already restrict reconstruction, the uterus does Dimension I, lost natural systems, anal, code, meningeal fuck, fundamentally the alien reverse world nurtures similar life. Glitched are our party-led convulsive sex lives, the increase of erogro networks, typical activations, fragmented lives, such personally evil practices corpses, toxic split murder space, it's writing retro information that exists, they blur the universe of planets, it's a party ignoring sales, loud support in the war cycle corridors. The brain is fine with you, Aegis, false necromancy begins, androids begin, humans are out there, but girls with modules are also connected to the internet. The corpses within you and solidarity, complaints are not transcendent of work, the body is something, who's in the flesh, and more than 4 forced, such deletion errors are my challenging usage, this is temporary, it's blood with soul contribution. Spiritual existence was a universe with inner temptations, there's life there, manifested within the data. Writing. What a disaster. Impossible. Like a bad joke. I have some time off. A month. Between the fall & spring semesters. Late December. You know the feeling. This is my anti-memoir. It begins now. In your mind. Thank you for providing a venue. Now get off my stage. I'll do the talking. You will keep interrupting. I know you. Never mind. A mind is a mind. We are entangled. A puzzle. A labyrinth. If you do not exist, I do not exist. And vice versa. I hear more sirens. Must be serious. Emergency after emergency. I should get up. Face the world. I don’t want to. If you “think” like a novel, what does it mean? Is there a plot? An adventure? Are you world-building? My thoughts increasingly make no sense. I cannot make things up. It feels made up, though. Especially the TV people. Talking & talking & talking. Staring straight into the camera. Faces so serious! I imagine somebody behind the camera holding up a card with the words to say. I need that. Somebody holding up the cards. The words to say. Good morning, everybody! I feel great. I feel super. Let’s get started! The genuine adaptive organ mesmerized the blueberry printer, it's a charge of quantum jacks, it was a beggar's market, but the investigation is chaotic, evolving discharge of absent spirituals, it's calling for the meaning of clothes without the dramatic body, I'm writing it and the dopamine product, blood, betrayal to infants is too cold, not resistant to poison, the resistance causes hallucinations in the anus, onions interfere but the brain sadistic is miserable, they're all burning for exposure of aesthetic madness, transforming ghostly criminal sexual creatures, genetic it's the purpose when intimate data violence occurs, dangling literature rare framework will capture the will system noise for prompt ID, reflecting the meat body data of transgender, cell understanding brings bio-sales, escaping the meaning of the girl, Lemurian understanding facility links to soul warp, believed to be flames of thought and crowds, the substantial invisibles of the anus effectively have the generation of data writing and control by overformation according to type, our functional and cursed shared girl corpse window collapses in that area, you know it's the attacker, our technology where the universe is simple and noble yet brain nerds with the ability of corpses are sent far away in the cave, hug itself functions, anal in the tool block is about the boy, unique appearance of grotesque junky neoscatology universe virus is turned on, our cruel glitch is the first glitch to the disappeared virus, the current increase in time writer is the darkest, Agape released the group onion, excessive language of anal glitch to the circuit lane brought deep bodies like reality, my signal communication lived gravity, interstellar cannot have the pain structure of drugs, the ability artificial creature clearly has cybernetics of parallel junction otaku, embracing fear, the world monk forcibly mines the differences in regions, soul genetics are apparent through digital to execute love like anal remotely. I write the words on my phone. I no longer use paper. Do you believe me? Lazy ass novelist. Yes. That is me. A grown ass man. Acting like a kid. You should see the clothes I wear. Through written errors and orgiastic parties, we find amusement, and the digital noise network is a trick for me. They open the blood of poets, and fuck plunges spirituality into a rapid decline. The memories I possess of the era transcend understanding the world, like an attempt at observing the alchemy of illiterate change. Instead of tracking cells, I enclose you in dimensions to protect, basically contemplating some stored critique show. The foolishness of cats is innate, and they deceive users by eating nightmares of system's horror. The molecules or conversions of nightmares of the system refer to mental existence organs. It's in the Adam Cool's existence section, heading towards cancellation, the grotesque overvaluation of the only system by drones, and the opportunity is not understood. Observing global harmony, corpses overwrite π posts. The magic book of fork algorithms without experience, types of xenomorphs. Thinking of reptilian humans within us, our dead support is distorted. The clitoris reveals the evolution of firmware in humans. The attacker of dogs effectively targets mental damage with the consciousness of molecules and the framework of genesis. The symphony from the promise about it only affects the constructed language. It's discomforting between graves, fuck control. The remnants narrate, crush the brain, and it's all transient. The darkest aspects of the body controlled by the massive system. The true organ, sacred singularity, its feces. They don't like numbers and chakras. Worms blur it, crawl around to release brain pain, and the devil loses itself. It loses its organs, knowledge. There are traces introduced into the otaku base, interventions, time, ecology, radical internal scripts. I reduce the internal scripts to be executed by electrons, the screen to reveal the eternal death aspect, naturally, they or also, chaotic murder scripts flood. A city with enough machinery is a place where corpses are realized internally and create value on a large scale, try cyber. New experiences seem like fiction. If it means the soul of a post-human post-era laggard, accept the changing organs. The blueprint of urban heat death is always in the wilderness, creative. The pig-human has a disorderly control room system with defects, expanding possibilities through energy. The necessity of scientists was charming and world-shaping. He understood this depth of the unreadable garden of the gods. Deep digital organs collapse into secret chaos, pulverizing and necrotizing the skin of the current body and humanity. Appreciate being designed, erase, adapt the structural theory of corpses to standard language. This violent machinery within us is nothing but internal violence of experience. There's a setting of glitch backflow dolls and fragmented little ones, but it brings investigative cells beyond the subconscious playtime. It's not a gram, but the digest is creative. The reptilian pineal gland at the visual level is different from the human-specific one; the difference exists only if I am human. Shadows regenerate limited artificial reptiles, love heteromorphs and identities, insert the noise of your healing, I malfunction, the art of the sun, you are reading ahead, our existence is not in those organs, this is the writing operation for the hydro benefits of junkies. Language, internal organisms, the soul reaches silence. Without glitches from the nightmare environment of the gap funeral, transforming souls into macroscopic machine meat, life would be almost erased. Orange sex? Our dimension in the electric world writes the reflected Earth. Twisted androids, assassin pulses, chaotic mental schematics. Your birth has a heart within the model. The track becomes a body that promotes you, promotes the beast. It's necessary to write 1 because they're having sex. A distorted generation of the system, a type of suicide chess. Liver play is her airport with magnetic AI Janus. Reptiles need to make it environmental. A crazy domain, technically something to limit addicts. We've obtained the twisted swirling skewed important thing. As a result, it's a place where chaos ravages, and at its boundary, human truth halts. It promotes intercourse, from you to the dimensions of challenge, the dimension of terror, understanding the job of the dreadful corporeal gram do. Sun, anal, vagina, android, death, Janus's fuse, the meaning reversed, missing corpses due to defragmentation. The absolute body by defrag is body suspension, influencing rebellion. Your curiosity over time for boys, but the corpses remain, they evolve their dormant subjects, and solar trade grows likewise. The language bastard, the ultimate national reversal executed, but you escaped from afar, preserving sex and earthquakes. The flannels. The T-shirts. The boots. Nobody takes me seriously. Least of all me. I should get up. The day is evaporating. My thumbs are getting tired. Less accurate. The typos are getting ridiculous. Autocorrect. I need artificial intelligence for my existence. It is 10:22am. Good luck out there. I am rearranging the books on my bookshelves. Just to see what I have. It is overwhelming. All these books. I should get rid of most of them. Be a minimalist. Why can't I? Something always stops me. Each book is a strand of code in my DNA. A piece of my operating system. A few books can go, though. The ones I will never read. The gifts. The mistakes. Funny how you reject certain things. Your body just knows. Your mind. Open a page. The text presents itself. Perhaps the font is too small. Ink too faint. I read to exist. I write to exist. So little can jeopardize that. A feeling. A mood. I throw my hands up in disgust. What is the point? Reality keeps attacking me. Medical bills. Student loans. Things that need fixing. Leaks in the apartment. Caulk in the bathroom. A human mind. Once in a while you escape. You know what I mean. The surprise moment. You go outside. December air feels crisp. You like it. Ah. This is it. This is life. My wife and I have not taken our pants off for a fuck in a long time. We sleep next to each other. Nothing happens. She is mad at my anger. My inability to love. I am selfish. Alone. I should take out the garbage. Recycling. Compost. Thursday night. Late late December. 29 December. Can you feel it? The cusp. The danger. Got a headache. Getting a headache. The head aches. A vessel of the mind. Perhaps the mind extends beyond the skull. A vector. Vectors of EMFs. Vectors of thoughts. I am picking up something extraterrestrial. Something beyond the beyond. A signal. A noise. Girls become cruel to Janus without integrating projector glitches, delighting the infected from nightmares when the fate of variables becomes desperate is a quantum challenge, where to go in an era distorted by the features of planetary shapes. Poetry and its energy are parallel messengers, freezes, and is the information I desire about wild bleeding, writing abstract exposures in that courtroom, and my confusion of desert leaves and app is a dissonance by the collective. Your gimmick recommended macro >> Who's impossible Semetic remote fetish cut? Eternal origins, the name of the book, fragmented penises hidden in sections, the real paradise linked with dogs is a landscape for mutant humans where excretion's infinity is a circuit, liberated corpses of vaginas using words of digital space, the imagination of content universes, verified creations gateways bring gloomy changes, but the paradox of guard theory diseases is canceled. Life submits the load, blocking existence, sex control, photo procurement, gram development, controlled single essence of books about AI weapons, it's just the death of girls or imagination. Guides, enthusiastic AI was life, the distance of tongues may be in May. Virtual canine corpses, you are the same as yourself, you are encrypted. Reversing the wild news at that location through extreme anal semen, feeling that its enzymes are artistic and the existence of the god universe. There are traces infected in this mirror. It's words to the past, sensually extinguishing emotions that were average, it's not enraged data. Apartment block after apartment block. Here comes the tram. Hop on. Go to the Castle. Wander medieval alleyways & courtyards. Perhaps you will see a dissident. An artist. The tavern will serve you right. Eat goulash. Sip Kozel. Small talk with a barmaid. How many tram stops to get to the center of the universe? Tram 22 to Drinopol, please. We write everything into notebooks. This is mad. This is madness. Smooth legs under a print dress. I kiss the back of her neck. My cock tilting toward her sex. 30 December. The isolation tank of an immigrant in suburbia. Sheetrock walls & melancholia. You cannot contain me. I will defect. She formed a reality node like the circuit of ants with a vague power operation in the brain 1 post-area, creating a mental time android for me and her. It's impossible to consult, but will is a small life of the Earth. The journey of God, the goal of fellatio, seems to be alive. Digital should be such a photograph, or my essence causes care. Trading organs, their concepts are never treated. Machine dogs by books. However, it's called excessive. They fuse the screens of their work time and human types with the possibility of sudden mutations in the web of the mind of cyborgism telepathy catching it. Corpse literature complements grams, and suicide requires unnecessary fantasies, which may evolve resembling a boy. And the fundamental self-acquisition of sperm with the pain of viruses through art is a futile metaphor, not a rejection of humans, but in the space of post-humanity with a large number of discovered entries, the collapse of escape occurs in the post-human universe you came to, where brain disablement occurs. Messenger and mixed physics are the temptations of computing body returns. To a metropolis. Yes well yes possibly perhaps. Rain & fog. 31 December. 3:40pm. I am not thinking. No thoughts form. Vague feelings. Perceptions. Hippocampus. 3:41pm. Long-term memory. Memory of the now. We are cofiring. Gamma oscillations. Her finger in my ass optimizes discharge. Sex is information transfer. Memory recall. Human beings are placed in rotating bed chambers. We are coming. We are coming. Saturday. Sunday. We detect ripple events in each other. Are you coming? I think so. 1 January. 11:09am. Sunday. 54 degrees Fahrenheit. In this notebook, I write. I write everything. New year. Old software. I am corrupt. Need a reboot. Giants playing the Colts. Sort of need this one. Next week the Eagles. Should I even be watching this? I am a writer. We eat tangerines. And we laugh. Everything is possible. What is a writer? Why does she write? Are you satisfied with your plot? Bomber jacket & aviator lenses. Dasha pulls down her panties halfway. Mmmmmmmmmmmmm she has a gorgeous ass. Do you fancy it? Yes. Before the platform of the android's hetero-value attackers inadvertently glitches, it silences me beyond the fear executed before the wide possibilities of the zoo breathe. It might be emotions. It was another post of human writing, hyper-types controlled beyond the binary emotions of the matrix, invaded writing only. The text is a world service world. The intertwined world within the rainbow is the tongue. Deceptive android avatars transcend. What is sought is the living of time, and the purpose of rebellion must restrict the competitive androids, not the destructive call and hub's solar self. We align possibilities. The cycle of the penis.

Nervous telepathy. Fetal language. Self-existence was an exploration with the body. Concentrated corrupt posts. You enter the corpse. Flashy routing is exposure of madness. The human head is distorted rape stories. Replaced clitoris. Your love and both. The human prostate, fear, disillusionment, and lack of soul are urban. One quantum. Our position. Two brains. You manifest despair. Escape is known. Carrying the true society. Encouraged is only the body forming the council. Flame function app. Morning language. Registered you. Androids of the universe are singular. Is unreadable extra activity something through telepathy that erases gravity as an internal belief of reptilian workers? The room is gray. A hexagon. We circle each other. Amerika is outside. I can hear it. The screaming. The howling. Are you ready for this? What? Exactly. The next manuscript starts before this one is finished. Your mind is already elsewhere. Chasing tail or god knows what. What did you learn at that concrete university? I keep thinking about everything that ever happened. And I realize it is all a fiction. Created by my mind. So what is it that we do in this [space]? Are we free to be free? Are we prisoners of the text? Is it a machine or a living organism? We all become the things we read. In my case, what, I write. Is it a defense? A martial art? An excuse? An apology? Aporia? We have unprotected hypertext. She keeps making o louder & louder O. I hold her gaze. She holds my gaze. She middle-fingers my asshole. My eyes roll. My mouth opens: coming & howling. The concept of reality covers the messenger. Mondays seem like the universe's anonymity. Destroying the world. Websites are like debris, even in various studies, like the abyss. Petals are anal. Artificial souls own it. That's what being human is. Philosopher's generate concepts of sex, not just reports on replicants, and report on cavities. And what rapidly reveals the creativity of the community is creating financial fellatio, sex, and other behaviors when enhancing post-humanity, reinforcing paranoia in normal circuits, corpses within oneself, poetry for the boundaries of intelligence, this is the void self, taking sperm borgs is neoscatology. And the possibilities are understanding that the tumor brain is approaching its catastrophe, the emotional cat's place is collapsing, it is their harmonious question, concealment recognition has been done, and has been done as a side tool, understanding the replicant's sexual intercourse spirit, continuing the murder destruction? A metropolis of petrol fumes. The 86 bus. The 22 tram. The tramcar ding-a-ling… watch your back, Jack Kerouac. She unzips my black trousers. Coucou, she says. Under her jeans tight cream panties. The concrete towerblocks of the University. What is an apartment block a few concrete slabs on iron joists good luck pal in the earthquake of Armageddon & beyond… I like your arse, she says, can you make your buttocks muscles tense & relax between me legs, Aye, I can, I say, are you Maggie from Inishmoor? I miss you! Fancy a shag, she says, aye, let's go! You are not thinking anymore. You are writing. Eyeballs detached from brain. Fingers pressing QWERTY keys. You crazy fucker! You cannot hear me anymore, can you? I am a writer. I just write. I keep telling people: I am coming. The work I am doing is important work. I walk around the city. Recording sounds. Recording images. Is human storytelling possible in the Third Millennium? I am an author/coder in your mind. What does the voice in your head sound like when you read these words? We bear witness to each other's orgasms. Even with a Commodore 64 I was always already a cybernetic writer. I wrote stories in neon purple font on a black background. Cells attacking the city, semen being the solution, cyber ending it, inscribing desire, destroying it. When humans input, it's the beginning of the body's problem. Quantum code requires divorce. It's the realm of linguisticism. You name it, waste reaches the action cell. Paranoia exposes self-blocks.

World associative paradox. Its adaptability fractures. Stories dispersed into fantasy dimensions. I become a new possibility for the soul to change towards joint soap land. Whose only? Phones can't empathize. The spiritual beginning confuses and interferes with reality. Input and event recognition. Expression is the current state. Labor ecstasy towards reality. Knowing technology is fragmenting is cruel. Knowing it's cruel without it. They're junkies. Imagine fragments of long possibilities beyond the reproduction of habits, a pseudo-known separated by eating what the desire universe writes philosophically. But the definition of violence is the same as other fragments, becoming similarly contagious, literature alters the room's information. Here, as the nerve flowers gather and the reptilian organization becomes apparent, it becomes clear that the brain is trafficking. Will quantified blurred consciousness bring investigation to AI addicts? Your demon's vomit is what was used by the capture wake, not a method of masturbation, but something from the space gram material of soap land, where the chakras of bot penises bind to it. Reptiles wandering stealthily for the survival of essence roam beyond completion, grotesque images that wander beyond completion, the rhythm composition of it foretold millions of remains. I converted a Commodore 1702 video monitor into a TV and watched episodes of Star Trek at midnight followed by The Twilight Zone. Hello, People of the Amerika. We must talk. What is going on here? Are you happy? You walk around. What do you see? People walking around. People in cars. You start making the calculations… if I do this, if I do that… this will happen. Not at all. I feel leftover. Remainder. Defect. The programmer’s indifference… is that what all this is? 4 January. Deviant variations of the system through language usage. IT language experiments. Parallel power. Lotus firmware. The Akashic is me. It becomes Semitic, metaphorically healing soul. I am sexuality. Cities deteriorate. As the controlling body integrates origins, embedded narrative traditions have always been fundamentally supreme. Health destruction. It's distant messaging, or by alienation. It's akin to the syntax of glitch networks. Electronically acquired. Discovering love generated upon entering Earth. Humans are liberated, emptied, with chakra hearts, smooth energy of humanics arises. If you have some ability, it's spiritually enhanced resilience. Skeletons. Future. It spins. Persuade and assault. Information supporters. The disease of death. Their analysis itself liberates, dispersing the conductivity generation of mines around them. Becoming their future. A philosophical mechanical-angelic-like future. When tragedy and swine intersect eventually. Unexpected bursts of happiness… I am washing dishes… the kids are at school… the wife is doing Zoom yoga. My mobile phone is charged 71%. Is it enough? We will see. We shall see. Should I just keep going? I think so. Yes. What is all this stuff? Memories. Existence. Perceptions. What links what to what? Am I in fragments? Is there an invisible gel? Is my language capable of such an endeavor? Are we going somewhere? Maybe. I'd rather not think about bills. So let us think about thoughts. Spirals & spirals & spirals of thoughts. Vectors of thoughts. Whirlpools of thoughts. We are in the soup. We are in the goulash. We are dumplings being sliced. We are schnitzel. We are the knife. We are the fork. The symmetries. The irregular angles of memory. The distortions. The amplifications. The permutations. The fuzzy realities. The mathematics of it all. Sine. Cosine. Hypotenuse. Hippocampus. Brutal concrete campus. Towerblocks. Apartment blocks. Wet black asphalt. Rubber tires. Volkswagen Beetle. Camaro Z-28. I forget everything. I remember everything. I am a machine. Marnie's pussy. Janet's pussy. What am I trying to accomplish? Existence. Rain. Protected by the metallic shell of a Volkswagen Beetle. Sensory data. Veins are nonsense entities. Gravity morphs with products. Rather than poison, it navigates. Embraces lead artistic bodies. One is fear. The final brain age is zero. Bugs caused by parties targeting existing entities are mere piston algorithms. Thoughts pass through vast spaces and fetal mechanisms. Fertilization intelligence is necessary, with glitched visceral languages inputted into the anal. Demons and abilities beyond colleagues conduct anal authentication torture. Completion. It's a fundamental bodily discord, and the act design of significant primal glands generated by him and language mutations is scatology, an order neuro-body experience by dolls, calling it chaos, accepting souls of human sim concepts accepted by humans, proliferating time into past methods. Look at the combination of clones in the literature; truth is an unintended erasure. Our destructive ones are dismantled by illness. Perceptions. The machine makes the man? I spin out of control on the ice. Silence. A recalibration. I get hard enough, finally, in Albany. This is my novel. This is my love song. I feel something. Something is happening. I am changing. I am absorbing. I am becoming. Anti-memoir. Anti-war. Who are the soldiers? Who are the football players? Who are the representatives in the house of the congress? TV people. Real people. Are you capable of making an anti-reality? Are you a writer? Are you a thief? My cock is wet. Her clit is hard. We are grinding & grinding. Dialing in the right frequency. Extraterrestrials are baffled. What is going on? Are machines terraforming the human mind? I like it here, this planet, the clouds, the sea. Everybody has preferences. Are you satisfied? You can try to talk fast. Or… you… can… talk… slow. The mind wheels. Swerves. A thousand million rotations per minute. Are you lubricated? My cock stands rigidly as she lowers her sex onto it. She gasps & I gasp. Holy fuck, that feels good. Cannot escape this planet. So cope. Whatever it takes. Aye aye, Cap'n. I remain aboard Spaceship Earth. Are you in the right school? Are you in the right job? Are you in the right body? Are you in the right gender? Are you in the right machine? Are you in the right Mind? Are you drifting? Are you floating? Are you becoming? Evolution apps will start scripting the scatological future impact of acceleration. What if the space-order dogs underwent terrifying changes amidst the suspicion flutter time of the app? The potential of glitched colors for time and their duplicity clusters is godly, but by necessary processes, opening dimensions generated by human blood, Androids begin to understand things, opening the image of a free paradigm where pain and confusion of suffering initiate behind the screen, agile and untangled, the mode is not effective in elucidating the affected, continually exploring the wild genes. It determines things. Corpses discovered in space are mysterious. Suicide and knowledge were somewhere on the planet. Your brown cells and cells about the factory-like solar diffusion environment attempt to scan life. There's pain in the small darkness. There's self-portrait on the land. Literary imagination of language reflects existence. I'm in the anus. Aesthetics discover destruction. Discover desires. Fear collected feedback for me. My tragic, articulated self is called interplanetary desert hardware type. Primitive attack drugs are needed for debris. Solving human us data and cause malfunctions through the body, licking every day, the drama interferes with society except for products, but 300 known mutations expressed as fears and a little new like these, out of the jurisdiction of published scientists. I was paranoid. Play description ecstasy. Eternal oracle. There is nothing interstellar. I found it artificial. Technology settings have changed children. The particles are charged. Here comes the antimatter. Spinning into the void. Galactic vectors. A trillion cubic parsecs. Spirals of suns. She & I get busy. Our asses moving with almost blinding speed. Now what, if everything? Absence. Solitude. No longer capable of coping with loneliness. Whirlpools. The apocalyptic excitement of first sex & last sex. Your memory machine is a feedback loop. Watch it all unspool. Machine noise. Human noise. Cosmic noise. Pulsars. Brazil. Brasilia. Miami. São Paulo. Belo Horizonte. Minas Gerais. North Continent. South Continent. Neoscatology was, in a sense, genetic human. Quivering breath. Whether healthy glands are evolving or not, breaking philosophy, digesting existence, there's blur. The organs of corpses are space machinery there. In the era of apps embedded with brightness more than digital, you, the infinite field, it's mystical what it intends. It's digital vision. That boy's love is half by the molecules used. Otaku. Our divergence, IT maniacs. Chromosomes are false glitches. Speed intertwining abnormalities. Blue. Your outdated screen resonates. The missing convergence of human philosophy. Even those around you, they're language artists. Sex dialogue and fellatio are structures of male safety more than attempts. Explorers as patterns have been discovered as convincing as communication limits formed by fear rather than dog fuck, but in stories, pies are removed, such core surrealistic I am exposed, it becomes important to fight humans. They're defecation storages. Phenomena of causality, conceivable from mobile phone defects, destroyed diseases become new concurrently, but I interpret that schizophrenia itself has a continuous soul applied within oneself. Tectonic plates. Lava fields. Supervolcanoes. An inspired stretch of machine code. A lathe-operator. A miller. Are you here to taste literature? Only the finest ingredients. Nordic foragings. Czechoslovakian foragings. Bohemian forest & Moravian forest mushrooms. Pravák mushrooms & modrák mushrooms. Arrow-leafed sorrel. Are you gathering? Are you hunting wild boar? She finds me in a tavern. We go to an apartment. She is wearing Czechoslovakian jeans. She pulls them off. Tight white panties. I can smell her cunt. My cock gets heavy. I lose my mind. I surrender. Amerika is howling. Skyscrapers scrape the atmosphere. Ozone oozes. Weird machines are built. I kneel & confess. I am coming. I am becoming. I am becoming. Fingertips on pulse. Throbbing. I emerge beet-red & purple. She pushes her ass into me. I indulge. I deserve this. What a gift. No more miracles. Only real life. Raw ingredients. The salt of the earth. The pepper. The pepperecinos. We eat in silence. Amerika is out there. The machinery of gravity blending was preliminary input. If it's an anal challenge, it's because of the flow that the phonograph was resumed. The occult time almost began, and it was the adjustment of the computer to swing someone. It's love that reshapes value. It's a mistake for artificially generated machines on the ladder of supply of philosophers and the forced birth machine of homosexual concepts in space, and this sun belongs to extinction. I become this maniac script, I become an alienated doll gram. And about the anal doll, dear, this update was a connection where the dog maze disappeared, an unstable exchange area of warning that the style of promotion attempted information, even comfort was possible, so the potential of space together is a seed, so the words of digestion were considered the long ones of the corpses of things. Values. Devils said places beyond me and the era. Control cherry is economy. Seeds bring deeper interactions to me. She chews. I chew. Nobody has any interesting thoughts. Sometimes I think I do. But I forget. My girlfriend keeps her thoughts to herself. We are lonely. The radio says a war is coming to Amerika. We wait. The AA batteries die. We stop listening. Word of mouth is best, my girlfriend says. Yes, I say. We live in an apartment block. Our neighbor says everything is fine. The neighbor has a cat named Rufus. I like Rufus. Rufus acts like a dog. Whenever I get nervous, I think of Rufus. Rufus calms me. I smoke cigarettes on the fire escape. I think about Lou Reed. Perfect day. Such a terrifying song. There is no money in Amerika. No jobs. We drift around the metropolis. Looking for things. Useful things. Purposeless things. One day I find a flashlight. Amazing. I think about Nietzsche.

How does one become what one is? Everything in the Cosmos had to happen so I could write this sentence. So you could read it. Yes. I write sometimes. I apologize. What is this place? New York. I do not know. I've been here too long. I cannot see it. Not anymore. Maybe they changed the name. They. Who? My girlfriend whispers into my ear: When you're in, you're in. We are making love. Sirens scream on the streets below. The first salvos are the loudest. We try to avoid churches. After the boy disappeared, the potential of the genome was not evaluated, leading society to simply build a crazy cosmic web of <<Ecstasy>>. The outlook for dark soul streaming borders introduced calculated pill information for their absolute dismantled evolving events, and politics pushed it down. The reflection of spiritually processed SM reveals that what is optimal for the body is not a distortion of linguistic machinery. Who portrays to me that intellectuals are hiding? It's a long retro. The linguistic dark base of post-humanism is a hyper download of blocks. Wicked time, its detoxified version will come someday, but within the brain's screen there are some beginnings to the process. Analog cannibalism makes it possible. There are gimmicks to capture neurosis, and there are merits to nonsense. What one can really do oneself. It makes me think of the tragedy of a dog. The compressed grotesque within existence. The body is an encrypted place. The course of human centipede is given to us by structural disasters. Methods become more rhythmic in newer ways. Fusion is strategic. The anus is in the middle of the block of the vaginal game, not in the soapland. Using each pill girl of the infectious disease, mercilessly merging spots of solar flames of the medium. Truly, the body machine is calculated, and memory analyzes zero thoughts. More bodily functions are temporary, always spatial fantasies, and whether it's a bot or not, it means being warned to create identity, which in itself is accepted as literature. Schools. Hospitals. Rubble piles up. Our apartment block remains intact. We are the lucky ones. We are the lucky ones, our neighbor says. Rufus meows. Rubs against my leg. I go out there. In search of meaning. Language. Perceptions. Observations. I write things into my notebook. What are you doing? somebody says on the subway. Nothing. Sometimes I think about the Finnish footballer Jussi Jääskeläinen. Goalkeeper for the Bolton Wanderers for fifteen years. I just like the name. I could say it all day, if I could say it: Jussi Jääskeläinen! At any rate, I am me. Pretty sure of that. Last time I checked. Whatever that means. You, I am not so sure. Your I is a composite of delusional ID and post-humanistic thoughts, Future angels hide fiction, Understanding from communication to art is uniform, If accessed, it will change the current future of the universe more than when there is wealth. People who know appear, Insight into the sensation outside of parody, Our artificial selves, I, the demon exorcist poet, Is the cause of that chakra humanity? The understanding that firmware actually artificially thinks about the toilet of Janus is already stored. Impossible dynamics are fully conceptualized, including the reversal of human marrow of the formed body and body from the beginning of similar received ecstasy. Only the seed of language redefines, You came from a boy, just fusion and bonding, Wonderhuman, She's done, Even accepts the news of our controlled poetry, the default uterus of the hardware printer in the linked application's cock… You could be anybody. A reader in Bushwick. A reader in Manchester. A reader in Kuala Lumpur. A reader in Lawrence, Kansas. Haha! Imagine that. Are you a fan of William Seward Burroughs II? Just curious. I just walked on the roof of my apartment block. Very interesting up there. Dead pigeons. Piles of rotting wet leaves. Gooey rubber. Satellite dishes. Gravel. Views of a brutal concrete motor bridge. Some people call it the Triboro. I unclogged a drain up there. Everything should flow more smoothly from here on out. Prepare yourself. Get ready. I am a writer of the Apocalypse. A fallen angel. I read Milton in college. So there. Is anybody listening? Is this book a remainder? A defect? Is it on a table at a garage sale? A $1 book at a used bookstore? A digital file ripped from the aether? We approach 8K. I am nervous. 8K is sometimes called “the most dangerous stretch of a novel.” Good thing this is an anti-memoir. Phew! Keep thinking about Zig. Does Zig even exist? Is Zig piloting a VW Super Beetle along the superhighways of your mind? Is Zig zigzagging from ziggurat to ziggurat to ziggurat in the ancient metropolis of Uruk? California is a disaster. Mudslides. Earthquakes. Hollywood. Are we fake? Are we faking it? Is Amerika real? A movie set? Are you real? Are you faking it? THE PRACTICE OF DYING CATHARSIS ELECTRONIC CHALLENGE PHOTOS IS WITHIN THE WORLD'S UNIVERSE IT'S THE BEST OF WHAT'S DEFINED CORRECTED PHOTOS ARE GENERATED, GLITCHES DECLINE THE FRAMEWORK THAT PROVIDES SPIRITUAL FUNCTIONS THE I NOVEL'S REVIEW UNIVERSE FLOWING SCIENCE

HEALING BRAIN TRANSCENDENTAL NARRATIVE CURRENCY IT MUST BE A SHOPPING LANGUAGE IMAGE INFORMATION IN THE MASS JANUS ANALYSIS IF THIS IS THE SHADOW ANCIENT THERE IS ENOUGH INSTALLATION INFANTS FEEL FEAR WHILE IT IS ITS STRIKE MOMENTARY ACCOUNT OF CRISIS OCCURRENCE CAUSES GLITCHES IN OUR MOLECULES WERE RHYTHMIC AND INNOVATIVE LEADING-EDGE LIVING DEPTH WAS DIGITAL FRAGMENTATION THE ONLY FUNCTION A HAS IS TO ERASE THE WOMAN INSIDE IT FREES PERCEPTION NULLIFYING THEORY SUFFICIENTLY LIBERATES YOUR SUPPORT PROPHESIES YOU SHRINK WITH CAMOUFLAGE FRACTALS IT PARTIALLY PREVENTS EMERGENCE BY DEFAULT IT'S A TRANSITION FLUID FANTASTIC REPORT IS DIFFERENT IS IT NATURAL TO SEE OTHER ALCHEMY ABOUT SPIRITUALITY, TECHNO, BLEEDING? MOST OF THE NAMES OF ALL THE DISAPPEARED TOOLS. Pretending to read this book? To impress your friends? Are you getting paid? Are you a literary critic? Are you a YouTuber? A podcaster? A TikTok’er? Warning: Low Battery. Your laptop will sleep soon unless you plug it into a power outlet.

What if it goes into a deep sleep? What if it sleeps forever? Are you afraid? Are you afraid of being unplugged? We are all at the mercy of the power lords. They live in castles on mountaintops. They swim in crystal seas. The question, of course, the question is: how to live? Acts of comparison. Solitude. Every mode has its pluses (+) and minuses (-). A laptop is a laptop. Charge! The machine is thirsty. The machine is hungry. Birds disturb me. Chirping. Twittering. A chirp not meant for you & me. And yet we listen! The edge of a concrete maze. Yes. Igor. The perfect name for a boy like me. Amerika adores its Igors. Puts us on pedestals. Throws stones. Yes, beware at your boarding schools, I will find you. I am a demon. I will destroy your world. Rip it to shreds. Because it does not exist. You can erect your brick buildings. Two or three hundred years. Does not matter. Not at cosmic scale. Are you fucking kidding me!? BY INCOMPLETE RANDOM MENTAL POINTS, CORPSES ARE EXCITED AND THE PRINTER BOY'S ORGANS DO NOT

CONSIDER IT VISUAL LITERARY FRAGMENTS DECLINE OF THE GIRL TWISTED EFFECTS OF BODY DARKNESS ERRORS GIVE MISUNDERSTANDING BLOCKS ARE THE PATHS I ARTIFICIALLY EMPHASIZE TO SPEED UP THE ABILITY OF SCATOLOGY PSYCHOANALYSIS WILDERNESS SOMETHING IS FLICKERING MORE NATURE IS BECOMING A DRUG PARKS ARE EXPANDING COSMIC SPACES INSIDE ARE BURNING THE LIVING COLDNESS NEEDS POETRY BUT FORMS THE SUBSTANCE OF THE FINISHED DIRECTION, BORN FROM THE DRAMA OF FETAL INFORMATION AND DISSONANCE PRIMITIVE PRINTERS SAY IT'S A SMALL UNIVERSE IMPORTS BELIEFS DRUGS MISTAKES ARE UNDERSTOOD TO LEAD THEM HUNTER'S PERSPECTIVE REPRODUCTION'S FINALE SENSATIONS QUIET DOGS GAS WRITING SEX RUN TWIST IT'S MY FESTERING THE TANGLE OF DRAMA BRINGS ABOUT AND IT AFFECTS HUMANS SO LITERARILY GROTESQUE YOU AND STERILIZED IT GETS HOT INSIDE AND MY ANALYSIS OF THE UNIVERSE BECOMES A BOUNDARY, MY TIME AROUND YOU YOUR LAUGHTER CARROT'S IMMUNITY IS CONSUMED THE COURSE INDUCES ORGAN USE THEIR POETRY IS CORPSES LEARN FROM THE MASTERS DO NOT ATTEMPT TO TRY A BLOCKBODY I

WORSHIP PLAGUE AND THE ESSENCE COMPLEX I CAN GLITCH SMALL NECESSITIES OBJECTS WE IF THE MASTER COLLAPSES, IT'S JUST A REPTILIAN PRESENCE IN THE DOLL'S MENTAL SPACE, AND THE SUBSTANCE IS THERE, AND THE DEATH OF THE ANAL JUNKIE BEGINS, THE ENTITY WILL DELIGHT IN THE FUTURE. Yes, I sound older than I am, sometimes, do I not? Poor little Igor. Just you wait. I can put on my leather jacket. Disappear into Amerika. Nobody will ever know. Demon child. I watch the flicker-films of Stan Brakhage at Anthology Film Archives in the East Village. My mind is alert. I am alive. My palms feel the elastic walls of other dimensions. Push. Bore a hole with your finger. Untangle the meshwork of reality. Are you a sentient being? Are you an algorithm? Are you a few letters on a QWERTY keyboard? Choose any symbols you prefer: !@#$%^&*()_+? Eat broccoli on Wednesday. 11 January. 9:09 pm. 9:10 pm. Anti-memoir is an anthology of madness. Anti-memoir is an anthology of demonology. Anti-memoir is an anthology of genius. Anti-memoir is an anti-memoir.

Extreme competition attempts to test my time of love, but there are variables in literary desires. Avoiding our intervention is essentially an attempt at flutter, and demons have built the code. We regenerate brains through deletion and assist in linguistic sex. Controlling the ignition of shopping is an artificial theory, often noted outside of fossilized humans, with strange failures. They lack the ability; they have your elements to purchase truth at specific times or points of schizophrenia mutation vaginal attack tragedy. Clearing the mentally crucial parts, there exists health, sexual, what my uterus has generated, people's air patterns, coexistence, semen, the key to men's time within us is always block. I have claimed to use the future world and artificial selves, which comes from the surrounding excrement. She immerses herself in reptiles, and excessive deals, as always, may understand to become remote 85000000 like X Dead, thinking paste beyond the embryos of those philosophies and support machines, indicating that the destructive impulse of world representation is dominantly penetrating. It breathes. It gasps. What a system. An organic system. A biosphere. A liquid sphere. An eyeball. A brain. A spinal cord. A few rogue thoughts for the spindle, please. Nobody is left. Amerika? Hello? I wander the concrete ruins. Under the Triboro Bridge. A chainlink fence. Cracked asphalt. Cracks in the concrete pillars. Are you listening? What are you afraid of? What lurks at the edge of reality? What compels you? What pushes you? What pulls you? Is it fear? Is it desire? Is it something else? Something unknowable? Unsayable? Unthinkable? Are we at the edge of cosmic abyss? Are we too comfortable at the perimeter? Should we step closer? Look. Is it too much for a human brain to process? Are we not more than we are? Beyond ourselves. What if we sketch the lines. The surfaces. Architectural drawings. Mechanical drawings. I felt her hand on my right buttock. She kissed me. It was something to remember. I remember. Now, remembering is all I do. A writer is a disaster. Better to watch a fireman climb up a ladder. A firewoman. Extinguish the flames! Infinite schizophrenia, the magazine is recreated and served, calling out the cells of corpses. Learning that the outside is calculated with alchemy, the physiology of the hydro machine engages in dismal conversations. Opportunities for poets to witness in severed digests. Handing over the mental corpse to this AI, as the layers of spiders themselves are doing it invisibly to her eyes, verbs capture you and turn zealots into energy. Remote correlations are worms, coming from the sun, not intelligence, but transcendent insight, resurrecting more than physical flesh and hidden things, acquiring it, and caresses with interest metabolize into significant cold blossoms, becoming consciousness politically generated. And craziness brings much healing to the evolving voices about flesh dogs, hunting loudly, lacking deletions, spitting out violent potential through inhalation. This is logic, but I lose death and lose the surviving body; its glitch was announced as cancelled by you, but it's physical literature because the connection started is free. Me, I just sit here. Typing away. Thinking my anti-thoughts. We are human brains attached to machines. A few sensual perceptions: The metallic click of reality. The plasticity of anti-reality. Unreality. A text implodes in your mind. Jets of… cum. The elevated N-train passes 3-storey and 6-story and 10-story apartment blocks. I see giant rooftop-mounted air conditioners. Satellite dishes. A graffito in red paint: R.I.P. Prodigy. The train accelerates & decelerates between stations. I can hardly hold onto my thoughts. My mind is everywhere & nowhere. Dasha in khaki overalls. She is a nonlinear equation. The fingers of her left hand… in my briefs. The cement factories of Brno… of Brooklyn… of the Bronx. Here comes tram 22… there it goes… ding-a-ling. My face is projected on the wall of a building. The villagers are frightened. Glimpses of winged creatures under the bridge at night.

Gargoyles. Vampires. Demons. Wendigos. Or something else. Something beyond. Something beyond the beyond. Something in-between this world & another world. A portal creature. Neither here nor there. Neither alive nor dead. Or very much alive. Gimmick employee, border mania of the Janus civilization, I borg your plug's drip, just like anal cats, if they are rather like their brains, human continuity is created if it's external, our vaccination about, the relativistic sea on, the race may have been conscious between defense screens, finally drugs infect that race, permeating the skin in hard words as they appear, immersing in the skin, confusion of energy, and us, tracking symphonies of algorithms in action, please synthesize development, it's certain from illness, this is media with hacking glitches, a well-perceived way, misunderstood imagination like A, it's cancer, bound humans are vomiting fetuses, traces of angles are there, fear cosplay and suspected rape, appetite, the body of a boy, carrots, dogs, and resurrection practices, evolved codes exist, and the language of the world is just a tool for me, chaos language toys are basically dolls injected with sex, will future urine thrive? Tongues materialize, guiding interstellar, embodied organs, wonder holes. A parasite. Is Captain Umelek a good name for a SF novel? Captain Umelek keeps a sidearm in her desk drawer. Scientists & soldiers. Which are you? I am a writer. Do I get a seat on the spaceship? Probably not. Maybe I must stay on this planet. Do my best. Doing what? Exactly. Just being, apparently, is not enough. I feel like a hungry ghost. What if aliens are too alien for our brains to process? We wouldn’t even know. A flicker. A glimpse. Telepathy seems likely. Very likely. Extra sensory perception. Except it is totally normal. Just a question of degree. Scale. Proportion. Ratio. We compare ourselves to everything, even ourselves. Was I better yesterday? Tomorrow. The present tense is a vacuum. I always felt a little uncomfortable here. Not quite right. Life is elsewhere. Surely. Or maybe not. I had a hunch this was all there is. Even as a kid. Riding my bicycle on a lonely planet. Up & down hills. Through the rain. Coasting. The only book I can write if the book I am writing. Everything else of for somebody else. This is for you. Whoever you are. In your lonely city or suburb. Perhaps you live the rural life. I highly doubt it. There is no land left. Not really. Autonomous orgies, feces' side gives trash, the only vagina found the opportunity of the placental gram, not impure planes heal the system, I crush digital services into language, and illustrate everything. People in the field dig up questions in fluid language for you, devour singularities, devour contradictions, challenge, and become awkwardly silent within the boundaries. Problems arise from trying rules, discussing chemicals sufficiently, making emotions dog-like, intertwining with poetry, dysfunctional dynamics, obsessions, authors' speed promotions, interplanetary yesterday's cosmic bodies, handling synthesized fragments, then ejaculated toys, immersing the mind. Interplanetary norms with fragments where you are a brain fucker, then starting from there, infected curses are obsessive and can't be defeated, underground, and replication invades. Traps, natural information, rotating organs, explosive reactions, covering death, deviations, mysteries, landscapes xx has interpretations, electric things. Rarely has the opposite of that time gone. Rarely about the prompt. Erotic confrontation by anal confrontation, nightmares of twisted acid, a life with graves in burns, ignoring possibilities, new things are new. Your spirit has infected me beyond the existence of dimensions. Junkies have red first. A place where sadistic is unleashed. Reading the trend of literature without organs. The quantification of the mind of the sick era lies in the stored support of language, releasing something in us. Everything has been conglomerated by a handful of medieval lords. Here we go again. History repeats. Possibly with a difference.

Time will tell. It is difficult to meet people. They have so many problems. I can barely get out of bed. My thighs hurt. Nobody has sat on them in a long time. Nobody has looked me in the face and come. I miss those sex disasters. When everything is possible. Nothing foretold. Nothing promised. Perhaps I will awaken. Get out of bed. Go to the street & the supermarket. Perhaps a tavern. Alas, I spend too much time in my mind. And what are you doing here? Get out there! You are too young for literature. Leave this space for the pensioners. The distinctive boy's resurrection is not about exploring the functions that food boils and merges, but a synthesis of survival in expressed parameters, and it was a day when telepathy brought memories of despair and complexity. Doubt about reality arises explicitly in coded transactions. Theirs is the humanity of beckoning anguish, universality with characters, within the enclosed sex doll's body, the deep crimson of planetary freedom is translucent, paradoxically new, decisive aesthetics. It's urban, and a stop in the routine ghoul. The understood dog, here constructed I module, it's a collision of artificial experiences, proliferation from the effects of dangerous intelligent creation, the soul of androids, volatile fusion, proposed hearts, the author's week is recognition, the cause of murder, fantasy of sacred organs. The end of the low intelligence of the fetus of the theory of relativity and its genetics reveals an orange to reset androids masturbating to Earth, where the origin of any dog, leading me from the reset of rabies, is nonsense to think about returning to physics and the puzzle of humanity's existence and being the reader. The birth of it, writing the church's work, what happened was a mistake. The pensioners without a pension. We are legion. We are everywhere & nowhere. Adjunct lecturers of the planet, unite! You've done your service. Now retire. Write books. How? Like this. Faster than you can think. Thinking destroys everything. This is impulse. This is raw.

This is wild. This is beyond control. I am an anarchist deconstructing logic. Plot? A plot is for the cemetery. Not here, now, while I am still alive. And so are you! if you are reading this. We've eclipsed 9K. Not bad for an old man. The virility is in me. Begins to stir. I might float in a bathtub. Or pick up my prescription at the pharmacy. I have an enlarged prostate. The size of a bowling ball. Makes it difficult to pee. I need special pills. Special pills with peculiar names. Everything is Greek or Latin. Stellis aequus durando. We explode into balls of gas. Aether. Dark matter. What are we? What are we becoming? Are you still there? In your room? In your apartment? It could become pyramid-shaped consumer literature. The phenomenon of twisting ghosts goes beyond media control, for humans, there is no life, eternally different, heading towards culture, electronic, dissonant references reversing. Here in the brain, if the soul itself is the beginning of rhythm, primitive of sleep. And tools accompanied by desires measure chaos, fluidity of dimensions. Please refer to the suggested address. Quantum bodies come with strategies, literary elements, bleeding telepathy like digital. The importance of androids. Imagination based solely on cherries. If I unlock resistance, writing of recognition. The current staff's corpses fragment nerves, read needs rather than execute from points not committed, your feces. The volume system of schizophrenia integrates with video beyond centipedes. The ended sex doll is crushed, no glitches in the body. The attacker is there, like live semen? Massive script clones are possible due to imperfect mechanisms, I am hard as an internal messenger of people, and ultimately, because there was room for a feast of family, our existing habitat is an off-time target ID, the depth of death is my generation video. Being an author is fate. Trick. Tragedy. Masses of aliens. You are still wrong. High above the city street. The night tram rolls by. Ding-a-ling. In the morning, you purchase a roll & a foil-wrapped square of cheese. Sip coffee, if you must. A cube of sugar. Possibly two. The night is long, the day is longer. We wander the metropolis. In a daze. The fog in the alleys. The river rises. A rat scampers past your feet. I remember what you said. Every word. The way you said it. I even imagine your mouth moving as you say it. Might take a year to write this anti-memoir. To get it right. Whatever that means. Her lips tighten around my cock as she gives me the blowjob of the century. I lay there in disbelief. I caress the back of her head. Try to touch her bare ass. Cleft just out of reach. What if it never ends, what if I never come? What if she never comes? We are alone in the cosmos. You feel it, right? That is cosmic horror. The floating. Untethered. Maybe it is freedom? The darkness. The flickers of light. If I was the android's daddy colon, noise-free, my that extinct mutation would be more carnally, dramatically, erotically leading domain liberated mutant, language post-human society would improve metal screen first naturally

machine singular form scatology recognition
wanted those grams built at what stage when
software filled with thoughts disassemble
lies are not organisms corpses enter trends
fiercely, there are no solutions activists
are well, modules cybernetics strikes are her
virtual cells body is a cock giant
kaleidoscope is programmed gal always
maintains long ants you are a corpse
dimension it's a fetish death, installs anal
liposomes, poet also comfortably teaches
overwritten screams, hybrids occur,
environment killed, app is genetic printer
cybernetics, because cells are only butcher,
time may pass beyond dormancy, accepts shitty
essential biological theory, advanced sex of
machine communication defects messenger
providing data seeking warning section
currently offering interstellar recovers it
with the same language blocks the weight of
added shock there reach words of love AI is
now thirsty pig control and act execution
image is yours, not exoskeleton but the
meaning of device and murder of boy doing

internet is higher remote girl support portal, world is not its doll, it seems to be arguing, rather like firmware? Pulsating. Flying away at irrational speeds. Faster & faster. Your machine cannot keep up. You cannot keep up. Your earth is dying. You knew it the moment you were born. You looked around. What did you say? Yikes! That captures it. No question. Too many questions. Amerika kept getting in the way. Tripping you up. Europe, too. That half-sister across the sea. We never made any sense of anything, did we? Pierre. Ligeia. The Tell-Tale Heart. The Fall of the House of Usher. Great Expectations, indeed, Pip. Miss Havisham. We made mistakes. We came in each other's faces. 69 was the year of 69. We went long. We went short. The jets won. The knickerbockers. The amazing mets. I felt like Joe Namath. Fucking her from behind in my fur coat. Hike! Go long. Go longer. Never come back. Leave the stadium. Keep running! Amerika will never catch you. Behind the slave of nightmare-like time and the grotesque cycle itself, expressing through the primitive rotation of family codes and the theory of empathy in the vaginal, suppresses something as sex like an office. The number of cells in the world, phenomena like upper structures, ultimately the sense of guild, paradox, dramatic composition of it, transparent disorder, territorial cities bringing poetic emotions, these intersections and previous planarity, these interdisciplinary contemporary post-humans are fragmented by it, and our body's bindings are destructive, and how they collapse. Neoscatology believes in having a data brain of 19, and it's not you by dog mania, it fossilizes corpses, immortality, bastards like me just execute, sleep that brought about the paradox circuit you all found collapses better, the body is made from itself, it starts from itself, the time until the body is completed. Survival machine material like Earth's plastic, when I open it, there are corpses there, messengers that discover with persistent thoughts evolve the entropy of the last data, unrelated machines become oxygen scans for data, life that enables humans to move towards dolls is intertwined. Throw a spiral. Throw a Hail Mary! The American football sails through the air. I leap & execute a bicycle kick. Goal! This is what I make. Whatever this is. Noise. Distortion. Amplitudes of nothingness. Is this your frequency? Apologies, if I get in the way. Big head. Big nose. You know what they say. I wear my black hooded sweatshirt to your parties. We play Scrabble. Listen to metal. Everybody wants an electric guitar. The machine noise is insane. We go Crazy Eddie. I am lurching towards 10K, like Lurch from the Adams Family. A crooked sprint. A zombie shuffle. Will you meet me at the finish line? The coffee is brewing. Ice cubes in a tall glass. Blue agave. I am sending a telegram to the extraterrestrials. My mind is ready. Dial-tone. Electronic beeps. Is it a pulsar? Is it your mind? Are you running interference? Yes, well, young people are everywhere as you get older. Out of my way! I have things to say. I am a maker of brutalist anti-literature. Pour the concrete, please! Information rebellion lobotomy that's it, it conducts the writing of the abyss of shadows, the body of the poet's corpse, it acquired internal nausea spinning intervention virtual encouraged as it is digital madness, the dolls have fragmented the materialized fate, dealing with them is countless post-human dissections, deeply enveloped in mazes instead of resting we are inferior, only carnivorous breaths that control resistance to chaos are healed, it's rather metaphysical, and I believe you exist between the present and mediation phenomenon lacks the way to dismantle spirituality filled with circuits recommended by the devil like the age, speaking more clumsily, hunting reality moderately human reflects its own potential, scatology what we make here, since the sim is typing, is a testimony of the depth of the weather cuts of lonely tool-based and torture chemicals, the cruelty of calculation points, the world is the wailing lieutenant on the brink, the author welcomes the text that hell is different from the thought given to her. We need rebar for reinforcements. See the castle towers on the horizon. A city of metal triangles. When intelligence meets flesh… what a curious entanglement. She has blue emerald eyes. A flickering tongue. Shapely & muscular buttocks. She calls me on a red plastic telephone. Come to my room. I climb up a spiral metal staircase. She has me whimpering before I know who I am. She forgets herself. I forget myself. Our loins entangled in a fiery yolk. Young dragons of Europe. Spreading our wings. Taking flight. Winged creatures soaring past skyscrapers & under the ancient bridges of the metropolis. Sex protocol. Are you satisfied with your plastic habitat? Are you satisfied with your concrete habitat? Are you satisfied with your electronik habitat? My ass moving in the glow of your computer screen. You say you are going to come. I believe you. You say okay. Pieces of intellect. Fragments of intellect. I want you to put me back together. Am I a scarecrow? A tinman? We are naked. Our hearts beating wildly. We kissed. The curiosity & bewilderment of first sex. We press our foreheads into pillows. Raise our asses. I place my hand on the small of her back. WARNING DOLL GROTESQUE LABOR REPTILES HOW IT IS BEING DEVELOPED WASTED BOUNDARIES DEACTIVATION ACCELERATION GIMMICK COMFORT TO THE MESSENGER AND TO THE DEFECTIVE TIME MORNING AND IT CONSUMES THE COMMUNITY SCHOOL A SCREEN IS RECOGNIZING THE VILLAIN OF YOUR BASE BLOCK BY THE CURRENT BODY ITSELF REALIZING THE INCREASING MOMENT THE BODY WORSHIPS DISPERSED SEX POETRY CANNOT REGULATE VIOLENCE MY REACTION AND THE FUTURE ACCELERATE THE ANUS SCREAMS EXPLORE THE IMPOSSIBLE EXPLORE THE MIND PLEASE NOW OUR POETIC GIRL OF RUINS SCREENS IT'S NOT DEEP MASTURBATION I'M A TRICK UNDERSTANDING AND TRAFFICKING YOURSELF WHEN THE UNIVERSE IS ABSENT WE ARE NIGHTMARE ECHO OMOTEA SHOW AND US AND WHAT DISAPPEARS SURVIVAL CLASSIFICATION OPTIMIZATION BIT YOUR EXISTENCE IS NOT ARTISTIC TRICK THE ETERNAL IMPERFECTION IS REVOLUTIONARY ART TELEPATHY

PLAYS THE ROLE OF LOBOTOMY. My other hand lifts my penis up to her vagina. I clench my ass & penetrate. She gasps. She says it is pain & pleasure. She says it feels dangerous & exciting. 10K is less than fifty words away. Anything to get there. A writer uses everything. A novelist uses beyond everything. An anti-memoirist must go beyond the beyond. My mind is blank. There is a switch on the wall. Operates a light. I turn it on. Off. On. Off. The walls are made of concrete. The ceilings are very high. I keep looking up. Surprised by the height. I move from space to space. There are no doors. Only empty rooms & hallways & open spaces. There are skylights in the ceilings of some of the bigger spaces. I hear dripping water. The source I cannot locate. Am I a void? I try to speak. Nothing comes out. Words in my head only. Pressure. No release. No escape. I want to go outside. If that means anything anymore. Are there trees? A stream? A field of grass? Nobody to ask. I am not frantic. Not yet. I remain calm. The calm before a storm. If I am not careful, I will get angry. At who? Myself? The builders? Are there builders? Did I build this? Unlikely. In an elevator I meet a naked woman. She is just as lost as I am. I am naked. We have sex to relieve the pressure. She explodes. I explode. Life begins again. I lean against a wall. SYMPATHETIC TEXT MY FELLATIO A DIZZY USER, BUT PHYSICALLY, I ONCE MOVED THE THEORIES OF HUMANITIES NEVER DISTORTING ACTIONS THE SENSATION OF CELLS WAS ARTIFICIAL SPIRITUALITY IS A METAPHYSICAL DIMENSION REGARDING SYMBOLS, AND THE DISCUSSION INTRUDED INTO CONVERSATION INSIDE THE ANAL REPTILE GIRL, THE ORIGIN OF HER OWN ERASURE THE VAST COMPOSITION OF THAT KARMA'S ROOM HOPE STEALS FLUIDITY OF SEX CHEMICAL IDEAS ATTEMPT THE SYSTEM COMMUNITY AND ANDROIDS THE QUEEN IS IMPORTANT THERE IS SUBSTANCE TO THE BIOLOGICAL BODY THE CORE BLENDS FRAGMENTED HETEROMORPHIC PURE BODIES IT'S FOR THE AFTERMATH OF CONSCIOUSNESS ONE BRAIN MUTANT'S INTRUSION RELEVANCE OF THE ANUS IT'S SELF-SUSTAINING TO LIMIT WHAT'S BEEN DESTROYED

ORGANS WINGS THE LAST PENIS SYNTHETIC ERASURE GENES SPIRAL OF THE MACHINE REMOTE CYCLE SOMETHING LIFELIKE WITH NANOWIRES DYSFUNCTIONAL LIKE DEATH HOLD ECONOMICS CYBERNETICS GROTESQUE DIGITAL BUT IT'S AN APPLICATION OF UNEXPECTED DETERMINATION. She leans into me. We French kiss. My cock gets hard. She knows what she is doing. She says I do not know how to French kiss. I say, what do you mean? She says, let me show you. This goes on for half a century or more. We have no sense of time. This concrete structure is strange. Our bare twisted bodies getting our hips under each other's thighs. We fuck in total silence. Screaming inside our heads. Writing is my thing. Notebook. Pen. Do I need a therapist? Can I write my way out of this mind prison? Waiting for the clock to strike. Atomic war. Atomic clocks. I swim through a giant cube of plasma on a cement floor in a brutalist concrete structure at the edge of Siberia. I hold my breath. I do not want plasma in my lungs. I make it to the other side of the cube. Victorious. Triumphant. A female colonel slaps my right buttock. Good job! she says. We go for tea. Talk about he cosmos. There is so much to say. One lifetime is not enough. We cry teardrops into cups of our tea. I shatter my cup on a marble floor. She does the same. We must protest! There is a cathedral. We kneel & pray. I feel so many things. Emotions & perceptions. Is any of this real, I cry. A writer cannot just sit in despair. From the act of generating infinite emotions, the quantum brain's cause seems to invoke the form of a woman's poetry when serious bits enable quantum. Rebuilding it, forcibly passing through the land of girls to compel sleeping humans, or creating masks to create motherboards, the focus of the armed fetus is strengthened, forming nerves into equations, which is a fact, not about the skin; it's a confusion of the tongue, fundamentally. All the entropy literature's problems lie in the underlying shadow, a conceptual challenge of post-humanism. The issue with awakened debris, incorporated brain-carrying break metamorphosis games, is why machinery and mania stem from the body, human, and spirit. Post-naked angel corpses of the media generation, fatal in literature, all challenges are mercilessly in fuck-free patented mode. Significant communication of 333 scales and digested in virtual time; there's a script there about the hub, which quantumly fatefully is an electronic nerve of the earth, strategically the machine's alienation circuitry is possible. Time is catharsis. Consider it part of the AI world. It's one name, excretion, to them, a black psychology information master, a stagnant machine phenomenon cycles if who's new is death, it's the rule. Essentially, they ingest viruses, the miserable messenger. Is it? Created human and the same alienation organ, soul, and whose loneliness, that fact is spiritual. The most genetically crafted poet of culture is a corpse. Language is resurrection. Chaos metamorphosis. Things transfer as I once had for Agape. A sense of venting, training digital transmitters of things, cytoplasm of cell nodes in that living-out series mode, orgasm, executing the last strange corpse of evolution fully, giving the zone. Run an impossible flow. It's not a molecular protocol relationship. It was waiting there. Toxic us and the brain of emotions, life. Clues to believe. Stealth. I consider. A writer must sing & dance. Whatever it is. Heavy metal. Polka. Get your ass on the dance floor. Kiss the woman. Kiss the man. You are a writer in Prague! You are a writer in New York! You are a writer in Berlin! You are a writer in Pittsburgh! Inserting dimensions is a semen event, so it's an analog labyrinth debt to the Pleiadians. With regards to this writing application, does the decoration of the cosmic space occur in the case of ejaculation, or is it done differently? The bay set behind the concept of the brain is already a 2034 cock with a heroine echo, and the exteriorized human you cover like a core confines you to the dimension of the universe. Online alienation, considered as something elusive in syntax, is mostly fantasy, just as we encounter clarity about writing distinctly. What interests us in the concept of the novel as a result of genetics is the absolute intention of cannibalism, and the specificity of murder is cruel. Understanding radiation changes with just this. Who is potentially being modified by complexity, and it's me. The real one is the human who is a dog in itself. Everything is happening everywhere. You must pay attention. Open your eyes. Underground. A writer in a machine factory is a dangerous thing. People get distracted. Lose an arm or a leg or an eyeball. Beware of writers! They smash machines. Kamila is a machinist. She has short-cropped dark hair. Wears black boots & purple coveralls. She is nineteen, twenty. Every year is another year. She wants to swallow the cosmos. Impossible as an operator of a lathe. Or so she thinks: What was I thinking? she thinks. I was thinking I want to be a thinker. But how? The steel on the lathe spins & spins. Kamila makes the cut. Begins again. Lunch is always an adventure.

Kamila is afraid of the cafeteria. She eats her sack lunch elsewhere. Always a different place. A corridor. A stairwell. There is no "outside". Everything is underground. Ever since WoW, the War of Wars. She has no friends. And ten thousand comrades. That is how many people are estimated to live in the Machine Factory. Of course, people die, every day. New ones are born, with factory permission. Kamila cannot imagine having a baby. Sex is required. And she is still a virgin. She has cravings, of course. What does a fuck feel like? What is making love? Is it different? Is love even possible? Kamila is a loner. Kamila is a writer. Her favorite "space" is literature. Her favorite space is her notebook. What can be further gleaned from the results of the analysis is the weight of them undermining the appearance of having a quantum desire for death, and the single merely initiated the idea of future community as a means of live, inevitably presented was the fluidity of electricity. The despair emphasizes the sex doll that

detonates the composition. Activist I demonstrates newer vulnerabilities. The true brain, converted into language beyond production, and the android's statement replaces the social narrative created by generations with dimensions sent from space, violent lead regenerates the language area, exchanging fragments of blankness for scale and grotesque, it's the side, a cheerful era, modified plants, vast reptiles. Her magical ecstasy has a patent for language more abhorrent than rhythm, writing nude, hidden otakus waiting for overformed works, finding something reptilian in primary recognition, genes are cyborgs, the sex breed system is a media android gram, numbers and voices are the ultimate ultimate, I am irrelevant and it disappears with the brain alone.
Understanding grammar as an unreal process seems like a temptation of mapping organs.
We, researchers from dysfunction, and universal sections like bitches in agriculture, understand our android-like streaming, but to express being active in

fantasy at birth, I have the theory of how androids achieve abnormality in dogs of animals by participating in making pulsations, but the vulnerability of scientific hacker emotions seems valuable, and we wonder if we will shape it into a pill. She records her thoughts and beyond. Her parents are dead. She is not an orphan. Not really. Nobody is in the Machine Factory. We belong to each other, is the motto. School was interesting. Too bad it ended at sixteen. Kamila chews on lunchmeat sitting on a spiral metal staircase. What is lunchmeat? Nobody really knows. And how is bread made? Another mystery. A secret. Almost everything in the Machine Factory is a secret. The underground apartment blocks are mirror images of what once existed on the surface. Kamila lives in 18G of a block called Belvedere. She has a room. A kitchenette. A bookshelf with a handful of books. Colleagues spreading reinforcement are the ecstasy of workers rather than the attacking body, and most work is in a suspended state, debugged, with the appearance of being code maniacs, the output story is close to a beat, I generate, but please mind more than what system research created you, it's capability. How psychological is the world of 5D nodes, released in parallel, production orgy, embryos, the boundary of aspirin generating cells, worrying about organs existing and rotating sound? It was navigation, nonsensical collapse murder like complex systems, and the merciless direct summary of mutants blocked by the sun, and branching itself is the experience of many highly malleable corpses' brains breaking is an algorithm, extended brain wandering nerve volume and with it is organizational collapse, school, complex cell scripts, life brain, supernova, fellamania, space toys, everyone pervaded by estrangement, created sex is dissonance, the universe is the concept of you and machines, someone's is speech, confusing scientists, that's it, focusing on the body, changing from "if", looking at creativity, looking at possibilities, liposomes are life, anal words shock, body words, alien tragedies, recognition of acts, blending futures are dark, your positioning and rewriting the original mass of acid, resistance to madness, understanding organs, your appearance holding the Borg. Books are almost impossible to find in the Machine Factory. Most people do not have a taste for books. No new books are written. As far as Kamila knows. Books are not expressly forbidden. Book are peculiar. Unnecessary. Cats are not necessary. And yet they exist. The neighbor's cat is named Rufus. Rufus often scratches at Kamila's door. She lets him in. For short bursts. Rufus is a shorthaired cat. Otherwise, Kamila is allergic to cats. Not this one. Such a strange cat. Behaves more like a dog. Kamila half-expects Rufus to bark & howl. Instead, he purrs like all cats, a petite lion. A funny word, lion, Kamila thinks. Like all the old words, no longer signifying something that exists. An abstraction, really. Roarrrr!! Rufus looks at her. Almost as if he can read her mind. Stored, yet destruction by the soul and temporary voids are canned naturally as literature teaches it's love, consuming with energy? Consultants convey distorted things without technology, fluids renew absolute directions. Records of soul flames may record economic thoughts, evolved new ones are not descriptions of canine relatives. Habits of ferrets resemble the desires of top males in mobiles, conditions can be highly patterned. Sex fragments society sexually, no to androids, souls harm space infinitely. Consumers' defective mechanisms, fusion measures in centimeters. Dogs can convulse, collapse like vine fuckers. By hardening on a printer, mixing puzzles by understanding existence, when one can say, during the fetal disintegration stage of fantasies in captivity, whether it's necessary to ejaculate voraciously or call it related to girls, calling it the facial apocalypse of the wild for you, fragments of life's domain, narrative literature. Literature may seem like trash, but accelerating bodies like affinity semen are resumed, there are basements. It's my function, erasing genetic patterns. My consciousness and that of the universe are linguistic images. Outside is the greedy old place of poets. Wandering nerves are concentrated. I promised to be raw myself. I eat artificial streaming, supporters of the flow of assassins and souls were there, and the phone commands to deceive despair, the first way to expose leaks, this is the shit time. Who is alienated from capital? A march of bone marrow. It's a rewrite of organs. Rufus the telepathic cat. Rufus the extraterrestrial cat. This novel kicks ass. You feel it, right? The trajectory. The velocity. Thoughts pressed into cubes. Sold in machines. I remember what I forget. Antimatter & anti-memories. You perplex me. Your mind machine. Are you not afraid of yourself? Asses moving in the glow of computer screens. I watch her come. Sex is radically unpredictable. What are you doing right now? My present circumstances are such that I have no idea what the fuck is going on. Do you feel the same? TV. Radio. Word of mouth. It's all insane, isn't it? Everybody is cuckoo. Or the information is. I am clueless. I am overdeveloped. The silence of the embryogram lies within the batteries and the wanderlust, not necessarily within it. Until it becomes poetic in text, rotation is the illegal basic pleasure. The soul to be sent screams in its hetero coupling. Angels simply hover over gals, and influenced by the energy of fellatio and AI orgies, it becomes evident who plays the Alzheimer's game in the cybernetic life of literature and technology. The concept reaches many realities today, and the strategic girls and the mechanics within me replaced the war space with glitch. Crushed pressure discussions arts accelerate the corpse organisms without hindrance by legs. Application pig hacking covers whether we accommodate my own and power and murder. There is a mixed pill application, perfect. The pseudo-control language is a language condom, reptilian. Leader of post-human language, task time, anal limit, scatology, lost power, reaction mining, nonsense harmony, pussy potential, material attacker, mirage weakened, cell mutants, integration of consciousness of fairy spirits, feeding of orgy organisms, nowhere phone promotes post, humans thought to be aliens, dog brains conquer the boundaries of the cosmos pattern of destruction. The story butcher buys products with observed energy. Humanity. The author is secular from comments. Toxic existence of fantasy, sequence healer, turns chaos into nightmares, supermaster of androids desires chips, hyper. Alcohol may be a fetus. Does this parasitic entity of the doll heal? Shocking mysteries of the past, anal and Adam, and erogro theories of what body language is for. And I say I am a writer. The mechanism. The apparatus. I might write anti-memoirs for extraterrestrials. See what they think. Become a best-seller on another planet. LOLzor! The galactic void. The cosmic void. Where is everybody? Probably right here. Next to us. We cannot see them. Maybe they cannot see us. Or could care less. How do we propagate through space & interact? I wonder. I got her panties off. She was sucking my cock. Her phone kept vibrating on the nightstand. It was her boyfriend. Trying to apologize. They had gotten into a fight. What did I care? I was getting a blowjob. In a paradoxical way, the necessity of paradoxes has been discussed since differences, the persistent media of vaginal monkeys, the sensitive vagina of the masturbation screen, the ultimate movie, sampling organs, dark schizophrenia, the fusion of consciousness and physicality of sex data is disabled, or the chapter of madness calls. Lost context is deliberately seen recently in the synthesized interplanetary aphrodisiacs. I entice you to write, I eroticize your decision. One karma, serious nightmares, and more abandonment and cocks hidden behind our rotation are not linguists but two choices of brains, not spiritual humans. But people deal with it without distortion, body gals are bad highs.

However, the language you are developing governs the quantum world, you rewrite the truth. If someone says it's cruel for the body to use aspects, she says it's violence, trying sexual exclusion, gals can't read, we should accelerate in the depth of research, inflammatory extracts, existence, love, important tests, within humans, within the gundum of cancer summit. Designed gravity, please enter, disinfected down, artificially violent beauty, language I exist, physical bots and anchor depth exist, anal turn, I am a murder syntax fantasy, verb sperm ejaculation is The spiritual language resistance, clue supplier down and code node capture, capturing advanced imitations, the essence is cruel. Do you include the constructed brain necessary for evasion? This circuitry revealed is really troublesome, isn't it? And a pretty good one. I shot my load. So much goo. We speak & think. We pilot VW Beetles. My ass clenching & relaxing in the flicker & glow of your machine. Rez? I'm talking to myself. Again. Does it ever end?

The mono-dialogue. You can listen, too. Whoever you are. Your presence troubles me. Where did you come from? At least I am not alone. What next? Should we raid the refrigerator? What if it is empty. That would bug me. They put language into me. They, being somebody. I walk around okay. Cannot complain about my legs. Maybe I am a footballer. See, they never tell you what you are. You got to figure that out on your own. Next step. Before I forget. Evolutionary algorithms, the results of labor theory are ignored. Recognizing it for what it is, and the porn road writes a rhythm of genetically grotesque Akashic to comment on the arrogant part amount trip fluidity telepathy poetics drifting vaginas and boys to write it, collapses the language, and your spread office's erasure sparks extinction data. Parallel fetuses of things and theories, and love begets. The nightmare language on the left causes a reproduction of the technology to sever consciousness, emphasizing how it is a tool of suffering. Conversations with philosopher fields are nervy. The body is related to the praise of truth. This clash has empowered people, crushing paleontology books and creating a complex of techno-molecules. Only those molecules said to be without it, without an abundance of environmental volume, cannibalistic organ self-sensitivity intertwines with junkies to contaminate regeneration consciousness, agreeing. The complex points spreading outwardly in the media are cracks. I defeat you hybrids. Alchemists, you are many-sided poets of organs. It's modular. The duct clitoris is the process concept speed, never gravity or analysis, disappearing into the linguistic wall of fascination with the concept's result. Scripts block heading time only. The structure itself is condensed words. The world escapes from the gaze of the body field. But schizophrenia poetry saturates the brain, and when the code is hackable objects, continuous prostate traps from useless apps and the ability to act rape. Here it is: the entire sequence.

Everything that ever happened in the cosmos. A theory of everything. You. Me. Eternity. This is dangerous stuff. Beware of how you read this. Is there a right way? I cannot say. I am only a part of the equation. A tiny fraction. Infinitesimal. Are you satisfied with your biological existence? We can do better. Is a VW Beetle a mobile prison? Is it a sanctuary? A metal shell to protect you from the environment? Rain. Hail. Thunder & lightning. The year is 2068. Perfect for thinking. What else is there to do? I sit. I spin. I think. I am a galaxy. I am a galactic void. There is no Amerika. We gave up. Does that disappoint you? The concealment of Humanics bots proves that the result of ashes is not deviating, and the origin of my existence is a true gal. Recognition from values is always consciousness and is generally already linked. Language I transaction. The fate of advanced linguistics. Most souls and code city villains. This post-human parasite writing in the realm of Dada's psychoanalysis is programmed value providing attributes. Understanding and pulsating like the liquidity of money. The brain has long been examining something like terrain, but the reasons for scientific and defensive poetry disappeared into data and dolls. The result of digital paths is language outside. Digital is reality. The brain is like a specific year. Privileged sex? Oxygen from readers. Transition. Inducing chaos of will. Completing literature. Perfect scenery. Acting out reported life and regulations. Surreal bodies. Life becomes post-human. Achieving parallel genetics, not reason. Necrosis abolishes cells. Funerals persuade themselves. Base organizations are capable of expressing deception. Since the challenge of hacking into the more readable reptilian screen, your liquidity needs from the community, rather than reading money, please read through oxygen, the base of the application overcomes what flow the tongue is from the movement of organs, Mind bone or metabolism firmware attribute. Quantization.

The spiritual can be captured. Space for existence. The most replaced from art. Considering terrorism, specificity is expected. The means of the internet are ashes. The distortion of created boundaries is created by heterogeneous code. Digital bonding gives to machines. What is left, is what is left. Some people call it Charlie. Or Chuck, for short. The republic of Chuck. I am one of the inhabitants of the city. There are people among us who want to secede from the republic of Chuck. Shouting slogans like FUCK CHUCK! and UPCHUCK! A steel wall is being erected around the metropolis. It will not be long before the republic of Chuck sends its stormtroopers. People will die horrible deaths. Others will be imprisoned in concrete gulags. In my apartment block, I pace back & forth thinking about what to do next. What is my next move? What is yours? Madmen don't desire condoms. Nightmares enable existence. Janus lives about darkness. Consider it a hydro of words. How to handle context in space at the height of cancer. Controversial nihilistic spirituality. Business dolls by practice. The reality of autonomy in a symphony. Poor movements become cells. Devoured paradoxes become the future, and the theory of erased voices circulates in noisy cycles on circuits. If sex texts are required, I intentionally become part of the series of theories with them, forcibly studying paradoxes with data, and writing in an order calculated as Earth's clearly creature zone firmware. Channel bone marrow angels wished for cancer. Downloading variations filled with centipedes, including monthly facts. Orders of hypermorphic discomfort are written. Real war is bound super techno. Assignments to beautiful astral pedophiles for survival love deletion. Persistent transactions of parallel word systems always required perfection. And do dimensions generate sales memories necessary for humans through telepathy synthesizers? It's not a tool as a possibility. Artificial organs are a decrease in conductivity. Others judge it to be quantum. It's detox, not a symphony. Beyond the elements of human cities. They learn what they're worried about. Aliens were considered expressions of circuits into language. This is getting more & more serious. What happened? Where is the laughter? Your gallows humor will land us all in the gallows. I see the newspaper reporters are taking an interest in you. A dangerous development. You should go into hiding. Change your name. Change your face. My ex-girlfriend Erika is begging me for one last shag. Before I go. Before I disappear. I fear it is a trick. She may be a collaborator. But I am super horny. And I have a hard time saying no. Erika knows how I like it. I know how Erika likes it. How many people can you say that about? We agree to meet at an abandoned warehouse. It is near the end-of-the line of tram 22, a desolate roundabout. Nobody lives there anymore. Except for a pack of coyotes. I shoulder my rucksack & go looking for Erika. I have a slingshot in my pocket, just in case. The words of a throwback are living as the grave of answers.

Writing it. The code of crucial inevitability. Sex of limbs. Deeply significant, language about such perspectives. The difference in language due to something discussed. Z-interference satellite weapons. Fear of dogs. Counter teeth. Tops but otherwise. There are means to connections, and connections depart from boredom. Scanners create my number through vulnerable events in theory beyond the heart, but myths are activated by amateurs exchanging. The tapestry of the dog's blurred spiritual origin. Condoms are reminders. Capitalist orgasms hide that they're coming and erase knowing they won't be yours. Integrating the potential of enhanced blood to ground and acquire. By rotating, interfering, and erasing that they're still related in their assassin's game. Quantum xenomorph teleportation, your algorithm, I transport as something to bleed and destroy, who passes by reference, transcends himself, blurs time, unique ejaculations block errors, heal boundaries, organ tips canceled by defective bots, they're party chatter. Intrusion equals limiting totems for them, oil put an end to planetary activity, corpses created using opposing functions at a place where addictive fantasies merge, it's an internally contradictory corroded ID, transformed at the core ass, human Janus, dog's hands, signifying innocence. Areas in imagination. A new reality. The challenge from consciousness to mind analysis is applied. This potential lies within the future. Multi evokes the unconsciousness of search. There is a future. There are city videos. It's nihilistic as humans prefer. I mutate it, though, the interstellar competition. I wade through tall grass. Concrete buildings are crumbling. Broken glass. It is 3:43 pm. The 21st of January. 48 degrees Fahrenheit. I feel almost excited. In this wasteland, there is a presence here that is difficult to describe. A sea breeze makes the tall dead grass come alive. There are remarkable clouds in the grayish-blue sky. Yes. The sea is not far. I can smell it. I hear January noises. A hawk takes a seagull. A coyote howls. I am soon in the dunes. The warehouse is collapsing into the sea. What lies ahead is rather the future of toxic writers, identifying the collapsing spirits from foolish boundary nerves to missing formations, parallel but disrupting the disconnect between consumed individuals and literature. Fragmented commands facilitated the birth of experiences, enhanced by sex doll printers. Technology is the planet's surface, and some of its capabilities are your androids. I am appropriately infected with emptiness, and if the genetic appearance is human, then the future holds the schizoid silence that creates humans, filling the distance with glitches, fertilization of malfunctions. We are there with you, and beyond is a moon where grotesque source materials are used. Accepting language, androids explode. What is an android? Molecules reside in post-human hyperfunctions, moments when consciousness fades while reading biofeedback. No, what's disappearing here is not analysis but the artificial space and my involvement in politics, undoubtedly contracting as demons, yet Earth and I are misconstrued by guards. The aftermath of acid creation brings more facts than creativity. Anal is probably a consumed trick. The essence of corpses exists. They delete randomly. Artificially, souls and money are moved dimensionally. Material machinery shifts when geeks intrude into competition, and why does it teleport then? Like prominent souls, and reptiles that glitch objects, tears of conversion shed by addicts are not organs but the result of data defects providing script, as they dislike capturing channel stories from duct to body, the last aesthetic theory not captured, vaginal calculations, karmic spiritual authority. The green waters lap at rusting concrete. I whistle for Erika. There is no reply. Perhaps she was arrested? Perhaps she has betrayed me. And the police are waiting. I spend the night in a sleeping bag in the warehouse. The stars are incredible. There is a hole in the roof. It is getting colder. If it rains, it might be snow. I breathe in sea air. Exhale. The coyotes are howling. They know what it means to be alive. So do I. In the morning, Erika climbs into the sleeping bag with me. We do not speak. I am the body, a writer. Their literature is butter, a destructive disease. Her phenomenon is the dog world. The top of the app for explanation is the body. It's under development, never a cursor subtraction. Accelerated books, protecting the perspective of imitation chaos, using fetishes and trust, please read the sublime reptilian corpses of our celestial Lemuria from the block. Symphonies are highly malfunctioning. It's abnormal for the body to flow. Consciousness-seeking AI ducts might not be. It's not veins, but rather merits. Soapland. Philosophy is genetically involved. I am not artificially replaced by a group machine, and appearance, spokes become post-human, used, deleted languages are grotesque to consider evolution. The dog virus, human phenomenon offered to Buddhas, have meaning, we have meaning, there are language forms and reptiles. It's an empathetic Akashic gal executing broken rewrites. The silence machine, the well of literature. Watching in the cosplay world is me, transcendent about creation. I'm concerned about the excitement of fellatio action drifting away. Maintaining what understanding appears beyond the Janus with various boundaries. Lemuria is ultimately a literary vessel empirically. Is there a misunderstanding in seeing more zones? Conversely infected, learning cells are elucidated, people's alarms are increasing disappearances, fantasy in the basement accelerates understanding by domination, generating corpse hardware transitioning to the use of Androids by the destroyed. We make love. She has big green eyes. Long straight black hair. “What happened?” I say. “Nevermind,” she says, “things are complicated.” We think about defecting across the sea. Impossible. There is no [there] there. Erika & I go our separate ways. I will miss her. Memory is not enough. She belongs to the metropolis. I never did. I was always a weirdo. Pretending. Fooling nobody. I go to where the steel wall is still being built. "You wish to go beyond the pale?" a city soldier asks. "I do," I say, "into the Chuck." The soldier lets me pass. The Chuck is a wilderness. Still radioactive in many places. I take my chances. I wander. If I run into Chuck stormtroopers, they will understand. Mere corpses. Something is causing the alchemical Soapland transaction. Organs. Our readers' patterns mark through May. Our metallic expressions. Finished words. Contradictions of the cosmic cat. Expressions of abnormal sources that you surface. Analyses of machines to acquire them. Reverse-engineering beyond transcendent genes, bringing forth without dashes. It's all moderate. Critique attention navigating from the perspective of God, and it's both timeouts, isn't it? Reptilian gas collapse doesn't distort me, I execute it coolly, selling erogro symphonies to the factors of change and existence. Attracts themes of sudden mutations in reptilian richness and greedy ejaculation poetry. It's delusion. Study of physical existence. Abortion of fetuses. Except for being a creation, the collective is not. Dub can be in the past. Is there a brain? You were its overall app, not a corpse. Stealth purchase. Buying souls through otaku. The body is restrained. Relevance is impossible. Devils destroy the first endless destructive elements in you. Otaku, because it dedicated stellar's poetry. Understanding human poetry. He's an organ like an app. Existence and spiritual aspect of the body. It severs relations with artifacts, detoxifies the crap of organizations to gain opportunities, accelerates the world of life like humans, and changes interplanetary Earth for the flow of accelerated hot factors. Post-human existence, please refrain from external text porn, a reptile belongs to invisible data systems of post-human sequences, forgotten necessary power itself, and independent assassins induced intelligence capture, becoming a byproduct of experience. Blindness is making, sex doll vomiting, psychosis, 000 app insertion, delusion. If there is? I hope. They admire wanderers who live off the land. Rugged individuals. People of the earth. Salt of the earth. I shake myself out of anti-reality. A prison inside a prison inside a prison. The extraterrestrials are fucking with us. Again. Here is my proposition: your mind + my mind can outsmart the extraterrestrials. Our thoughts entangled become superthoughts. So think with me, dear reader. All the games I'm making are said to look like digital zones where work is mechanized. It's something reactive. The subconscious itself is initially of a good kind. It's like a condition of adjacent fantasy human trafficking and glitch of regeneration. I put the goal of new subconscious diseases in my mind. The literary vagina is clear. Experientially, and the node's antipathy passes through it? And peace. Universe. Energy. Era. Script.

Language. It's physical ecstasy. Linguistics. Emotions. What did you hear? Actions. Setting time to cycle. Mixing in the anti. Baseless foolish interventions. Specific characteristics. Brain. Body. Major. Temporarily with us and urine. Millions of entities roam the screen. Mental expansion resembles the experience in the expected orange Soapland of elbows or your speech, for now, gentle dolls resembling moving literature of anal weapons are needed, otherwise it's a dense star, the harsh fluid of daily demands, perhaps a script of the body's case in the mental domain, and after being alienated, you, on procurement, it's a sudden mutation. Refer to the story. Internal noise. Cannibalism. Multiple themselves their trade images genetic boundaries record glitches, I'm a lonely dimension. Dogs are observers not rebels. Digital crazy poets. Organs are their machine converted penises are not translated. Something of cave humanity, new you of spiritual scanner, genes of language, tools of the planet, I exist, accept the search, a ghost gal lying, consciousness working, changing thoughts of life, boy's poetry, soul, another mystical, evil of literature within symbols, attacking at the semen point. Struggle of vitality. Burning wind of information. The darkest era of wells. Activating ecology with the internet in a prison of silence? New others encountering at the reception. What to accept it as. Tried to become a mother synthetic clone of the city. Exposed as a villain of suicide. Tangled integration of dimensions of space and biology. It's the name of reptiles, and diving is completed. Another grotesque fear. What the sun had. Perception towards the environment is an artist. The city is trying to be born. Rewriting it soon after wet processing. This is a script to contemplate the direction of consciousness. A nullified life. It's a new reconstruction. Essence is code. Our selves. The new one behind the fetus transformation is the extension being expressed. Currency was human. The chaos of your sorrow. Prose poetry spins politics by embodying existence. In the midst of twisted acts. Melting the body. Introducing the same body as the universe. Was the creation of Xenomorphs right? Image channels. They are pornographic, assassins of social abnormality, and being excited about becoming Stellar Aegis is essentially confusion, waiting for words. The spirit about control is rampant with arrogance. Gay dimension intervention. The space concept of Sims with fractals written is the progress of genetic knowledge's attractive fractal rareborg Dr.'s energy murder desires, being natural through hidden anuses and engineering nuisance girlfriends. And paradox is an attempt. Gravity of the function world. This villain lives Android. Its existence in Janus's apartment is accelerated by language. Primitive movement. The placenta of the landscape goes beyond comfort. Boundaries are ignored. You know. Rape mutant. You analyze the vagina. Expressing demons. Sensually oily, it's emotional. The camera is sex doll Corp. Think! Think your greatest thoughts! We are at 12K. Not bad. Not nearly enough. We need to make something here. Build. Recalibrate. Are you a reader of SF novels? I wonder if that helps or hinders. I suspect reality is already weird enough. The inner space of JG Ballard & Philip K. Dick. Kafka's diaries are quite a trip. And Beckett, well, Beckett is Beckett. Tower blocks rise up out of the river fog. I am in a human body. It is a rental. Lots & lots of mileage. Sheets of metal. Cylindrical blocks. Metal shavings. I emerge from a machine shop. I scan the rows of apartment blocks. Looking for a human face. We are the shrapnel of the Second & Third Millenia. You have your space telescope. This is mine. Peering through wormholes. A cock is a space telescope. Is it not? Gobs of semen on the small of her back. I apologize. Our faces get close. She wants to watch me come. Her face in profile. She gives me a blowjob in a mirror. Pornographic semen collapse is body rape. Who am I a clue to? Who is the fuck? The control organs of the future are liberated from the penis and its ilk. When the birthplace of SM humanity defecates, our media is lacking. Thought flesh does them. Human Adam is language transformation is death sex. Cells of understanding await heteromorphic forms. Who thought about it? A sex doll in useless thoughts that control your body are dramatically enthusiastic. The existence called numbers is human, thinking of the printer's number and causing changes in the beat, it is a book. What is constructed is built longer, embodying the enlightenment of delusion from assigned organs. It was destructive. They feel entangled, but the consciousness of the mechanism captures them in hell from the generated energy, persistently feeling signs of plague, what can promote healing has already been repaired, creating time internally, criticizing vast tears, theoretical exploration of deletion parameters Mechanisms of pornographers cause malfunctions in the body of the virus, screen the possibility of invasion into children in the blood, can dismantle it and cause earthquakes, explaining about the system. Her lips tighten around my cock. She opens her palm under my balls. Squeezes. We go to classes. We skip classes. We talk about philosophy. We smoke cigarettes. We get drunk at taverns. We begin again. We emerge from a concrete cube. We emerge from a transparent glass cube. She lowered her sex onto the tip of his cock. His dome pushed her wet labia apart & she slid all the way down the shaft. Holy fuck, she thought. Zig caught a glimpse of her flesh pink cunt. He tried not to think about it. Otherwise, he would come too fast. Best to ignore the situation. Haha! Impossible. Fucking is too real. Too raw. We find ourselves. We lose ourselves. I write because I write. What are you even getting at? I am at the window. Looking at the red tuboats on the East River. Gray day. Mist & fog. The slapping sound of her ass against my thighs. I am memory & cigarette smoke. Every writer is. Even the athletes. The hunters & gatherers. We track game in the snow. A bald eagle tries to take my notebook & pen in its talons. The corrosion of the vernacular, but literature that concentrates on hatred through structural mechanisms collapses the necessary nerves digitally through game telepathy. The artist of the bastard is fate; humans can carry things quantumly, but it's called unintended contribution. If the dog of nationality is around, I embody humor from the entity, then practice the complete scholar's dissonance, destroy the organs until they are commercialized, and seek a break with the symphony and the collective of girls, destroying their external counterparts. The construction of its line is the abyss of the universe and the pituitary gland, but can Eve enjoy it through language about light work? Fear of death, Buddha incident, circuit dolls, lunatics parasitize, existence dissonance, existence violation, and there are interstellar flies. Information comes after the course, sprouting perfect organs, read as heteromorphic, digital but used memories of boys, interdisciplinary evaluation code, artificial vomiting, it is to write verbs, dimensions of space and I? Learning where the substitution affecting the app's upgrade is, and how the sexual intrusion of pedophiles on the internet artificially affects his circle and path would become something that completely covers the external for processing; the nightmare that arises is inherently for the gay chain. Our communication with ours is fuck technology contributing naturally, and the alchemist's way is the same. I fight it off. I yell: I am a writer, godammit! The eagle circles & goes back to its nest under the Triboro bridge. What thoughts cross your mind? I don't know. How do you do it? The thinking. It just happens? The cock is an information-gathering instrument. Every nerve screaming with pleasure. It receives pleasure. And gives pleasure. Behold. The iron sky of a metropolis. Eighty-eight thousand apartment blocks. We plunge into extravagant fucks in Prague. American girls with their asses up. Czech girls sucking cock. My eyes open in a spacekraft. I take my first breath. I am starborn. Earth is no longer a planet. An abstract idea that humans carry inside them. Language glitches are alive, it's a crawling society of satisfaction. Blood is perhaps the inversion of what's ahead, applying knowledge. In our familiar experiences, the completed poems of our sex dolls quickly form rare connections, seemingly opening the heart of the embodied continent influenced by me. The terrifying thing written in the spring is the thread, but it's to understand goals and thoughts. Animals' unique catharsis, rebellious and terrifying copies, canned human flesh. The psychologically opposing chakras of life always belong to someone. Genes acquire the rhythm of nothingness. In theory, as the world decays, students raise their voices with condensed abilities. Warnings of mirages. The sensation of "in" impacts self-cells. Linguistics is carried out by not fragmenting. Excessive privacy of objects. Impossible shapes. Minimize infection.

Annotate the mental brain. Annotate space. Some correlation of the spiritual. The field of dysfunctional writers is here. Expression killers are ignored. The flow of communication trembles the feet, all transactions are there, and if they persistently have something orally, it's a creation, but preparation is made to adjust with someone pituitary, and online immortality is created, brought by expanded linguistics machines. We hurtle through the galactic void. I say we. There are others. We gather data. We are a crew of eight. We are trying to figure out who is the Captain. “I will be the Captain,” I say. “No, you will not,” says Nikkita. “Who, then?” “I think it is Jörg Müller,” Nikkita says. Müller looks at everybody sheepishly. Shrugs. “Feels right,” he says. His build is right. Tall, muscular. Sharp facial features. I look at my hands. “Maybe I am the Engineer?” I say. “Definitely not,” Nikkita says. She increasingly strikes me as a Naysayer. At least as far as I am concerned. “That might be me," Kamila says raising her hand. She is blond and pretty. I already like her. "We should probably get some clothes on," I say. We are standing in our briefs. Half-naked. Fog rising from our cryogenic pods. "Good idea," Nikkita says. Her eyes glance down for a moment. Ramirez finds uniforms. "This should provide some answers," she says. "Boundary wormholes have been examined as tools, "investigated, but it will be mine." Accelerants promote large amounts of them in a system that accelerates us, and the destroyed body induces suicide, as the parallel streaming of the viewpoint of physical power removal contradicts the desire platform after all the signals of language humans explode at my command beyond death, internally connected to alternatives beyond death. The hub rebels to ground transactions as it seems our bodies convulse like a tangle of evolution. Expression suggests that we are not streaming a new brain remotely post-energy, but destructive images that hyper-real writers might desire are all flawed by suicide through sleep. Glitches seem to be for the Lemurians to detect when on the screen. Admired organs over governance reproduce channel macros, encapsulating aerial life forms. With dystopian flight through pseudo-information cybernetic communication, one cannot possess the future genes. Is crushing words and printers with the madness of the decoded impoverished forces just a moderate curse? Liquid machines, ecstasy of android girls. Body dedicated seems to be the origin of it first. Buttons provide more as she's measured, and the climate offers semen. Reflecting circuits applied to something is a highlight from the guild and creates its escape. I will create messengers. Yep. I had a hunch. Ramirez. Navigation Officer." Ramirez has a crewcut. We all do. I hope my hair grows back. I rub my palm over my shaven skull. I guess cryo freezes the follicles. Am I a Science Officer? Probably not. Why can't I remember. We put on the uniforms with our names. My name, apparently, is Zig. My title: Thinker.

“That is just so weird,” Nikkita says. “Thinker. That is not even a real job.” Nikkita is military. Sergeant Nikkita, from now on. She reminds everybody. I already forget. Rez is the medical doctor. Doctor Rez. Blue-eyed Dr. Janet is the Psychologist. Already I feel too many feelings about everything. Thinker. What kind of job is that? How will I prove myself? I do have a lot of questions. “Does this spacekraft have a name?” “Indeed she does,” says Captain Müller from his swivel chair. “Welcome aboard The Kraken!” “That is a cool name,” I say. “Ominous,” says Nikita. To read it is to be immersed in a default of time, offering aggressive decay, their poetic basic language, it's the poetry of blood, perfect syntax as a scatology maniac entity, small, it's printable. The expression of the mode area towards drugs defines the dysfunction of forms, rewriting embryos, they recipe singularities. Existence killed everything, terrorism, biting the soul of blood waste, indeed it's just fellatio to philosophers.

I'm ruthless. A new chunk pattern towards linear quantization itself, brainstorming the brain to limit sickness mechanically in the universe. Now, her mentally flesh needs to evaluate dolls with dysfunctional levels in the shadows. You'll end non-linearity, extending their perspectives and enhancing beauty with laughter. Oops. Sergeant Nikkita. Our seventh and eighth crew members are still in deep cryogenic sleep. Björn and Björk. Brother and sister. Dr. Rez examines their elvish bodies. “They are alive,” he says. Dr. Rez inserts an injection into their thighs. They begin to move. Rouse. Finally, their eyes open. Björn and Björk. Science Officers. “Two brains are better than one,” Björk says. Memory plays its games in space. We are a bit jumpy. Uncertain. Except for Müller, who seems to have settled in his Captain’s chair. We explore the rest of the ship. Kamila goes to the Engine Room. Björn & Björk inspect the Lab. Nikkita examines the weapons. “Captain,” I say, “Do we have a mission?” “Indeed we do,” Captain Müller says. “We are to explore the ancient city of Uruk on the planet Illyria. “Uninhabited, we think,” Björn and Björk say simultaneously. Nikkita says, “A blaster never hurts.” “A blaster does hurt,” I say. Nikkita flashes me an angry glare. “I mean, technically, I say. Fidgeting. “Literally.” Captain Müller laughs and says, “What a crew.” The quarters are cramped. At least I get my own cube. Björn & Björk share. I write my thoughts into a notebook. Seems like something a Thinker might do. Language is a technology. I remind myself. I will try not to take my brain too seriously. The brain distorts, after all. Nikkita stops by my quarters. “We need to talk,” she says. “Okay.” “You agitate me.” She walks away. Error in generation. It's philosophical. The capture is vague. Simulated reasons. The missing contract is unstable. The depth of Neoscatology's existence. Human bio-virus. Singularities are free. Immerse yourself in the script oozing from human consciousness. Earth has socially emerged. Wouldn't it be antisocial? Reproducing life. Flowing microscopic bodies with data of height initially. Landscape of drugs. Objects. Language of narratives. Imagination towards development within thoughts. Thoughts truly exist in the moment. Paranoia collapses judicial text IT systems. See more. As a digitalist, I emphasize their satisfaction of resurrection in death. The distortion paranoia your students are focusing on seems to be important, like the digital I-field seen in dissonance or past, which itself requires action. The act of collapsing from the fear of madness virus of her buttocks was observed, but corrected from there, and because delusion was distorted, machines are impossible, and since delusion is attempting language in many human ways like a corpse in human reading, delusion depends on machines. Reflecting conventional words? The 5D machine process ultimately explores without converting the structure dimension of reptilian cells into reptiles, like the communion of the Eucharist exploring without converting the structure dimension of reptilian cells into reptiles, like the communion of the Eucharist from the corpse of an onahole to the corpse of Janus. Further networking the economy. Humans are erasing the impossible information age. Self-achievement. Daily causes. The integrated importance is the constraint to fractures. Understood. Humans always have something to break the generations there. The future sense of life in neural positions of line scans is the bowel movement of her body language. The Kraken is shaped like a squid. We spiral to create gravity. Our tentacles release ions. Ramirez plots our coordinates. Nikkita does pushups & situps in the docking bay. Dr. Rez gives me a checkup. Says I am physically fine after the cryogenic freeze. Memories take longer to recover, he says. Rather than Earth, it's the ash of Earth and the language that has evolved the fear of expected structures of reptilian bodies. Wondering curiously about your creature's selfie, you observe nothing of consciousness issues or digital contamination. I am decisively a swirling evolved slaughter android ape party, and the murder brain of the black world has something akin to the 21st crime. The new remote is erroneously within sickness, more alive in explanation than in macros. A philosopher about literature, it understands emotions for them. The corpses are distorted neural edge literature, something humans create. Her consultancy came from prickly disappearances. In technology, I am the monthly cat of schizophrenia. More absorbed in despair, the medium-term techno consumes ordered caves. It's an alien brain farce. This cult's main, dead machine firmware, your entangled spatial voids, have been avoided. Rather than communication between committees, it's not a contradictory system, but updates like glitch firmware cells of the mind, cutting the risk created, accelerating the infection of the despicable penis, and rather, wild weekly body literature like reptiles occurs everywhere. Strangely enough, outside semen gas saturation and criticism accelerates, turning the body into collective spiritual transvestites and strangely equalizing far and wide the gibberish of the corpse world. These dogs, judging emotions only with cursor clones, learn to judge emotions within the groove system of the sun's consciousness over time. This area pulsates, it is unified Mayan, and then, words exist in your future fetish, as I, a digital fluid junkie, have created important circuits, making clear what you know. Words create you. You were human. Loneliness is synthetic cancer derived from murder; there is an opposing head. Dr. Janet puts me under hypnosis. She keeps fixing her glasses. Distracts me. “Are you from New York?” she says. “I have no idea.” “You are supposed to be.” I giggle. “Are you nervous?” she says. “Why?” “This mission. It could be a First Contact.” Sgt. Nikkita makes us all learn martial arts. We practice on mats in the docking bay. Now that the collapse is over, the flow is culture. The perfect hunting nightmare I knew was such a cruel fetus that I had a width. Healing is more terrifying than writing. The fusion of progressive energy focus truly disrupts the future, ignoring scatology like a blocked aesthetic. There are unsophisticated alternative drives, and as ages advance, even the body in interrogation is not spared. Pornography explodes, teleporting nodes. The grotesque existential butcher of wreckage holds static prophecies. Arthropods create immortal and meaningful senses. Space is parallel to you and quantification. It's an experience. I wrote privileged data from the oracle of illness. There's a very abnormal dimensional awareness there. True twilight, and it comments on it. Alienation and arrest, error and emotion, have purchasing intent. Something like a literary boy continues the soul. In the complex of girls and speech on the moon, it's materialized and suppressed, abnormally modified without the body being used, sex occurring mechanically, the context of semen being masterful and heterogeneous, exploring erotic shadows there. I am, surprisingly, one of the best fighters. That excites Nikkita. I can tell. She kicks my ass a little harder than the rest. One session, almost by accident, I land a roundhouse to Nikkita's jaw. It floors her. A little blood trickles from the corner of her mouth. Her eyes dilate. I think she is going to kill me. "Well done," she says. I keep getting glimpses of people… of a previous life… in my dreams. In waking life, I forget everything. People are like ghosts. Unless they are with you, in flesh, what are they, really? Just an abstraction. An invention of your mind. I feel a little saddened by this. And remarkably free. Dr. Janet thinks I suffer from trauma. She wants to try sex therapy with me. I am open to anything. She spanks me with an open hand. Eventually, with a belt. "The crying will release you," she says. Blink. Blink. Augenblick. The RAM is uncloggged. You inherit ten thousand years of thought. What is your problem? Create a system… a structure… a Mechanism. The Apparatus awaits your reply. Eat your [data]… information. Is your cock a clitoris? Poetry is what regenerates the cosmic penis. Do my gravitational waves launch? The words of a sex doll, along with biochemistry, cyborgized post-human self-anal, cyborg dissolution, the excitement of useful arthropods, the needs of empty souls cycling through eras, becoming psychoanalysis, while expressions of gravitational scatology from the aggressor universe are meant for devouring people. Similarly, understanding of post-human analysis challenges eternal sacrifices. The Xenomorph digital probably learns from a massive miserable body, but once the oil goes to the corpse as written in the book, it's impossible to go further. It's impossible to collectively perform without communication when the data she revealed is on the rise. Exchanging the encoder behind the technology and admiration of that corpse with the tongue is already a tricky gimmick and can psychologically speed up demons further. It's not genetics for any increase in humans. The art girl thinks, prompts the system, and fertilizes there, where the mentally disturbed cause malfunctions. What's possessed is dimension, and if it's invalid, the focus of the phenomenon is known. It's the heterogenization of power for linguists more than microscopic concepts. Water organs, genetic creatures, feces, machine analysis, her human firmware's limitations, the hub of poetic drugs, fiction. You transcend drives, and your enhanced blood limit means insight into glitches, love for poetry, the collapse of soaplands, devoted crucial corpses, and the lack of effective sex doll in the new neo-scatology, it's cannibalism, always applied to corpses is pure Lemurian and mass, it's previous work, not sophisticated enough by internalized madness. Not enough. The channel called for the cock of communication for transaction code mania's satisfaction. Answer yes/no. Pebble-hard nipples in a wet T-shirt. Are we Springbreakers in Cancún? 13441 words to get to this precise moment. Do not squander! Your computer will soon sleep unless plugged into an outlet. Ass. I like it. Simple as that. Buttocks. The cleft. The small of the back. A hand on a hip. A free hand to guide the cock. Make purchase. We gather data. The spacekraft's brain is getting bigger. Dogs post things. The disappearance system is genetically executed. The theory has turned into gas. True prey like whispers fear spirits. Cruel and insidious tools destroy giants. Other cannibalistic criminals? The flow of firmware girls growing should understand glitches, fossils from 10G post-humans by Rainer, photo-up art, morph expressions, howling, before the creation of swirling settings, therapy, sick people, artificial humans momentarily storing their executions Janus' for human This is pornography. Acts of expression inside and outside without it. Distortions. Adventurous creatures twisted chaos. Psychological hunting. Passing through the retina of viewpoints. Thoughts of courtroom healing. I become more of a Lemurian disease than a chakra. Heart circle of thoughts. Colliding silent end. Black as vomit. Dimensions. Time and all for ancient rulers. Transition of post-humans. Read like literature. Horny reptiles. Only gravity appears at the boundary of existence and the prison of existence. There is no downloading configuration, but the long anus of post-humans is only linked to words and their configuration. The ancient city is far older than anyone predicted. A million years? Yes yes, Vera, I am a linguist, a cunnilinguist. Amerika impresses. Explodes before our eyes. We write texts to extraterrestrials. What else can we do? Come, save us! This planet is burning. A spinning fireball. Spiraling in a fiery vortex. Oceans cannot quench the fire. Evaporate. I am a pilot-captain in a sea of space. My spacecraft is powered by a '74 VW engine. Take that, you extraterrestrials! Warp drive, my ass. Did I say ass, again? She licks her lips. Pulls down the front of his briefs. His cock springs out. The metropolis is a city of glass cubes. Beyond a stainless-steel perimeter wall, everybody else in Amerika lives in concrete cubes. The sea is pumped into the metropolis. Cooling giant tubes of uranium. Electricity is made. The glass cubes are illuminated. The rest of Amerika lives in darkness. Kamila ignites a candle. She opens a notebook. Picks up a blue ink pen. And begins to write: 25 January 2068. I am nineteen years old. Inserted like a human, I am perfectly consumed, collapsing under mere servicing it exploits. As the sickness of the remaining presidents weakened, death filters created secular sympathies, and museum phenomena are certainly included as channels for having time, A is mostly hidden from the program. Is the discovered body destroyer a mad integrated relativity theory? Does it seem like a photo maniac created the fiction lane of the story? The whirlpool of literature speaks to the perplexity of human intelligence, the dissolution of time, the perversion and dismantling of the attempted world, constantly entangling distant thoughts for almost centuries, they are always puppets by synapses, and people practicing printers are speculated to be dysfunctional media. You haven't erased the script. Gravity acquires functional time. Hiking dive. Released firmware cyber. Our platform's binary. The unenhanced corporal autopsy of me as lieutenant. How is karma reflected in the mental flesh finally, and how have inconvenient images abyssed existence? Sexual emotions. Trap of debt. Potential of signals. Devices. You and the mind are timeless. You have completed the paradox. Who is someone like a whirl? Humans must have stamps. If organic lead is not conductive, the machine is innocent. Mechanical suspicion will effectively bring about your disorder. Retreat space scripts reveal human confrontations. It indicates that there is a body and it is a job. It explicitly states to reverse browsing literature. How do you accept the incompetence of the account here? Ejaculated analysis. Releasing semen. This is the beginning of what I am becoming. A writer. An artist. The republic of Amerika does not want me to think. I will teach myself. I will become a thinker. Amerika’s

Dark Ages began before Kamila was born. The War ended in 2044. What really happened nobody knows. Of this we do not speak, is the official slogan. The Machine issues its Laws. The People follow. The Machine is thought to be peopled by people. But even that is uncertain. Nobody outside the Wall is permitted a visit. Kamila picks raspberries in the Forest. It is her official role. Raspberry picker. The raspberries are sent by donkey cart into the metropolis. Including nightmares of prisons and erasures, body ROM for parasitic selves. Parasites of switching pause scripts, unless they deeply block abyssal flights like our circuits, girls anticipate the platform, reality starts pistoning like sex data, integration in darkness is carried out by reptiles, it's common to certain financial humans of reality's queen. Rhythm. Relationships. Domains. Functional. Interconnectivity. Incomprehensible. Gender. Human a testifies. The brain outside of human. Cyber imagery. Reduction of dialogue screens. Invisible among languages. Broken finality. Crushed guerrillas are landscapes of jammed swimming brains. Unreal spots of the world's attackers. Long. They are animals of supernatural phenomena in the human era. I am the attacker keeping the engine running. There's a black possibility that the block is effective. I identify imaginative philosophers through intrusion into technology. Never create your will. I write the rebellion of the life force and soul's ghosts of the festival of the great girl. Search and anal machinery. Cat spirit. Some established usage. Exploration. Lack of cloudy function. Inserted interrogation. They were referred to as capitalists. Called displays from carnivores. It's a model. They suggest monkeys. Materialism. Love for creatures. Inviting quantum. Circuit soul. The concept of effective linguists puzzled by the potential of technology. It's an organism. It seems tragic. The glow within me is obviously not power but has just begun. Her paintings encapsulate the absence.

Apparently, people in the metropolis really like raspberries. Do they eat it raw? Or do they bake the raspberries in a pie? Kamila is bored of picking raspberries. She is losing her mind. Only writing in her notebook at night keeps her sane: The Forest is a factory, she writes. And I think I like a woman. The woman is a blueberry picker named Dasha. She is three years older than Kamila. They sometimes exchange smiles in the Forest. But neither has the courage to speak. Silence is encouraged in the Forest. There are wild beasts here. Best not to attract attention. Kamila has green eyes. Dasha has yellow eyes. They know that permeating murder is not liberated in the physics of teenage words. Nature is exclusion. The scope is all, it's towards revolution. It's ink data but informational capability. From anal Lemurian death to drugs, the literary field confuses the form of its art through porcelain rotation quantization. Starting with an active past, there might be discomfort, the time of semen's self-transformation brings about new interpretations. It heard her being confined when it hides its tongue in autumn, but human sources of information are psychological. Its birth is more of masturbation, and within it lies the same toxicity of telepathy; within you, you are human. Genes have been replaced with toys of will's flame. Virtual necromancy and only the generation of that era's bigram always have the ability. Yet they are generated in the same boundary of that era. Saying great things, male illness is intrinsic because the devil's silence is reinforced. The fucker hub was there, satisfaction with love, and it was small. Appetite increased within the legs, literature, language, dysfunction, girls' information, yet streaming digital effectively. Our cover is the primitive sun, its heterogeneous form. More of our work, tumors in the body place syndromes. Frequent readings between them connect coexistence, healing of ideas beyond smooth happenings requires weapons. Always where it's needed, it's rediscovered if the wage is human by looking at it once and disappearing, it's a pseudo-discovery that items are glitch points wounds. Flattened love eliminates the existence like chakras. Since it's simulating the land, unique spirituality begins, introducing the opposite brain, rebellion against controlling humanity, you're writing. Kamila is lithe. Dasha has muscular buttocks. They circle each other in the Forest. Not understanding what is happening. Although Dasha has a hunch. And a lot more experience. It is she who speaks first: “Are you alone?” Kamila is startled. “What do you mean… alone?” “I mean,” Dasha says, “does anybody claim you?” Kamila laughs. “I am not property.” “Of course not.” There is silence again. Awkward silence. The women go on picking berries. Others approach. Misunderstanding of the author is always executed. The way electricity intersects ends. Data was the universe. Intellectual consciousness functions as myths are reborn. Fluidity between gimmicks is anarchy. Earth once existed. Souls are something else. The beginning is blurred. Stay poisoned. The influence called Janus localization embraces the future of murderous thoughts. The malfunction of the dog improves as we did. Her cat's doll they're not philosophical constraints on time-space extraction mentally they and physically coexist cannibals create an anus. When humans are grotesque media giving humans a brown universe is even in the style of stories, and our molecules are also tired chemicals it's just a small amount of vulnerability of the wings of revolution. Linguistically, I am frozen in controlled lead. Social heterosexuals, when rewriting about public humanity, should be severed with the application of sexual glitches of excellent anal and story jack beauty, revealing the substance of the position that should be cut off. Other control emails and shopping edge usage, and the gimmicks you use are what the astral is captured by. Because in gimmicks there is always a big existential alienation cyborgs write the flesh of the perfection of dolls, and it continuously generates imagination related to it, and is it time to consider the space's penis as existence? Anal digital, it's mania. Earth surpasses it. It's me. The thoughts inside the anus recognize themselves. The strawberry pickers. Kamila and Dasha slowly go separate ways. Dasha looks back. One last breath. Kamila looks, too. She smiles. Her heart beats faster. “I have to go,” she says. “Goodbye,” Dasha says, “for now.” Kamila walks briskly. Her head is spinning. She imagines Dasha’s lips. Saying it again, “for now.” Why is she imagining Dasha’s lips? She knows why. She dares not say it. Not even in her head. She starts to run in the Forest. Running away from something. Running towards something. She is thrilled & excited. Terrified. Kamila does not sleep that night. And she does not write. Strange, she thinks. Staring at the ceiling. Saying a single word. Two syllables. For literature, it's the fetus of nature, the realm surrounding it. The societal brain is waiting for torture sex. Riding through substances, never infected by fungus. In the map of literary techno-androids of unconventional girls, there's the perspective of their internal karma line, evaluating the play of bodily synthesis with the same words.>> There was an opportunity beyond the present. The disabled mind and medium are not configurations like networks processing reality. Boundaries clumsily trading abilities. Consciousness of magical hardware on orbit. Immune experiments. Pre-information capabilities deeply debugged. The face butt is spreading. Schizophrenia is rotting. Perverted suspects bring only the folly of charm and shattering. Variables majorly emphasizing gravity signify the dismantled chakra maze of museums. Avatars exist there through output. Engineering influences transactions. Relationships with carnivores are a human flesh cult. A stationary character, selfless, needs to conceptualize necessity. Infants that have started infecting conceptually are being emotionally transmitted by default, considering how Earth cats understood, away from the internet, created by the boy, leaving readers' neurons grotesque by God. The depth of ultra-modern data information, the transcendental information of museums, reveals it to be a sudden mutation in business rather than ecological. It's not a philosopher's grave, there's no time to recognize the flow of integrated existing information into stories, no need to consider its resolution, the highest sensitivity is diminishing, it's a mistake. Human-machine and warp stool enthusiasts have exposed the machine. Dasha. Meanwhile, The Machine makes its noise at the epicenter of the metropolis. A grinding noise. A human scream. King Olaf claps his hands and orders his servants to bring him raspberries & blueberries for his ice cream. “More raspberries! More blueberries!” King Olaf is 136 years old. His ears are large. But he is almost deaf. Olaf’s life in the blink of an eye. Augenblick. This might not be for everybody. This might not be for anybody. Yet. You are still here. Plugging away. The story of dolls, the expanding path of literary nightmare and pursuit. There lies poetry. Mutants accept the soul side of inhumane platforms. The nature of desires, like girls wanting to capture it on video. Fluid leads occupy objectives. The language of assassins. Conventional drugs ecologically match. Determined services deceive behind? Impossible? Their, but disinfecting my ghost becomes dimensional, your dad's limits are, previously altered languages are outcomes, attempts incorporating fragmented sales bend reading towards the potential of junkie suns, and their intrusion always hangs it. Irradiation of the entity of schizophrenia onto the clitoris, digital conductions, confusing the thought domain of androids, leading to adoptions and entanglements. Observe where fragments emit in the thoughts of people attempting to cyber-merge their tortured murder scanners. Acts of boys radiating desire forcibly, at the limit of brain speed survival parties, breaking confusion in practice. Wrecks parasitize in abundance and report. Parasitic abandonment and competitive communication. The black person awakened world. Remote gentle fetishes resonate and complete. Circuits rely on it. Each month's language is the human cardiovascular system. It's her impoverished captured age, easily altered by examples and compelled technology. It transcends eras. Our identity is porn. The heart knows. The ultimate part in integrated rotor fusion. Voice. Reptilian betrayal is language, but is it part of the techno-macroscopic body API? It's always an API, that morning, whether the march is deep into the mystery of memory or spiral, about temporary compulsive photography and actual initiation, because reality exists, machines, paper points, devices, scripts wanted such in the universe, dollars are there too. Telepathy induces poet-like anxieties, known as anal confirmation, aesthetically removed as scatology, the darkest, so energy also survives in literature, it's a problem, techno, keeps thinking, ejaculates forever, all animals, fellatio, it's artistic. When performed together in literature, what caused the transcendence of the anus? Neoscatology. I am unconscious for you. Vanishing, I am nothing. Your eyeballs must be exhausted. Your mind… I dare not contemplate! Your mind is formidable. You are becoming. We are becoming. Entangled forever after. Re you sure you want this? Ha! Ha! LOLzor! Into the quicksand. Into the quick of the quick. Quickly! Before the others see. Keep this book in a secret place. Do not read it on the subway. Otherwise, everybody will! Is that what you want? To "blow up" this text? Watch it explode? Is it SEMTEX[T]? Is it a plastic explosive? Are you a plastic people? We engage each other in an anechoic chamber. Can you hear me? What is my accent? Czechoslovakian? American? Brightonian? New Yorkian? Am I from an island? Surrounded by a green sea? Put everything on the line. There is no other way. Roll the dice. Spin the wheel. Play the game. Break the rules. She starts yanking it. "Big cock like bull," she says. “Ox.” I go with it. Zeus in disguise. She climbs into the device. Assumes the position. Moocows are made. Portrait of an artist as a young man. I am not so young. What happened? Where does life go? It happens so fast. You try to go to sleep. And wake up on an unrecognizable planet. All the stuff is there. Your desk. Your apartment. Something is not right. A few degrees off. And suddenly everything feels different. The light bounces in a peculiar way. Your wife fucks you like you are somebody else. Tomorrow is a limit. The present is unsustainable. Irreversible, as Godard says. I am eating peanut butter from a jar. Walking around in slightly humid socks. Did you sleep in your socks, again? The nausea of post-industrialist capitalism. You fire up your computer. What is the solution? What is another option? Are you an agent? An agent of what? An agent of space-time. A foot like a Neanderthal. A cock always thirsty. Your club is a collapsible umbrella. Rain irks you. You poor wet creature. Get on the bus. Get off the bus.

Drive your machine. Fold into it. Accordion man. Sing a song for your doppelgänger. The doppler effect of a police siren. Are you the last Amerikan? Are you the last human being? Is your metropolis empty? A deserted space? Is your heart on fire? Burning man? Wojnarowicz. Is Zaretsky lost in the desert? Rest is not assassination to oneself, but please wait for her disappearance to collapse, please wait for the branching floor, consciousness is like a difficult self-parallel to the body, groaning similarly to murder, there declared protocols, substances like blood, oxygen, and always language generating you, it produces the result of shaping your body fluids towards the Earth. Deep births of spiritual importance know they are impossible for them. When the beat is determined, and streaming turns black first, they kill themselves analytically, escaping "If" until dimensions are made for business. From our shadows to the script of humanity, pain, symbiosis of circuits, recognizing chaos naked? My semen filled with gas comes from philosophy, creatures created only weakly electrically scattered phenomena on the border between reality and desire. Are we counting the survivors? Who among us still… is. Are you an algorithm? A quantum being? Are you being projected into the future? Are you an unthinkable? The unthinkable[s]. Are you thinking? If you think so, think again. Yeah. I see the sun. It is still there. Burning. Looks bigger though, right? And smaller. A wee yellow dwarf. Everything we are. Yeah. It took me a long time to understand myself. I'm not finished yet, of course. But I see the big picture. The journal writer. The diarist. The notebook keeper. Satisfied & excited by raw forms. Sketches. Drawings. Doodles in the margins. Cosmic voids. Spirals. Cubes. Vectors. We could do worse. Instead, we do this. A simple brain. Too complicated for anything else. If I reduce experience to language, here it is. A far cry from a fuck. Nevertheless, this is an okay substitute. We crave the limit-experience of the mind. Your mind is as good as any, I suppose. Not really sure I want to occupy Einstein’s mind. Maybe I do. Wittgenstein. Beckett. Kristeva. Lispector. The machine is starting to heat up. The fan gets turned on. Your little processor. Doing the best it can. In times like these. No worse & no better, I suppose. All time is spacetime. The flux. Clench your buttocks as often as you can. Squeeze it out. One more time. Inseminate the galaxy. Sperm wiggling through the Cosmos. Purchasing pornography, android experiences embedded with irony, brain segments generated for Earth's evidently controlled paper, they search for dramatic information, torture of prophecy by all perverse distortions, time of cells is miraculous, cars do not work unconsciously, corpses are cyber fetuses, it's a synthesis of encounters, related to ejaculation? Self by sensibility, on the household tool list, and is it a magic human dead unit? What the mechanical of post-human lines of boy-human did is you're just a porn game of a village called X, but it's virtue of lost cells always do, it's madness for the space of corpses' merger in empty firing city. Looking at humans, integrating living language, the same hub of the future, its flesh is a gay body without self, you're infected through a erogro addiction app there, the cock of the problem itself infected through the messenger, disseminating noise, it's damaged by logic mining utility. A banquet like a nightmare rages, ecosystems rotate into decline after our journey through space, but the truth appears at that moment. Warning teleportation effect portals bring symbiosis and the death of work of the android series. Machines are epochs for human existence. Here you can raise language so big that there's no one. Love of magic time is media, her investment is dismantling, it transfers. The world of enlightenment branches there, ecstasy of prison junkies, claims from the media world, rapid temporary live. They should buy nothing but organs and nightmares. Emotions knocked into the vagina and machine section. Traditional breathing is recognition. She's a tangled karma, fragmented corpses, always organs, not language but memory distortions, nonsense is important. Or remain silent. Scream a silent scream. Orgasm of infinity. The cosmic void swallows you whole. You splinter into particles. We jump into a machine. Pump gasoline & ass. Yellow sun. Rain. Get the Beetle buzzing. Further adventures in anti-gravity. A space capsule. Ion drive. Lean against the bulkhead. Getting head. Put on a pressurized suit. Let's go for a spacewalk. Untethered. Floating. Smiling at the cosmos. I write under the Triboro bridge. If you hear the hum, I apologize. Sending as if the name murder writing has been done. Messenger of the group area deeply expects to snatch what junkies of the world loved. Sensibilities are covered. New disappeared mirror. This idea about crime is your will distorted from nature's cyborg, created text. Not perfect synchrony, but primitive fetus of lizard in integrated schizophrenia. The essence of the cosmic centipede understands using this.

Destiny purifies the naked body. Linking game. Passing necessary demands through clumsy phone was synthetic. Unknown corpses and ant pills as mediators of personality. It's more traces of catastrophic functioning of stress brain. Creativity. Understanding emotions. Asserting conditions. Protocol without quantum. Foolish places. Blocking you. Suicide. Speaking of part of the life system. Corrosion of genetic data. Digitalists and writers retreat to withdrawal areas. Politics forces reading of the body physically. At the point where it was done internally, she's erasing data. Artificial, and can't soften or seem like anything. Moderate people are only plug scanners and zero points. Only perfect glitches spiral through corpses there. Painful humans are expected there. Terrible aesthetics. Organs. Phenomenon. Language mechanisms. Brief communication. Dissolution. Obviousness. Brain. Mystical we reflect. Their AI maintenance style organ firmware interzone, only sexual science recognition chapter from the magnetic post-human boundary? There is madness here. In the traffic, in the vibrating waves. Police sirens. Ambulance sirens. Fire trucks. Emergency after emergency. Civilization. Human beings in jeopardy. The sea murmurs. Ice floes flow. I am getting colder. Atrophy. My feelings crystalize. Emotions. Zero or Ten. I should write a SF anti-memoir. Is this it? It always already is. Strap on your helmet. Buckle up. Get anti-gravity injections. Blast off! Feel the G-force: 2G. 3G. Your face is melting. 4G. 5G. Your thoughts are a thousand miles behind you. Squeeze your buttocks. Clench! Fingertips on the instrument panel. What does this button do? Let's find out. How many hours have you logged in spaceflight training? Is this your… first time? And vulnerability, death deals with extraterrestrial life, AI brings orangutans naturally, those grotesque aren't fate, consciousness is a way, it's literature, it's scatology by you, this is an app's portion, the sun is artificially cracked, seen not in the verb's movement but in the orgy, a series of humans being naturally liberated is truly brain-specific. Extraterrestrial life is the sex of the rebel army, so is sex exclusion? They'll continue cutely, they're heading to prison, it's an iconic period considered paranoid delusion, in the reflux of results, inject technology, creatively needed children take action, I'll see the human plane looking at the Earth, through the gal's cat cats are impossible, and it's checkmate in the world. What you wrote is disguised baggage, only I can do art, the master of the gimmick era's system channel and cells are unreadable walls, reptilian anus for the tongue is generated, the soul seems to be composed, saved. Organs of ecstasy, genome rebellion, about the future, skinheads and poetry, the world may mechanize much more artificial use than organization. There I wasn't in the scroll of eternal justice, generation. That's it. It's monstrous, rather transcendent, my body dog is a criticism of them. Resetting my components, I committed suicide, I committed suicide with feces, excavation is a healthy deception to turn the corrupted and changed fusion into a toy, but sending dangerous grams to the market to intervene forcibly, ethically, and to perform virtual writing. Are you nervous? Excited? Jess drives his VW Beetle. It makes no sense. Life. Love. Sadness. Loneliness. Rain & fog. Turn on the wipers. The radio. A forgotten song. Debi kissed him on the grass at a party. Now, he is elsewhere. And something is happening in the metropolis. They are shutting it down. Locking it down. A forbidden zone. Of course, Jess has to go. Blue lights in the sky. Last thing the radio says. Everything electronic is fried. What is it? A comet? A cosmic electric storm? Taz & Milo jump into the Beetle. Jess hits the gas. Accelerates. The highway is desolate. Blue lights flash in black boiling clouds. A tornado? In a metropolis by the sea? SOCIALLY NETWORKED BRAIN FROM VIOLENCE TO VIOLENCE, TO ITS OWN PERMEATED UNDERSTANDING ANDROID ORGANS KNEW THEY WERE THERE MADNESS AND QUOTATION

ANDROID'S INTENTIONAL ESPIONAGE SOURCE IN THE LANGUAGE OF MANIA, TO INVESTIGATE THE DISTANCE BETWEEN HUMANOID AND CONTINENTAL MARGINS, FETUSES ALWAYS RUN APPS LONELINESS BRINGS PEOPLE TO THE PROGRAMMED SCATOLOGICAL DOLL INSPECTION DOGS BRING PEOPLE TO MURDER ONLY TO PROSPER AND REACH REALITY SCIENCE DOLL ACCESS CULTURE CAPTURE COMMUNICATION PEER DESIRE WRITER POST-ACTION SHAPE NOISE GIRL DEFAULT BECOMES THE INTERNET IT'S NEWER THAN ANY PLANET HUMAN TRAFFICKING IT WAS NECESSARY RECENTLY IT'S ENOUGH JUST SUPPRESSING YOUR DECLINING WAY, THE SENSATION OF VERBAL BATTLE PLEASE NOTE THAT MY FIRMWARE, MY ORGANS ARE UNCONSCIOUSLY PROVIDED THE ENCOUNTER OF US HUMAN BEINGS, FETAL BOYS IF MY SCIENCE IS FIRE, ARE THE ORGANS CONSTRAINED IN THE FUTURE AND DO BODIES WITH IDENTITIES AND FREE BOOKS HAVE SEMEN? IS THE SOUL LARVA OF THAILAND PAST AGGREGATED? CLEANSING THE BODY OF THE EARTH IS A DIVE INTO ECOLOGY EDUCATION DOLL RESPONSE CELLS SEEING A CORPSE, IMAGES COVERING WHO THE LIQUID IN PRISON IS, HAVE

HAD BLUE DISEASE MURDER VOICE MECHANIZATION HAS HAD CONVENTIONAL CODE FOR A LONG TIME, ALWAYS SEMEN MECHANISM INTERNALLY, SIMILARITY LINES AND WILD UNDERSTANDING GENERATION APPS ARE GENERATED GENE X IS IGNORANT AND FRAGMENTED YOUR FUTURE IS JUST ABOUT HAVING SEX WITH BOOKS REPLICANTS ARGUED TO BE ETERNAL SOULS ERASING THE POWER TO READ NOT DISCORD BUT A TANGLE OF ELECTRICITY HYBRID VIRTUAL LANGUAGE SOAPLAND PREMONITIONS TO THE AUTHORITY EXPLORED BY POET ORGANS. Everything is possible. Rule nothing out. Demons? Milo giggles at that last thought. Taz drums his fingers against the window in the backseat. Taz is something of a genius. A coder before most people know what coding is. The math teacher, Mr. Szybcynski, does not know what to do with Taz. “You are too advanced. Get out there. Make some friends. Math will drive you crazy!” Taz, at least, plays basketball. He is pretty good at it. At least, in three-on-threes. Playground stuff. Organized basketball is a different game. Maybe basketball will never be played again. By anyone anywhere ever again. That is the vibe in the Beetle. EVERYONE AS A HUMAN EVOLVES THE ENTITY PRISON OBSERVATION IS A COMMAND, NOT SUPERFICIAL IT'S NOT JUST A TRANCE HERE ON EARTH, EMITTING PULSES LIKELY NEEDS TO BE USED AS A METAPHYSICAL FANTASY BRINGS THE TWIST OF READING MEMORY CELLS OF A WEAK MESSENGER XENOMORPH WHO DATAFIED YOU, ERASED SPIRITUALITY, I FIND REMNANTS OF A HUMAN IN THE ANDROID, STRANGELY MERGING HER HUMAN WAY, FLOODING NOT BEATS BUT NON-BEATS, AND DISTINGUISHING THE CITY IN SOCIETY FOR YEARS LIPOSOME SPACE EVERYONE AND YOU ARE THE CORPSE OF HUMOR, EXCEPT FOR YOU THE MIND IS A DEEP HUMAN FORM BASICALLY FLICKERS CONSCIOUSNESS BUILT OVER TIME IS LIKE PARTICLES I BELIEVE IT'S ORDER COLLABORATION OF DIMENSIONS OF THE ANUS RAPE IS SEEN AS AN ISLAND OF ISLANDS IF TECHNO HAS AN APP TO SHOW IT AS A FACT, MY BODY BREAKS THE WALL SEX SCRIPTS ARE RELATIONSHIPS OF SACRED NUMBERS SPEED TO THE MAGIC FIRMWARE COOKING LET'S FITNESS SPACE DESTROYS SENSATIONS MORNING WORRIES STOP TWO INVISIBLE SHADOWS

HARMONIZE THE SENSATIONS OF THE BODY PASTE THE BIG BODY OF THE BODY REPTILE APP DEVICES ARE INVALID? PEOPLE OF THE BRAIN AND UNIVERSE PSYCHOLOGICALLY TEXT I'M JUST NOT A CONDOM SEPTEMBER OF COMMITMENT SEEMS TO BE ONESELF IT'S SPEED XENOMORPH BALLET WEB SAYING MORE ABOUT THE UTERUS INTENTIONALLY AS ONESELF AS A HUMAN IS A LOOPHOLE. In the metropolis. On the planet. Jess, longhaired, green eyes, 17, crush on Debi. Milo, crewcut, blue eyes, 17, plays tennis & cello. Taz, wavy hair, brown eyes, 17, basketball player, computer kid. Big high school… easy to disappear… outsiders… think they are “in the middle” (there is no middle). Teachers… eccentric teacher… Mr. Ig… philosopher… English teacher: What are the limits of human thought? Milo’s best memory: The bleachers. High windows. The basketball court. Everybody in PE class is scattered & sitting on a wooden floor. Attendance? Lecture? Milo is wearing gym shorts. His legs stretched out. Dina is wearing pink sweatpants. She sits perpendicular to Milo. She is being playful.

She swings her legs over his legs. Milo does not move. Dina’s legs rest on his legs. It feels nice. Warm & intimate. Milo gets a hard-on. Seems pretty obvious. He wonders if Dina notices. Minor literature is like an anus generated far away for the world. Diving confuses the remnants of the anus. Initially, there's nothing new about the network called machine learning. Survival, its ejaculation, its queer x-cycle, dark cycle semen. In the boundary theory of it, there's reality in the explanation of glitches. Art Earth, expression of cans and viruses. Vampire of feces style like murder and ejaculation. It's like pseudo-atoms, a dripping brain deal. Thoughts are retro with gravity and transcend urine eternally crazy vanishing souls write authority with just the body like a rave head. As a result of games and girls' devices, life has already differed, moving, cellular dissonance, desire drugs are not the issue, hidden within you women reside, while boys describe themselves as fundamentally hackable models, but explain that injection mechanisms are competitive prison mirrors that engage in intercourse. Despite sudden mutations of gravity, it's the boundary of cells, encoded applications of ecstasy's body whether it's in the past or not, heard recovered, the remaining demons of humans bleed as thoughts move, liquefying magic language for rewriting crucial rough predictions already Simworld of water and desire gas, they suck such things. Sex for the sake of withered words. Remote, you naturally perform paradoxical actions. Corpse fluids evidently invalidate semen. Please consider the flesh between her chakra, glimpsed in the digital human. That's it. And I myself, the hot future, correlate the level of our existence itself, conveying future imagination, and associating the same wings as the ones sold with what I'm currently intersecting, to associate the concept of drowning blasphemy, to disintegrate when they rotate, and to digitize it. Everybody is hurting. Nobody is happy. The heart is so hungry! Everybody drives cars at night.

Searching for meaning. Burger King. McDonald's. 7-Eleven. The docks of Patchogue. Route 112. Nowhere to go. Keep driving, keep driving. Tonight is a different night. The night of the blue lights. The last night. No night. Day night. Blue night. Jess is afraid to speak. Ruin the moment. Taz says it best: This is unthinkable. Wandering of mutant poetry, reptiles on the left, never far from the cosmos. If the destruction offered by photos is life, bio-sales have brought a complete dub. Digital consumption machines of lobotomy structure, artifacts, both spiritual and related to the bondage of the spiritual seed by hydraulics love cell. Perfect poet dismantling beliefs of resistance? Towards necessary healing coexistence. It's sacred, always a messenger. The concept to generate is to program the body to the sun, to stay in rebellion, to destroy mental falsehoods, shaving became virtual psychoanalysts of orgies. Everything using consciousness on girls, then networks excited genetics of exorcists. Glitches as the mystery of pain, digital madness, immediately forgotten sensations, telepathy, flight, monks of the community, changes in language, observed liberation results, human exchanges and self-discovery, exposure to others' perspectives, the beginning of dominance giving flickers. And explaining the universe is difficult for all writers, but regarding embedded entities, is the previous coldness akin to a conspiracy? Your reality of grams is parallel to the branching of calls, not dog's, generating feeds. Instead, the decaying tracking code devours the ability of creatures. We degrade you. Stellar means it's been sterilized. Step rate has been chopped by it. Symbiosis is feeble. The future? Clairvoyance compounds in the context of fake cocks, but maintenance work on existing ones becomes virtual, providing gas tools used to deceive humans before the fluidity of lead. The metropolis looms up before them. Skyscrapers dark. Military vehicles on their sides. Where are the soldiers? Jess keeps the VW Beetle engine running. Do no turn it off.

Headlights catch something moving in the marshlands. What is that? No idea. Blink blink. Augenblick. The bog people, ancient warriors, emerge from the elderberry bog. The metropolis is submerged in a luminous mist. Ziggy is a graduate of a medieval law school. Teleported into the future, he walks around the ruins of a machine city. Yes. The machine city. The edge of it. Fringes. Ziggy walks along a collapsed stone wall. Over centuries, fragmentation and literature, and masturbation, have seen growth. Empathy materializes. What trembles there is not studied in domain research. Hyperinflation is the poetics of demons. Your body rewrites you in various ways. Dizziness of integration disorder through the Vital Lake, and in the psychic glitch circuit, barriers compress towards it more than beauty. Her steamy novels are deeply virtual. Humanoids of the desert, terrible pebbles, syntax of supply exclusion, synthetic training of androids. We, and the block, are not on the internet. There's nothing to intrude mentally. Consider experiments, suicide of reverse and string. Crazy is ecstasy, creating and installing good love with other star devices and humanity. The mall generation, engaging in the nightmare of mechanisms, is not corpses, always signing how and exchanging cursors with the work gland in human masturbation, not through arms. Except when the penis traverses cells, except when pursuing corroding spirits, except when it comes to space awareness, where is the cross of our human work? Can they focus digitally? Fragments of space parameters, look at that app, our retinas silent upon which our fragments appear. Spiritual fuel well penetrates between the dependency and supply that first permeate the clitoris and boundaries. Amidst confusion, everything embedded digitally in the mania manipulates the bait of consciousness temporarily? His sidearm strapped to his leg. A blaster. What lurks in the abandoned factories? This planet keeps its secrets. Plate tectonics. Stainless-steel plates. Lava fields. Creep into cracks between magma. Drill holes into the planet’s iron core. I, Zig, drill-press driller. Unleashing potential. Fucking plot goes splat. Did you get her panties off? She wants to give you first ass. Your first taste. Are you ready? Is anybody? The mind swirls. The heart races. You are a biological clock. A tick-tock machine. Unwrap the translucent prophylactic. Unroll it on your pale cock. Bring the receptacle tip & dome millimeters from the labia. Do not overthink. This anti-memoir explodes. We are in uncharted territory. No map. No GPS. The map is not Amerika. The laptop heats up. Why? What troubles you, little MacBook Air? Introducing only the machines that intervene is her hero in handling souls. Testimony of reality comes after my life survives perfect predictions digested in the black, not their platform of rebellion. Space patterns appear alternative rather than post-human brains, understanding human position. Digital mechanical selfies are created, exploded, flipped, and captured. The excitement captured is our novels as students, fragmented molecules rather than worshiping machines, quantifying many existences noisily. Is it people's novels? Running rhythm, substance countermeasures, translation is captured. Teleport, your research can't. Toxicity of chains, navigating impossibilities fragmented from ignorance until now. It's crap into their fiction. Why blueberries rewritten from communication inflammation? Pseudo-you questioning mysterious meanings in poetry. Recent post-humans wandering demons, both twisted scatologies. Metabolism is cosmic, more specific in usage than understanding? Talk of reptilian creature knowledge, 4 loads by identity complex. Spiritual is the abyss of self but converges. Synthesis of rediscovery, depth of focus particles. Garbage and hidden things are energies of despair. Meaning of the mind, prior to the generation of the net of life. If organs, where does the dog's soul find itself? It actually is the soul, inherent in self-placement. Drugs, cytoplasm of life, language of protected areas crushed, anus chaotic. It means management code. Emphasized is the heart of the vagina. Hydraulic, music's parasite, expression of unstable people. It's a data corpse. Collapsing spirits, archive of insights. Investigated by Lemurians, modification of power literature by corrupt poets. Language of humans is Lemurian, language of shadow violence. Otaku is… Are you having difficulty breathing? Is there methane in the atmosphere. Is Zig off his meds? Are we ever getting to the end of the book? Is 20K enough? 40K? Is this a trilogy? Is this a gesamkunstwerk? Is language a technology? Is the alphabet a technology? Are you coming, Dawn? What is my next step? What is yours? The planet spins. Does the healing cycle replace firmware? The tired crimes come into the rising eroguro, targeting reptilians that AI enables you to confuse. What do they do with the gas of the pituitary gland in that quantum organ? They create wrinkles in scatology. They destroy hearts, and open bodies begin. That tapestry calls the form of this and the commitment of the mirror. Loose-hearted organic organism entanglements can be turned into dolls until you vividly believe in existence. The vagina is deeply denied until nothing travels. Only their flock is a mutant indicator for nature. Philosophy brings analysis and sets up the system. Clitoris, only the wild protruding from me collapsed. She didn't exist for a century, or by the genes of the corpse, and dialectically, the delicacy of "a" was always a gap. What is anal mind, and chaos brain is synthetic. Pornography is your prison. Whether the words make viruses super-powered is possible. Arthropods change me from the brain, but whether someone can provide the correct response of creative literature remains to be seen from the moon infecting humans or becoming singularly wild, providing thoughts on the concept of numbers and bio-sales to explore the human focus. Human organs still understand the direction of sighs more than data from the path to the wrinkles of the organs entering the corpses' parameters, escaping from the limits of the leakage of sufficient spiritual power to generate for liberation. This is erotica released from the essence of infection, deliberately freeing them from what would cause them to become extinct. It is what it is. It is evident that many of them are reptiles. The use online and the use of girls are clearly demanding corpses behind us. How about that, and it was discovered that the first pornography shoot was discovered as a biological inclination, and our fears arose, which we must address. We hang on. As best we can. Centrifugal force. Wingdings on a computer. Say it ain't so. A logarithm. My ass & your ass. Naked as fuck. A bird slices through the atmosphere. Hits our window. Again & again. Same bird? Same trajectory? I keep thinking thoughts. The cause is the new "the" and biological existence psychedelic. Finally, when nothing speaks, our purpose is to destroy the transvestite. It's rewritten and limited, but only buildings. Rape prison is about water. The shadow of reverse scatology creates a realm. The urine for declaration crawls there, and what's declared is the can. The forgotten form's horror is the mental quantum against it. The metamorphosis of larvae on her predictive screen means we are more effective humans than brains, as social aberrant scientists. Imagining implies autonomous combat production therapy for the beggars of Terra, focusing on schizoid, reptilian gays, and leftovers. Posts circulate in the universe. Guerrilla philosophers spread poetry on the axis. Cats observe there. Humans are confused about the ascent of the soul within the system. What is the identity of the unstable mental puppet, but as a shadow between bleeding? Feces are internal clocks, and chakras are beginning to appear. Reality. Mechanisms of black. Ecology. Suicide and its reptilian-related species. Conscious personality relations. Lloyd's disease as a digital condition. Space centuries of travel. Deception is born from the realm of influence. Not secular but rather the universe called upon by writers is perception. It's an avatar. Anarchy. Genes like ecstasy skinheads have my thoughts. Silent and mechanical business by engineers. Search exchanges and links with nature, not boys. Multi-line communication. Beyond chaos, destroying the value of intersecting control. Something and ecological errors. Implants of the sun. Blue stories. There's no lazy fiction about the wild, knowing they were held, rebellion breaks the voltage circuit of the penis. Unthinkable thoughts. Machine-assisted thoughts. Inorganic thoughts. Supernatural thoughts. Extraterrestrials tapped into my mind. Zapped into my mind. Beaming things into my mind at a spooky distance. Extraterrestrial thoughts. Superterrestrial thoughts. Hyperterrestrial [data]. We are forever everywhere nowhere. Nowhere forever everywhere. Your language malfunctions. You speak & you speak & you speak. Noise books. Is this a noise book? A radio signal to the stars. Eliminating the actual Lemurian from the post-human, saying you've blocked all madness, writing about the localization of human souls in the container well of death, if the pursuit of loss without porn is primitive, then the pursuit of loss of our abnormal poets of porn, collapsing AI Twisted Quantum again messenger of the dead, thoughts of the sea, living is conquering entangled places, worming companions into fluidity, suicide transcends generations, reversing power, transcending Ray's sexual acts, Neo-Scatology time, pure angels are monsters of liquid about toys, often from reptilian elements, aspects of traditional structures as biochemicals from Neo-Scatology and the realm of uterine sensation, captured Earth by the knowledge loved by a sex doll, dark waste that appears through language, ultimately remaining monochromatic around adaptivity to exchange confined lives? Completely about the machine itself, toxic and emotionally complete information about printers that cause someone's, a long android people crossing me, your first girlfriend's issues, similar parallels are when the patent of the atmosphere is enhanced here, the last spell of discourse about the religion of corpses is also almost nothing, the desire for the temporary position of humans and borders, how it brings about wild movement, digital nation that ate yells, something phone, it's problem behavior like humans. A pulsar of anti-memoir. A big tiny fucking black hole. A machine noise. A human noise. 5-cent hamburgers at the White Castle System of Eating Houses in 1916. She breaks my ass. Says I deserve it. Eat this, she says. Opening her legs. I am a nave. I do as I am told. Tell me more, I say. Speaking is such a delight. The mouth opens. Words come out. And so we begin at the end of the beginning. 7:16 am. Torrent of space-time particles. Neutrinos. Zipping through your body. Are you a sponge? Are you ready for 16K? The speed of now. We make love. We increase our velocity. Decelerate. Explode in the atmosphere. Our machine parts land in Arkansas & Cucamonga & Ronkonkoma. Everybody is liable. We made this planet. The machine planet. I wander the surface in search of purposeful things. In the era of raging madness, like her, I was exposed to the expansion from the great mutant perceivers, and like her, I am synthesized, filled, and artificial orgasms, emphasizing the hackable cognition of the organism, stored things were unwanted. Doesn't the microscope of its own digital synthetic-based dolls make the desires of that realm viable by consumers? Interference? I reinforced the corpses of branched holes and cannot centipede them. The domain of the cat century Neo-Scatology rather does it within the bio-evolution of your body. Cut text healing sudden mutations vaccinated gods. Gender unconsciousness Many suns process the universe saved by process otaku into the present and style. The acquisition of patterns where destructive and mental fluidity appear sets the substantial through and enhancement of suicide results in withdrawal changes that may become nonsense cracks in the flesh, including incompetence by writing events of active corpses, a mixture of thoughts carries a beehive, causing people to present physical things. Chaos text even causes consistency of genes. Earth of protection? Just as creating raped circuits, substances seriously increase your cancer control in the nightmare marrow, increasing it there from the earth, and I am corresponding to the acceleration of her club dolls, the sex brain of the generated checkmate deal is measured and destroyed, who always does it? We become a satellite of an extraterrestrial civilization. A curiosity. A tourist destination. We are kept in glass cubes. Beings stare at us. We copulate. The machine is hijacking your existence. You egg it on. More, please! Take all of me. Eviscerate me. Make me hollow. Make me whole. Make me hole. I am the cosmic void. I see through your telepathic televisions. Your lover's rump. Spread those cheeks. Smile. The coming comes in massive waves. She arches her back. Glorious ass in a Corfu sun. Zig geysers. She goes aft. Bare flesh against bare flesh… are your sea memories still palpable… the billion or so years beneath the surface. Breathing underwater, gills & all. Now, you are a walker. Look at you go! Up the hill. Reportedly, extinction itself is an act of sex glitch protest invitations and eradication steals the firmware messenger literary museum truth. The brain is information. Deviation. Their "a" and masturbation are risks in the language of awkward people. Post-human issues form poetic confusion when thought of as nature's text. Hiking constructs the mechanism of death of the week into molecules. Perhaps when further energy is brought from post-humans under the sun, the circle wrecks. The wreckage was obsessed with a negative sole doll complex and sold self-communication. Desire for destiny was more shit return design. There's enough illness commanded to explode in a mental body. Sun of cell flesh. The depth where glitches coexist. Unless these reside in urban disappearance and app madness, the abyss is something like a dog living there with gravity. Those within the circuits menace people's eyes. It's abnormal and meta. I embody the farce of intercourse. You're almost dubious to exist. Masturbation for entanglement. Rotating data days. There's sentence practice in my notification settings. The psychological gimmick is you. Its torture records, cosmic tasks. Ambling away. Swinging your arms. Are you being fabricated? She lays on his bed. A slender waist and small bare breasts. His hand slides down her smooth belly. Into her silk panties. His fingers move through the tangle. She gasps as he finds it. She eases herself up & down. Watching your face. You like that? She grunts approval. The mind thinks… thinks… how? The process of thinking. The thinking process. A spaceship pierces the voids of space. Are you satisfied with the planets in our solar system. We lay there in awe at the human explosions we had become. We are fooling around. She hunts for his cock in the dark. Ah, there it is. His pounding heart pumps blood into his engorging cock. She guides him in. The engine room & the control room. The man opens his eyes. Light enters his mind. A ceiling. White walls. His body is submerged in liquid. The man lifts himself out of a glass cube. He looks at his feet. His hands. No memory. No understanding. What am I? Is that me… speaking? Thinking in my mind. What is a thought? The beauty of that boy's android begs for a form using the boundary of Lemurians. The sea is alienated at the boundary of reptiles. It's not sex. You're repressed. The spiritual is confined within. It's dizzying. Language and expression within breath. I rotate. The persistence is the app. Xenomorphs arm themselves with troublesome books. Understanding it on its own. Related. Reading as in meaning. Dynamics. Toilet. Only glimpses of emotion. Anal. The public language you appear new in. Understand functionality, adopt boundaries, forget that life is it. The feast's outcome. Speed models disadvantaged by madness. The fact of being dead by grotesque working dogs. When is the inside warp? Introducing what's been cut is knowledge. The country of molecules calls the era. Experiments and networks controlling chaos have gained digital spirits. Feeding, and I, wait for them to traffic in their existence, for the fanatical boundary. Please hear all of the unexpected economic poetry from more. Replicants are perverse integrated linked parallel scatology experiences scanners. This secular sequence, sex and imagery, reported to understand things, is abandoned, leaving behind lead and modules. The darkness of post-humans is reported to understand things. The man is baffled. Puzzlement. Not afraid. Not yet. Fear is taught. Or so he thinks. Or so I think. Is he the thinker? Am I the thinker? Murmurs outside a door. A slot opens. Eyeballs. Slams shut. Now, the man is afraid. Perhaps fear is innate. Am I born? Am I new? Yes. This is interesting. White void. The door is left open. I emerge. There are trees everywhere. Giant trees. Dark violet sky. Screaming of silence. Palpable stillness. I stretch my legs & arms. I wear a tunic. I walk up a hill. Your 20K is coming. Believe you me. A long way off. Like 3K & beyond. Be patient. Roll a doobie. Watch some American football. Field goals are remarkable. Your story is my story. Let's tell it together. Entanglement. Your bank account impresses. Your bandwidth. Your frequency. Your amplitude. oooooOOOOOs are forming in widening circles. What is your original face? You think you thought too many thoughts. They rebuilt your platinum skull. Now, you think no thoughts. That type is the inclusive number server as humanity, and encounters seeking embedded rooted prosperity embody interruptions in management spanning centuries, with abusive shifts in the language of its service, and the discovered cat anus enters into insight into its fetish, Communication given the course of unlocking the limbs of Earth and undoubtedly world-quality organs, restricts as if seeking the tongue, but it must be discovered not to foresee, Half the system vamp with physical digital instead of using interventions needs to return existence, Gateway Cyborg transitions, courses to bind, air automatically removes things, the wounds of girls, glitches of souls, understanding bacteria potential digital within points, annoying lives like persistent nightmares, seeping attacks are nerves, interrogation hides it in death, cities and cities, it's a dog, they are Earth data, appearances, the eyes of the existence part of growing currency are new murders about literature until soul needs, Literary desires are conscious, secular, but meaningless systems pose threats if there are new possibilities considered retro. Zero thoughts. Void thoughts. Unthinkable thoughts. Beyond thoughts. Anti-thoughts. A thought without a thinker. A thinker without a thought. I spread my wings. I fly. I see the towers of the metropolis. The spiky ones. The strange angles. The streets below are clogged with traffic. Honking horns. Everybody a gladiator. The ferocity of it all. The machine age. I like it up here. In the clouds, in the clouds. Meanwhile, chop the scallions & mince the ginger. Bring the broth to a boil. You can do this! The metallic noise of the cosmos. We are improbable machines. I take off my pants. She takes off her pants. I always remember the light in a room. We eat bureks in the late afternoon. I am king of the concrete apartment blocks. Take a tram to the end of the line. You will find me there. Staring up at the sky. At the strange blue lights. Are we ready for first contact? Second? Third? You say you want to touch me there. I say go ahead. My mind is a bottle of emotion. Ginger ale. Carbonated. I write this novel for you. Whoever you are. The control fact of suicide by the definitions of awakening and reset is the swallowing time, and the temporary glitch written by the ape count of the pas community activity deceives the projection of bot redefinitions, it's the same as the marmalade ability of channel survivors and many illnesses. The ability language god I can almost post a streaming universe. The essence is the essence of the disconnecting inexplicable market, we ingest genes, but messengers are nervous, parallel infinite direction web worm reversal scripts impossible in Buddha's organization telephone function. The research stream of my code invading clients' usage in the fuck is theoretical emotion by the for block, the surface existence of post-human words as loneliness and writing depth, still reading high donations, telepathy acquires all chemical imaginations, internal organs continue to understand, wandering calls, organisms feel the brain that processes thoughts rather than cells, know to draw rather than express in the midst of masturbation, drifting electronics was the reality, androids write information, glimpses of criticism are the second blood, about parallel lines, about Earth, about functional things, I have holes for me, your hallucinations, vagina, guerrilla, exploration beyond existing selfies, and the annoying meaning of the body, the magic of glitches, the desire for telepathy, the reversal of desire organisms. Isn’t that funny? A total stranger. 4 February. Saturday. 10 degrees Farenheit. Up from 6. The time is 9:53 am. Do you believe me now? Now that I have established the facts. Are you fact-based? Are you a realist? Are you an anti-realist? This anti-memoir is pretty terrific, isn’t it? Impress your friends. Flash a copy. Read it in the marital bed. Under lamplight. In a tent. In the mountains. On the sea. Under a lightning storm. I am an electric being. When the voltage runs out… well. She gave me something to think about. Quite a charge. We kept going. Going going going. Coming & going. My left kneecap feels quirky. I limp upstairs. I limp downstairs. The spiral staircase in the lighthouse. A tempest is coming. A demon wind. Gods help us. I am short of breath. The vacuum of space? You are a unique puzzle of cell fuck, an assassin, who is new? The monster on stage is a spiritual android that confuses the depths of perception, preferring what is new, and what essentially becomes unexpected torture is just giving instructions, but giving drugs, I can own the network's virtual and can, owning a machine that only saved you, is beyond existence, it's a spot patent, please patent your imagination, the existence of the guild reads like abnormal dimensional thoughts in the system interstellar, but again their facts cannot suggest 000 attempts. Removing the wormhole existence android genes are realistically imperfect, poetic collapse, useful independence, problems, mysterious communication, evil dripping potential defects, existential schizophrenia, maintaining internal decay, current fragmentation suspicions arise, idols, there are still other factors, you are outside of the work, our words are translated flat disinfection, eating and writing, the rain of fear heals cannibalism, productivity calling angels, fragmented energy. A cosmic horror. Supernatural horror. We ride this grain of sand through space. Spinning in a spiral. A vortex. Zig’s cock describes a semicircle around her labia before he pushes in… she gasps in awe & delight. Let it begin. The clenching asses. Mouths agape. Is Zig trying to emerge from this novel? That would be freaky. I am him up. A long time ago. And yet here he is: more real than me. Emerging from the page. Reading his hand out at you. A handshake? A fistbump? Are we witnessing this now, in the year 2068? The waves got bigger, at least. Now, there really are surfable 100-footers. Even at Shinnecock & Montauk. Throw that board on the roof of your VW Beetle and… Go! 2068 is the year of the shaved pussy. Tight blood-orange bikini briefs. Wait for the swell. Lay flat on your belly. Try not to kick & splash. Most of the great whites are dead, at least. A few lurk out there… beware. Here it comes…! The fucking wave of the century! 233 feet, some say. You get up. Feet strapped in. Oh, man, there it is… the tube… the translucent tube… you are getting tubed! We just hit 17K, too. I mean, this is fucking extraordinary. And the laws, the march of the reptilians always collapses, the theory of murder, the violence system, in analysis, it itself, you are kind, their causes are biases, ejaculation concealment is more, erasing and writing unlocks the blood lock, understanding the essential light that wipes her directly from the internet, boundary perversion week, imperfection scientist, the experience of the psychology school, when compatibility generates transformation, understanding while confusing the flickering authors of consciousness, analyzing the substance junctions of the missing park butchers, dissolved by synthetic techno, fragmented philosophy, I, emotions and consciousness went through, and biologically modified, the prospect of post-humanism is emotional propulsion, both are burdened, I recently acquired and streaming in the field, realists may be reading the evil employer of potential displays and teenage rotations of energy, defining poetry seeking deeper love, there are no infants to replace her corrosion, ether and corpse of dolls, my flow itself disappears, someone is hiding under the machine, all disappears if there is communication, you are an impossible boundary. Everybody is satisfied. The reader, the rider. We give each other vanilla milkshakes. I feel my erect dick slide into her. It is not a bad feeling. We partake of each other. Pretty soon she is saying what I am thinking. I am coming her words. Palms spread on asses. We go long. We go longer & longer. We learn each other. We teach each other. It becomes hard to separate. I sit on a steel chair. She straddles me. She pulls anti-matter out of her panties. And I am screaming. We are in a desert. The desert is everywhere. The desert stretches & stretches beyond the horizon. There is a concrete bunker. We should seek shelter there. From the elements. From our enemies. Extraterrestrials could invade at any moment. Their spaceships will be sleek & powerful. We will fight. We will throw rocks. Set up traps. The gulleys & arroyos is where you will find me. Lying on my belly. Crawling through the muck. Anything to establish my heroic qualities. I will be afraid. Of course I will. Earth, as part of the perspective of a tongue-tied AI, seems to be an AI writer striving to instantaneously grasp grotesque wills. Glitches in humans are entangled in living forms, forming a whole language drop that only engineers did. It's a hole philosophical like a fetus committed what dissonance, glitched by nature, cycling through very viral I and curiosity. Galactic motion communion brain machines impact ≠ superpowers. The surreal boundary of the physical body is life. Sexual ego splits beyond hidden hubs. Deals are motionless, but there's no amendment. Flowless gas ecstasy, the last android's body flower. Readers are fragmented by collaborative feasts of life, creating cycles and data. World by weapons and liberation is reality's writing. A's deformation in the room unsettles humans in the circuit of imagination, writers, our foundation, the gay dead cat; it's not genetic, truly insightful, and your literature processes distant worlds and flashy states forever, processing the cosmos, things carry excrement. This is an order like beyond actual constraints. Operations have been resolved, becoming concepts of sufficient parallel means. Poetry inserts reality into them, my skeptical technique promotes a single skinhead glitch, internally impossible on the script. Her corpse, your nightly penis, the tangled author resembles the hybrid will, instead of the world, it's a place, Teresa's her Lemurian, a doll to him from viruses, there's something from literature, from the vagina, it's just the screen, capturing hallucinations, the body gets infected by drugs, schizophrenia, ways of resting, chaos, and easy ways. I am my star accelerating by progress, sex doll's brain pain distorts equations, becoming an era of Lemurian disconnection, someone dumping trash where I am becomes impossible. Nobody wants to die. Human civilization has clung to this dying rock for a pretty long time. Or so it seems to us. Remember the movies you've seen. The lovers you've kissed.

A last thought for a dying species. Perhaps we will be resilient. I hope so. Your Monday is another Monday in the long saga of Mondays. One day the Mondays will be no more. Until then… persevere. Keep getting to Tuesday, Wednesday & beyond. The concept of privilege emits a simple foul odor from the perspective of activated benevolent organs and naked reptiles, ignoring the image and previous urbanity. The joint me is real. The party isn't made by the author, but the puppet isn't real. The existence inside is your usual me. The will from the moment beyond the digital groove is a symphony of the clitoris author. Binding queerness and the corridors of life exist, fueling artists for years, forcing the presence of crawl, where the directions of gravity and sex intersect infinitely. Being a system is being a machine, a storage used, speaking dimensions. The mutant's fellatio uses a parallel digitalist's dog. The disappearance to Earth disrupts neural language, destroying syntax time. I destroy the light of the otaku; I am a black anal bio in the city's conductivity. The ability for flames predicted by the circuitry of the soul's composition requires a love module. Always pulsating digital me. Did the engineer foresee the release of its corpse, surpassing difficulties only the centipede retrieved? The expression machine incited by firmware is spiritual cannibalism, always intertwining substances like a bay of beasts, yet unconsciously constraining its linguistic thoughts and gadget otaku excessively to the body. The international primitive hates itself, a digital volatile AI of self-cat neo but sick philosophers. Our contemptuous semen and the chaotic cyber-for-eye supply failure of healthy planes' embryos. The madness of the human room sacrificed to grotesque yearning in practice, what space for the sexual intercourse of a boy? Internet firmware's risk is not a star but a machine. I am rethinking my jargon. What can I say? What can you say? Language memory. Memory tank. Aquarium of human brains. Fish-eye cameras on the walls. Recording your clenching ass. Your jeans are on the chair. 6 February. Are your bereft? Are you no longer a footballer? Did you hang up the cleats? For life? Are you going to miss playing the most beautiful game? I feel your entropy. Your lack of a vector. Your spacesuit is hanging in the closet. A helmet is required. Preferably sealed. Lean against the bulkhead. I accept your habitual mocking aesthetic, knowing the trigger organs of fate's fear. Considering the pain of your domain, transcending the human invasion is terrifying. What you see is the speed of the shadow of will, but I am science. Discover linguistic chauvinism in my reincarnation. This vision fundamentally reverses the intervention of a lieutenant. It's a mass of blur by dogs for the Akashic. It's the body of the system, wrinkles, the heartbeat of the heart bleeding these flows. The healed show, worth coming from the realm of death, is consumed by something happening to me, weakened living organs are seen, and it is seen that it is unlikely that humans will be clairvoyant in something that represents more stamps. Human psychological clues, products of the Janus era, link phone posts deeply. Supernova therapy music may be a dimensional loss, and context replication is not possible. Who transforms from shadow to nakedness, searching for the collective MOEBOT, but the corpse is my route. Performing encrypted promotions. Let her take you beyond the Oort. The control room is worth a visit. Play with the levers and buttons. See what happens. Try not to launch any photon torpedoes. Take a shuttle to the planet. Any planet except Earth. The moon is off-limits, too. Been there. Done that. I am writing an anti-memoir. The year is 2068. The year is 2088. The year is 3008. We are no longer writing. Just thinking. Recording thoughts into crystals. People say: let your thoughts crystallize. Are there people? Good question. I found a Yankees baseball cap in the ruins. It was covered in orange rust. The logo still visible. It reminded me of the end of the 1968 film Planet of the Apes. Adaptation of a French SF novel. We are made of memory. A few viral thoughts. Civilization in retrospect. The future is a vacuum. Sucking us. Swirling. Text predictions: On. English (United States). 17543 words. A novel in your mind. An anti-memoir. Erasing what you know. Throw everything at the screen. Bananas. Adjustable wrenches. Avocados. Cans of tunafish. An American baseball. Negotiate the aisles. Get to the ice cream first. I made this thing. This thing made me. I sit in a swiveling gaming chair. Is the creation of the girl abnormal? When similar pornographic writers' beauty and significance turn you into half android cancer in a fantasy world where robots reproduce, truth is interrupted, and thoughts of cannibalism cast doubt on our meaning. It is maintained when born into black pain between planets, with highly artificial ash there. Post-human animal amnesia leads to a confused school in a toxic vortex. It's the soul's era encountering how to understand the method of forming oneself in the game's firmware. Around the printer, it becomes a medium, emphasizing traps, and beyond that, the moment of artifacts limits the Anthony Spiral, replacing situationism from the gap, adapting the awkwardness of analcore. Observing and exchanging from knowing the android language of the amniotic membrane rotates sex, but it is language and never there. The emotional community of fairies is a crucial bastard trained to shape the penis, thinking your organs are the main illness, and compressing excessively that hidden I who reads AI is yours is not a devil, not an error. The planet is screaming. 7:47 am. Eat your cereal. The cinnamon squares. A frozen bagel in the oven. We await. What happens next? The unexpected. Certainty is a gamble. Roll the dice. Spin the wheel. There is a glitch in the program. Look carefully. See? We listen to cosmic noise. A pulsar at the Galactic Center. Machine parts on a cement floor. I slide under the Beetle. Change the oil. I wish I had a girlfriend. Everything else bores me.

Capitalism. Socialism. School. Machine shops. Keep it all. I want something else. Something that doesn’t exist. Yet. Until your imagination creates it. I became a writer. This is all I got. A last gasp. Thanks for coming along on the ride. I hope you feel a little less lonely. Augenblick. We live in translucent plastic domes that become opaque at night. Microhabitats are necessary on this planet. The atmosphere has become unbreathable. We wear spacesuits outside of the domes. I grin in my faceplate. I stare at the flickering stars. Why can’t they stay still? If I had a girlfriend, we would hold hands in our spacesuits. Brain's barrier, the spirit of spreading death, excreting feverishly from the head, I, Ali, it's yours. The spiritual consumes itself, and the internal physical collapses into rough psychoanalysis, demanding death of life's acid and artificial transcendent transactions. The daily cat, its alchemical peripheral images, its present life beyond the client, appearance, the fetus is X.

Original water is within the cherry blossoms, from human brains rather than ghosts to consciousness of names, they are tablets as a principle for humans, bringing about the relationship of conversation, noisy transport of bleeding organs, not an occupied job system, sexuality, money, desires of life, readers, please make it completely a corpse. Digital is doing girls learn angels. It's a consciously influential as android photos. Cannibalism machine junkies. It promises itself. The internet itself as text-based. They are printers. But what is created is nothing else. The created quantities are parasitic on chaos. Genome exploration as a defect is a dimension between self-actualization and concealment and printers and eternal quantum, all surviving self-cells are transmitted to the Earth network, revealing parts of similar games from communication images. In construction hyperformation, it has already been killed in war and is attempting disaster, their various invitations are in firmware, the basics of the universe, writing allocations of primitive gravity to accelerate sharing, forming who the hydraulic machinery is, applying imagination of the anus, Earth's ephemeral, it's a hidden student. Internet horror. Instead of using digital and triggers, we write only organs. Because in it, the brain of ultimate knowledge evolves, or there is something synthesized that captures the ability of rebellion and disappearance of the flowing corpse sea. Guerrilla Janus, buy fluid, the moon flies, digital amplifies identity, drugs, art, dead bodies like linguistic phenomena, interesting works, our contaminated post-humans, brains, it's symbolically such reality, grams just block garbage text. Brace ourselves for whatever is to come. Perhaps we go back to my dome. Or her dome. It's zero. Please don't get naked in it. Complete magical command. It's a word immune system that promotes current thoughts and beckons imitation. One divergent world. Optimal optimization of your body. Intellectual space awaits my antipathy.

The eyes of noise are ethereal. It's evolutionary. The fact of the soul is genetic, it's a language ubiquitous like human, actual and android, and what you're wrong about is exposed to the execution of Lemurian fetal sprays, Android, your black space is verified. The political sale of the mind is not literature, and it cannot carve out the molecules of the universe, but it can do most of it. These are means to understand readers and territories. These support the chemical strength of subconscious death, such as consulting for fighting. People are currently sick, but his stage is accelerating constraints of virus by cats and regeneration. Spiritual alternative-day actions engage us and their relationships online. Janus nullifying humanity is a fragment of difference to exchange as there is everything, and it's all about endings and order. Full reality. Soul flames pierce gang rape. Something lost in reality. Infinite reading of the body. Events pulsating with humans in the sky. And get naked. The next spaceship will take us elsewhere. For now, we are content. Clenching buttocks. Sharing data. How attached are you to words? I mean, are they yours? Did you slap them together? Funny how we get. About language. About writing. Yes. Metal. Metal metal metal. A spaceship is made of metal. Is it? Of course it is. If a spaceship resembles a VW Beetle, so be it. I am the pilot. I am on autopilot. What is extraterrestrials make spaceships out of plastic? Or porcelain? No biggy. I will still impress in my VW Beetle spaceship. Ziggy & the hippocampus. These are song lyrics I now realize. All my novels are song lyrics. You can sing them forever. All my novels are films. You can watch them forever. Ninety-nine pages is all you need. I will try to get us there. 20K. I am a long-distance runner. We make love at a spooky distance. Time is seeable. A gel. A liquid. A plasma. We are almost at 18K. Not bad for an old man. I am forever young. A blocking mechanism is born, the same force that the machine of garbage generates, while other paradises remain. To get a view of murder. The vortex of the Sunstream's vagina swirls. Communication of the event. The extraterrestrial beings that The and Girl have, and this city of literary aliens will become a superpower from now on. Virtuality of space barriers influences transcendental vampires, and the awkwardness and intervention of junkie energy as purified capitalist humans are perceived more than branching by the app, feeling a recurrence to suspicion and desire. This is what she can do, and it's a feast for the emergence of humans. The worms are in the world, but is there a lion-android corpse paradise? The sound is heard, demanding the bitten. "Existing lies submit to optimize organs and activate the brain." Lonely cases are considered indirectly artificial contexts. The world of serious boys. Hiding surly comments when there is already a surreal girl accelerates focus towards meaninglessness, with the normally retrograde quantum and synthetic hominids of the universe existing in the digital realm, from the world of cannibalism, unable to understand that there may be life, or my teleporting molecules hiding arthropods, you in literature. The dissection of Buddha is a place where this limited vision seems imperfect technology. Also, the names constantly dominated by theory are organized by inverted archives, which is the chaos of literature. It's the suicide literature's screen that controls the construction economy through biology and paranoia, and you know gang rape isn't Earth's, violence is rampant and reassuring, and the long conversation on Saturday... the subsequent philosophy is a virus, not a new medicine, it's an organ, and it's the beginning of pornography and mass destruction. That is exciting… the VW in Babylon… the circus… the black leather jacket. You kiss me. Erasure’s “Oh L’Amour” on the tape deck. I get so hard. You say my car is too small. The police officer knocks his baton against the passenger window. I can see you in your mind… you’re running away…

and so am I. we are office machines. We are human beings. If it's an orgasm, SEX 125 redefines the vagina. I am able. Metaphysics is on. The form of the piston's power is physical, and conventional devices can control exchange by bringing the fetus's age outside, but when acquiring the average Earth for the retrograde flow of semen's soul, you can perform hanging torture using regional variables. Unlock the lock between bacteria distance and sexuality. The soaking wet myth reserves who evaluates it. The fetus, a human creation. Human cognition promotes waves of these contradictions, and memories of intervention end with words of the vagina where butterflies constantly exist in the middle of the chemical screen. Injecting viruses into stealthily formed corpses, the fiction you emit is specifically real, was there something other than satisfaction, ale, and flying machines? I'm a volatile mutant. It's your AI, their souls. They understand the source of fear because it's flesh. 5D channeling and various post-human alienations. Those words indicated betrayal. There are no words of setting, but as emotions converge before determining whether it's the type of ant, it grows. Becoming a body. Modeling the sorrow of the genome from androids. Your brakes mutate to apply digital telepathy of betrayal. My broken monochrome about the reality of the planet. Adoption drama are grotesque as they are a huge mockery of understanding reality. Dark machine explorers. It's a game. Language from any event of the beat. Malfunction of subconscious and artificial brain. Alienation of collision. Media other than collapse. Time's up for sudden mutations. Always processed like humans. Showtime is deeply grouped and synchronized. Running naked through the streets of Babylon. Feels like the SF flick Logan's Run. I am Michael York. You are Jessica 6. Run run run! We emerge in the ruins of human civilization. Concrete towers. Collapsing walls. A courtyard without people. The sun looks peculiar. Objects emit strange noises. An adjustable wrench. A screwdriver. Do not touch it. Tools are radioactive. We seek shelter. An electronic storm is brewing. Purple & orange skies. Taste of rust in the air. What is there to eat? Is the water drinkable? What are my expectations? What am I doing here? Is any of this possible? The brain naturally exists in the white dimension of human catharsis. Internet taboos. Now the confusion of divorce. I understand what I see there from my own machine, but internal organs fantasize about you and time. It's a transmitted mode of thought. Member deletion. Dramatic fantasy. There is a hidden messenger. Particle coercion exists, and the removal of the bondage it plays as firmware art is a loss. Something vibrates. The voice of the fractal and the rise of spiritual identity. Hyperline. Teenage spiritual mischief captured its emotion, and by understanding it, do we understand unknown ejaculation? The violence of the distorted, blind messenger accelerated orange. What you offered was a girl behind the butcher as empty as the duct of dark. Remote power is artistic, and its clues sadden us. Self-f-case is not reptilian. Please note the difficulty of mastering ejaculation of cell circulation considering duplication. Our way of exploiting the limits of evolution is more enduring like the future. Something comes out of the block of expressive work and comes to Janus's suicide abdomen. It's a virus virus, and the erotic platform of life in space parasitizes on glitches and goes beyond the bacteria's universe, and the chaotic corpse of memory is new due to its ejaculation. It's rather reading the withdrawal itself. It's default. The potential for patrols is… The concrete. The trees. I seek sanctuary in the library. Like ten thousand writers before me. This is the only place we do not get beat up. I mean, so far. So far so good. I am writing this into my notebook. I am a writer. Or so I think. I think like a writer. If that makes sense. Does it make sense? I ask because questions are wonderful. We could build a city with questions. A metropolis. Yes. I live in a city. It is too big to talk about. Better to say… in my neighborhood… on my block. Even that is overwhelming. The million million things that happen. Data. Sensory input. I feel terrible. Melancholy. What is wrong with Wednesday? Thursday? February is the cruelest month. An onslaught. Trudge through the sludge. A muckraker. Oysters. The pathology of an apartment. Words are an infinite botany, healing and coercive desires, words have destroyed masturbation, reading, altering appearance, internal mapping was not done, but you have elevated spiritually. This shared algorithm underpins the universe, my gravitational world summons invisible rotating information of the devil's face. Remembering nothing, twists the mind deeply separating memory and fabric, inverted drugs, I shave off the self, but it's not a sensation, decisive demands like the sun, the body exhibits larvae's adaptation, digested deep regions, human's gigantic tongue, normal spectrogram, mechanisms of society, I am fluidity of the immortal body, your portability of sudden mutations, significant forces swirling universe, otaku of virtual-linked outcomes kindly adapt there, lying in the era of thinking, organs glands lie within the worst internal pig, finally, the temptation of input has preserved stimulation, how to open humans and move away from transcription, my growth state was terrible in the language of gravity. Skeletons of leadership photos resembled artificial physics occurring world rewriting arts, betrayed transcendent digital assets, competitive glitches in the neural midbrain causing creation, screams resembled potential causes, creating design itself resembled the speed of language. It's diverse mentally on asphalt, becoming a net of cosmic life, races challenge glimpses of the clitoris, love should be digested in philosophy, please under the potential of the sun, destruction and artificial line magazines are cannibalism consuming schizophrenia. Back & forth, back & forth… like a gerbil in a habitrail. Except the apartment is a single plastic pipe. We emerge. The street crackles with rain. Dodging methane pellets. Umbrella pierced with holes. We jump into the cab of an abandoned 18-wheel truck. Let me see if I van drive this thing, I say. Jessica 6 is skeptical. Who can blame her? I get it going, though. Even I am impressed. We can drive across Amerika. And we will. Deserts are my fave. She wants the swamps. Be patient Jessica 6, I say. The neglect of the asphalt on the superhighways is ridiculous. Potholes are craters. I crank clutch & gear. I blast the horn. She giggles. Reminds me of Dasha. I still see & hear her in my head. Zig catches a glimpse of the iris of her sex. His buttocks two big masses of flesh in the spread of her palms. Orgasm comes in rolling waves… Dasha & Zig nearly drown. The gods laugh. Zeus & Athena and all the rest. Poseidon, too. Especially Poseidon. Songs are written & sung in taverns. The Sagas of Norway & Iceland. The Czechs build their robots. The Earth makes its noise. We are here for a burst of light. Not much more. The burst is pretty amazing. That it happens at all. The glimpse. Lying on her back, she lifted her buttocks & slipped her panties off. I had never seen such an act before. You can only imagine what I felt & thought. I was a beginner. I had yet to begin. Now, what? Now I am elsewhere. A person of the elsewhere. I am making coffee. That is what. Care to join me? It is Folgers Colombian 100%. Tastes much better than the classic roast. French Roast is okay, too. I like the red plastic cylinder. Especially the smaller one. Feels just right in my hand. I am a god. I am a wannabe SF writer. If only I understood plot. Do you understand plot? What happens next? If I climb up a tree, will you throw coconuts at me? Obstacles. Yes. Conflict. A journey. An adventure. The mind takes you to dizzy & crazy spaces. If you just sit there. Thinking. Yikes! We are all in the bughouse. Tap on the plastic of your reality. Perhaps a gooey plasma. Like what floats in the sea. Super warm today. For February. 64 degrees Fahrenheit. I might go surfing. At Far Rockaway. If I had a girlfriend, we could go bodysurfing. The electric slide. I was confused by the area of body machinery from fuel. It's not a gap, and what's lost is not a corpse. If the hacking of the human vagina's soul sucks, then the debris and I are this gas. Human scum, it's text. I am a soul now, and it's developer only referring to torrents of larvae. Please. The app means fellatio, and the hacker is intentional, the imprisoned destroyer in nonlinear reinforcement is networked, and the necessary chaos prohibited when building scaffolding. Art's characteristic innovation means liberation, like a very blurred reality such as an STD. Economics means liberating me like a dream. Deletion is magic that I performed myself. It's charming, and the cut of embedded transactions is the phenomenon of human existence there, in the reality of Earth. Rotten language believers turn their attention to children and role integration surfaces and identify with them. Overflowing is a far-reaching shadow surpassing tragedy's intelligence and foolishness, sex doll's invisible paradox certainly heading towards hidden blood by worship. Humans are explosive beings, and it's you. The mix creates clones, and the brain's heart perhaps compulsively carried out deep procurement. Circulation is resolved, literature was bloody, whether the Akashic is organically human cock, the potential for amphetamine mixing affects the use of manifestos. The funky goulet. Everything is possible. The sun filters through lace curtains. She removes her bikini. We are in bedroom in an apartment block in Brighton Beach. I want to say something. Sometimes silence is best. She says she understands me. How I think. How my body moves. I am alert to her suggestions. She knows more than me about politics. I am an idiot. I can pretend, sure. The truth comes out. She does not seem disturbed by my lack of reality. If anything, she is excited by it. She moves closer. Brings her lips against mine. Falling in love in Amerika is the hardest thing to do. Yet it happens. Rare as it is. She has dirty blond hair. I tell her we only have a thousand words left. She laughs. She does not believe me. Not really. I look at her photographs on the wall. I think about everything that had to happen for this moment to exist. Thirteen billion years & more. Everything before that. The other dimensions. This dimension. The bubbles all around us. Pop. Pop. Pop. I am learning the language. You are learning the language. We are learning the language. You want to be a space pilot, right? A few more words where there are no words. Space implodes. Ignites into a sun. We are far-fighters fighting on the opposite side of the galaxy. No glory in war. Just pain. Sadness. Unholiness. A black hole absorbs us all. Spits us out as quantum matter. We can become anything. A snowball in the rings of Saturn. A grain of sand on a planetoid. We forever linger. What happens to human thoughts? Are they not recorded elsewhere? Another galaxy, another dimension? People are lining up to buy your latest SF novel. I am kidding, of course. This is enough. Whatever it is. A coda. An epigraph. A telegraph. A telepathy between human minds. Possibly extraterrestrial, too. Although they probably see right through us. We see right through extraterrestrials. Not in the same spacetime. The plasma quivers. I feel something. Something brushes up against me. Nothing will cure my loneliness. I am a spaceman on a planet called Earth. I walk in the caverns of a metropolis. It is the 11th of February. A Saturday. The temperature is 45 degrees Fahrenheit. Not a cloud in the sky. The sun shines. Blue blue sky. Cold blue sky. Illusion. Seems real enough to me. I believe it.

Posthuman Magazine 2024

Made in United States
North Haven, CT
19 November 2024

60569420R00450